PAUL FITZSIMONS

BURNING MATCHES

For Michael.

My Collaborator, My Friend.

My Dad.

Acknowledgements.

Creating A Novel is a collaboration.

Writing a novel can be a lone practice. I can sit, I have sat, in my quiet corner and produced ninety-thousand words. But to make those words good, to make them great, to turn those words into an edited, honed, formatted and produced novel that you might want to read, takes collaboration.

Collaboration on *Burning Matches* started in 2005, when early drafts were shared with my first Creative Writing group. I would like to thank everyone in the Naas Harbour Writers, especially Margaret Scott and Paddy Carroll, without whose guidance I would not have had the confidence in myself and this story to continue.

Later drafts involved invaluable direction and input from Laurence O'Bryan and *The Dublin Crime Writers Group*, a group that has helped the careers of many of Ireland's current generation of crime authors.

My advice to anyone even thinking about writing a novel is to join a writers' group. The advice, support and, most importantly, friendships will be invaluable. You won't regret it.

I would like to thank the experts who advised me on the technical aspects of *Burning Matches*. John Higgins (retired) and Damian Hogan of *An Garda Síochana* advised me extensively on the processes, procedures and culture of Ireland's Police Service. Chef Patrick Guilbaud guided me on the running of a five-star restaurant and kitchen. Paddy Carroll advised me on the financial aspects of the story and I was guided on medical issues by Dr. Greta Rafter.

I would like to thank my agent Ger Nichol whose unwavering faith in me and this book and her tireless efforts to secure a deal in the traditional publishing industry made me believe that this is a story you would enjoy.

I would like to thank Mark Dawson, James Blatch and the behemoth that is *The Self-Publishing Formula* for helping me realise the merits and potential of this relatively new industry. Without their assurance, technical insight and resources, advice and humour, *Burning Matches* would still be sitting on the virtual shelf.

I would like to thank my Dad Michael FitzSimons who was an active collaborator in the development of *Burning Matches*. It saddens me deeply that he is not with me to watch the fruits of my labour, our labours, finally come to life.

I would like to thank my mother Ann FitzSimons for proofreading and helping to put the final touches to *Burning Matches*. Her years of being an English teacher and a language enthusiast helped me ensure that, whatever about the story, at least the spelling and grammar would be sound.

Both Mum and Dad have been avid supporters of all my writing pursuits.

Stuart Bache did an amazing job on the cover art design and promotional materials for *Burning Matches*. And *Draft2Digital* and *IngramSpark* who formatted, converted and distributed the book.

I would like to thank my team of Advance readers who helped my put the few final touches to the book (and correct the occasional typo).

I would like to thank my ever-patient and amazingly-supportive girlfriend Jennifer who has listened to me rattle on about 'my process' for six years and has held my hand during my more difficult creative, professional and personal times.

I would like to thank the rest of my family Samantha, David, Paddy, Greta, James and Alice for their support of my stubborn

insistence on being a writer. I would also like to thank the fantastic writers who have become my friends since this thirteen year ordeal began, including Jax Miller, Louise Phillips, Sam Blake, Ellen Dunne, Catherine Ryan Howard, Liz Nugent, Margaret Scott, Laurence O'Brien and Cormac O'Keeffe as well as Vanessa Fox O'Loughlin of writing.ie for her continued and extensive support and for allowing me to exercise my creative muscles by publishing my writing on the website.
I would like to thank all my extended family and friends such as Rick, Siobhan, Alison, Sarah, Louise, Hugh, Caragh, Antonio, Craig, Rachel, Sonia, Scott and Thyrza for their support, guidance and friendship. You guys rock.

Reader Reviews.

-

- "Fast-paced, well-plotted, terrifically written."
Jo Spain ('The Confession')

-

- "In his debut novel, Paul has created a world of intrigue, credible characters and a compelling story that will keep you guessing to the end."
Liz Nugent ('Skin Deep')

"Gets under your skin and you don't know where it's bringing you next."
Patricia Gibney ('No Safe Place')

This is a work of fiction. Names, characters, organizations, places, events, and incidents are either products of the author's imagination or are used fictitiously. Any resemblance to actual persons, living or dead, or actual events is purely coincidental.

Text copyright © 2018 by Paul FitzSimons.

This edition contains editorial revisions. Logos are trademarks of the book's publisher or its affiliates.

Kindle ISBN-13: 9781386355854

Trade Paperback ISBN-13: 9781527232563

Cover design by Stuart Bache.

Cover photographs © Shutterstock

Burning Matches.

Lou didn't bother talking. Left to his own devices, he could never think of anything to say to the boss. It was rare that he was in this situation – he had always been told what to say, when to say it, how to say it. That was the arrangement and it suited him just fine.

The boss was nervous, even more than usual. They walked in silence, Lou more conscious than ever of his own shuffling.

Fuck, this guy has good posture.

The boss caught him staring and Lou looked away. He sniffed and tried to appear chilled, relaxed, like he did this 3am-walk-along-the-river thing all the time. He patted his pocket for his smokes, not because he wanted one, just to know they were there. His gaze was drawn across to the Four Courts, casting its ominous reflection on to the river. He'd never actually been inside that building. Still, it always left him uneasy.

They crossed the deserted Church Street Bridge, picking up pace to clear the road and the bin-truck heading towards them.

A few steps onto the footpath, Lou glanced over as his companion took a deep breath. He took another, which turned into a gasp. He wheezed and coughed as he put his hand to his chest.

"Eh, you okay there, bud?" Lou asked, forcing a grin, even though it wasn't really the guy's style to mess around.

The boss wheezed again and dropped down on to one knee.

Lou could no longer deny that something was wrong. "Jesus, what's wrong with you? You having a heart attack or some –"

Whatever remained of his slurred concern was lost as Lou suddenly felt a tight grip on both his ankles. He tried to shake it off but he was already being lifted off the ground.

"What the fuck –" His body cleared the wall between footpath and river and he was falling backwards. He reached out for anything to grab but there was nothing. Passing that point of no return, he felt the grip released.

What started as a cry of anger became a terrified scream as Lou fell away and down towards the river, desperately clutching the air as his speed increased. He hit the water and the impact pushed the air out of his lungs. Opening his mouth to breathe only meant he swallowed and inhaled the filthy grey water. He surfaced just long enough to emit a retching cough before being dragged back down by the river's current and his own heavy clothes.

This fucking coat.

As he swallowed another mouthful of river, Lou spasmed as his vocal cords constricted, sealing his airway. He looked up through the murky water and could see the stars glimmering in the clear sky. He thought of Aileen and the boys, that life he had forced himself to forget. When he got out of here, he'd give her a call.

He knew then that he'd be okay in a second, as soon as he

resurfaced.

Just a second now.

He felt his eyes closing and he let them, knowing that, whatever happened now, he would be okay.

And then nothing.

Chapter 1.

October.

Daniel was careful not to stare, although it would not have been noticed if he had.

The dance-floor below was packed and nobody cared about anything that was happening outside their immediate radius. And singling out someone on a mezzanine twelve feet above would have been a challenge for a sober person. Which nobody was. Not even remotely.

He blended in easily in this crowd. His short black hair with the occasional grey strand was perfectly ruffled. The *Jaegers*, *Façionable* shirt and *Cole Haan* loafers were as close to a uniform as made no difference in a place like this. Added to this was Daniel's sultry expression, which suggested a certain unapproachability. Stylish, aloof, *chic*. A façade that had taken years to perfect. One of *The Beautiful People*, he had been told more than once. And in those days, he had liked it. When stuff like that mattered.

But not anymore. And definitely not tonight. All he cared about was what he was looking at. One group of people.

Not even a group. One person.

He knew the others vaguely. Those two girls from the choir – what were their names? Angela was one of them. And he knew Alice of course. He was okay with Alice, still appreciated what she had done for him.

But Daniel was barely aware of the choir-girls or Alice. Or anyone else in this stupid place.

As ever, he was in awe of her. Every time he looked at her, he felt it. That rush. She was perfect.

Perfect? Really? He tried to be objective. It was an extreme word to use, he knew that. But he couldn't deny it. She was.

She was happy too. Drunk, no doubt, but it wasn't just that. And Daniel felt a sudden urge of resentment. He wanted to be a part of that happiness. For a second, he wondered, if he went down there, would she talk to him.

He felt eyes on him and realised that Alice was looking up towards the mezzanine. He backed away from the steps, so he was no longer visible from the dance-floor.

Fuck! Well done Danny, way to be invisible.

He went to the bar and ordered another drink, even though the bottle of Heineken in his hand was still half-full. He tried to neck the beer but it tasted sharp, unpleasant and he winced. Catching the eye of a tall girl in a lime-green beanie-hat perched at a nearby high table, he smiled an embarrassed smile. If she smiled back, Daniel didn't see it. He had already turned back towards the dance-floor.

It took him a second to find them again, the tide of the crowd having moved them towards the exit. But now, where there had been four people, there were five. Daniel moved down the steps, trying to get a proper look at the new arrival. But he knew who it was. The black leather jacket, the goatee beard, that undeserved smirk of self-approval.

You lying prick, Daniel thought, *I should have known better.*

Barely acknowledging her friends, the guy kissed her. Tender at first, then passionate and intense. The others watched, unsure how to react, amused or embarrassed.

Daniel stared, willing her to pull away, smile politely at him, maybe make an excuse. But she wouldn't be doing any of that. She'd be reciprocating, maybe arching herself closer to him, arms around neck. Whispering 'Oh yeah' when he asked her if they could go soon.

Daniel backed away from the handrail, closing his eyes in a fruitless attempt to prevent the inevitable.

The dizziness came quickly, like someone had grabbed his shoulders and sent him spinning. He extended one arm and then the other as he tried to regain his balance and, feeling a cold surface against his fingers, he opened his eyes to see a pillar covered in yellow mosaic tiles. Both hands flat on the pillar, he stood there, and recited the mantra.

It's a panic attack. You and it are separate things. It is not you and you are not it. It only exists because you allow it. So don't –

"Hey, are you okay?" The words, yelled over the music, smashed into his head. He turned to see Beanie-Hat-Girl standing beside him. He stared at her, his mouth open, even the simplest one-word response failing him.

The girl's smile changed quickly from flirtatious to polite to awkward and she glanced back towards her friends.

She tried again. "I said, are you –"

"I'm fine, thank you," he managed, adding a detached smile to the end of it, hoping his abruptness would have the desired effect.

"You look like you're about to faint, man. Whatever you're on, you might have taken one too many." She tried to guide him towards her table. "Maybe you should sit down. My friends are –"

He shrugged her away. "I'm fine, I said. Leave me alone, okay!" Daniel's voice rose in anger.

Beanie-Hat-Girl pulled back. "Jesus! I was only trying to help!"

"I'm fine, thank you," he managed, adding a detached smile to the end of it, hoping his abruptness would have the desired effect.

She turned back towards her friends, shouting 'Freak' as she left.

The word still bouncing around inside his head, Daniel walked unsteadily to the other end of the mezzanine. The last thing he needed was to draw attention to himself.

It's a panic attack. You and it are separate things…

But it wasn't working. He couldn't stop him picturing her, down there on the dance-floor. That vivid picture and the word 'freak' – at that moment, that's all there was.

That fucker looked you right in the eye and lied, he thought. Right in the eye!

His head was suddenly clear, anger rushing in to replace the dizziness. The urge to rush down there and pull them apart was overwhelming. He could see himself, sitting on the guy's chest, slamming his fists into that lying smug face. *A prick like that, the world would thank me.*

He turned back towards the stairs, not exactly sure what he was going to do. But he couldn't find them. Panicking, Daniel's eyes flitted through the crowds, dismissing one person after another. *All of them different, all of them the bloody same!*

And then he was running down the stairs, any fear of being spotted forgotten. As he willed the throngs to vanish or least clear a path, the anxiety closed in around him once again, his skull shrinking against his brain, that voice shrieking at him that he's fucked it up again. He tried to see past all the drunk and happy faces. They looked at him and looked through him, he pushed past them all. He reached the edge of the dance-floor – and found her.

She was at the door, putting on her coat and saying goodbye to her friends, as they playfully pulled her back towards the dance-floor. The Prick stood nearby, holding the door open and glancing into the street, so keen to move the date somewhere more intimate.

~ ~

"Follow that car!" Daniel said before he had even closed the door. He pointed to another taxi, in front of them on the rank.

"Yeah, very funny. Where to?"

Daniel thrust two fifties over the seat.

"I'm serious. Just go!" he shouted. As they pulled out into the street, his glare remained fixed on the other car.

But he didn't really need to follow her. He knew exactly where she was going.

Chapter 2.

"Kieran."

"Who is this? Mia?"

"Kieran, help me. Fuck!"

"What's going on? You okay?"

"I need you…I –"

"Mia, what's wrong?"

"He was trying to kill me!"

"Who?"

"He broke in, he actually broke in! He was just there, sitting at the table –"

"Slow down, slow down –"

"I stabbed him, Kieran."

"I told him to leave me alone. That it was over. Why wouldn't he just listen to –"

"Mia! Who did you stab?"

"Daniel! I stabbed Daniel!"

~ ~

Kieran Temple was definitely awake now.

He thought he'd been awake when the phone rang and when he had heard Mia's voice, a voice he hadn't heard for nearly six months. But as he sat on the side of the bed, staring at his phone, the conversation had felt like the end a bizarre dream, that bit just when you're waking up.

Daniel…I stabbed Daniel.

It was real, no matter how surreal. And he didn't have time to be sitting on the side of the bed, staring at his phone.

"You going in?" he heard from beneath the duvet. For a second, Temple considered being up-front, telling Yvonne who had been on the phone. But he knew she'd make it mean something, even despite the circumstances. "Kieran? You going in?"

"Yeah," he said, hoping a vague response might not result in any follow-up questions. The duvet folded back to reveal a thatch of dark matted hair and Yvonne's brow furrowed as her half-sleeping brain processed the situation.

"Awww, poor baby," she said, patting his back. "Jesus, are you sweating again?" she said, rubbing her fingers together.

"I'm fine," Temple said, standing up.

"Kieran."

"Just leave it, please." *Quarter to four in the morning, for fuck's sake.*

"I'm the one who has to change the sheets every day. You any idea how hard it is for a small woman to change a duvet cover?"

"I'm sure I'll read all about it in your memoirs," Temple said as he put his trousers on.

"Don't be a smart-arse," Yvonne said before the duvet was pulled back over her head.

"Damn, you're sexy when you're being crude."

"Hmm," he heard from under the duvet. "Make sure Alfie doesn't get out."

He glanced over at the Red Setter, lying beside the radiator, snoring away. Not exactly the look of someone about to make a break for it.

Temple finished getting dressed and glanced in the mirror. Her timing aside, Yvonne was right. He was sweating, his bald head sporting three static beads. He wiped them away with his hand and left the room.

He resisted the urge to think about the phone call. He wanted to actually talk to Mia properly before coming to any conclusions. But, with the final mist of sleep finally clearing as he got into the car, he started putting it together, he couldn't help himself. The call had come in at around half-two and, according to Mia, she had attacked her boyfriend Daniel a few minutes before that.

I told him it was over.

Or ex-boyfriend Daniel, it would seem.

Remembering something else she'd said, Temple pulled his phone out of his pocket. She hadn't called 999 before she rang him. And she hadn't wanted to call them at all.

"It doesn't matter Mia," he had said. *"Whatever happens, you need to call it in. You can do it now or after I get there, but if you wait, the first thing you'll be asked is why."*

He called the Control Centre and was told that a call had just been logged into the PULSE reporting a stabbing at 195, Connaught Street A unit from Mountjoy was at the scene and two more were on the way.

He forced himself to relax, relieved that Mia had listened to him, had followed procedure. She was an off-duty Garda detective who had just stabbed someone in her own home. God knows it was going to be complicated enough.

Chapter 3.

As he turned on to Connaught Street, Temple pushed away the vague memory of the neighbourhood. The two-storey Edwardian end-terrace house was already flanked by two Garda Mondeos. A third patrol-car was positioned across the entrance to the street and had to manoeuvre awkwardly to let him past.

The blue lights had naturally attracted a crowd and as he pushed through, he could already hear them all guessing and surmising and assuming.

As he approached the front door, he recognised the face on sentinel duty.

"Garda Yeats, the only one doing any real work, I see."

"D.I. Temple?" As expected, she was surprised to see him. "O.C.U. have an interest in this?"

"Someone's had her Weetabix this morning. Let's just say I have an interest in this."

"You want us to pretend you're in charge until the real detective gets here?"

"If that wouldn't be too much of a stretch. Mia Burrows. She's inside?"

"Mia…" It took her a second. "The occupant? No, she's across the road. Number Eleven. The resident, Barbara Caldwell and Goff are over there with her."

"Okay. You been in?"

"Sir. We were the first on scene. D.O.A., I'm afraid. You want to go in?"

"Not right now. I'll go talk to her first."

"I don't think so." The voice behind him was slightly high-pitched with a soft Kerry lilt. Temple turned around to see Detective Inspector Michael Hodge, not looking too happy.

"Michael," Temple said. "How are you?"

"Imagine my surprise to be told there was another detective en route," he said. "Until I saw that it was yourself, of course."

"So you know who it is then?"

"Of course. And something tells me she called you before she called 999."

Yeats frowned, not happy at being left out of the loop. "Eh, mind if I ask -"

"Look, I don't know why she called me either," Temple said quietly, stepping towards Hodge and out of Yeats' earshot. "But she did."

Hodge looked at him as if to say 'Sure you don't know'. He turned away, towards the neighbour's house. "Well, let's go find out. Number Eleven, wasn't it?"

Temple put a hand on Hodge's wrist. "Let me talk to her."

"Absolutely not," Hodge said, trying to brush Temple away. "You shouldn't even be here, Kieran. I can understand Burrows, in her altered state, calling the one friendly face that could get past the blue tape. But that's all you are right now. Someone to help her get through this." He smirked. "Unless you think Al Capone was involved, of course."

"Well let me be first in the door at least. Just so she knows she's not just being treated like any other witness."

"Right now, Temple, she is exactly that. Like any other witness."

Temple kept hold of Hodge's wrist as the tension of the stand-off mounted. Hodge eventually shook himself free. "Fine," he said. "She can see your smiling supportive face first, if you think it's so important. But that's where the special treatment ends."

~ ~

Temple led and Hodge followed through the hall and into Barbara Caldwell's kitchen.

Mia Burrows was sitting at the kitchen table with a mug of green-hued tea in front of her. Yeats' partner, Garda Goff, and a woman in her seventies, presumably Mrs. Caldwell, sat on the other side of the table, looking distinctly uncomfortable.

"Kieran," Mia said with definite relief as she stood up to greet him.

"You okay?" Temple said as she hugged him and held it slightly too long. She visibly tensed when D.I. Hodge entered the room.

Maybe noticing this, Hodge turned his attention to the neighbour. "Mrs. Caldwell, isn't it?" he said, extending his hand. "This is D.I. Temple, I'm D.I. Hodge. Many thanks for being here. Very neighbourly of you. Don't see it enough these days."

"My pleasure," she said and then blushed. "Well, obviously

not pleasure. I mean –"

"Can you give us a minute to talk to Ms. Burrows?" Hodge said. "You'll have your kitchen back very soon, I promise."

"Of course." Mrs. Caldwell emitted a definite sigh of relief. "Unless you need me to stay with you, dear?" she said to Mia half-heartedly.

"I'm fine Barbara, really," Mia said with a forced smile. "Thanks. I really appreciate your help."

"Would you like me to call someone for you, then?" she asked. "Maybe your gentleman friend –"

"No, I'll be fine now, honestly." Mia said as she glanced at Temple.

The woman's expression showed a hint of disappointment. She exchanged a polite smile with Temple and left.

"I swear, she knows more about my life than I do," Mia said with a frustrated shake of the head. "The downside to having a neighbour who looks out for you, I suppose." She looked up at Temple with a lukewarm smile. "Thanks for coming."

Temple blushed and glanced at Hodge, who was gesturing to Garda Goff to leave too. The young guard hurriedly obliged.

"Mia, have you met Michael Hodge? We worked together in Mountjoy a thousand years ago."

Hodge extended his hand. "Good to meet you, Ms. Burrows."

Ms. Burrows. Witness first, cop second. Or maybe suspect first.

"You too," Mia said, as they shook hands. "Michael, is it?"

"You can call me Hodge. Or Inspector."

If that was supposed to put Mia in her place, she didn't seem to notice.

"You're with the N.S.U," Hodge continued.

"Yeah, just over a year now."

"She was too good for us," Temple said, as he crouched to take a proper look at her injuries. Her right eye was blood-shot, and a black-blue bruise was taking shape below it. The abrasion on her left cheek and cut on her lip, combined with the deep bruising on both sides of her neck, showed that her attacker favoured either hand.

Most of the front of the stretched-out tee-shirt she was wearing, originally grey, was now a pastel-shade of dark-red, and blood-spatter was visible on her track-suit trousers.

"Is there someone you want to be to call?" Temple asked her.

Mia shook her head weakly.

"Your mother, maybe?"

"No." There was no ambiguity in that answer. "Definitely not. This she doesn't need."

"Come on, she's your mother."

"Yeah, she'd love to find out that another member of her family might end up in prison. Husband, now daughter. Maybe we'll get Granddad busted for speeding in his wheelchair. Cover all the generations."

Mia rarely mentioned her father and maybe this was why Temple hadn't thought about that whole affair for a long time – the man's incarceration twenty years ago for drug-dealing and causing the death of a teenager.

"Don't ring her, Kieran. Please," Mia said. "I mean - I'll do it myself. When I know what I'm going to tell her."

"Okay, I'll leave it with you. For the moment," Temple said, trying to combine softness with authority. "Look, the ambulance will be here soon. They'll take a look at your injuries."

Mia looked at him, confused. "My injuries? What about Daniel?"

"Well I haven't seen him, but I understand he didn't make it –

"What? You haven't seen him? Why?"

"Mia, D.I. Hodge is the *kig* on this. I'm here because you called me, because you asked for my help –"

"Yeah and how can you help me unless you believe me? That I had to do it! You won't get that unless you see him."

"So, it was self-defence?" Temple asked and immediately felt Hodge's hand on his shoulder.

"Inspector Temple, if you don't mind," Hodge said.

"No, he's right," Mia said hurriedly.

Temple stood up and took a step back. There was no point pissing off the man-in-charge before they even started.

"Maybe," Hodge said, sitting down across the table from her. "But I really think we should hear it in your own words, don't you?

"But Kieran – D.I. Temple is right, it was self –"

"Unless," Hodge cut in. "You'd like a solicitor in the room before we talk?"

Mia was shocked. "What? I don't –"

"Michael, come on," Temple said. "Is this really necess –"

"D.I. Temple, could you step outside please?"

Temple put up his hands in submission. "Okay, okay. I'll be good. Mia, Hodge is the D.I. on this. I'm here in a supportive role. You understand that, right?"

Mia looked from one man the other, momentarily confused, before nodding her understanding.

Hodge forced a smile. "Ms. Burrows…can I call you Mia?"

She nodded.

"Mia, you're a detective. And, from what I hear, a pretty good one. So I'm going to extend you the courtesy of not patronising you. You've been on my side of something like this before, I assume?"

"Something like this?"

"Domestic abuse?"

Mia thought for a second and then nodded.

"So put yourself in my shoes," Hodge said. Temple had to

admit, the man had a point. This wasn't exactly going to be straight-forward. Domestic abuse cases were tricky enough. And here was one involving one of their own. He didn't envy Michael Hodge at that moment. "So why don't you tell us what happened," Hodge said. Mia was looking at him, Temple could feel her stare. He resisted looking back, so as to show her that she was on her own, for the moment at least. After a few seconds of silence, she sighed in resignation. "Daniel Summers, my ex-boyfriend, illegally entered my residence at approximately 2.25 this morning," she said, adopting her best officious tone. "I discovered him in my kitchen and threatened to call the guards, at which point he attacked me, striking me about the face and upper body. He then proceeded to put his hands around my neck and…" Her officiousness vanished. "And…I knew he was going to kill me…" She stopped and sucked in a quivering breath "– The meat thermometer was on the kitchen counter and, intending to scare him off, I accidentally stabbed him in the side. I was just trying to get him to stop. I didn't mean to –"

Mia was looking at Temple and this time he reciprocated. The tears in her eyes belied the calm in her voice. "Of course I didn't mean to kill him. But he…he wasn't going to stop, Kieran."

"So this wasn't the first time?" Hodge asked. "That he was violent?"

Mia averted her gaze and nodded, a gesture that Temple had seen so many times before, from so many victims. A gesture that said 'How could I let it happen?' and 'He wasn't the man I fell in love with' and "Why didn't I leave him long ago?'. A shake of the head for questions that would never be answered.

Temple's stock-answers – all those 'it-was-not-your-fault' and 'you're-the-victim-here' - would be of no use here. Hodge clearly knew it too, Temple could see him searching for something original to say.

Temple pulled a chair from behind the door and perched on the edge. "When did you two meet anyway?" he asked. "You barely mentioned him last time we talked."

Hodge visibly relaxed as the pressure was taken off him.

A brief smile came across Mia's face. "That was nearly eight months ago, Kieran," she said. "We met in March, a few weeks before that. Against your good advice, actually."

"My advice? When have I ever given you advice about men? Except don't pick them up at weddings."

A short laugh from Hodge. "Been there."

Mia was smiling too, but hers was laced with embarrassment.

"Really?" Temple said. In different circumstances, he might have been amused. "A wedding?"

"Yep. Feel free to tell me you told me so."

Chapter 4.

The Previous March.

"Now there is one other person that I need to thank. My *husband* and I need to thank."

The bride, Kate, giggled as a cheer erupted around the room

"As some of you know, I had no desire to meet Stephen that night –"

"Thank you, darling," her new husband interjected.

Kate placed a hand on his shoulder. "But one particular friend was persistent and made sure we got talking. So, if I can step away from tradition for a second, can we all raise our glasses to one of my best friends in the world, without whom we wouldn't be here. Alice Miller."

Hearing her name, Alice glanced up and realised she hadn't been listening to a word of Kate's speech. She half-stood, gave her best surprised-and-embarrassed look and, once again, glanced at the door.

Jude? I so hate you right now.

It had been the same argument that morning as ever. With the same outcome – Jude went to work and she went alone. He had made a half-hearted promise that he'd get to the wedding before the meal but it was now seven-fifteen, the food had long been cleared and they were deep in tedious-speech territory. And she was still alone. No Jude.

She wasn't really alone in the room, of course. The fact was she knew almost everybody here today, well enough, in fact, to know who was worthy of conversation and who of small-talk. And, vitally, who was to be avoided.

Top candidate of the to-be-avoideds was Bill Pryce, Kate's uncle, a lecherous boor of a man who liked to say hello, goodbye and everything in-between with his hands. And he was now meandering towards that conspicuously empty chair beside Alice.

I so hate you right now, Jude.

~ ~

"Three Gnocchi, one Sea Bass and two Rongoncini!"
"How many scallops?"
"Chef?"
"I said 'How Many Scallops?'."
"No scallops, chef. Three Gnocchi –"
"Yes, I heard you. And well done for selling the Gnocchi. That's a challenge for you, I know. But what did I tell you –" A glance at the clock. "– three hours ago at the start of service?"
A blank face stared back from the other side of the Passe.
"Chef?"

"Sell the bloody scallops!" Chef Jude Miller roared. He threw what was in his hand at the waiter, wishing it was something heavier or pointier than a tea towel. "See all those beautiful fresh sea-scallops sitting in that fridge? Well we are going to serve ALL OF THEM today. Whatever is left you will personally eat before you go home! Raw! You like that idea?"

"Yes Chef! I mean, no Chef!"

The idiot didn't move, just stood there looking at him. Jude gave his best 'Well, why are you still standing there?' glare and the waiter bolted through the swing door. Jude turned back to the Passe.

"Okay, Amy, three gnocchi, let's go, let's go!"

"Yes Chef!" Amy, ever-competent, had already started.

"Order Up!"

Jude spun around for a look at the plate going out. "Ah for Christ…What's your name?"

"Eh, Fintan, chef," the commis stuttered.

"And Fintan, did this particular customer sexually abuse you as a child?"

Another vacant stare.

"Because I can't think of any other reason you'd subject them to this, Fintan. This is supposed to be a fairly straightforward Rognoncini Trifolati! As in thinly sliced? What did you use, a cleaver? Amy!"

Amy appeared and pulled Fintan away from the Passe.

"Not to worry, Chef," she said. "He'll do another one. Two minutes, tops."

"No Amy, you'll do it. He had his chance. You have about thirty seconds," Jude said, picking up the plate and throwing it at Fintan who somehow caught it in his arms.

"Yes Chef!" Amy said.

~ ~

Fintan spun around and let the plate drop into a sink, breaking it.

"Fuck," he said under his breath, as he started to clean it up.

"Leave it, Grasshopper," Amy said. "Just make the new one."

"He said you were to –"

"He doesn't care, as long as it's done. I'll plate."

"If he sees that, he'll –"

"Right now, just focus on getting food out that door. Here." Amy reached for a fistful of parsley.

"Start with that, and this time do it the way I showed you."

Fintan took them and started. "Why does he have to be such an asshole? It's like he trying to be –"

"He's not trying to be anything, Fintan. Don't be a moron. If you took five seconds to realise how lucky you were –"

"I do know how lucky I am. To be working for Renato. He's not Renato."

"As far as you're concerned, he is. He's worked his ass off, doing all the shitty jobs that you're barely capable of doing. For the last four years here and before that –"

"So he works hard. Big deal. Doesn't make him God. He's not the boss –"

"Stop being an idiot. Do you know where Chef Miller worked before here?"

"I know, he was at the Dorchester. He was Ducasse's right testicle."

Amy grabbed a couple of plates from the rack and started plating up her dishes. She glanced over to see what Fintan was doing.

"That's fine. Get on with the kidneys. Your problem is that, while you're busy sticking your tongue up Renato's arse, you forget that he hasn't got a clue who you are and probably never will. And –" She paused as she finished plating, wiped the edges with a tea-towel and slid them on to the Passe.

"Order Up!" she called.

She turned back and started wiping down the prep counter. "And, more importantly, if you opened your eyes, you'd see that Chef is the only reason this is a bearable place to work. Can you imagine someone like Renato in here every day? Eh hello, why are you stopping? You have about ten seconds before he'll be screaming for that."

~ ~

At the Passe, Jude could hear snippets of the conversation as he inspected the plates going out. He was going to tell Amy to shut up and let Fintan finish the damn kidneys but, as he listened to her, he realised that there might be one person in this kitchen still in his corner.

Jude was, in essence, a victim of his own success. He knew that. The Michelin star that he had killed himself to win for *La Bocca* was proving to be little more than a curse. The standards set to earn the award now had to be maintained and, despite his efforts to do so, he remained Renato's *second*, even day-to-day. It was the Dorchester all over again. Worse maybe, now that Renato was so much more in his face. *Do you want someone like Renato here every day?* He *was* starting to be here every day. He had even robbed Jude of what was his favourite part of a service, getting out of the kitchen for twenty minutes to chat with the clientele. *A chef's place is in his kitchen,* he had announced. Bullshit, Renato just wanted to bask in the glory.

Worst was the night Renato had taken over a service completely, accusing Jude of 'not exercising the restaurant's philosophy'. Jude's unilateral decision, the same day, to change one of Renato's ridiculously complicated recipes, had resulted in a very public clash and Renato had actually fired Jude on the spot. A humble apology in front of the entire staff, followed by a proclamation that Renato was the superior chef and his creations were never to be questioned, were required to reinstate him.

But the hostility remained, intensified in fact, exacerbated by a feeling that Jude couldn't shake – his staff didn't respect him anymore. And he realised that he could no longer work at *La Bocca*.

Jude's plan – the Big Plan – had existed in the back of his mind for years, to be realised at some date in the far-off future. But suddenly it was right there, shouting at him, every day.

He couldn't shake it. He didn't want to.

That was nine months ago. Progress had been slow – it had to be, last thing he needed was Renato getting wind and showing Jude how vindictive he could be. But now Jude was here, less than a day away from a meeting that would change everything.

"Order up!" Jude heard behind him and spun around to see Fintan holding Attempt-Number-Two of the Rognoncini Trifolati. There was a shake in his hand as he laid it on the Passe.

"Okay, okay, that's more like it," Jude said. He was impressed – the dish looked perfect and had been produced in just a couple of minutes. Jude glanced at Amy, who was conspicuously being not-involved.

"Order Out!" Jude barked.

"Thank you, chef!" Fintan beamed.

"Don't thank me, just do it again. Three more times," Jude said. "And you might still have a job by the end of the day."

As he turned back to shout for the status of three overdue

desserts, Jude felt his phone vibrating in his pocket. He fished it out and the ever-familiar 'Alice Calling' was on the screen. Out of habit, he almost answered it, but stopped himself. He looked at it for another second and put it back in his pocket.

~ ~

Alice didn't bother leaving a voicemail. She wasn't even sure why she had bothered ringing. They both knew he wasn't coming, so there was no real point making him come up with a vague excuse.

"By the way, Alice, did I mention that you look ravishing tonight."

On the other hand – *Jude? I hate you right now.*

Bill Pryce had always talked as if he were on American day-time TV. He flopped down into the empty chair, leaned forward and put his hand on her knee.

"Yes, Bill. Several times," Alice said with a fixed smile. "I do like your tux, you look just like our waiter. Except for that gravy stain, maybe." She gestured with a how-embarrassing-for-you grimace.

The put-down was either missed or ignored as he smiled drunkenly at her. "You know, every time I see you, I think you look more beautiful."

Alice tried again. "How's your wife? Karen, isn't it?" She hoped that his recent divorce, brought about when wife Karen finally found out about his series of affairs, was still a touchy subject.

"She's fine, Alice, just fine," Bill managed, the lecherous smile fading and his neck taking on a sudden reddish hue. "Speaking of better halves, didn't you have a beau the last time I saw you?"

"Jude's working today, Bill, thanks for your concern."

"Well if you need someone to dance with later –"

"I know where to find you, thanks," she said, pointedly pushing the man's bloated hand off her knee.

"Well actually I didn't mean me," he said, the full grin returning to his fat face. "The ex will be here later and I'm sure he'll make space on his dance card for you. God forbid you'd be left all by yourself." His gaze momentarily dropped to Alice's breasts.

She tried to ignore the man's lechery. "What ex is that?" she asked, and then cursed herself for engaging Bill in conversation.

"Kate's ex. What's his name? The solicitor. We're in the same business network. He was feeling very happy with himself at this morning's meeting."

"Daniel?" Alice forgot that, moments earlier, she would have walked into a kebab shop to get away from this man. "You sure?"

"Quite sure, darling, quite sure." Bill smirked, relishing being the bearer of gossip.

"Does she know?" Alice asked, gesturing towards the top table.

Bill sneered. "Of course she knows, it's her wedding. Too nice for her own sake, that's our Kate's problem. She'd have invited Bin Laden to this thing if he wasn't six feet under."

Alice considered reminding Bill that Bin Laden had been buried at sea so wasn't actually 'six-feet-under' anything but decided not to bother. An idea flashed through her mind and she couldn't resist a brief smile.

"Excuse me." She stood up and walked away without giving him an excuse.

~ ~

As she touched up her make-up in front of a huge gilded mirror, the concept continued to develop. "Perfect," she whispered and took her mobile out of her bag, smiling at herself in the mirror.

"Hi, what are you doing?" she asked when the call was answered.

"Staring at the front of a pub on a small screen in a smelly office. The drug-dealing will start any second now, I'm sure."

"You're still in work." *So much for Plan A*, Alice though, disappointed.

"Only for the next…four minutes. Or sooner if Detective Barely-Out-Of-Nappies-Pressman gets his arse out of the tea-room and gets up here to take over."

"Oh. Does that mean you're no longer the new-kid-on-the block?"

"Like that's going to make any difference. So, what's going on with you?"

This was all the encouragement Alice needed. "Fancy crashing a wedding?"

Chapter 5.

Their sex tonight was wanton, carnal.

Not like their more recent liaisons, for which the best description would be 'going through the motions'.

Like the other times she had played her game, Alice came away from the wedding ravenous. Jude had not disappointed and tonight, for over an hour, it had been just like old times, like before they were married.

Afterwards, they lay in silence, listening to their breathing regulate.

Alice was the first to speak, her eyes still closed. "So thanks for abandoning me today. You know how much I fucking hate weddings."

His smile was a curious mix of amused and content. "Well stop fixing up all your friends then. You're just a victim of your own success."

"Speaking of which, I might have –" Alice pulled herself up and hoped Jude was still drowsy enough to have missed it.

She was brought back to the hotel function room five hours earlier, where she had initially regretted her compulsion to invite Mia to crash the wedding.

But then she'd seen Daniel, remembered him, remembered what he was like. And had known instantly that Mia was perfect.

She had watched Mia arrive and make a beeline for the bar. She was half-way through a gin-and-tonic when Alice had pushed her way through.

"Nice to know you have your priorities sorted," she said.

"Are you kidding? The only thing keeping me out of my pyjamas was the promise of a full bar," Mia said. "Anyway, I didn't want to cramp your style. You were deep in conversation over there. You in the market for a bit on the side or something? I'll never tell."

"Pass," Alice said, trying to catch the barman's attention.

Mia peered over Alice's shoulder. "Cute, though," she said. "What's his story?"

Alice had felt a rush of exhilaration and had to force herself to seem indifferent. "Who, Daniel? Kate's ex."

Mia had glanced over again and Alice noticed that she was blushing. She turned to see that Daniel was already looking back.

It's now or never.

"Come on," she said. "There's a couple of empty chairs at his table. And my feet are killing me."

In the following hours, as Alice watched Mia and Daniel, these two beautiful people, chatting and laughing and dancing, the adrenalin had cleared away the champagne-and-wine-cloud. They hadn't kissed – no physical contact at all in fact – but that didn't matter. Just their body language was enough. It was beautiful.

Can I pick em or can I pick em.

"You might have what?" Jude asked now, rolling on to his back.

Alice didn't reply, instead waiting for him to get it.

"Ahhh, now it makes sense," he said. "You were at it again, weren't you?"

"These people are destined to be together," Alice said. "I am merely the conduit by which the inevitable comes to pass."

"Very poetic and me without a pen. So?"

"What?"

"Don't keep me in suspense. Who was it?"

"Your bestest buddy," Alice said, hoping she could spin it into a 'I'm-helping-your-friend-because-I-love-you' story.

"I have a lot of bestest buddies." He finally opened his eyes and was greeted with his wife's cynical raised eye-brows. "What? I can't help it if everyone loves me. Come on, who?"

"Oh Danny boy, the pipes, the pipes are.....something." Alice sang.

"Daniel?" he said. "You tried to get him and Kate back together? At her wedding? That's ambitious, even for you."

Alice laughed and playfully bit his nipple. "Not quite."

"Who then? Anyone I know?"

"Mia."

Jude looked down and waited. She held out for as long as she could before looking up at him.

"Please tell me you're kidding," he said, his joviality fading.

"What? Why? You should have seen them."

Jude propped himself up on his elbow, that deep frown line appearing across his forehead. "What...what was she even doing there?"

"I was on my own. I was pissed off. I rang her," Alice said and gently brushed her lips against his. "Seriously, you should have seen them, Jude. It was amazing. Don't know why I didn't think of it before."

Jude's response disappointed Alice and she stared into his eyes, waiting for him to realise she was right after all, or at least to relent. But instead he turned away and stared up at the ceiling.

"What?" she said, trying not to sound like she was asking for his approval, pleading for it.

"You know Mia, Ali," he said. "She'll just –" He stopped himself, probably looking for the right way to, once again, express his disdain for Mia. Eventually, he just closed his eyes and exhaled. "I just don't see it."

Of course you don't, Alice thought, throwing back the duvet and sitting up. *You have no fucking imagination.*

Chapter 6.

October.

"Is anyone going to get that?" Temple had been staring at the PULSE for a while before he realised that the ringing phone was distracting him.

Nobody responded and the phone kept ringing.

"Hello? Anyone at all," he said more loudly.

"Temple, that's you."

The ringing did seem to be coming from the direction of his desk. He was there in three steps and grabbed the receiver. "Temple."

"Well someone's Mister-Gruff-and-Grumpy this morning."

"Sorry…hi, yeah, my brain is already on go-slow and it's only – what time is it?"

"That's why I'm ringing you," Yvonne said. "It's half-eight and I wanted to make sure you've had your breakfast."

"Yeah, of course I have," Temple said and knew instantly that he shouldn't have bothered.

"Don't lie to me, mister," Yvonne said. "Don't forget which one of us is the better detective."

In Yvonne's defence, Temple couldn't deny the reason he wasn't able to focus on the PULSE. He was hungry.

"I'll have something now."

Temple opened his desk drawer and found a Snickers. He picked it up and started to open it.

"Not that." Yvonne said.

Temple dropped the bar back in his desk. "Of course not. Proper food. You on your way in?"

"Yeah, Stillorgan Road's a nightmare. Would you arrest me for using the bus lane, Detective?"

"I have Donnybrook station on speed-dial. You know I'll do it."

"Thanks," She was smiling. "I presume, since you didn't come home, that phone-call turned out to be something?"

Temple sighed. She'd asked him directly – well almost – he was going to have to come clean. Yvonne was pretty much a human lie-detector and he had only got away with the vagueness that morning because she was half-asleep.

"Yeah, sort of," he said, taking another stab at vagueness.

"What does that mean?" *Human. Lie. Detector.*

"It was Mia."

Silence.

"The call this morning. It was Mia."

More silence. Temple wondered if they'd been disconnected. Hoped, more like.

"Mia?" No such luck. "Mia rang you at two-thirty this morning? For what?"

"I can't say much –"

"You better say something."

"All I can tell you is that she's involved in something and she needs my help. It's work, I promise."

"What do you mean 'It's work, I promise'? What other reason would there be for her to be ringing you at half-two in the morning?"

"Exactly."

"Why didn't you tell me that this morning?"

"It wasn't –" Temple noticed a few heads turned his way and realised that his wife's voice was travelling. He turned so his head was between the phone and the audience. "It wasn't a secret," he said, dropping his voice. "But it was half-two in the morning and I didn't feel like having this conversation. Especially when I didn't know exactly what was going on."

"So what is going on?"

"I told you. I can't tell you."

"Well is she involving you in one of her cases? Because –"

"Honey? I really can't, okay? All I can say is, I won't be involved for long. Isn't *that* what you want to hear?"

Temple glanced at the opening door and, possibly for the first time ever, was relieved to see Detective Superintendent Hickey walk in.

"Is that true or are you just saying it because it's what I want to hear?" Yvonne asked.

"Both."

"Kieran –"

"Yvonne, I have to go. The D-Super is here."

"To talk about your work? As in, your own cases."

"It's funny that you're happier with me dealing with drug dealers and hijackers than with my ex-partner."

"Don't be an asshole," Yvonne said and was gone.

Temple shook his head. She was always good at the dramatic hang-up.

"Kieran," The superintendent did not look happy.

"Sir."

"How did you end up involved in this Burrows situation?"

Never one for pleasantries, this guy.

"She rang me and begged for my help."

"Begged? What does that mean?"

"She was panicking. Given the circumstances, is that so hard to believe?"

"And I gather she hasn't been arrested? I know I've only been a guard for twenty-five years, but isn't that kind of the done thing?"

"Sir, this isn't as cut-and-dried as any domestic abuse scenario. It –"

"Thank you, D.I. Temple, I'm fully aware of how un-cut-and-dried this situation is. And you managed to make it all the more un-cut-and-dried just by being there, out of jurisdiction, in order to…what? Hold a suspect's hand and put words in her mouth?"

"I didn't put words in –"

"Who was the first person to mention self-defence, Detective Inspector?"

Thank you, Hodge. Temple locked eyes with the D-Super. "Sir, I called it as I saw it. She had injuries, I gather there was evidence of a break-in –"

"That's it though. You didn't even see it. And then, based on a few cuts and bruises -"

"Sir -"

"And on her say-so, you decided what was what."

"You're right, sir. Burrows rang me in a panic. I helped her out but I had no business being there. But the proper personnel are on it now so I can just –"

"Oh no, you don't, Kieran," the D-Super sneered. "The second you pulled a favour with your buddy Hodge and made him follow you into that kitchen? That was you becoming involved. His D-super has already been on the phone, having been reminded by none other than the Assistant Commissioner herself not to 'balls this up', to use the vernacular. So, as you can imagine, he's been busily passing the buck."

Hickey's verbosity left Temple dizzy but there was no doubt what was being implied. "What? No. sir, you said it yourself. I have no jurisdiction on that."

"And that will continue to be the case," Hickey said. "Hodge is still in charge, it'll be his name on the paperwork. But this is a potential embarrassment for the Gardaí, I don't have to tell you. And D.S. Burrows called you for help. So let's use that to get this thing wrapped up, okay?"

"What does that mean exactly?"

"You're a smart fellow, Temple. You know what it means."

Chapter 7.

Temple laid his cup on the table and watched Mia glancing around the room, like she was only now realising where she was.

The interview room in Mountjoy station was small and grey. It looked small and grey and it felt small and grey. The window and glazed door might have let in more light, grey light, from the office, if Temple hadn't lowered the blinds.

"Who'd have thought you and I would ever be on opposite sides of this table," Mia said, managing a smile. And it was a real smile, one that threw Temple – despite her bruises, despite the gruesomeness of the situation, despite the greyness of this room, she was able to manage a smile. It also bothered him that it could have the same old effect on him. The next few seconds, his mix of embarrassment and frustration, were also the same.

"I…I figured you'd appreciate the privacy," Temple said. But he was already wondering if putting her in here was a bit confrontational, a bit accusatory.

"You ever bring Yvonne to one of these rooms? Try a bit of 'bad-cop' role-play? I bet she'd…" Mia faded off, maybe realising that her attempt at procrastination was pointless. And crude. "Okay," she said. "Where do want to start?"

"With what happened last night."

"Well –"

"Did you hear the victim enter the house?"

"Jesus, I wish you'd all stop calling him a victim," Mia said. Frustrated, she pointed aggressively at her own face. "You can see what he did to me –"

"Give me a break, Mia. He's lying on a metal tray with a big fat hole in his abdomen," Temple said. "He's a victim, okay?"

Temple's aggression clearly surprised her.

"Maybe I shouldn't have called you," she said. "I'm obviously putting you in a position you're not comfortable in. And D.I. Hodge's nose is out of joint –"

"Just answer the question. Did you hear him enter the house?"

"No, no I didn't," she stuttered. "I was out –"

"With?"

"Alice. We were in *Café En Seine*. You remember Alice?"

"I don't know, maybe. Just Alice?"

"Kate Dobson and Blathnaid Reynolds too. And Ben Jameson."

"Ben Jameson. Is he a friend too, or –"

"He's someone I'm seeing, yes," Mia snapped, although she really didn't need to. "He arrived. We stayed a few more minutes and then left. Went home. To bed."

"Did you go into the kitchen when you got home?"

"No. Definitely not."

"So the vict – Mr. Summers – could have been there since before you got there."

"I suppose. Alice might have said something in the pub, about seeing him there. But I couldn't really hear her."

"So he might have followed you home."

"Yeah. It's possible."

"And while you were upstairs, you didn't hear any noise coming from the kitchen? Breaking glass?"

"No. We were…to be honest, we were making a lot of our own noise." She tried to look embarrassed but it wasn't convincing.

"Okay, so after you and Mr. Jameson were finished making noise, is that when -"

"Ben left pretty much straight away –"

"Really? That his idea or yours?" Temple asked. "It was late. He wouldn't just stay till the morning?"

"It's not that kind of relationship. We don't snuggle."

"Fair enough."

"So Ben left and I went downstairs to get some water. And he was there. Daniel. He was just sitting there at the table, blood all over the place."

"That was from breaking the window? The…door?"

"I mean, he just put his fist right through it!" Mia's eyes flicked left and right, the reality of what had happened hitting her, maybe what kind of person Daniel Summers was. "What kind of person does that?"

"And what happened then?" Temple pushed, keen to keep Mia focused.

She looked at Temple, glared at him. "What happened then? I told him to get the fuck out, is what happened then. And he just sat there. Calm and serene, and –"

"Was he on drugs? Prescription meds, maybe for –"

"Drug..." Mia was surprised by the question. "No."

"Are you sure?"

"No, I'm not sure, okay?" Mia said. "I hadn't seen him for a while. But I've seen enough users to know one when I see one. Look, I'm trying to tell you what happened, Kieran. Can I just...?"

Temple gestured for her to continue.

"He started asking me how long I'd been seeing other men. Other men! Like it was a new guy every night. Anyway, I told him that it was none of his business, that who I see is none of his business. He just kept asking the same question over and over. How long have you been seeing other men? So I said I was calling the police. That's when he...." She faded off and fresh tears appeared in her eyes.

"That's when he?"

"That's when he lost it," Mia said, shaking her head. "Hit me. Grabbed me –" she showed him her wrist, which had two purple marks the shape and size of a man's fore- and middle-finger "– got my phone, threw it against the wall. And –"

"And..."

"And hit me again. And again." She gestured towards her face. "It felt like...I mean, he really put his back into it." She automatically touched her cheek and winced.

"So he hit you three times?"

"I don't know, yeah. I screamed at him to leave me alone..." Mia stopped, suddenly out of breath.

"Okay, Mia. Pause," Temple said quietly. "Just take a second."

"I'm fine," she snapped and then forced a thin smile on to her face. "Can this please be the last time I have to do this?"

"Come on. You know how this works. I can't guarantee –"

"But I've already been through this! You say he's the victim?

I'm the fucking victim!"

"Look, do you want to be treated like a suspect, Mia? Is that it?" Temple stood up. "You called me, remember? I have a job and this isn't it. But you asked me for help so now here we are. So can we please cut the bullshit drama? Or I'll just call Hodge now and he can arrest you. You know he's dying to."

This had the desired reaction. Shock, then realisation, then understanding.

"Is that what you want to do?" she asked.

"You would," he said before he could stop himself. "If you were in my position, I bet you wouldn't hesitate."

That expression, that mixture of curiosity and contempt, was Mia's favourite. She used it to unsettle people. She was now trying it out on him. He didn't like it.

"Can we continue?" he said. He gestured for Mia to sit.

After a second of stand-off, she relented. She sat down and took a deep breath. "He was shouting at me, you know 'How could you do this to me?' 'Why were you with that guy? I have a right to know!' I wanted him to calm down. I was about to try…you know, to reason with him."

"Except?"

"Except he hit me again. If I thought it were sore the first time…it felt like my head was going to come off." Mia touched her bruised neck. "I managed to push him away, don't ask me how. And the meat-thermometer was there, on the counter and I grabbed it, I just wanted to scare him. But he was…"

She trailed off and looked Temple in the eye, her expression suddenly eerily neutral.

"He was right behind me, and when I turned around, the spike just….it went in."

She was looking at her hand which was closed around the imaginary display of an an imaginary meat thermometer. She quickly opened her hand out and pressed it down hard on the table.

They sat in silence, Temple fighting the sudden wave of sympathy he was feeling towards Mia. Right now, she was as vulnerable as he had ever seen her. Her body was speaking its own articulate language of helplessness; shoulders forward, head dropped.

"We just stood there, looking at each other," she said. "It felt almost, I don't know, familiar or something. And then he just…lay down on the floor. Like he was just going for a sleep, like it was okay. I couldn't stop it. Did I even try? The thermometer…was in my hand…so much blood."

"Let's just –" Temple started but then had no idea what to say. He had been in similar rooms with similar victims over the years, but it was never someone he knew. It was never Mia.

He watched her running her finger over the back of her outstretched hand. She suddenly looked up at Temple, her eyes glistening.

"What the fuck have I done, Kieran?"

Before he could stop himself, he took her quivering hand in his and gave it a reassuring squeeze. He wanted to hug her and tell her that everything was okay. But, as ever, common sense kicked in just when he needed it to. Or, just when he needed it not to, maybe.

Temple could see that she sensed his hesitation, his awkwardness. Pulling her hands away, she tried to smile. "This is something you're not used to in your job these days, I'd say," she said. "Tears, hysterics."

"Are you kidding? Trevor Fagan bawls like a little girl every time I bring him in."

Mia managed a short laugh. "Yea, probably. Hey, did he ever manage to get rid of that tattoo? What was it? Kat and Trev 4

Ever?"

"Sort of," Temple said. "He got his brother Malachy to have a go at it with an industrial sander and ended up spending a night in James's. Last time I saw it, it looked like something between a birth-mark and a burn-scar. Poor fucker won't wear speedos ever again." He smiled mischievously. "He asks for you, you know."

"Fuck off."

"He does! He says he almost enjoyed being arrested when the 'bird with the great tits' was doing the questioning."

"Nice to know I'm missed for my exemplary police work.".

The smile faded from Temple's face. "You are, actually. Missed."

"Don't."

"Seriously, it's gone back to being the old boys' club in there. Farts and dirty jokes."

"You're such a prude, Temple. Besides, the farts and dirty jokes happened when I was there. I miss it actually."

"Yeah, right."

"You ever work in NSU, Kieran? It's not exactly –"

Mia stopped herself and looked immediately guilty. Actually, Temple recognised it as her trying-to-look-guilty face. They both fell silent and he knew they were thinking the same thing.

Mia sighed. "I just wish I hadn't fucked it up –"

"You know what?" Temple interjected. "You're right, Mia. Let's not go there."

Not waiting for a reaction to his brusqueness, he clicked his pen, which he hoped suggested that they continue with the interview.

Mia closed her eyes, exhaled and put her hands over her face. "I'm so tired."

That was fair enough. Combined with the sleep-deprivation,

Mia had just gone through an extremely traumatic event. That she hadn't gone in to shock at the time definitely spoke to her strength.

"Tell me about him."

"What?"

"Daniel."

Mia looked at him, back to annoyed. "He liked Pina Coladas and getting caught in the rain. What do you want?"

"Well you went out with him for, what, six months –"

"Four."

"For four months. And you ended it?"

"Of course. He never would have."

Temple shook his head. "I don't get it, Mia. You're a good cop and you've seen your fair share of..."

"Of what, Kieran?" Mia said, with a Go-on-just-say-it look on her face.

So he did. "Fucked up relationships. Abusive pricks beating their wives. How did you not see it? See something in him, long before four months."

"You think I don't know that? That I haven't been kicking myself? Every time he told me he loved me, or gave me a longer-than-normal hug. I'm now thinking 'Is that when he went nuts?' Even on our first date, I..." Mia tutted and shook her head. "See? This is what he's turned me into."

"What about your first date?"

"Let's just say, a red flag should definitely have come up."

Chapter 8.

March.

Before a word was spoken, she had kissed him.

The anxiety that had been there all day dissipated instantly as he felt her lips on his, sensed her apprehension. Even still, his hand went to the back of her neck and she seemed to emit a slight shudder as he ran his finger-tips over her smooth skin.

Despite the electricity between them at the wedding and despite how much he had thought about this kiss ever since, it still took him by surprise.

When he eventually and reluctantly broke the kiss, she looked into his eyes before giving him a cheeky smile. "Oh I'm sorry, wrong guy. I really should have put in my contacts."

He laughed and, as she confidently looked back into his eyes, he had to admit what he so didn't want to. He was already mad about this woman.

It wasn't so much those 1920s film star looks that was

bowling him over – those unbelievably green eyes, her warm smile, that dainty nose. It was more the kindness behind the eyes, the boldness in that smile, the tiny line under her nose when she was really laughing, not just polite-laughing, that really caught him. And he had noticed all this about her in the first thirty seconds at the wedding. This never happened. Well, not very often anyway, Daniel wasn't generally interested in people. People bored him.

"How embarrassing for you," he said. "But I hope my wife didn't see it. She's not crazy about me kissing strangers on the street."

"Women. We're so unreasonable," Mia laughed and hugged him. It surprised Daniel how happy she seemed to see him.

"So where you taking me for dinner?" she asked. "Somewhere ridiculously expensive, I assume?"

"Well of course," he said. "There's a lovely little place just down the street, do this thing called a 'Big Mac'. It's bread, then meat, then even more bread.

"Wow, sounds amazing."

"And they don't just have chips. They have *French* fries."

"You really are pushing the boat out."

Her hand brushed against his and he had wrapped his fingers around hers before he knew it. And she didn't pull away.

He leaned in and they kissed again.

~ ~

It was one of those tables that normally annoyed Daniel, where the occupants sat at right angles to each other - a space-saving exercise made to look as like an attempt at intimacy. But right now, he loved the idea.

"I was starting to think you weren't interested, you know," he said as they sat down.

"Why would you think that?"

"It took you – I don't know – how many subtle hints and at least two direct requests before you agreed to go out with me. I haven't had to work that hard since I became partner."

"Well, you know, I didn't want you to think I was desperate." she said, playfully running her fingers over the hand.

"Good point. Nothing puts a boy off more than a girl ringing every five minutes with 'Whatcha doin?'"

"Very true," Mia said. "But I would never be so uncool. Actually, it was something Alice said to me."

"Oh? And what did she have to say?"

"She told me about Kate."

The tightness in Daniel's stomach was instantly back, but it wasn't nerves this time. "What about Kate?"

"That she's your ex?"

"Alice told you that Kate is my ex," he said, trying to sound casual but failing miserably. "And why ...why were you..."

"It's okay, I've been there." Mia was clearly thrown by his reaction. But he didn't like that Alice had been talking about him, gossiping about him. Even if she was the one who had introduced them.

"You...you know," Mia stuttered. "You come out of a long relationship and you're not used to being on your own. And when it ends suddenly like it did with Kate, it can be quite a shock to the system."

"I think you might have –"

"So I really don't want to be a rebound for you. Don't get me wrong, I believe in the rebound, I believe in it big-time, but –"

"Ok, whoa whoa whoa," Daniel interjected, managing a smile. It was time to clear this up. "I don't know what you think you know but.....what did Alice tell you about me and Kate?"

"She was kind of sketchy on the details."

"First of all, we hardly broke up today or yesterday. It was, like, nearly two years ago. She just got married to some other guy!"

"I know that," Mia said. "But a bad break-up –"

"It wasn't a bad break-up." Daniel's raised voice caused a glance-over from the next table. He told himself, again, to relax. "It had reached….you know, reached its natural conclusion. I mean it wasn't a good break-up. There were rows, lots of rows, especially in the last few weeks, but, at the end of the day, we were both adults. We realised – we were in love and then we weren't."

"That's it?"

"That's it. So I don't know what bullshit story Alice Miller was telling –"

"She wasn't, I promise," Mia leaned in and touched his hand. "I'm sorry I said anything to you now. We weren't gossiping, I swear!"

"It kind of sounds like you were."

"No, Daniel, Alice was just looking out for me."

"*Careful with the bad man Daniel*, was it?"

"Of course not. Why would she think that? She was the one who dragged me to that wedding, just to meet you."

This threw him. "Did she?"

"Yeah. I guess she thinks we'd be good together. And I, for one, thought she was on to something."

He watched her pull her hand away and fold her arms. Daniel closed his eyes and cursed himself, realising that he'd blown it. She was about to tell him as much, wish him a happy life and leave.

But he knew he should say something, try and apologise maybe.

"I'm sorry."

He heard the words but it wasn't him saying them. He opened his eyes to see Mia still sitting there, not reaching for her bag or her coat. In fact, she looked embarrassed. "I should never have brought it up," she said. "It's none of my business and –"

"No, I'm sorry," Despite everything, he still owed her an apology. "I over-reacted. I mean, you were bound to find out sooner or later about Kate and me. Like, I'd have told you myself eventually."

"Not on our first date though, right?"

No, but it was out now. He might as well just deal with it. "Look, I admit it. I wasn't good to Kate. She deserved better. I was uptight. Obsessive and – "

"Hey, watch it, that's my date you're talking about." Her hand was back on the table and she squeezed his. "And right now, I like him."

"So this isn't the bit where you make a lame excuse and bolt?"

"Nah," That great mischievous smile was back. "I'll let you buy me dinner first."

~ ~

His intensity, his passion, his hunger had overwhelmed her as they kissed outside the restaurant. She couldn't help but reciprocate. She hadn't meant to, it certainly wasn't part of the plan. But she had done it anyway, as if not kissing him back wasn't an option.

As the taxi took her home, Mia thought about this instant attraction she had to him. It had come as a surprise. And a guy rarely surprised her, even when she had dated him, even when she had let it stretch into a relationship. It was like there was a catalogue of gestures and actions and statements. Every man apparently had a copy, had read it and always used it.

Like tonight. Anyone else would have quickly brushed away any mention of an ex, dropping in something like 'Oh I don't want to talk about her, I want to talk about *you*." Straight from the catalogue.

But not Daniel. Daniel had reacted. And that reaction had brought something else surprising. Desire. The likes of which she hadn't felt for a long time. Not since London, maybe.

So familiar and yet so scarily new.

Chapter 9.

October.

"I think you're being a bit hard on yourself," Temple said.

"Maybe."

"Come on, Mia." Temple remembered this particular trait of hers. The self-criticism that could only have come from a Catholic upbringing. It occasionally worked for her but more often held her back. The speed at which she could blame herself had always been impressive.

"So you knew about his ex-girlfriend and he got defensive. That's hardly the first sign of a violent psychopath."

"Violent psychopath?" Mia snapped. "Who ever said he was a violent psychopath?"

Temple was surprised at her. This was one of his standard tests for victims of domestic abuse – paint the attacker in a bad light and observe the reaction. Occasionally, the victim would agree that her husband was indeed 'a monster' or 'pure evil' but, mostly, she would rush to defend the person who had just beaten her half to death.

Temple had almost not tried it with Mia – as she had said, she was privy to his stunts and she wouldn't thank him for using it on her. So when her reaction was the same as all those victims, he realised how vulnerable she actually was.

He decided to come back to that later.

"What about this friend of yours? Alice?" he asked.

Mia was clearly surprised by the change of subject. "What about her?"

"She played a part in getting you and Mr. Summers together?"

"Yeah, I suppose," she said. "She asked me to come to the wedding, she was bored without her husband there. She introduced me to Daniel, yeah. But she wasn't exactly locking us in a cloakroom."

"But she was okay with you two getting together."

"Of course she was, she's my best friend. She was happy to see me getting together with someone. But…"

Temple gave her a second to continue. "But?"

"I think she was short on coupled friends to have over for dinner. She loves having people over for dinner. Can't say I blame her."

"How come?"

"If I lived in that house and had a world-class chef as a hubby, I'd have dinner parties too.'.

"Well you would need to have the world-class chef hubby. That Chicken Korma of yours? They're serving it to the inmates in Mountjoy these days."

Mia gave Temple her not-in-the-mood look.

"So, Alice had this fabulous house and fabulous chef-husband…what's his name?"

"Jude Miller. You heard of him? He's borderline-famous."

"Can't say I have. What's he like?"

"What's he like? Get to the point Kieran, please. I'm tired."

"Hey, you brought him up. So what's the fabulous house and chef husband got to do with you and Mr. Summers?"

"Because me and Daniel were just finding our feet, trying to decide what we were. But Alice, God love her, has the silverware out and invited us over for dinner almost immediately – suddenly I'm part of an 'us'."

"Not keen on that?"

"A bit too quick, that's all."

"You and Mr. Summers?"

"No, he was okay with it. That's kind of why I went along with it. He wanted us to be this public couple from the start. I'd have just preferred to be doing stuff, just the two of us for a while. I should have followed my instincts."

"Why's that?"

"Well that first dinner party…it was supposed to be a cosy and friendly even-numbers get-together –"

"Except that…"

"It was the most awkward dinner party I've even been at."

Chapter 10.

April.

"Look at you, all proud of yourself."

Alice was sitting on the large cream couch, a glass of wine in her hand. She was looking, with increasing amusement, at Mia's smug expression.

"It's not pride, it's just…" Mia took a sip of wine and smiled. "We've only been out a handful of time, it's been fun but –"

"I've already been on the phone to Phillip Treacy, got my order sorted for the wedding. Wide rims are back in, apparently."

"You're just loving this, aren't you?"

"Don't I get to enjoy the moment a little bit? I did introduce you –"

"And I thought we were here to celebrate my smugness, not yours."

Alice raised her glass in Mia's direction. "To your happiness, m'lady," she said with a wry smile. "Among other things."

~ ~

"Are you sure you're not over-cooking the meat?"

Jude threw his eyes to heaven as his mother once again opened the oven.

"I don't know," Jude said in his slow I'm-just-an-idiot voice. "Because I've never cooked lamb before."

Geraldine let the oven-door close and poked her son in the rib as she passed. "Don't be cheeky," she said. "You know how your father likes it, nice and rare."

She immediately blushed and, noticing it, Jude did too.

"But I guess that's not my problem anymore, right?" she said.

"I didn't say anything," Jude said.

"You're right, Mrs. Miller." Daniel, sitting at the table, must have sensed a changed of subject was needed. "You need to keep these so-called professionals on their toes."

"Exactly," Geraldine said and started tidying the counter-top. "Look, you still don't know how to keep a tidy kitchen. How many years –"

"Mum, please," Jude said, trying not to sound annoyed as he took the bag of flour out of her hand. "Why don't you go inside to Alice? You know, relax. You're a guest, remember?"

"I'd be more relaxed out here," his mother said defiantly.

"Come on. Please. I thought we agreed we were just going to get on with it. Put all that behind us."

"Jude." Geraldine muttered through gritted teeth, gesturing towards Daniel, who was now reading, or maybe pretending to be reading, the newspaper.

"Don't worry about him. He's bound by lawyer-kitchen

privilege." He lowered the heat under a pan of asparagus and turned around. "Anyway, come on. Time for the bubbly."

"Shouldn't we wait?"

Jude glanced at the kitchen clock. "I told him we were doing the champagne at eight. It's now quarter-past. This new being-late thing of his isn't as fashionable as he thinks it is."

~ ~

Jude tried not to dwell on the fact that, by opening the bottle, he was breaking a long-standing family tradition. As the cork popped, a glance at Geraldine told him she was thinking the same thing.

"You know, your father always opens the champagne," she said with a sigh and then saw the nervous glances around her. "But I suppose things change, right?"

Jude gave her a proud smile as he poured the fizz. "Maybe that's what we should be toasting. Change. You know, for the better?"

"If you say so, dear. I suppose we should officially recognise that you're now the man of this house."

"Well, maybe," Jude said. He glanced nervously at Alice, which she didn't see or chose to ignore. He handed around the glasses, leaving an empty one standing conspicuously on the table.

"The first thing worth mentioning," he said with a bright smile as he tried to curb any mawkishness. "Is that two of our best friends, Mia and Daniel, are here tonight, but more to the point, are here tonight *together*."

He looked inquisitively for confirmation from Daniel who, having said little since he arrived, now broke into a bright smile. "Safe to say," he said and looked at Mia. "Right?"

"It's early days," Mia looked less certain but she forced a smile too. "But it's, eh definitely worth of a bit of bubbly though."

"Absolutely," Geraldine said and clinked Mia's glass, giving her an encouraging smile. This started a barrage of clinking. A few sips were taken before Jude got a chance to speak. "I have a bit of a news myself, actually."

"Oh?" Daniel said, looking somewhat deflated by the too-quick subject change.

"Yeah, I've kind of left my job," Jude said.

"Jude!" The exclamation from his mother made everyone else jump. "You did what?"

Alice laid a reassuring hand on her mother-in-law's arm. "He's just being dramatic. Jude, don't give your mother a heart-attack. Come on, tell them the rest."

Jude waited a few seconds, deciding to be selfish and enjoy the anticipation.

"I'm opening a restaurant."

Chapter 11.

The hugs from Daniel and Mia were as expected, but it was of his mother's reaction that Jude was understandably wary. It should have been both parents he'd have been nervous of but, with his father a no-show, his eyes – all eyes in fact – were on Geraldine. She also didn't rush.

"Well," she said, setting down her glass and fixing her son with a glare. "It's about time." Her face broke into a bright smile.

Jude felt tears come to his eyes. A smile of any nature was not something he had seen on his mother's face for a long time. And he found himself relieved too. Relieved that his father wasn't here. If Geraldine was getting to enjoy this moment, then she deserved to enjoy it without reservation or self-consciousness.

As he reached for the champagne bottle, Jude felt a wave of anger towards his father wash over him – anger for robbing his mother of that smile, for pretty much every decision the man had made over the last six months.

He took a moment before turning back to his audience and topping up glasses. "Thanks," he said quietly when he got to his mother. "I knew you'd get it."

"Of course I do," she said. "You're too talented to be under Renato's thumb. Way too full of himself, that man. If he was half as good as he thinks he is, he'd still only be average."

Jude laughed. "You're right there."

He stepped back and raised his glass high.

"It's about time!" he exclaimed. Everyone else laughed and repeated his toast.

"So come on," Daniel said, putting his arm around his friend's shoulder. "Details details."

"Well, I don't know what else to say really," Jude said as he sat down. "The fact is, I have landed on my fucking feet."

"Jude, language," Geraldine and Alice said in unison and looked at each other, embarrassed.

"Sorry," Jude said. "But it's warranted. Two magic words. Silent. Partners."

Daniel's eyebrows raised. "Meaning?"

"They're a small venture capital company, just two guys. Met them at the culinary fair in January. And there's no other way of putting it. They loved me."

"Of course they did," Alice said and kissed Jude's cheek. "Because you're brilliant." She took a sip from her glass. "And you should see the space he's got, it's great. Bit off the beaten path but I'm sure –"

"Actually, there's been a change of plan on that front," Jude said.

"Oh?" Alice raised an eyebrow. "Something you didn't tell me?"

"Well, yeah. One of my two new guardian angels, Mr. Lewis,

broke one the basic rules of being a silent partner. But am I glad he did."

"Why, what did he do?" Geraldine asked.

"Suggested I use a different building."

"What do you mean, 'suggested'?" Alice's disconcertion was clearly increasing.

"Eustace Street, twelve thousand square feet, newly renovated…." Jude trailed off, the excitement getting the better of him.

"Eustace Street. As in Temple Bar?" Alice asked. "Nice of him to make the suggestion. How are you supposed to pay for it?"

"It wasn't just a random suggestion, to be honest. He owns the building. Well, his property management company does. He tells me that, in the current climate, it makes more sense to rent it to me than to sell it. And for less than I'd be paying for Francis Street. He said he doesn't want me distracted by having to entice customers to an 'up-and-coming' area."

"I'm waiting for the 'but' here," Daniel said with a laugh. "Because no-one is that jammy." He thought for a moment. "Actually Jude, you probably are."

"No, I'm sure the 'if's, 'and's and 'but's will follow," Jude said. "They're probably waiting until I'm nice and comfy before they spring it on me. 'My son wants to be a chef, you must give him a job. By the way, he's thirteen and he has no arms.' To be honest, I can see –"

The doorbell interrupted him. Jude traded an uneasy frown with his mother.

"Here he is now," he said, laying down his glass. "My ever-fashionable father."

"It's okay, I'll go," Alice said. "You're in mid-flow."

The doorbell, or more to the point, the knowledge of who was ringing it, had robbed Jude of his impetus and his mother, normally a master at breaking awkward silences, was also lost for words. Instead, everyone listened as Alice opened the front door and greeted Jude's father.

But not just him – there was another voice too. A female voice.

Oh God, no.

Jude looked at his mother. Although the glass held to her lips hid her face, the shake in her hand betrayed her.

Alice walked into the room, followed by a man in his early sixties, wearing a cream jacket over a navy polo-neck. Holding his hand was a slight blonde woman. Nervous smiles adorned both faces.

"Daniel, Mia, I'd like you to meet my father, Brian." Jude stood up. "And, for some reason, Suzanne. His girlfriend."

~ ~

The next hour-and-a-half had been the most rushed and yet slowest time in Jude's recent life. The hushed promise from Alice in the kitchen that she had no idea his father was bringing 'that woman'. Jude demanding that they go, before Alice managed to talk him down. And, knowing his mother would not show weakness by leaving, the fastest served meal since he worked in that Taco place in Sydney.

As dinner was being hurriedly consumed, Daniel and Mia bravely tried to make small-talk until every attempt to ask Geraldine about work or compliment Alice on the house were greeted with a single-word answer or a scowl from Jude. Realising he had been left out of Jude's announcement, Brian made an attempt at being offended, but it was short-lived. He then tried to raise a toast, but its lukewarm response only served to increase the tension further.

"And, of course," Brian said, taking one last stab at civility. "We should toast the new happy couple, right? Daniel and Mia?"

The 'new happy couple' smiled politely, now neither of them relishing being the centre of the man's attention.

"Oh I didn't realise," Suzanne said, trying to conjure up as much enthusiasm as she could. "When did you meet?"

"Couple weeks ago," Daniel said, obviously starting to enjoy the limelight, however tainted. "Alice was –"

"Actually Geraldine?" Alice cut in loudly, causing everyone to jump. "Did you see the new en-suite? You probably haven't been here since we put it in."

"Eh no, you're right," Geraldine said with uncertainty. "I'd like to see that."

"Oh yeah, it's very impressive," Brian chimed in. "Actually, Suzanne, you're thinking of installing an en-suite, maybe you should have a look."

Everyone, including Suzanne, glared at Brian in disbelief, disgust or a mixture of both.

"I'm sorry, I…" Brian said, for the first time showing any real embarrassment. "I must have misunderstood."

Alice and Geraldine hurriedly left the room and that awkward silence quickly returned. Jude, knowing that a conversation with his father could not be avoided, pressed on Daniel's foot while gesturing towards the door.

"Why don't we make some coffee, Mia," Daniel said, standing up. "I think I remember how to use that machine."

"Sure. Good idea," Mia said with relief.

Jude waited until Daniel and Mia had pointedly closed the door behind them. "What the fuck!" was all he could manage.

Brian would not meet his son's glare.

"So, I'm right then," Suzanne said. "I wasn't supposed to be here."

Brian looked at her and shrugged.

Typical, Jude though. *Never your fault.*

"I'm sorry, Jude. I really am," Suzanne said and it was clear that she meant it. "I asked him to ring and make sure. But he was so bloody adamant Alice had invited me."

"I am in the room, you know," Brian said defensively.

"Well speak up for yourself, then!" Jude shouted. He forced himself to lower his voice almost to a whisper. "How could you possibly think that this was a good idea? That this could ever have been what we meant by inviting you?"

"Alice –"

"Alice nothing, Dad. Don't even try to blame this on her. Even if she had invited her, surely you could have known to just bloody-well say 'No thank you'!"

"I know and I'm sorry –"

"You're clearly not sorry!" Jude's cheeks had turned red. "And so-fucking-what if you are? That's all I ever hear you say. Just fuck everything up, say you're sorry and it's hunky-dory –"

"Hey!" Brian barked, pushing his chair back as he stood up. "I am still your father!"

Sure enough, Jude felt like he was ten years old at that moment.

"I will not be spoken to like this," Brian continued while he had his chance. "Not by you. Yes, I messed up tonight. Fine. And it's not the first time. Fine. But grow up, for Christ's sake!"

Once again, father and son engaged in a heated stand-off. And, once again, it ended with the son backing down.

"Okay, okay," Jude said. "Just sit down. Let's just have coffee, okay?"

Brian held his position for a few more seconds before relenting. He sat and put a reassuring hand on Suzanne's.

"Suzanne would prefer tea," he said gruffly.

Suzanne, embarrassed, started to say something but realised there was no point.

"Em, okay. I'll…eh, go tell your waiter," Jude said, trying to lighten the mood, and was relieved when he saw a brief smile break on his father's face.

"If it makes you feel any better –" Brian started but was interrupted by Geraldine storming into the room, carrying her coat.

"Mum?" Jude said, startled. "Where you going? What's the matter?"

"The matter is I'm leaving." Geraldine was clearly upset and Jude cursed himself.

"I'm sorry, Mum. You weren't meant to hear any of that. That's why I didn't –"

Geraldine looked confused. "What are you talking about? I didn't hear anything."

Geraldine turned to leave and smiled politely at Daniel and Mia, who were standing at the door with the coffee, looking confused.

"It great to see you again," she said squeezing Mia's hand. "A word of advice though – choose your friends more wisely."

"Mum! Will you please tell me what's going on?"

"What's going on? Ask your bloody wife!"

Chapter 12.

Jude stared up at the small protruding rock two feet above him. Pressed against the cliff-face, both feet and one hand were secure. He was sure he could stay in this position for a while, before the build-up of lactic acid demanded that he move. Yes, he could stay right here.

Except that a certain someone, looking up at him from a few feet below, was getting impatient.

"You going to flirt with that grip all day," Alice said. "I would like to get to the top of this mountain before I die of boredom."

Ordinarily, Alice's jibes had little effect, in fact he enjoyed them. But, this morning, he was in no mood.

"If you don't mind," he said. "I'd like to make sure it'll take my weight, unless you want me falling to my death and taking you with me."

He knew he was being snippy. He also knew that Alice wasn't really the cause of his bad mood. That was very much his own doing.

He could have sorted it out the night before, after his mother, and then everyone else, had made their hasty exits. He could have pushed Alice for more when she brushed off his mother's storm-out as a misunderstanding. But he hadn't and now, here he was, climbing a mountain, in a sulk.

"Well at least we'd be doing something," Alice shouted from below.

Jude emitted a sigh. He wasn't just in a funk, he was also nervous. Logic told him that he knew what he was doing. He'd been climbing for years. But all it took was a flash of him losing his grip or missing a footing and he was suddenly on edge. It was the reason he would never be the climber Alice was. She didn't have the fear. Or, if she did, she was able to ignore it. She was able to use it.

"Look, staring at it isn't going to do you any good. Just go on, will you?"

As admirable as Alice's confidence and ability were, right now they were making her a pain in the ass. Jude looked at the potential hand-grip above him, bent his knee as much as he could and launched himself upwards. He grabbed the small protruding rock with his left hand and inhaled sharply when it moved under his weight.

But it held. He hung there for a moment, enjoying this minor victory. Then he reached up with his other hand and quickly pulled himself up to the ledge.

He looked down at Alice as she deftly and effortlessly climbed up towards him. It wasn't so much her ability he was jealous of, more so her confidence.

"Bravo, Hard Man," she said, glancing up but barely slowing. "Osman would be proud of you."

Jude smiled and shook his head. She was really enjoying this.

Actually, she was. Once again, it struck Jude as odd that someone could be so content hanging off the side of a mountain.

"Thanks," he said. "Now I have a nice rope here, you want me to drop it down to you? You look like you need it."

"Aren't you Mister Cocky now that you're sitting comfortably."

Alice grabbed Jude's foot and gave it a shake, making him grab the edge with both hands. Laughing as she reached the top, she swung herself around and perched beside him.

"Yeah, really confident, my man is." She leaned in and kissed his cheek. She gestured to the view of the sea in front of them. "Now aren't you glad you came?"

In answer, Jude glanced at his watch.

"It's half-eight in the morning, Jude," Alice said. "And it's Monday. We'll have you back in your smelly kitchen in no time. Let's just enjoy this, okay?"

For a few minutes, they sat in silence, Alice leaning her head against Jude's shoulder. He even closed his eyes briefly. He then remembered what needed to be said. "So are we going to talk about it?"

"About what?"

"About the other night?"

He turned to look at her and watched the unmistakable tension returning to her face.

"Not now, please," she said quietly. "Don't ruin this. We've been through it all anyway."

"Eh, no we haven't. I remember asking you why my mother stormed out in the middle of a dinner party, and I remember you not giving me an answer."

"I told you, it was just...it'll blow over."

"What will? How am I supposed to deal with it if I don't know what it is?"

Alice sat up and readjusted herself, slightly apart from Jude. "She found the scan, okay? It was in the back of my book."

"Scan? What scan?"

"You know what scan!"

It took him a moment. "Ah Jesus, Alice!"

"What? It's not like I had it stuck to the fridge!"

"This is all we need now," he said under his breath, shaking his head.

"You said I could keep it," Alice said, her voice cracking.

"I know, but..." He sighed. "And she definitely saw it?"

"Oh, yeah."

"And she –"

"Freaked out? Tried to tear it up right in front of me?"

"And?"

"And I grabbed it off her. She started yelling at me, saying that I couldn't have it, that I had to live up to my end of the bargain. I told her to mind her own business, that she had already done enough damage –"

"Christ!"

"She overstepped! Do you not even see that?"

Jude tried to respond but nothing came and an ominous silence descended between them. Jude stared out over the Dublin landscape and pale blue sky and wished he was back in his smelly kitchen.

"Look," he said eventually. "I'm not telling you to get rid of that thing, but – "

"No, you can't."

"How can it be helping?"

"It just is, okay?"

"But –"

"You agreed and I'm keeping it."

"Fine."

The ominous silence resumed.

"Anyway," Alice said eventually, some confidence returning to her voice. "That wasn't why your mother stormed out."

Jude looked at her in shock. "Of course it was!"

"No, it wasn't. She started asking me about Daniel and Mia. How they met, had I anything to do with it."

Jude was confused. "Why? What does she care –" Then it hit him. "Ah come on, she doesn't still think…I thought she had agreed that you had nothing to do with it."

"She was never convinced, Jude," Alice said. "We both knew that. All we did was persuade her to leave it alone."

"So what did she say?"

"Oh, you know. What happy relationship had I destroyed to get Daniel and Mia together? Was I enjoying the misery I was causing? Same as before."

"Typical. My father has an affair and it has to be someone else's fault. He even has her believing it."

"Maybe she has a point. I mean, I did introduce them –"

"At a party with, what, sixty other people there. We've been over this. He's a sixty-two-year-old man. What he does is his own responsibility."

"Suppose."

Jude closed his eyes again and tried to enjoy the supposed tranquillity. But he knew where the conversation was going.

"They still hate me, don't they?" Alice said.

There it is.

"They never actually hated you. They were angry."

"I feel there's a 'but' coming."

"You know what they're like. They might go on like it's all

forgiven –"

"But…" Alice said.

"But it's not forgotten."

Alice sighed and shook her head. "That's fine for your mother, I suppose, she has a right. But Brian? Doesn't it kind of make him –"

"A total hypocrite? Oh yeah."

"So what am I supposed to do?"

"You know we don't play happy families. We don't pop round to each other for tea. And we definitely don't talk about our problems."

"So, what? We don't say anything? And the whole thing becomes yet another skeleton in the Miller closet?"

Jude wasn't surprised by how much this annoyed her. In more maudlin moments, it bugged the hell out of him too. He reached out and took her hand.

"What's one more at this stage?"

Chapter 13.

October.

Alice adjusted herself on the uncomfortable plastic chair, her gaze wandering around the bland and utterly joyless waiting room.

"Simon, please," she hissed into the phone, glancing towards the reception hatch, where a Guard was busy pretending not to listen. "I know you're new, but I think you can hold the fort for a few hours…..I don't know how long I'm going to be….just call me if there is any problem…okay, bye."

She sighed as she dropped the phone into her bag. *For fuck sake. Why did this have to happen today?* She thought and then immediately felt guilty. *Guess it's my own fault for hiring someone who can't find his nose to scratch it, let alone house-sit an art gallery for five minutes. God, I miss Suzanne.*

A pretty girl, three, maybe four years old, was walking around the room, flying her Barbie-doll like Superman. She had been sitting with two chatty women, who seemed perfectly comfortable with being in a Garda station waiting room, and Alice had watched the girl getting increasingly bored and restless as the women did an admirable job of ignoring her. As she approached with her doll, the girl noticed Alice and boldly stared at her.

Alice smiled. "Hi," she said. "You flying?"

"I'm Wonder Woman," the girl said proudly, holding the doll up for Alice to see. She then noticed the thin sterling-silver Tiffany bracelet on Alice's wrist. "That's pretty," she said, walking up to her and touching it.

"Thank you very much," Alice said. "That's a very special bracelet."

The girl's eyes opened wide with excitement. "Do bullets bounce off it?"

Alice laughed. "Maybe they do. I've never tried that. But –"

"I'm sorry, I'm sorry!"

Alice looked up to see one of the women rushing over. "Jayziz, she'll talk to anybody, this one."

"No, not at all. She's beautiful. And very friendly. Aren't you?"

"Look Mommy, Wonder Woman!" the girl said excitedly, pointing to Alice's bracelet.

"She's obsessed with Wonder Woman, wherever she's getting that from," the woman said, perching beside Alice on the sofa. She pulled the girl to her and started fixing her clothes. "You have any yourself?"

"Hmmm?" Alice said, distracted by the fidgeting girl.

"Kids. You have any?"

Alice opened her mouth to answer, but no words came. She'd answered that question countless times since her mid-twenties, everything from the dismissive 'No, thank God' and 'Not yet, we're both focussing on work at the moment' to 'What, and ruin this figure?' and 'No, we actually enjoy our lives' when she was feeling more broody and defensive. Maybe she was sick of these ready-made answers or maybe she didn't want to share even a cliché with a stranger she just met in a Garda station waiting room, Whatever the reason, none of these answers came to her and Alice realised that, to her annoyance, she was actually welling up.

She quick closed her handbag and stood up.

"Excuse me," was all she could manage to say before standing up. She walked briskly towards the exit. She couldn't be in this room anymore – they could just come find her outside when the time came. She was running by the time she reached the door, barely hearing the woman's confused apology behind her.

~ ~

"Alice. Thanks for coming. I didn't know who else to call." Mia hugged her friend and immediately seemed galvanised. Of course, no longer being in that interview room probably helped.

"Hey, of course," Alice said. "How are you? I mean...I can't believe it. Daniel's..." She blushed, unable to finish the sentence. "Have they, what...have they arrested you?

"No." Temple stepped forward, which seemed to startle her. "No-one's under arrest."

"Alice, this is Kieran Temple," Mia said.

"Oh, right," was the curt response.

"Detective Inspector Kieran Temple," he said, shaking her hand.

"We used to work together," Mia said, almost defensively.

"This is that Kieran," Alice said, visibly relaxing. "And you're investigating –"

"Just offering my support. Mrs. Miller, isn't it?"

"Alice," she said. "I don't think I'm old enough to be a 'Mrs' yet."

Alice's almost-flirtatiousness surprised him. Mia clearly noticed it too as it was followed by a moment of awkward silence.

"So I assume Mia will be cleared of any wrongdoing?" Alice said. "She should get a medal after what he put her through."

"There is, naturally, a full investigation on-going," Temple said. "Despite whatever opinion you might have of him, Mr. Summers is dead. The investigation will be thorough and will include finding out everything Mia – I mean, Ms. Burrows – knows."

Alice Miller blushed. "Sure. Sorry."

"And you."

"I'm sorry?"

"We'll need a statement from you," Temple said.

"From me? I don't understand. I wasn't there when –"

"You knew the victim," Temple interrupted. "And you know Ms. Burrows, of course."

The woman took a second to regroup. "Oh right. Sure, I'm available any time." She opened the handbag and pulled out a business card. "My details, if you want to pass them on."

"Thanks, I'll do that," Temple took the card. "And thanks for putting yourself out today. For giving Mia somewhere to stay."

Alice Miller covered her surprise quickly but not quickly enough. She then nodded slowly, as if finally realising why she was here.

"Right, well I need to talk to Hodge," Temple said to Mia, in an attempt to dispel the awkwardness. "I'll let you go. Get some rest."

"Yeah, okay," she said, giving him a quick hug. "Thanks for…thanks for everything."

After Mia had pushed through the door on the street, Temple turned to Alice Miller. "May I ask you one question before you go?" he asked. "I didn't want to bother Mia about this right now."

"Sure," she said, wrapping a strand of hair behind her ear.

She did seem to have the look of the wife of a becoming-famous chef. If there was such a look, she had it. The clothes, prim and conservative, were understated and could have been bargain-basement or haute couture, as far as Temple's untrained eye could tell. But it was her jewellery that stood out. A tiny stone, that could only have been a diamond by how it glinted even in the Garda station's dull light, sat comfortably on her neckline, held by a barely-visible silver chain. It was accompanied by two equally perfect diamonds in silver settings on her earlobes. Temple couldn't see her hand without pointedly looking at it but he could imagine a formidable piece on her ring finger.

Even more than the jewellery though, it was a certain air emanating from Alice Miller that Temple noticed. An air of confidence, an answering knowledge that where she was in life was exactly where she was supposed to be, where she was entitled to be.

Temple hoped that he was imagining all this about her, but he knew that, when it came to people and his first impressions of them, he was rarely wrong.

He pushed it away. "We're having trouble tracking down Mr. Summer's family and I was wondering, maybe –"

"His parents died when he was seven," Alice Miller said. "He has a sister, I think."

"She's his next of kin?"

"I've no idea, I'm sorry," she said. "My husband might know. He was more friends with Daniel than I was."

"What about previous girlfriends?"

The woman looked confused. "Previous...my husband?"

Temple forced a laugh. "Sorry, no. Mr. Summers. I'm trying to get some idea of his background –"

"I thought you were here as Mia's friend."

The woman's change in tone, now rough, defensive, surprised Temple. "I'm involved, in an advisory capacity. You know how it is. So, girlfriends?"

She squinted. "I'm not....sure.... I can help you, to be honest."

"Why's that?"

"Like I said, I...he was more my husband's friend."

"Oh, okay. Well, someone will be in touch about getting your statements," Temple said, gesturing towards the card she had given him. "And feel free to contact me here. You know, if you think of anything."

Without another word, just another tight smile, Alice Miller turned and left the station.

That first impression was holding fast.

Back in the interview room, Temple flicked through his notebook and thought back over Mia's statements. Her story was consistent – what she had told him just now tallied with what she had told Hodge earlier. The few variations merely proved she wasn't reciting some carefully-practised speech. Her statements also corresponded with the physical evidence – the position of the body, the amount of blood, the nature of the injury. As far as he could see, Mia had done what she had to do.

As far as he could see. That was the first thing that bothered him about this whole situation. He couldn't trust himself to be objective. He couldn't just use his best judgement. For someone who always relied on his instincts, this felt like he was missing a limb.

Something else was unsettling him. Alice Miller. Or, more to the point, what she had said.

I didn't really know him.

It wasn't so much the words, but her change of stance. The averted gaze, the stammer, the defensiveness. It all pointed to one thing.

Alice Miller had just lied to him.

Chapter 14.

"Returning to our lead story, Gardaí at Mountjoy Station in Dublin are investigating an incident in which a man died from a single stab-wound, during an apparent break-in at a house in Phibsboro last night. The man, whose identity cannot be released until family have been informed, is said to have illegally entered the house on Connaught St at approximately two thirty this morning and subsequently sustained a stab wound. He was pronounced dead at the scene. It is not yet known whether any arrests have been made or if foul play is suspected.

And now the weather. Squally showers are to continue throughout the after –"

Temple tapped the remote control and the TV went black. He didn't need to know at what time squally showers would stop and the rain would start.

Today was turning into a day of reminiscing, he realised. The visit to Connaught Street that morning and now sitting in

Mountjoy Station, the location of Temple's first posting as a Garda. A shiver went down his back as he thought of it, as the memories came flooding back – the rumours, the taunting, the practical jokes – the cost of being his father's son. All that hard work and recognition in Templemore, winning the Commissioner's Medal – it all meant nothing once he was out in the real world. Especially in North Dublin, where dealing with the reputation of his name was a daily battle. His strength and aptitude over the following years had helped stem the tide, but it was never fully forgotten, certainly not by anyone who had known retired Sergeant Roger Temple.

Although he had visited the adjacent prison half-a-dozen times over the years, this was the first time he had set foot inside the station since his move to Limerick in '95. And, for no reason in particular, he wasn't really enjoying it.

Temple's phone rang. It was a mobile number neither he nor the phone recognised. Ordinarily, he let these calls go to voicemail but, given the day that was in it, he didn't have that luxury.

"Kieran Temple."

"Kieran? It's Michael."

First name terms. Maybe Hodge didn't mind that Temple was being forced on him by the higher-ups.

He decided to let Hodge lead the conversation. "Hi Michael."

"Looks like we're partners."

"Seems so, yes. Just so you know, I didn't push for this –"

"Relax, Kieran. I didn't just get off the bus from Leitrim. You got a phone-call from Miss Posh-Britches at three o'clock in the morning and the D-Super sees that as some sort of divine intervention."

"Something like that. So you're okay with it?"

"As it happens, yes. The way I see it, two D.I.s are better than one. And you obviously have a rare insight into what's going on with this woman."

"Do I?"

"She rang you. That means something, in my book. But Kieran –"

"I know, I know. You're the *kig*. I do the work, give you the rare insight, and you get the glory."

"You know me so well," Hodge said. "Look, it's a political move, we both know that. The boss wants it nice and public that there's no cronyism. And what better way than having Burrow's own superior officer –"

"Former superior officer." Temple cut in.

"Whatever. And a D.I. with a certain reputation to be seen getting his hands dirty. It'll certainly help the GSOC folks sleep at night."

"Maybe. But seriously, what investigating?" Temple asked and immediately felt that twinge of unease again. "You've interviewed her, I've interviewed her, the physical evidence –"

"You interviewed her? When?"

"Just now. I wanted to see if her story was different when it was just me talking to her. Or if she's using me to create some sort of smoke-screen."

"Is that likely?"

"It would seem not. He broke in, attacked her. She thought he was going to kill her, so she killed him. That's what she told you and that's what she just told me –"

"And that's what the evidence points to, yeah, I get it. Well, keep her there till I get back –"

"I've sent her home. Well, not home, to a friend's house –"

"You did what? Kieran, you're coming dangerously close to treading –"

"Michael, you know what she's been through. She needs to rest. She's not going anywhere."

There was silence on the other end. Well, almost silence –

Temple could hear Hodge clicking his tongue the way he did when he was thinking. "Okay, fine," he said eventually. "You know, if this was anyone else, I mean not Mia-Burrows-the-Garda-Sergeant, we'd be done by now. But instead, we must look like we're turning over every stone, while also not looking like we're dragging our heels. It's a shitty deal, especially for you. But if you think sending her off for forty winks is the best move –"

"I do."

But Hodge was right. A woman is attacked in her own home and kills her attacker. Ordinarily, pretty straight-forward. It's investigated and statements are taken, the victim is pointed in the direction of a counsellor and that's it. But, because the woman is a Guard, with all that training given to her by the state, suddenly its two D.I.s walking the streets where it should be one, interviewing the neighbour's dog, worrying about transparency.

"So when are we going to bang our heads together on this?" Hodge said.

"No time like the present," Temple cast his gaze around the open-plan office. "Except I don't see you at your desk."

"I'm still down at the house," Hodge said. "The tech boys are giving me the final run-through. They do love talking, three-syllable words and everything."

"I'll buy you a thesaurus for Christmas. When –"

"Just find yourself an empty chair," Hodge continued. "I shouldn't be too long."

"I'll go get a cup of tea," Temple said.

"The Café Sol in the hospital does takeaway," Hodge said. "Just remember to look both ways before you cross the road."

Temple started towards the back door and the car-park, the way he'd come in. He then told himself not to be stupid.

The Garda station front office had changed very little in the sixteen years since he had been there, which wasn't really surprising. The walls might have got a few coats of paint over that time – one quite recently by the smell – but it was all just so-the-same.

And it was just as he feared. This was the one part of the station that brought it all flooding back. The memories might have been sixteen years old, but they were just as vivid, as discomforting, as ever.

The guard behind the counter barely looked at him. "Yes?"

"D.I. Temple. I'm working with D.I. Hodge on the Connaught Road thing. Can you tell him to ring me when he gets in, if I'm not back."

Another brief glance. "Sir."

"Inspector?"

Temple half-turned to look at the stocky individual standing behind him. The khakis, checked shirt and satchel-strap across his chest identified him as a journalist but strangely not one that Temple recognised. Unless he was new, he certainly wasn't a crime-corr.

It then struck him – the man did look familiar. And that flicker of recognition wasn't missed.

"Don't worry, I'm not here to review the canteen," he said with a smug smile and then waited for Temple's certainly expected laugh.

"I'm sorry?"

"I'm Ben Jameson? The restaurant critic?"

He was a restaurant critic alright. One for whom nothing was more amusing than destroying a decent restaurant because it didn't meet his whimsical needs. And he did it all with such arrogance and self-importance.

"Mr. Jameson," Temple said. "I'm honoured. We so rarely get celebrity visitors."

"Well, I'm not sure I'd call myself…" It took him a second to pick up Temple's tone. "Ah. I said something nasty about your favourite Chinese takeaway, is that it?"

"It was Indian. Cost my niece her job when it closed down."

"I'm sorry to hear that."

"I'm sure. So I'm guessing you're the same Ben Jameson who _"

"Are you involved in this investigation? I was told to speak to a Detective Inspector Hodge."

He decided not to bother explaining the chain-of-command. "You have something you'd like to contribute?"

"Do you mind if we discuss this in private?" Jameson interrupted as he glanced at the guard at the hatch. "I'm already taking a risk by just being here."

Arrogance and self-importance.

Temple opened the door that led to the rest of the station and gestured for Jameson to go through. "Sure. Why not."

Chapter 15.

"So what can I do for you?" Temple asked, gesturing to the other chair in the interview room, the same chair Mia had sat in.

"Well I'd like to make a statement, obviously," Ben Jameson said, sitting down. "You know that I was with Mia Burrows last night."

"She mentioned it, yes."

"And I wanted you to fully understand....the timeline of events."

"In other words, you want to clear yourself of any involvement."

The man's attempt at embarrassment fell short. A vague smirk broke through. "Something like that, yeah. Because I had left long before she...it happened."

"Well, time of death has yet to be determined so –"

"But I'm telling you, I wasn't there," Jameson said, sitting forward, almost aggressively. He then remembered where he was and quickly reversed course.

"Mr. Jameson," Temple said, busily ignoring the outburst by inspecting the statement form. "Who are you worried will find out? Your readers? Your colleagues?" He looked up. "Your wife?"

The colour disappeared from Ben Jameson's face. "All of the above?"

Temple almost felt sorry for him. Almost. "Can you prove you weren't there?" he asked. "At half-two, let's say. Can you prove you were anywhere else but in that house?"

"You think I'd be here if I couldn't?" The false humility was gone as quickly as it had arrived. He opened his satchel and started rooting around inside. "This is why I love technology, Inspector. Big brother is watching over us? No problem. When I was in the taxi on the way home – around half-two, I checked my email on my –" he pulled out a tablet. "On this. I even replied to one or two." He started tapping. "Sent the last one…yep, 2.39am. Not the kind of thing you do when you're watching someone getting stabbed. Wouldn't you agree?"

"Perhaps," Temple said. *Maybe you would if you were trying to establish an alibi.* "That it?"

This time, the humility looked real. "Well, when I got home just a few minutes later, my wife was up with my three-year-old son. He was sick."

Temple couldn't resist. "Using your wife to prove that you weren't with your girlfriend. Classy."

Jameson shrugged his shoulders. "Desperate times." Then it dawned on him. "But…hang on, you're not going to contact her, are you? My wife? You can't."

"Hey, you're the one who put her forward as an alibi."

The look on Jameson's face was now sheer terror and Temple enjoyed the moment. The fact was, unless further evidence came to light to suggest his culpability, Jameson's wife could probably be left out of it. But Temple didn't have to tell him that straight away.

"When did you meet her?" he asked. "Mia."

Unsettled by the change of subject, Jameson squinted. "How's that relevant?"

"Indulge me."

Jameson stared at him for a moment longer, still uncomfortable. "About six months ago. I was at another opening of another five-minute-wonder. Sixteen Eustace, you know it?"

Temple shook his head.

"Mia's a friend of the owner, Jude Miller. Waste of a perfectly good building. Damn shame –"

"Miller?"

"Yeah. You know him? He's kind-of-famous too. Or he was, for about a week." That shitty smugness was now officially annoying.

"I mean, he's okay," Jameson continued. "You know, as middle-management. He was good when he was Renato Rossi's second. But when he went out on his own?" He shook his head like a disappointed father. "Out of his depth. Plus I don't think he's getting on very well with his business partners, I overheard a –"

"So how well do you know him?"

"Who, Jude?"

Temple nodded.

"Em, let me see. He got back to Dublin when? Five years ago, maybe? Since then. Can't say I know him well. But crossed swords more than once, as you can imagine."

"Is he married?"

"Married?" Jameson looked disappointed as the conversation was veering away from being interesting. "I don't know. As I said, he wasn't exactly inviting me round to his house for tea." He squinted again. "Actually, yeah, now that you mention it, he did introduce me to someone at the opening. Might have been a wife. Very thin, if I remember. Still a ten though, don't get me wrong. Well, nine – the tits a bit small –"

"Okay, if we can just get back to your statement, I can get you out of here," Temple said. "We're both busy. I have alibis to check."

"My wife doesn't really need to be involved," Jameson said, trying again to be polite but forceful. "The thing with Mia, it was casual, just a bit of fun!"

Ah, the next stage. Bargaining.

"For you?"

"For her too. She wasn't after anything serious. I mean, I wouldn't have minded staying over last night, I was wrecked and I didn't really fancy schlepping all the way home. I could have come up with something to tell the wife. She's a trusting soul, God love her."

God love her, indeed.

"But Mia would never have let me."

"Did she know you were married?" Temple asked.

"Are you kidding? She fucking loved it."

Temple felt his ears go red. "If you say so."

"I'm serious! She got very....vocal. I mean, she tries to pass herself off as so refined." Jameson picked up Temple's pen and started rolling it over his fingers, as if no opportunity to show off could be passed up. "You know, like the night we met, and when I took her to lunch a few weeks later, you'd think butter wouldn't melt. But get her into bed with a man with a ring on his finger? 'Incorrigible' would be the word. And she even wanted me to call her my wife's name. I mean, what kind of sick bitch –"

Temple had had his fill of this and put his hand up to stop Jameson. Before he found himself using more forceful means.

Jameson sat back and tapped the pen off the desk, pleased

with himself for having this effect. "I think I have scratch-marks," he said, determined to finish his little soliloquy. "It really is hard to believe Mia took that brain into work with her. I hope she used it to good advantage?"

Enough.

"Can you show yourself out?" Temple hoped the droplets of sweat on his forehead weren't visible.

Jameson was surprised, then annoyed. "Sorry? What about my state –"

"Detective Hodge will be here later," Temple had had enough. "Drop back then."

"But...I..." Jameson stuttered but Temple was already standing up.

"It's fairly straightforward. End of the desks, left, straight until you get to the waiting room." Temple stood up. "And then, keep walking."

Chapter 16.

Temple was standing at the gate of 98 Orwell Park, looking in at the large Victorian.

The encounter with Ben Jameson, the guy's blatant disregard for Mia, had left a bad taste in Temple's mouth. But then Jameson's mention of Jude Miller had changed things, piqued his interest. Suddenly, the two people who possibly knew Mia best, the two people who would know most about her relationship with Daniel Summers, were, in fact, living under the same roof. That warranted a home visit.

He could probably have just guessed what the Millers would tell him. In the two years he had worked with Mia Burrows, Temple had himself been witness to, or heard reports of, a number of her ill-fated romances. She had even managed to get herself involved in a 'thing', as she called it, when she was in London for just six months. He had hoped that, since then, she might have become wiser, or at least warier. But as her most recent conquest was that asshole Jameson and the one before him had tried to kill her, it seemed not.

So there was a pang of guilt as Temple stood looking at the Miller house. He was about to ask questions, the answers to which he already knew and, in the process, further upset two people who had just found out that one friend was dead and another friend had killed him.

"I think you'll find I'm not in."

Temple spun around to see a man getting out of a taxi. "Mr. Miller?"

"Detective Inspector Temple, I assume."

Temple realised that he had had a picture of Jude Miller in his head and this was not it. Tall and with a faded tan of someone who had travelled in his younger days, his unkempt black shoulder-length hair had hints of grey running through it. In addition to this, a small black stainless-steel 3-pointed star earring suggested final rebellion against inevitable ageing.

As they shook hands, Jude Miller tried to smile but it barely broke through. "Sorry to keep you waiting. A restaurant kitchen – not the easiest place to escape from. Especially when it's your own restaurant kitchen."

"At least it affords you certain luxuries," Temple said.

The man looked confused for a moment. "The house? No, I inherited that. Been in the family for four generations." Any other day, that might have been said with pride.

Temple gestured towards the taxi which was still trying to negotiate its way back on to the street.

"I meant that. Hardly the cheapest mode of transport."

"Oh, right. No…my car is, em…" Jude Miller looked even more uncomfortable. "I don't have a car at the moment."

"Ah."

"Sorry to keep you waiting," Jude Miller said again, clearly keen to move the conversation on.

"Not at all. I was just…you know, taking it all in."

"Yes, it's a bit in-your-face alright."

"I like it," Temple said as he approached the front door. "Fits in well with its, you know, surroundings."

Jude pressed the button on a fob and the gate emitted a short squeak before gracefully sliding sideways. "Gate's new, I admit." he said, walking through in to the gravel driveway. "It might just be me today, if you don't mind. Haven't been able to get in touch with my wife. I'll try her again when we get in –" He stopped as he noticed a black Mini outside the front door. "Or…not." He didn't sound too happy.

"Alice? You h…you here?" he called as they entered the large hall, any ease in his voice gone.

"Jude?" The voice was coming from the room on the right. A moment later, Alice Miller appeared at the door, a silver picture frame in her hand. "What are you doing here?"

"Funny. That was going to be my question," Jude asked, accusation in his tone.

"Well I was just –" She stopped when she spotted Temple on the step. "Inspector."

"You know each other?" Jude asked, surprised.

"Your wife and I met this morning," Temple said. "At Mountjoy station."

Jude Miller looked even more annoyed. "You went."

"Why wouldn't I?" his wife said defensively before her husband could speak. "She's our friend, Jude."

"After we agreed to –"

"No, we didn't. You told me to…I still can't believe you did that –"

"Ah, just forget it, forget it," Jude Miller waved a dismissive hand. "Inspector Temple wants to talk to us about Daniel. You weren't answering your phone."

Temple tried to pass her into the room.

"Not in there," she said a little too quickly, before quickly regrouping. "It's a bit of a mess. Spring cleaning." She looked at Temple. "Only six months late." The laugh that followed was forced.

Jude turned on his heel. "You'll have some coffee, Inspector?" he asked, crossing the hall. Temple gestured for Alice Miller to follow her husband and she replied with a fixed smile.

The kitchen was a stark contrast to the very traditionally-dressed Victorian house he had entered. Bright, slick and modern, it sat in what had to be a recently-added extension. He sensed a certain pride on Alice's face as she noticed him taking in the room. He concluded that it was her design, her contribution to the 'Old-Miller-Place'.

"So what would you like to ask us?" she said when they had sat down at the large glass-and-steel table.

"Straight to the point," Temple said, pretending to be impressed. "Fair enough."

"You'll have to excuse my wife, Inspector," Jude Miller said, distracted by a complicated-looking coffee machine. "Never has been a big one for pleasantries or small talk."

"Thank you, Jude," his wife said in a gruff 'I-can-speak-for-myself' manner.

"Well I'm sure you're busy," Temple said, opening his notebook. "This won't take long."

Once again, she cast her fixed smile, clearly a thinly veiled expression of irritation or embarrassment or both.

Temple returned the polite smile. "But this is important, as I'm sure you understand."

He turned in his chair. "My first question is for you, I suppose, Mr. Miller. I was wondering –"

The man put up his fore-finger as he pressed a button on the coffee machine. It started making a loud buzzing noise. "Not the quietest of things." He raised his voice over the machine.

Temple wondered if this was a stalling tactic but it didn't bother him – he could sit here for the day if need be. The noise eventually stopped and Jude set an espresso cup in front of Temple. The smell was damn good and Temple had to remind himself that he didn't drink coffee anymore.

"Thanks." he said anyway. "So, as I was saying, Mr. Miller –"

"Actually," Alice Miller interjected. "Would you mind calling us Alice and Jude? I feel like we're being interrogated otherwise."

So it was nervousness, not coldness, that he was seeing, Temple realised. He was suddenly conscious that he might have been projecting some aggression. "Sure," he said, trying to sound light and casual. "There's no interrogation happening here though. I just need to clear up some things."

"I know. It's just…if you don't mind."

Temple looked over at Jude, trying to see if he felt the same.

"What things, Inspector?" the man asked.

"Has Mr. Summers ever done anything like this before?"

Jude was clearly taken aback. No, not taken aback, annoyed. "Has he ever…" he said. "Has Mr. Summers ever done anything like what before? Been stabbed to death on a kitchen floor? No, this would be his first time. What are you talking about?"

"I'm trying to get an idea –"

"I mean, why are we talking about Daniel like this? He's the victim!"

"Yes, but –"

"What about Mia?"

"Jude, stop." Alice cut in.

"No Alice, I won't. What about Mia, Inspector? What is she being charged with, for example?"

"Mr. Miller – Jude – the reason we're talking about Daniel is that, as it stands, Mia Burrows most likely won't be charged with anything."

The man's mouth dropped open. "You mean – what, she's going to get away with this? Are you fucking joking? What, just because she's one of your crowd, she can literally get away with murder?"

"Will you calm down!" his wife said.

"No!" Jude was on his feet. "I don't believe this! Daniel is the victim here. He didn't deserve this! And the very first question you want to ask is 'What did he do to deserve…" He faded off.

"Look, I know this is a shitty deal," Temple said firmly. "He was your friend. And I can tell you that we are investigating all possibilities," Temple decided he better include this reassurance. "But if he attacked Ms. Burrows, as she claims –"

"Yeah," Jude scoffed. "As she claims."

"And as evidence suggests, then she had the right to protect herself. So, if you can look at me and tell me that Daniel would never attack her, then we can take that on board as we proceed."

Jude looked at Temple and started to speak but only a brief sound escaped, as if the man's belief in his friend had just vanished.

"Can you?" Temple asked. "Can you tell me that Daniel would never hurt her? That he never did it before, for example?"

"You know what?" Jude said. "I'm not going to sit here and hand you what you need to let Daniel's killer go free. I'm just not."

"Mr. Miller, if you are purposely concealing something from this investigation –"

"That's not what he's doing," Alice interjected. "But if what you're saying is true and Daniel attacked Mia, what difference does it make whether or not he did it before? It's not like he can hurt anyone else."

"Because it is my job to know everything there is to know about a victim in a situation like this. And, besides Mia, you two seem to be the people who knew him best."

"He wasn't a bad person, Inspector." Alice said. "He wasn't. He was a bit intense and, in hindsight, maybe a bit unstable but –"

"For fuck sake!" Jude said, glaring at his wife. "You're turning on him now too? Are you saying he deserved this?"

"No, of course not! But maybe, yeah, Mia did what she had to do. I saw her face this morning, you didn't. And she –"

"Oh big surprise!" Jude's aggression was back. "Fuck Daniel, right? Never your precious Mia's fault. Why don't you just erect a fucking statue to her on O'Connell Street!"

There were tears in Alice eyes. One escaped and meandered down her cheek. She slowly stood up and Temple realised that it wasn't sadness he was seeing. He knew that look, he knew it well. But he was still too late to warn Jude before she slapped his cheek. She slapped it again. Temple looked for the hurt to show on Jude's face but all he saw was acceptance. The man knew he had overstepped some line.

"I know you're trying to hurt me right now," Alice said. "You're entitled to. But how you can say that to me? Do you not think I feel guilty enough?"

She backed away from Jude and then seemed remembered they had company. She stood in the middle of the kitchen, maybe searching for that right thing to say, something to justify her actions or at least ease the tension.

Instead, without a word, she turned and left the room.

Chapter 17.

"She's right about one thing, Inspector," Jude Miller said, breaking the silence. "He was a good man."

They had stood and listened to the front door slam and the Mini being driven angrily out of the driveway. The moments that followed might have seemed, to the casual observer, awkward but not to Temple. The silence was important. He needed Jude to be the first to speak and he'd happily wait as long as it took.

"He was," Jude said as if Temple had tried to disagree. "What he did to Mia – I don't know – but he's been my friend for nearly five years and he was decent."

"I take it you're not a big fan of Mia's though?"

"Yeah, look, I'm sorry about that. It was uncalled for. She's your colleague, your friend maybe and –"

"Never mind that –"

"But I'm probably not being fair. I don't know her all that well. But I've always felt that…" He faded off, embarrassed.

"Forget that she's my friend, okay?" Temple said. "Really. I need you to be honest."

Jude looked at him for a moment, maybe trying to decide if he could take him at his word.

"She's hot," he said, almost blurting it out. "I won't pretend I haven't noticed."

Temple nodded.

"But, Jesus, how well she knows it." The sudden spite in Jude's voice was surprising. "I've never known anyone to have so much self-confidence and so little self-awareness."

Temple was about to get defensive, 'Mia's one of the most modest people I know ' or something like that. But he didn't. He had just told Jude to forget his friendship with her and he couldn't really take that back. It didn't really matter anyway. This was Jude's opinion, he was entitled to it.

"She's always been Alice's friend. But when she got together with Daniel, I probably should have paid more attention, made more of an effort to…"

He faded off again and Temple let the silence happen.

"I know it sounds like an excuse," Jude said. "But I was opening the restaurant around that time, it was all I could see. Everything else was, you know, in the fog."

"What did Alice mean there? 'I know you're trying to hurt me'?"

"Ah nothing. We're just….working through some stuff. I don't want to talk about that."

Temple nodded. He could come back to it later if he needed to. "Okay. So, this restaurant."

"What about it?"

"Is that going well?"

Jude looked surprised by the changed of subject, but then relieved. "Well, it's still open," he said. "Nearly seven months now. I should probably get an award for that or something."

"Yeah, not exactly the best time to be starting any new business, I'd say."

"Ups and downs, I admit. It was good at the start. I mean, really good. The novelty of something new, especially nowadays. But that wore off and it's been a bit…quiet since then. Plus, the reviews…they haven't been great"

"But who reads those, right?" Temple said. He vaguely remembered reading some of those reviews and 'haven't-been-great' was being generous.

"So how long have you been with the Gardaí?" Jude asked.

"Eighteen, no, nineteen years, fifteen as a detective."

Jude was suddenly nervous again. "Something you might know –" He stopped himself, as if changing his mind a little too late.

"Please." Temple gave him a reassuring smile.

"Any idea how you get a background check on someone? Like on TV?"

""You know, you should probably have got to know your wife before you married her."

Jude forced a laugh. "Damn. I knew there was something forgot to do." And then he was serious again. "But…is there a way?"

"Background check on who?"

"Just, you know, generally speaking."

"Not really, no," Temple said. "Our vetting unit does clearances, of course. You know, teachers, care workers, that sort of thing. It's not available for the public though."

"Right. Not to worry."

Temple tried again. "Who are you looking to check out?"

"Ah no-one really, I'm just curious."

It didn't take a detective to know that that was a lie. He waited.

"It's just...my new partners in the restaurant. I know, I should have done it before I shook their hands. But I met them at a trade show, they offered me a lot of money and it was all so fast, you know...."

"Too good to be true, right?"

"Don't get me wrong, there's no problem or anything. It's all going great."

"But contracts are signed and suddenly you don't know who you're getting into bed with."

"Something like that, yeah."

"Well, you could hire a P.I."

"Really?"

"Of course. Go on the internet, you'll find a few. They're not cheap though. How's that Dire Straits song go? 'The usual fee plus expenses'."

Jude looked disappointed. Not the reaction of someone for whom there was 'no problem or anything'.

"You know, there are a couple of strings I could pull," Temple said. "Make some unofficial enquiries, under the wire. What are these partners' names?"

"Ah look, forget about it," Jude said. "I don't want to make a big thing of it."

"But maybe just to be sure?"

At the sight of the Temple's notebook being opened, Jude was suddenly very nervous. "Actually, they insist on being my silent partners and I'm sure they have their reasons for that. I'm just being paranoid."

"But you obviously –"

"You're reading too much into this, really. It's fine."

Temple stared at him for a few seconds. "If you're really sure –"

"I really am."

Cursing himself, Temple put away his notebook and pulled out his keys. Jude took the hint and gestured towards the door.

"Maybe they'll move on to pastures new," Temple said.

"Don't want them to. They're very generous. This –" Jude paused at the kitchen door to pull his sleeve – "Was the latest treat." Expensive watches might have been out of Temple's budget these days but he still knew a Patek Philippe Calatrava when he saw one. And the one he was looking at had to be worth at least three grand. Not for the first time since he met this couple, Temple wondered if he had made the right life choices.

"They weren't exactly confident that I was going to be ready to open on time," Jude said. "This was my reward for proving them wrong."

"Like you said. generous."

"Yeah. Good customers too. Buy the expensive wine."

"And pay for it?" Temple asked. "Not much good having investors if they're drinking the profits. I had an uncle, drank two farms in Wexford."

"They pay their bills, Inspector. Seriously, I shouldn't have said anything. God knows what you must be thinking of me. Of my business acumen."

Jude opened the front door and shook Temple's offered hand. "Look, I really should apologise for Alice's little outburst," he said. "She's pretty upset by all this. I mean, we both are. This is just all so surreal."

"It is that, alright."

"And, like she said, she obviously feels guilty."

"Yeah, why does she?"

"You know, for her part in it. That whole match-dot-com thing she does."

"What, like matchmaking?"

"I suppose you could call it that. But she's good at it. Look at Kate and Stephen."

"Who's that?"

"Oh, sorry. That wedding where Daniel and Mia met? That was Kate and Stephen. Alice got them together. And plenty of others." He sniggered. "Maybe she was getting tired of creating all these boring perfect couples. Decided to mix things up."

"What, you think your wife purposely got Daniel and Mia together, knowing they'd be bad for each other?"

"I'm not sure I'd –" Jude stopped as Temple's implication dawned on him. "Jesus, no! I didn't mean…fuck…I was kidding!"

Temple felt guilty for indulging in this moment of mischief. "Of course. Sorry, I –"

"No, it's my fault. I shouldn't be making a joke of it."

"Hey, we all have to treat ourselves to a bit of gallows humour," Temple said.

"Daniel's death is one thing – it feels weird even saying it – but how it happened…I mean, Mia…."

"Did you approve of their relationship?"

"I didn't give it that much thought," Jude said too quickly for it to be true. "As I said, I was distracted with work."

"You must have an opinion though. He was your friend."

"I was okay with it, I suppose. But that was naivety on my part."

"Why do you say that?"

"He was always an in-with-two-feet kind of guy when it came to relationships but I just assumed he'd take it slow this time. Allow the relationship to take shape at its own pace."

"But?"

"After a week, Daniel was in love, Inspector. And that did scare me."

Chapter 18.

April.

Daniel was miles away. So much so, he nearly missed the conversion.

And the first one of the match too. Leinster had been doing okay, having scored three tries in the first forty minutes. That would have been great, except that none of McFadden's kicks had been on target. Thankfully, minutes into the second half and after try number four, Isa Nacewa had finally anticipated the wind and sent the ball gracefully between the posts.

And Daniel had almost missed the whole thing. Because he was, once again, thinking about Mia.

Since the night in Jude and Alice's when they officially became 'a couple' – or maybe even before that, since their first date – he had been distracted by her. And every time he saw her, whenever they talked on the phone, any time a text from her popped up on the screen, the excitement intensified that little bit more. And by now, a month in, he'd been at the point of hyperventilation more than once.

He had needed a distraction and rugby should have been it. It had always worked before. But, he just couldn't get into it, despite Leinster's dominance.

Daniel could always talk about his feelings. Of course, of his gender, he was in a minority and, over the years, when he tried to open up, his friends would mock him until the subject changed to something more innocuous. Thankfully these days, he did have one friend with whom he could have a frank conversation without fear of reprisal. Unfortunately, at this moment, he had no idea where that friend was.

In his usual manner, Jude had been very vocal, and optimistic, in his Leinster support during the first half, not even getting too bothered by those missed kicks. The attempts to bolster and engage Daniel had been starting to grate and he was relieved when the half-time whistle blew and Jude had offered to get the pints. But now, the second half was well underway and Jude still wasn't back.

Feeling a bit detached from the match, Daniel decided to go look for him. He figured he might be able to persuade Jude to duck out early and have the pints in the pub instead.

He made his way out of stands and headed towards the bar. As he pushed through the door, he spotted Jude, with his back to him, in the middle of what looked like a serious conversation. Daniel didn't recognise the other person, a rather stern-looking middle-aged man. The man wore a tailored charcoal suit which, by its cut, should have made him look formidable, important. Instead, he looked he had stolen it from someone formidable and important.

"I can assure you, Mr. Lewis," Jude was saying to the man as

Daniel approached. "It's all in hand. We still have a few days before we even start the soft-openings. And you couldn't really expect a hard-core fan to miss this match, could you?" Jude laughed nervously and, even a few feet away, Daniel winced when the laugh wasn't reciprocated.

"What we expect, Jude," the other man said. "Is for the person who is supposed to be getting this thing off the ground – that would be you – is making sure that it happens. Me and Mr. Curtis, we've sunk a lot of money into this, you know."

"I appreciate that and it will, of course," Jude said, a lot more timid than Daniel was used to. "We're pretty much ready to go anyway."

"Ready to go?" The man's sneer was unsettling. "I was there four hours ago. Didn't look ready to go to me –" He suddenly stopped and glanced over at Daniel, who immediately felt a bead of sweat on his neck.

"Can I help you with something, friend?" the man asked.

Jude looked over his shoulder and turned abruptly. "Dan, hi. Is it over?""

"No...no, of course not," Daniel stuttered. "I was getting thirsty. Everything...eh...everything okay?"

"Yeah, sure." Daniel knew Jude's relaxation sounded unnatural. "I'll grab the beers and –"

"Look, I'll leave you to it," the man interrupted. "You have a busy few days ahead of you." He looked at Daniel, a long glare. Like something was his fault. "But, you know, enjoy the rugby, by all means."

"Eh yeah," Jude said. "You too, Mr. Lewis, and thanks for your advice. We'll be ready."

"I hope so." The man's tone left Daniel cold.

"Sorry," Daniel said, watching the man leave. "I obviously interrupted something there. I thought –"

Jude was deep in thought. "What? No, hey, not a problem," He shook himself off, smiled.

"Who was that?" Daniel asked.

"That was Mr. Lewis," Jude said nervously, "They're the silent partners. Him and Mr. Curtis."

Daniel sniggered, seeing an opportunity to lighten the mood. "Do you really call them 'Mr. Lewis' and 'Mr. Curtis'? Isn't this the twenty-first century?"

"With the money they're giving me, I'll call them God and Jehovah if they want me to. Right, come on. We're missing it."

"Meh. Were not missing anything. I was thinking we'd just head over to the Horse Show House. Beat the crowd."

"Yeah, right," Jude said and started towards the stands. He turned back when he realised Daniel wasn't following. "What, are you serious?"

"Well....yeah," Daniel said, suddenly embarrassed.

Jude folded his arms. "Okay, what is going on with you? You barely said a word since we got here and now you want to leave probably the best match we've played all year. What the fuck, Dan?"

Daniel couldn't help himself. "I think she's it, Jude. I have met the perfect woman!"

Jude looked around, embarrassed by Daniel's eruption. "I presume this is Mia we're talking about?" he said quietly.

"Who else! I've never felt this...this...I don't know, I -"

"Okay, go easy there, Romeo. You'll give yourself a nose-bleed."

"I'm serious, man."

"Serious about what?" Jude said. "You've only known her five minutes."

"A month. But yeah, I know, it's ridiculous. But when it's right, it's right."

The smile was gone, he wanted Jude to know he was serious. "And this feels right."

"We do need a proper pint," Jude said to Daniel's relief.

They started towards the Merrion Road exit.

"You know, I have this vague recollection," Jude said as they walked. "Of having this conversation with you before. You do remember Kate, right?"

"This is different."

"How, exactly?"

"It's totally different. Kate and me were stupidly complicated. Even before we were together, we were complicated. This is the opposite, it's simple and straightforward. I met her and I fell in love."

"Fell in love? Is that what it is now? Do you not think – "

"It is! There's no mixed signals or he-said-she-said. And it's clear in my head. When was the last time you heard me say that?"

"Em…"

"Come on, you know Mia, she's –"

"Yeah, I do know Mia. And yeah, she talks about you too, to Alice. But that's why I'm telling you, take things slow."

"Mmm," was the only response Daniel could manage. He knew Jude might not be ecstatic about the relationship but he had been expecting a bit more support than this. Not that it really mattered, he didn't need Jude's support or his permission.

"Actually," Daniel said. "I might call it a night."

"What, you're sulking now?"

"No. I've just…well, I've to go into the office in the morning." He pointed back the way they had come. "My car's over here. I'll see you."

He started walking. Jude shouted after him. "Are you even going to think about what I said?"

Daniel's response was to keep walking.

"Or am I just wasting my breath?"

"Yeah, sure," Daniel called over his shoulder. "I'll think about it."

~ ~

She thinks about me!

By the time he was getting into his car, Daniel was confused about confiding in Jude. He was disappointed that his friend hadn't just slapped in on the back and said something like 'Job well done, you've got a good one there'.

Mia thinks about me!

In fairness, it was Jude to whom he always turned for the more articulated advice, so he couldn't give out too much when he got it, even if it wasn't what he wanted to hear. He –

Mia's talking about me!

That was what Jude had said. "She talks about you too, to Alice." That's what he said.

What does that mean? Maybe…

Daniel tried to push that thought out of his head but it was already there. As he drove out of Ballsbridge towards home, he turned the music on. *Massive Attack*. Loud.

But it didn't drown it out. It was bouncing around his brain and it was going nowhere. So he just accepted it.

She loves me. She loves me like I love her!

Chapter 19.

The smile on Renato Rossi's face was wide. And it almost looked genuine.

"Per favore, will you welcome," he declared through perfectly-accented English. "Chef straordinaria, and now Restaurateur straordinaria, Jude Miller."

As the applause erupted, Alice could clearly see Jude's nervousness. It was to be expected - his plan was finally a reality and he was the man of the hour. And he probably hated it.

Alice was looking at her husband with a renewed surge of pride. She knew she hadn't been paying enough attention over the past year as his disillusionment with Renato and *La Bocca* had reached crisis point. So when he had told her that he was leaving once-and-for-all and going out on his own, she hadn't exactly been thrilled. Not when she could see so many restaurants going under and all the others struggling to survive.

Not when the whole country was proudly announcing they were staying in at the weekend with a meal-deal rather than eating out. Not when she was in a job that, as much as she loved it, was never going to bring in the big bucks. And definitely not when she had a responsibility to adopt a certain lifestyle, one that Jude wanted them to adopt even if he would never admit it. So, no, the thoughts of her husband struggling with a new business, one which might not bring in a decent salary for years, did not fill Alice with enthusiasm.

But she had kept her counsel, thinking it would pass, a few bad weeks with Renato that had brought about this knee-jerk reaction. She watched him go to meetings with bank managers and business advisors, estate agents and mortgage brokers, to be told by all that 'it was inadvisable and commercially unsound to be starting any new business, especially a new restaurant, right in the middle of the worst ever global recession'. And, despite feeling sorry for him every time he walked, dejected, through the front door, Alice had been relieved when his enthusiasm for the idea waned.

Then that chance meeting at a hospitality fair had changed everything. Jude suddenly had himself two new 'angel-investors' – two very silent partners, so keen to remain silent that they hadn't even attended the opening. They simply believed in him, Jude told her. He was an outstanding chef, so they believed that he could be an outstanding restaurateur. And right now, in the moment, she believed it too.

There was a laugh from the crowd and Alice cursed herself for, once again, not paying attention.

"So please," Jude was saying. "Have a glass of wine, enjoy the food that my talented and attractive staff are serving and, don't worry, when you're paying for them, the portions will be bigger."

More laughter and applause marked the end of Jude's brief speech. Alice pushed through the crowd towards him, wanting nothing more at that moment than to hug her brilliant and under-appreciated husband, to show him the pride she was feelings. And hoping that he'd see that she meant it and it would make a difference.

But by the time she got to him, he had been accosted by Renato.

"Well done, Jude," he was saying. "Nice and short. I was afraid you were going to go on and on, just like you used to do at the staff meetings, *si*?"

"Grazie, Padrone," Jude said. "And thanks for those kind words. That can't have been easy."

"It's okay, my friend," Renato said. "I have new boyfriend Nicolas. He has just moved here from Amsterdam. He tells me, live and let live."

He pretended to only now spot Alice, as if she had just walked in. "Ah la bella ragazza Alicia! Come stai?" he said and kissed her cheeks with such enthusiasm that Alice might have felt special, had this not been the way Renato greeted everyone. "I was just congratulating the chef."

"I know, I heard."

"But I can't help feeling happy with myself too, no? For helping you get here, Jude? Especially when you have been stealing my staff." He gestured towards Amy, who was momentarily visible as the kitchen door swung closed. Jude just shrugged.

"You think I would not notice, eh?" Renato continued. "As always, you underestimate me. *So tutto, vedo tutti!*" He took a sip of his champagne, never breaking eye contact with Jude. He tut-tutted and shook his head with his usual over-affected manner. "I guess she will never be the perfect chef that she might have been. Such a shame for her, si?"

Jude started to retort but obviously decided not to bother. One last departing blow, Alice figured, maybe we should let him have it.

Then again, maybe not. "Perfection is over-rated, Renato," she said. "The rest of us put happiness first. You know, that whole 'job-satisfaction' thing? You wouldn't deny Amy that, would you?"

Renato, surprised by this challenge, looked at Alice, probably trying to gauge if she was joking. She held his gaze.

"Of course not," he eventually said stiffly. "Scusi."

Alice tried not to enjoy the moment too much as she watched Renato walk away, pretending not to look put out.

"Why does he insist on calling me 'Al-eee-sea'?," she said and took a sip from her glass.

"You just couldn't resist," Jude said. Alice wasn't sure if he was impressed or annoyed. Maybe he wasn't sure himself. She decided not to give him time to decide, pulling him to her and kissing him. It was a long, impassioned, kiss and Jude looked surprised by it when Alice eventually pulled away

"Your mother seems to be having a good time," she said. She gestured towards Geraldine, who was chatting animatedly with a group of attractive people. "Who's she talking to?"

"I have no idea," Jude said. "Trust her to find the rent-a-crowd and make them her new best friends. She'll be meeting them for lattés within a week."

Alice noticed that sad-little-boy look. "What?"

He shook his head. "It's weird seeing her out without him."

"You were right to tell him not to come, though. Both of them couldn't be here, Jude. Not after the last time."

"I know, I know. And she actually looks happy."

"She does," Alice said, forcing a smile. "But it's going to take time. Let's not proclaim her cured just yet."

"Funny, I'd have thought you'd be the first person to want her cured, after –" Jude caught himself but it was too late.

Even tonight, she wasn't going to let him away with it. "Oh, thanks, Jude," Alice felt herself blush, her cheeks suddenly roasting. She shoved her glass into his hand. "Really. Thanks very much."

"You know what I meant –"

"Yeah, I do."

She pushed past him, not really sure where she was going. Not to the toilets, she told herself, not by herself. She wasn't going to be in there, with just Jude's opinion of her for company.

But that was where she was heading. She couldn't seem to stop her feet from bringing her there.

"Oy missiz, are you sneaking off to do a line of coke?"

Alice turned to see a grinning Mia as she and Daniel arrived, looking slightly drunk and very content. Alice suddenly had somewhere to direct her anger.

"Where the fuck have you two been?" she snapped and enjoyed the over-reaction.

Daniel was taken aback but still smug. "Whoa. We were having dinner. Jude's finger food is good but not exactly filling."

"I'm delighted for you, Daniel, but you missed it."

Mia gestured towards the very full and boisterous room. "Eh, hardly."

"Jude's speech?" Alice felt her annoyance growing by her friend's lack of contrition. She didn't exactly feel like being in her husband's corner at this moment but they didn't know that. "You missed Jude's speech. You know, there is more going on in the world than you two and your little romance."

Mia looked confused. "Okaaay. Well I'm going to get some champagne while you calm the fuck down."

Before Alice could respond, Mia was gone.

Daniel was still smirking. "Feeling a bit side-lined, are we?"

Oh no you don't.

Alice leaned forward and, almost seductively, whispered in Daniel's ear. Then she pulled back to get a proper look at the result.

The smile was gone. The smugness was gone. And, knowing Daniel, they wouldn't be back tonight.

~ ~

Jude felt annoyed, mostly with himself. He had made a promise to himself, about Alice, and he seemed to be breaking it a lot recently.

He watched her scolding Mia and Daniel and silently apologised to them for bringing on this wrath.

"Taking it all in, are you?"

Jude turned to see the small and stout Ben Jameson approaching. "Ben, glad you could make it," he lied. "Sorry, I was miles away."

"Don't be sorry. This is the best day of your life," Ben Jameson said. "Of any chef's life. You're the king of your castle today. You might as well enjoy it."

"I don't get to enjoy it tomorrow?"

"Tomorrow? Nah, tomorrow you'll be too busy trying to control the speed at which everything goes to shit. And you'll be doing that every day for about nine months until you hand the keys over to the next poor sucker. You know, when you realise that you, my friend, are a chef, not a businessman."

"You know, I'd forgotten how much crap comes out of your mouth when you're not staring at my wife's tits."

Jameson grunted. "Don't flatter yourself. So does she not

mind supporting you during this little mid-life adventure?"

Jude felt his jaw clench. "She's not –"

"That eighty-two that Renato is now *not* paying you…that's got to be leaving a hole in the push-up bra budget."

Jude wasn't sure what infuriated him more, the slur against his wife or the fact that Jameson knew how much he had been earning.

"Here," he said, grabbing the plate of au d'oeuvres from a passing waiter. "Try the anchovy and truffle terrine."

"Truffles? Really, Jude? Seriously, when are you people going to wake up and smell the mould?"

Eat it before I jam it down your throat.

"Pleasure as always, Ben." Jude walked away but Jameson, not getting the hint, followed him.

"So what's the deal with you and this place?" he said. "The usual grapevines have been very quiet."

"What can I say, I don't engage in idle gossip."

"Or maybe you just weren't worthy of idle gossip. You know, when it was going to be that cosy little non-story in Francis Street. But then something – or someone – happened that put you here instead."

Jude stopped and slowly turned, again surprised by the extent of the man's knowledge. If he wasn't so repelled, he'd have been impressed.

"Yeah," Jameson said, the smugness oozing out of his pores. "Don't be so naive as to diss the grapevine, Jude. Especially when your boss - sorry - *ex*-boss sustains it singlehandedly."

"Funny," Jude said. I thought it sustained him."

"It's…a symbiotic relationship."

Jude said nothing. He knew all too well that people mostly fell afoul of Ben Jameson when they answered a question they weren't asked.

Jameson was waiting but starting to look uncomfortable. "You don't want to tell me?" he said eventually. "Fine. Not to worry, I'll find out anyway."

Jude sniggered. "Yeah, I'm sure you will. I reckon…"

He noticed that Jameson's smugness was gone. In fact, the man wasn't even listening to him, his attention had been drawn elsewhere. "What are you staring at?" turning to follow Jameson's sightline.

"You know, you might not have to make me eat mould to render me speechless," Jameson said. "Do you know that one?" He gestured to someone across the room. "Or is she just one of the nameless beauties you hired to make this place less mediocre?"

Jameson was looking at Mia, who was weaving through the crowd with two glasses of champagne. She responded to the man's leer with a polite smile before turning towards Daniel.

"Aren't you married?" Jude asked.

"Yeah, sure," Jameson said with a dismissive wave of the hand. "So, who is she?"

Once again, Jude couldn't decide if this man amused him or repulsed him. "Mia, my wife's friend. And sorry to disappoint, but not available. She's with him." Jude pointed towards Daniel and then leaned in towards Jameson. "My friend."

"How very cosy," Jameson's tone was of disbelief. "Hardly the most loving couple though."

Jude glanced across the room, ready to accuse the journalist of wishful thinking. But, actually, Daniel had his back to Mia and roughly pulled away when she tried to take his hand. And then Mia looked confused.

Oh great, he thought, *their first fight and they've picked tonight to do it. Well they better not be one of those shout-y couples.*

"So maybe she'll be available one of these days," Jameson said.

"You scratch my back, Mister I'm-Looking-For-A-Glowing-Review, I'll scratch yours."

Jude was surprised by what was being suggested, but also by Jameson's arrogant forthrightness. "What are you saying, Ben?"

"We both know what I'm saying," Jameson interjected. "I'll leave you to work out the details. Don't forget to read my blog tomorrow. You might get a mention."

Before Jude could say anymore, Jameson was gone. He watched the highly respected food critic squirm through the crowd towards the exit.

And wondered what the hell just happened.

Chapter 20.

"Okay, what is wrong with you?"

Mia and Daniel were having coffee. It was one of the first non-rainy days of the summer - it would have been an exaggeration to say that it was sunny - and Daniel had agreed to sit outside. He hadn't really agreed, more like shrugged his shoulders when Mia suggested it.

Since the launch party, he'd been like this. She barely got a goodbye kiss that night and he had given her that horrible answer 'Fine' when she asked if he was okay.

The following few days were the same. Unanswered calls, two-word texts, more grunts and 'Fine's. So when he agreed to meet her today and then sat there pointedly ignoring her, Mia had had enough.

"Seriously, Daniel, what?" she said, enjoying the strength in her voice. "And don't tell me 'nothing' or 'I'm fine', or, not kidding, I'm going. You can walk ho –"

"Do I mean anything to you?" Daniel blurted out, a definite growl in his voice. "Like, at all?"

Mia was taken aback by his aggression more than his words. "What does that mean?"

"It means...just that. That everyone seems to know you. That everyone wants to be your friend. And that I....I'm supposed to be your boyfriend and every time we're in company, I feel completely unimportant. Like you could take me or leave me."

"I don't know what you're talking about. Is this from the other night? I was just chatting to people, being sociable. Isn't what you're supposed to do at those things?"

"Yeah, all men though. Or did you not notice?"

"All men what?"

"You were only talk –"

"I was only talking to men, is that what you were going to say? No Daniel."

"Okay, what women –"

"You know what? I really can't remember every single person I talked to. But I very much doubt that's true."

"Talked to? Come on. You weren't talking, Mia. You were flirting."

Mia laughed. But it wasn't funny. "Seriously, what you...you think I was flirting with other men?"

"As if I wasn't there. Worse – you didn't seem to care if I was there or not. They were lavishing attention on you and you were lapping it up. Alice noticed it too. She was the one who pointed it –"

"First of all, Daniel," Mia sat forward in her chair and then realised her tone was drawing attention from other tables. It took every bit of effort to stop herself from just walking out, as she had threatened. "I was talking to plenty of women," she hissed. "Alice, Jude's mother. And..." Something Daniel said suddenly hit home. "Wait. What do you mean 'Alice noticed it too?"

Daniel looked embarrassed. "Nothing. She just pointed out that you were enjoying the attention. Which is true, you were. This isn't about Alice. It's about – "

"It is about Alice if she's saying something that's making you *this* crazy."

"What's that mean? Please don't use that word."

"I'm not. I'm not saying you're crazy, but these aren't exactly rational thoughts I'm hearing, Daniel."

"It's just…okay, maybe you weren't flirting. That was an exaggeration. But one thing's for sure, every male pair of eyes was on you."

"So? What's wrong with that? Surely that's a good thing, that your girlfriend is someone that other men look at."

"There's nothing wrong with it, if you weren't enjoying it so much. That's the bit that doesn't do much for a guy's self-esteem."

"What about my self-esteem?"

"Yeah, right."

"I'm serious. You know, maybe it makes me feel good about myself."

"What, you're saying I'm neglecting you now or something? I'm always telling you how beautiful –"

"For fuck sake, it's not about you. It's even not about us. I'm just not as confident as you think I am and sometimes I need some harmless – *harmless* – eye-contact with strangers. But it doesn't change how I feel about you. It really doesn't."

Daniel sat back and took a slow sip of his latte, looking calm. Placated maybe.

"So how do you feel about me?" he said.

Or maybe not.

"How do I feel about you? What, you want me to quantify –"

"Because I love you."

A lump instantly formed in Mia's throat. She tried to appear cool but her inability to look him in the eye was betraying her. She fiddled with her napkin. "Do you?" was all she could manage.

"Definitely."

"Definitely? We've known each other less than –"

"What difference does that make? You've told me yourself that you've fallen in love in days."

"Yeah, when I was sixteen! We're not sixteen."

"Doesn't matter. Look, I've been over and over this in my head, okay? And there's no getting away from it. I love you and you're just going to have to live with that."

He wasn't looking at her, instead concentrating on stirring his latté, first clockwise, then the other way. He seemed transfixed with it and jumped when she leaned in and took his hand.

"I love you too." She said it so quietly, she wasn't sure if he had heard her. "I said I love –"

"I heard you. But don't."

"Don't what?"

"Don't say it just because I said it. Just because you think you have to."

"I'm not. I've wanted to say it. But I needed to hear you say it first."

Daniel clearly didn't understand that.

"What if *you* didn't say it back?" Mia said, impressed with how exasperated she could sound when she needed to be. "I couldn't take that chance." She pointed at herself. "I told you. No confidence."

Daniel was already off his seat and leaning across the table to her. He kissed her gently and, once again, she felt that lump in her throat.

It dawned on her that they were in the middle of a very busy coffee-shop veranda. She pulled away and glanced around, feigning embarrassment. No surprise that everyone was doing their best to ignore them. Apart from one small boy who was boldly staring.

Daniel, on the other hand, didn't look one bit embarrassed. "So, do you think," he said, sitting back down. "We should think about, as they say, going to the next level?"

"What do you mean?"

"You know, you and me?"

Mia laughed. "What, get married?"

Daniel looked shocked. "Well, that wasn't what I meant but –"

"Hey, I was joking, I was joking!"

Thankfully, he looked relieved.

"But maybe what I want to suggest won't be as much of a shocker now."

Mia eyed him with overstated suspicion. "Go on."

"Move in with me."

He was wrong. It was definitely as much of a shocker.

"I'm serious. Move in with me," he said again, as if he was afraid Mia had been imagining it the first time.

"You want to live together?" she said.

"Well, yeah."

"Like, now?"

Daniel didn't try to hide his disappointment at her less than enthusiastic reaction. "Yes, like now."

"Daniel, we – "

"We've only been together a month. I know. We covered that. But we work, Mia. We do. I love you, you love me, so why not? What's the point in waiting?"

She wanted to interrupt him, tell him all the reasons why not, make it clear to him how far from ever-happening that was for her. But she didn't. Instead, she let him get excited. She let him think it was possible. And, worst of all, she started thinking about it herself. Wondering if maybe she could live with him, be with Daniel on that level.

"You're right. Let's do it," Mia heard herself say.

What? No!

"Seriously?"

No, not seriously. I was joking. Ha ha, got you!

But it was too late for that, even she couldn't be that cruel.

"Yeah, absolutely," she said as this staggering lack of self-control made her dizzy. "Probably going to happen sooner or later, right?"

What the fuck are you doing?

There were tears in Daniel's eyes. Actual tears. Mia sensed an assortment of emotions emanating from them – the obvious ones, delight and relief, but also gratitude, longing and even fear.

Or maybe those are my feelings, Mia thought. *That last one certainly is.*

Chapter 21.

May.

"Yes, I know that Miranda, but I did tell you three days ago that I had this meeting," Ben Jameson spoke on his mobile as the taxi crawled along in the heavy Wednesday evening traffic. The taxi driver smiled and shook his head. Jameson ignored him.

"I told you," he said. "I agreed to go and meet this chef to discuss my review…Because they're never fucking happy with their reviews…it wasn't that harsh, actually….Have you eaten there? No, well then….I don't know, I might need a pint afterward…. tell him Daddy's working….he's three years old Miranda, I think he'll be okay with it ….goodbye."

Jameson threw his phone on the seat beside him and breathed a sigh of relief. Thankfully, Miranda hadn't asked him the one question he couldn't answer. Why was he giving Jude Miller a second chance? It was something he never did, it didn't matter who he was dealing with.

He knew the reason, but it wasn't exactly something he could tell his wife.

"Trouble and strife with the trouble-and-strife, wha'?" the taxi driver said.

"What?" Jameson said with some irritation. "Yeah, whatever, just drive the car."

The taxi suddenly jerked to a stop, jolting Jameson forward.

"Hey, will you watch what you're doing!" he shouted.

"Eh, sorry there, but you really should be wearing your seat-belt."

"You know what, where are we?" Jameson wiped the condensation from the window with the side of his fist and saw that they were approaching Christchurch. "Just stop here, I'll walk."

As he stepped out into the unyielding drizzle and almost got knocked down by a bicycle, he made a decision that made him instantly feel better.

Jude Miller was going to pay for this.

~ ~

Not for the first time, Jude told himself he was nuts.

The last time Jameson had been here, he had not made his presence known to the staff. Jude had only become aware that he was there at the end of the frenetic lunch service, by which time the damage had been done.

Jameson was not yet famous enough, or notorious enough, to be recognised on sight, not by waiters. So it was the head chef who stayed ensconced in his kitchen throughout a service who most often suffered the man's wrath.

"That the staff don't know me means that I get a more genuine and organic feel for a restaurant," Jameson often boasted in his column.

The 'organic and genuine feel' that Jameson had left with that particular day had been less than ideal. His column in the next issue had the headline 'A pedestrian effort at Fine Dining...so keep on walking". And in the days that followed, most people did.

So, as Jude put the final touches to the 'You-better-wow-me' starter, he asked himself again why he was engaging in this tête-a-tête with Ben Jameson. With everything else that was going on, did this really matter?

Yes. It did.

That's what Jameson had said. "Okay, I'll give you another chance, Chef Miller, but you better wow me."

What a prick.

How about a good kick up the arse? Jude had thought at the time. *That will 'wow' you and I promise it will feel genuine and organic.*

"You know, you really need to get a louder door-bell."

Jude turned to see the critic standing at the Passe. He was wet and not-too-happy.

Jude took enjoyment from it. "Still pretty bad out there then?"

"No, I took a shower in my clothes. You know, the taxi drivers in this city are all idiots. I could be at home right now. I have a ton of work to do."

"Well you can thank me later. This will be a damn sight more exciting than sitting in front of a computer."

"Yeah, if you say so," Jameson said dismissively, glancing around the kitchen. "I have to warn you, whatever happens tonight, I won't be retracting or apologising or anything like that."

"Never say never. You know, the *Times* were in the next night and they gave us a rave."

"Like I give a damn what they think," Jameson said. "So, what am I choking down?"

~ ~

As he waited to be served, Jameson's mind wandered again to his real motive for being here. He wondered how long he should wait to bring it up.

He realised that, the two times he'd been here before, he hadn't really taken in his surroundings. It was significantly different to *La Bocca* but that was to be expected. All that burgundy velvet, pile carpet and gilded picture frames weren't really Jude Miller's style. Renato Rossi, definitely – they were right up his street. And right up the street of Dublin's restaurant-frequenting community. Well, a certain cross-section of it anyway.

Jude Miller was clearly not trying to attract the same clientele. Maybe it was out of respect for or fear of Renato, but it was more likely because Miller, for all his faults, was not into all that headache-inducing pretention shared by the Italian and his patrons. Renato only got away with it because, it had to be said, the food at *La Bocca* was unparalleled, possibly the best in Dublin. That Michelin star had been truly deserved.

And now Jameson was sitting in the restaurant of the man reputed to have actually earned that star for Renato, done the work for it. Jameson wondered, not for the first time, if Jude Miller could achieve the same plaudits under his own name.

The interior of the dining room was certainly up to the same standard as *La Bocca*, even if it couldn't have been more different. The principle colour in the room was silver. It was in the soft leather of the circular low-back chairs and in the wide masculine stripes of the wallpaper. Much of the wall-space was out of sight however, as it was adorned with large rectangular white-framed mirrors. In contrast to all this lightness, thick oak flooring and unclothed oak tables gave the restaurant a much-needed bit of maturity. The pieces de résistance though, to Jameson's mind anyway, were the lights – huge glass globes hanging from the ceiling by silver chains.

This ultra-clean-and-contemporary interior suggested that Jude Miller was trying hard to show that he was not Renato Rossi. A little too hard, perhaps.

Jameson had just taken out his voice recorder to start notating his thoughts on the design and its significance, when the door from the kitchen swung open.

"Okay Ben," Chef Miller said as he approached. "Get a load of this and remember that 'retract' is spelt with a 'c', not a 'k'."

Jameson emitted a short snigger. "Yeah, right."

The dish of Pithiviers of Smoked Crab with Forest Mushrooms was laid in front of him and Jameson had to admit that it looked impressive.

"Your presentation is certainly up to a more expected standard, Chef," he said. "It was all a bit thrown together last time."

"Well that's a cloaked apology if I ever heard one," Jude said as he sat down opposite Jameson.

"You're joining me?" Jameson asked, surprised. "Don't you have the main course to do?"

"In a second," Jude said. "I wanted to ask you something."

"Sounds ominous," Jameson said, cutting into the pithivier.

"About what you said at the launch."

"I'm sure I said a lot of things, each more clever and witty than the last."

"Something about having to scratch your back?"

Jameson tried not to smirk. "Oh that," he said. "Well I was –"

"Excuse me," a voice at the door interrupted him.

Damn.

Jude was squinting, looking in the direction of the dimly-lit entrance. "Yes?"

Jameson turned in his chair to see who it was that had such terrible timing.

"Mr. Curtis?" Jude said, standing up and approaching the

new arrival. "How are you? Great to see you."

Jameson got the sudden sense that Jude Miller was nervous.

"I hope you don't mind me dropping by unannounced," the man said. 'Mr. Curtis', whoever he was. "Could I have a word?"

"Sure, sure," Jude said. "Come through…come through to the office."

Jameson stood up, expecting an introduction. But Jude just walked past him.

"Eh, I'll be right back, Ben," he called back to him as he and the other man disappeared into the kitchen.

"What the hell?" Ben said out loud to himself and dropped back into his chair. "I haven't got all bloody night."

He decided that this would be a good opportunity to sample Jude's fare without distraction, so he took a mouthful. "That's definitely a bit more like it alright," he said to himself.

He picked up his voice-recorder but, before he had spoken a word, he was distracted by Jude's voice emanating from the kitchen.

"Yes, I am aware of that, Mr Curtis, but –"

He was being interrupting by this Mr. Curtis, but that voice was not loud enough for Jameson to hear.

"Well," Jude said. "We are only open, what, less than two weeks, you can't expect –"

Another interruption.

"Well I'm trying to remedy that right now sir, as it happened," Jude said. "And I'm sure we'll be back on track very soon. So you don't have to worry about –"

Jameson would have given his two back teeth to hear the other side of the conversation.

"I know it is your job to worry," Jude was saying. "But it's also mine. My reputation is on the line."

A door opened and Jameson could now hear what the other man was saying. "I don't care about your reputation."

Mr. Curtis emerged from the kitchen, Jude a couple of steps behind. As they approached him, Jameson suddenly felt very self-conscious.

"This is fantastic," he said enthusiastically, gesturing towards his plate, in a hope to lighten the mood. Mr. Curtis stopped, as if only now realising that Jameson had been there. He then walked on towards the door.

"I'll talk to you tomorrow, Jude," he said brusquely. "Think about what I said."

Jude stopped beside Jameson's table, clearly thrown by this brief but aggressive meeting. "Okay, Mr. Curtis. I will, of course," he said. Jameson was surprised to hear a shake in the chef's voice.

For a few moments, Jude stood motionless, staring at the door, before Jameson felt he should say something. "Everything okay there, Chef?"."

Jude turned on his heel and tried to smile, but it was closer to a grimace. "Sorry about that," he said with a little too much gusto. "What were we talking about?"

"Everything okay?" Jameson tried again, wanting to sound concerned but coming off more as curious.

"Of course!" he said. "Everything is perfect! That was Mr. Curtis. He's one of my silent partners in this place."

Silent is right, Jameson thought, *I couldn't hear a bloody word.*

Jude sat down and absent-mindedly took a sip from Jameson's glass of water.

"So, the food…Pithivier is okay?" Jude's enthusiasm was very much forced.

Jameson realised that this was a perfect opportunity. Whatever they talked about now, Jude Miller would embrace the change of subject.

Jameson put down his fork. "So we both know why I'm here, right?" he said.

"Do we?" Chef Miller did look relieved.

"The cute blonde? At the launch party?"

"Cute blonde? Place was full of cute blondes that night."

"You know who I'm talking about. Your wife's friend."

Jude Miller looked uncomfortable again. "What about her?" he said.

"I'd like to meet her."

Jude smiled. "And I'd like a Michelin star and my own TV show. I told you the other night, she's seeing someone."

"And, as I said the other night, things change. Today she's seeing someone, tomorrow, maybe she's not. I reckon you have the power to change things. You're an influential man."

"What are you saying? That you want me to break them up?"

"Well I'm trying not to say it."

"Why would I possibly want to break them up, especially –"

"You know the reason. As I said, that's why I'm sitting here?"

"I thought you were here to give me a more fair and balanced –"

"To give you a chance, Jude. And to do that, I'm going to have to be pretty creative so it doesn't look like I'm doing the old flip-a-roo. Things that ask that much normally come with a price."

Jude stood up. "Tell you what, don't bother," he said, reaching for Jameson's half-full plate. "I wasn't sure you'd turn up tonight and, when you did, I actually thought you were an okay guy. But, of course, I was wrong. Your reputation remains intact. You are a dickhead."

"That might be, but right now, you need this dickhead."

"I don't think so. One bad review, I can live with."

Jameson put away his recorder and looked at Jude.

"How about two, or three, or twelve?"

"What?"

"How about three bad reviews? From the same magazine,

one issue after another after another. That'd be it for you. See, I expended all this time, energy and dry hair to come here tonight, so I have to write something. And I have something to write. Yeah, I really do."

"What does that mean?"

"You and your buddy there, your partner. You might think you were keeping your voices down," Jameson said. "Unfortunately, those walls are very thin. And I know what I heard."

He hoped his poker-face was holding. "That was a boss, or silent partner, or 'angel-investor', or whatever you want to call him, getting antsy because his investment isn't performing to his satisfaction." He put his hands up by way of concession. "Admittedly, I may have had something to do with that. But it is what it is. It would go something like this – '*Not only is the menu uninspired and the fare substandard but managerial in-fighting and power-struggles would suggest that Jude Miller is as ineffective a businessman as he is a chef.*' Pretty good, huh? That just came to me. Seriously, my talent even scares me sometimes."

A bead of sweat finally broke on the chef's face.

It was time for the final blow. "Then I'll recite word-for-word what you and your boss just said to each other," Jameson said.

The sweat ran down to meet Jude's eyebrow. "He's not my boss," he said.

Jameson sniggered again. "He is so your boss."

He enjoyed the moment of helplessness on Miller's face.

"So, what?" the chef said. "I introduce you to Mia and in return, you don't publish that column?"

"I'll go you one better. As I said, I have to give them something. You do that for me and I'll run with a very favourable article. You'll be the hottest place in town by next Tuesday. You haven't a lot of time though, to make sure…what's her name, Mia is available, so better get cracking.

My deadline is the end of next week."

"Available?"

"You know, single? She has to be single. It's just too complicated otherwise."

Jameson stared across the table at Jude Miller and for a second, it really wasn't clear what way the chef would go.

Eventually, he pushed back his chair and picked up Jameson's plate. "You ready for the main course?"

"Are you kidding? I've been starving myself all day for this."

Jude turned and headed for the kitchen.

"You know," Jameson called after him. "Your food is spectacular, Jude. It is tonight and it was the last time I was here."

He always enjoyed that look on people's faces, that mix of surprise and disgust.

"And yet you trashed me anyway." Jude said.

"That's the thing about being a critic. It's all so subjective."

"You really are –"

"A dickhead? Yeah I know. But it comes in handy. Don't feel bad though. If all goes well, I'll be printing three words I have never used in my entire career."

"Oh, yeah? What are they?"

"I. Was. Wrong."

~ ~

As he plated the Pieds de Porc à la Sainte-Menehould, Jude sighed with relief and allowed himself the briefest of smiles.

That had been easier than expected.

Chapter 22.

Mia was perched on a bar stool in *The Old Bailey*, speedily working her way through her second Gin-and-Tonic.

"I mean, we're only together two months! It's stupid!"

Alice laid a comforting hand on her wrist. "It's hardly stupid, is it?" she said. "He loves you. And you love him too so –"

"Do I? I mean, I barely know him!"

Alice sat back, not happy. This was typical Mia. "You told him you love him."

"Of course I did. That's what you say. Someone says 'I love you' and you say it back. I mean, what else are you supposed to say? 'Thanks'? 'Okeydokey'?"

Mia went to take another sip but stopped before it got to her mouth. "I mean I like him. And sure, maybe I was convincing myself that it was love…but if it is, then why am I reacting like this?"

"You're scared, that's why. But the fact is, you've no reason to be. You're so close! So just go the last bit. Take the chance."

"You make it sound so simple. The last bit, as you call it, is the difference between 'Let's-both-stay-living-in-our-respective-places-of-residence' and 'let's-shack-up-and-play-happy-families'."

"Yeah I know that. But you know what this really comes down to?"

"What?" You've built up a nice little barrier over the years, protection against another crap attack."

Mia looked slightly offended. "Is that such a bad thing?"

"You're not worried about whether you love him," Alice said.

Mia looked sceptical.

"You're not," Alice said. "You're worried that, now that you do love him, what's going to happen to your safe little universe? *Oh shit, what corner am I being backed into?*"

"I don't know," Mia said.

"So maybe it's time to give up some of that control that's so precious to you."

As she sipped her wine, Alice watched her friend carefully.

"You mean, give it to him," Mia said.

"Yeah, it's called a committed relationship. Giving the other person some of the control you have over your own life. Not always being able to do what you want, when you want. Being there for the other person when they need you, or maybe when they just want you. But also – and this is the really good bit – knowing that he's doing all those same things too."

Alice paused, mostly to catch a breath, but also to see if she was having an effect. "This isn't rocket-science, Mia. Every couple goes through it."

"And you think Daniel is the person I should be doing all this with?"

"Of course I do." Alice grasped Mia's hand and looked at her, pleading. "Come on, Mia. You're so close."

Alice couldn't tell if Mia was looking at her or into space. "I just don't know why he wants to move so fast. Surely he knows the risks –"

"He wants to establish a stable home life for himself," Alice said. "You can hardly blame him, you know what kind of childhood he had."

"Hmm. How many of us can say we had a stable home life?"

"Yeah but he has this completely utopian idea of the perfect family. Maybe if his parents had died when he was twenty instead of seven , he might have a more real idea of what they were like. But to him, they're exactly the same people, the same perfect couple, from when he was seven."

"And how can I even compete with that?"

"That's the thing, you already are and you're winning. It's why he wants to move in with you. You should see it as an honour - the guy seriously needs some positive female influence in his life and you get to be it."

"Is that what I am?"

Alice sat back and watched her pep-talk sink in, watched Mia consider her options. She had dug herself into a nice little hole and, whichever way she went now, it was going to be dramatic. It was going to be fantastic.

Chapter 23.

"You were right about Daniel, apparently," Alice said.

She was standing at the door of the bedroom, looking at Jude lying on the bed. He was watching TV, which meant he was stressed. He had watched a lot of TV lately.

"Jude? I said you were right –"

"Right about what?" he said, not looking at her.

"He's just asked her to move in with him."

"Ah Dan," Jude said, shaking his head. "What're you like?"

"She said yes."

"She what?" That was more the reaction she was looking for. "What the hell is she doing?"

"The right thing, maybe? They're good together, surely you can see –"

"Okay," Jude said, sitting up on the bed and turning off the TV. "This has to stop right now. Seriously."

"I don't think so," Alice said. "It's actually getting interesting now."

"No, it's not, Alice. It's getting dangerous. And you have to –
"

"I have to what? This is nothing to do with me."

"Like fuck it's not."

"Jude –"

"No, Alice!" Jude's outburst threw her. "Don't try and pretend...You're going to put a stop to this. I'm serious."

"What do you expect me to do, exactly?" she said.

"I expect you to use the gift God gave you, the one you've been using so well since college."

"My gift, if that's what you want to call it, is to know when two people suit each other –"

"And then to go to whatever lengths necessary to get them together. Yeah, I get it. So all you have to do now is reverse it. Work out how to split them up."

"It's not as simple as that," Alice couldn't believe she was hearing this from her good-as-gold husband.

"Course it is. It's just about manipulation."

"You seem to know a lot about it, all of a sudden."

He looked at her, a cold look. "What can I say, I learn from the best."

"Well then, you do it. Because I'm not –

"Yes, you are. You got them into this, you get them out."

She stood at the end of the bed, glaring at him, waiting for him to retreat.

"I will help you," he said instead.

"Help me. What does that mean?"

"It means that Mia's going on a date with someone else. You can make that happen, right?"

"What are you talking about? Like, with anyone in particular or are we just grabbing someone off the street?"

"Ben Jameson. The journalist."

Suddenly it all made sense. "The restaurant critic, you mean," Alice said. "This isn't about saving Daniel from the big-bad-Mia. This is about you pimping out your wife's friends for a good review. For Christ's sake, Jude!"

"Why is it you're a matchmaker and I'm a pimp?"

"Motivation, that's why."

"Yeah, sure. Shall we talk about your motivation?"

"The guy's married, for fuck sake!"

"It doesn't mean he's not willing. He's a weasel-y toe-rag, devoid of morals and led by his libido. Perfect for Mia."

"Jude, stop –"

"Getting the two of them together will get her away from Daniel, which *is* my motivation." Jude smirked. "But, hey, if it gets me on the cover of *Gourmet* at the same time, sure what's the harm."

He's actually serious.

Jude stood up and came around the bed to her. "Look, you don't have to worry," he said, cupping her face in his hands. "This has to happen. So just do what you do best."

As she looked at him, so confident and poised, Alice could feel the anger, the rage, building up and she couldn't push it away, didn't want to.

"You asshole!" Alice could feel nothing but hatred for Jude at that moment. "I can't believe you're…things between Mia and Daniel are just getting good, getting…interesting. And you want to spoil my…you want to spoil their happiness just to help your fucking career!"

But, this time, losing her temper wasn't helping. It always did before, always helped her gain control of their arguments, swing the balance back in her favour. But this time he wasn't budging and it scared her.

She turned to leave.

"Can we not just talk about this?" Jude said.

"Talk about it?!" she came back at him but, again, he stood his ground. "There's nothing to talk about. Don't ask me to interfere with Daniel and Mia. Do you understand?" she hissed. "In all the years I have been doing this, this is the best relationship I've created."

"Best relationship?" Jude laughed. "Best for you, maybe."

Alice didn't know what to say and she knew the battle was lost. A few options came to her but they were either extremely hurtful or completely innocuous.

"So just leave it alone, okay?" was all she could manage. "Just leave them alone."

Before he could respond, or worse, laugh at her again, she walked out of the room, down the stairs and out the front door. She was halfway down Orwell Park, heading towards the Dodder, before she realised she'd left the house. Walking along the riverside always helped to calm her down. She'd walked there often enough recently that it had, apparently, become an instinctive response.

That said, she had never been down there after dark and she almost turned back. But, instead, she decided to just trust her instincts and keep going.

"If it gets me on the cover of Gourmet at the same time, sure what's the harm?"

"Best relationship? Best for you, maybe."

Alice closed her eyes as she heard Jude's mocking tone inside her head. She couldn't believe he was doing this.

This is so not Jude, she thought. He'd had always proclaimed that he didn't care about what the critics thought about him, that they were 'all wannabes who couldn't get into proper journalism'. Of course, this was when he was comfortably ensconced at La Bocca, where a bad review would be rare and of little consequence. But now, he was all alone in the big bad world, right there on the raggedy edge, where any morsel of positive press was key to survival.

But to make deals with these morsel-givers, especially someone as repugnant as Ben Jameson? Alice really didn't think Jude was so desperate. And she certainly never thought he'd stoop this low. Mia might not have been one of his favourite people but Daniel was. And this would kill Daniel.

This would kill Daniel.

It's not just about the review, she told herself, it can't be. There's something else going on.

Then it hit her. It was so bloody obvious.

He's doing it to punish me.

"I promise you it's forgotten." The more he kept saying it, the more adamant he was about it, the less she believed it. That morning they had climbed together, she had realised how little she believed it. His disappointment that she still kept the scan, his inability to ever take her side these days, and his will, above all else, to keep his mother placated. Each of these, on their own, were nothing but, together, horribly significant. There was no getting away from what she knew – that Jude still resented her and, most likely, always would.

Back when it all happened, when things were at their worst, Alice had taken some comfort in the knowledge that she'd had no choice. That she'd done what she had to do. But even that wasn't working anymore. Of course she'd had a choice, a big, life-changing choice. And she had made it.

It wasn't perfect, not for anyone. Everyone got something and lost something.

So why am I the only one still being punished?

She was at the river now but the idea of walking along the unlit path left her cold. She stopped on the bridge instead, leaned against the metal railing and looked down at the black water of the Dodder.

So why not just refuse then? She asked herself. *You know what he's playing at, so call him on it. Tell him that you're not going to set*

Mia up with that pig of a journalist just so he can take some obscene pleasure in it.

But Alice knew that she wasn't going to do that. In fact, she was going to do exactly what he wanted. For one very simple reason.

She wanted it too.

Chapter 24.

October.

The Dublin Outdoor Pursuits Shop did exactly what was suggested on the sign over the door. According to their website, it supplied equipment to enthusiasts of outdoor pursuits – canoeing, hiking, mountaineering, mountain-biking. *Dops*, as it was affectionately known, was owned by Llewellyn McNamara, a former canoeist who had taken a bronze at the '92 Olympics, as well as winning countless races around the world. He was regarded as an authority on the sport and had run the first ever canoeing school in Ireland. The shop in Howth, in addition to another in the UK and the very profitable online store, had become a healthy empire and allowed McNamara time to pursue other pursuits, not least an enviable pundit slot with Eurosport.

Nestled snugly between two similar terraced-houses-converted-for-business-use on the main street of Howth, *Dops* was now in the capable hands of Llewellyn's daughter, Kate.

With her husband Stephen Dobson, she had continued to grow the shop's revenue, despite the rumoured downturn in popularity of outdoor pursuits.

Temple entered the large but claustrophobic space and was hit with the warm smells of wax and rubber. As he approached the counter, he enjoyed the look of bewilderment on the face of the twenty-something shop assistant, who clearly was not used to dealing with people in navy suits.

"Hey, whassup," the guy said.

"Hi, I'm looking for Mr. or Mrs. Dobson?"

The bewilderment was now outright confusion. "Eh…who?"

"Kate or Stephen?" Temple said.

"Okay, cool," the guy said. Then, in an affected officious tone, "And may I say what this is in reference to?"

In the interests of discretion, Temple decided not to identify himself as a Guard. "I'm Kieran Temple, they're expecting me," he said instead.

"Okay, cool," The guy said again, happy to be able to pigeon-hole Temple as a non-customer.

"Garda Temple?" he heard to his right and turned around, ignoring the shop-assistant's step-back on hearing the title. A tall, lanky man with a head of thinning ginger hair stooped under the doorframe of the adjacent room and hesitantly extended his hand, as if he wasn't sure that it was the appropriate greeting for a Garda.

"I'm Stephen Dobson," he said and gestured towards the other room. "Would you like to come through?"

"Sure," Temple said, momentarily feeling that he was here for a job interview. Temple followed Stephen into the other room and up the stairs, passing a faded 'Private – Staff Only' sign on the wall.

"Kate's just on the phone, she'll be finished in a sec'," he said as he strode up the steps two at a time. He wore an ill-fitting button-down and even more-ill-fitting chinos.

It must be difficult, Temple figured, *to get clothes when you're as oddly-shaped as this.*

"…okay, that's grand, Byeeeee." he heard from the room in front of him as he reached the top of the stairs.

"Katey, Mr…Garda…Temple is here" Stephen said and entered the room.

"Oh right, cool," she said, already starting to stand as they entered.

"It's Detective Inspector, actually," Temple said, trying to be helpful but just sounding defensive.

Kate McNamara was dressed much more how Temple expected an outdoor-pursuits enthusiast to be dressed, a pair of khaki combat cut-offs and a grey tee-shirt with 'Liffey Descent 2007' on the left breast. The shirt was stretched at the front by a much-defined bump.

"Hi Inspector," she said with a quick smile. "Thanks for meeting me here. I'm not exactly mobile at the moment." She pointed at her stomach.

Temple gave her a warm smile. "That's no problem. Congratulations."

"Plus," she said with a huff as she lowered herself into the chair. "I'm pretty much going to be here every waking hour now before Mister Kicker gets here."

"When are you due?" Temple said, sitting in the chair opposite, as gestured by Kate. "If you don't mind me asking."

"Six more weeks," she said and then sighed. "A honeymoon baby, as they say. Of course if he wanted to pop out now, I wouldn't mind at all."

"Well I appreciate you taking time to talk to me when you're –"

"Hey, of course." The chipper tone was gone. "It's just so unbelievable. How did…I mean…what happened?"

"We're still trying to determine that," Temple said, not keen to divulge too much. "I gather you and he used to be...an item?"

Kate blushed and glanced at her husband, as if her relationship with Daniel Summers was a subject of embarrassment. Maybe it was.

"I really don't see how that's relevant," Stephen said. "They broke up years ago."

"Well, what I can tell you is that Mr. Summers was stabbed and that the person who did it is claiming self-defence."

Stephen looked confused. "I still don't see how –"

"Oh my God," The colour had drained from his wife's face. "It's that girl, isn't it?"

"What girl?" The look on Stephen's face, a mix of fear and responsibility, was one Temple had seen before. Expectant father. "Shit, Katey, are you okay?" he asked, like he was certain she was about to go into labour at any moment.

Kate waved him away. "That girl he met at the wedding. Mia something, right? Didn't they start going out after that?"

"I really can't confirm anything right now," Temple said. "As I said, we're trying to establish –"

"That's why you're here, isn't it? To establish some kind of pattern in Daniel's behaviour. God, he attacked her or something?"

"Sorry Detective Inspector," Stephen said with a mixture of embarrassment and concern. "Katey watches too much C.S.I. Problem with pregnancy insomnia."

"Actually, your wife does have a point," Temple said, annoyed by the man's patronising tone. "Mr. Summers was attacked by the woman he was seeing" – he was careful not to mention a name – "and, given this person's claim, I felt it was pertinent to establish if Daniel has a history of violence."

"No, of course he doesn't," Kate said.

"Katey, come on."

She looked at her husband as if he was betraying her. "He didn't. One time does not count as history."

"Yeah, it does, actually," Stephen said, getting annoyed. "One time with you. You have no idea what he was like before that, or since –"

"Hold on, hold on," Temple put his hand up. "Mrs. Dobson, please. What do you mean by 'one time'?"

The woman's gaze dropped to the desk. "He hit me, okay? It was a slap. But it was only once and –"

"It was only once," Stephen said. "Because you walked out and never went back –"

"Are you planning on letting me finish one sentence today?" Kate snapped. It reverberated around the small office. Stephen leaned against the wall and folded his arms, like a scolded child.

Kate brushed her cheek, as if she felt a tear on it. "The fact was, we were already kind of broken up at that stage. Daniel was always a bit intense and became totally obsessive when I asked for the break."

"Why did you?" Temple asked.

"Ask for a break? A lot of reasons," she said. "This place was getting very busy and I just had less and less time. But, mostly, I just wasn't feeling it. He took care of me when I was very sick – I got Malaria when I was travelling. I mean he was brilliant. But I think I confused gratitude for love. I made it work for as long as I could, but in the end…"

"You can't fake it forever," Temple said.

Kate shrugged. "He had been getting more anxious that I wasn't around and when that turned into jealousy and paranoia, I told him we needed some space. I needed some space. But that just made him worse, more obsessive. You know, he'd ring, call around, at stupid-o-clock in the morning, ringing the doorbell incessantly. And one of those times, we had a bad fight and I said some pretty mean stuff."

"Like what?"

"I don't remember specifically, but –"

"I think you do," Temple said, seeing how guilty she looked.

"Inspector," Stephen said quietly but firmly, pushing himself off the wall. "If she says she doesn't, then she doesn't –"

"It's okay, hun," Kate said, giving Stephen a grateful smile. "He's right, I do remember. Like I'll ever forget." She looked at Temple. "I said that I was happy that his parents were dead so they didn't have to see how fucked up he was."

"Oh," Temple said. "Okay. That was…"

"Horrible, I know. But I hadn't slept for a week, because of him."

"That was when he hit you?"

"And it wasn't a little slap either," Stephen piped in. "Tell him, Katey."

"It was a slap, Stephen. It's not like he used his fist or anything. But…let's just say he didn't hold back. I had a bruise for a week. Everyone wanted me to press charges. I didn't see the point, it wouldn't have made things better. But I did make it clear to him that we were finished."

"Did he accept that?"

"Yeah, yeah, he did," she said. "How could he not, right?" Her expression was begging Temple to just accept that and move on. And, for that reason, he didn't. Siting back in the chair, he folded his arms and waited.

"Okay no, not right away," she said. "He was more like a man possessed. If I thought the 4am phone calls were bad before the break-up, they were a million times worse after. Begging me to forgive him, take him back. I tried honesty with him, I tried reasoning with him, I tried screaming at him. Nothing worked. Eventually, my Dad got involved, threatened to…well you know."

"Get violent?"

"'Talk to him in a language all bullies understand' I think were Dad's words. Thankfully, the threat was enough, Daniel backed off. Didn't hear from him after that."

"Until?"

Kate looked confused.

"Well how did he end up at your wedding?" Temple asked. "If things ended so badly."

Stephen looked at her as if to say 'Yeah, how did he end up at our wedding?'

"Don't look at me like that," she said. "You agreed!" She took a deep breath. "Look, he wasn't a monster, Inspector. He was a decent guy with a lot of problems. But I met him a couple of weeks before the wedding and he was like a new man. He had a new job, he was just back from skiing, he was just much happier." She then seemed deep in thought for a moment. "But he didn't change, did he?" she said quietly. "He got worse. I mean, that's why he's dead, right?"

"As I said, I –"

"Inspector, please." There was a tear in her eye. "Help me understand this. I knew Daniel for a long time, even before we were together. He wasn't perfect but he wasn't a psycho either and if that's how it looks, then…"

She looked down at her bump and then back up at Temple, tears in her eyes. "I don't know, it just seems unfair."

"This is not in any way conclusive," Temple found himself saying. "You understand?"

She nodded.

He looked over at Stephen. *What I'm about to tell you doesn't leave this room.*

He nodded, message received.

"All evidence so far points to a relationship that ended badly, similar to your own, and that maybe he wasn't taking it well. Daniel went to plead with the woman maybe, going as far as actually breaking into her house, and when he didn't like what he heard, it would appear that, yes, he attacked her.

"God," Kate laid her elbows on the desk.

"He was killed accidentally in self-defence."

"Oh Daniel."

Temple watched Kate carefully. She could no longer distance herself from Daniel Summers' death.

Stephen could see that too. "Inspector, if there's nothing else," he said, pushing himself away from the wall.

"Of course, yeah," Temple stood up. "Mrs. Dobson, I am sorry for your loss. I can see you were still fond of Daniel, despite everything."

Kate nodded and smiled in appreciation and Temple turned towards the door. It was only then that he remembered the other thing he wanted to ask. He glanced at Kate.

She sensed his hesitation. "Inspector?"

In for a penny...

"The people who were telling you to press charges against Daniel? Family? Friends?"

"Yeah, both."

"Alice Miller one of them?"

Kate looked surprised. "Yeah. She was the first to suggest it. How did you –"

"We've been speaking to her about this. And her husband, Jude."

Kate was suddenly annoyed again. "Oh, I get it. It was Jude who put you on to me, wasn't it? I must be somehow involved. I broke the heart of his best friend, poor, innocent Daniel, something like that?"

"Well, no, I'm just trying to –"

"He's been gunning for me all this time, no surprise he's trying to shovel some of this against my door."

Temple was surprised by her sudden venom. "Gunning for

you?"

"You'd think they'd known each other since birth. Jude and Daniel. But they only met when he got together with Alice. I mean, it was great that the two boyfriends got on but what wasn't great was Jude, wading in to Daniel's defence, anytime he and I had a row. And, then, after we split, he became a proper asshole."

"Jude did?" Temple had only met the guy but 'asshole' wasn't a word that sprung to mind. And Temple knew how to spot an asshole. Ben Jameson, for example – there was an asshole.

"I actually knew Jude, from before," Stephen said, clearly in an attempt to take the tension down a peg. "It was when he was still with Renato Rossi and I was Renato's business advisor. Anyway, me and Jude used to go for pints now and then and one night, sitting in Kehoe's, he turns around and tells me that Kate is doing the dirt. Jut says it casually, like he's asking for the time or something! I'm raging of course, and I ask him what he's talking about, and he says that he saw her in a restaurant in town with some guy and that Alice had seen her with the same guy a few times before then."

"And were you?" Temple asked her. "Seeing someone else?"

"Of course not!" she almost shouted. "For fuck sake!"

"Katey, please," Stephen said, embarrassed.

"So who did Mr. Miller see you with?"

"I have no idea. I have loads of friends, Inspector, men and women, but I'm not having sex with them. Jude could have seen me with anyone. Or maybe he just made it up. Anyway, Stephen and I had this huge fight. We nearly broke up before I convinced him that it wasn't true. He confronted Jude and Jude just accused him of being naïve. That was it, they never spoke again. I emailed him, told him not to come to the wedding."

"And what about Mrs. Miller?" Temple asked.

"Alice? What about her?"

"Did she know what Jude was doing?"

"As in, was she involved?"

"Well, Jude did say that Alice also saw you with whoever it was."

"That's probably nonsense too! Sure, why would she want to break us up? She got us together."

"I suppose," Temple said. He glanced at the clock on the desk and remembered he needed to call Hodge before he went off shift. "Look, let me get out of your hair," he said. "I'm sorry to drag you into all this, but –"

"I'm glad you did, Inspector," Kate said. "Because I'm not sure many others will be telling you that Daniel did not deserve this."

It was obvious that she believed that. Somewhat disconcerting was Stephen Dobson's expression. He didn't share his wife's opinion.

Chapter 25.

"D.I. Temple," Michael Hodge said after Temple answered on the second ring. "You've been using your female intuition, I see."

"Ah right," Temple said. "That's funny because it makes me a woman."

"I just got off the phone from one Jude Miller, friend of the deceased?"

"I spoke to him, didn't have much to offer." *Apart from sending me on a wild-goose chase in the boondocks of North County Dublin.*

"I know you did," Hodge said. "Three hours ago, apparently. What brought you to him, exactly?"

"You want me to bore you with my investigative process?"

"Oh yes, Sensei. Please share."

Temple really didn't feel like going through his every thought but he also didn't want to get into a pissing contest with Hodge.

"Him and his wife are friends with both the victim and Mia

Burrows," he said. "Making them two of the best witnesses we have, since we don't have anyone who actually saw what happened. And both swear they have never seen any sign of violence from either Burrows or the victim. I also had a conversation with the victim's previous girlfriend."

"You really did have your Weetabix this morning," Hodge interjected. "And what did she say?"

Temple cleared his throat. "That he was violent with her too but only the once, it was just a slap and he didn't deserve to be dead. So all-in-all, despite suffering from significant emotional and psychological issues, Daniel Summers was loved by all, including a woman he slapped in the face once."

"Is this an epidemic of never-speak-ill-of-the-dead syndrome, do you think?"

"I didn't get that impression, no. The previous girlfriend even hinted that Daniel Summer's psychotic break was inevitable, that Burrows was just unlucky to be in his life when it happened."

"That's one way of putting it. I mean, did nobody think to warn her?"

"Apart from the ex, I don't think anyone knew. And she'd convinced herself he was cured. Even invited him to her wedding."

"Ouch. Maybe that's what broke him. Seeing your former lover walk up the aisle? Ouch."

"Don't think so, that wedding was eight months ago."

"Right. So what you're saying is, you spent the day driving around, interviewing the victim's spurious friends and lovers, finding out…not much. Solid police-work there, Kieran."

"You know it had to be done."

"Do you want to hear the pathologist's preliminary report? Just came in."

Temple steered the car into his driveway. "Just give me the

highlights."

"Victim sustained injuries as a result of one stab wound through the left lower quadrant with a straight un-serrated blade, length approximately six inches. Blade penetrated skin and adipose tissue, into the abdominal cavity. Cause of death was extensive blood loss as a result of an incision to the abdominal aorta. There was some expected dovetailing as the blade was extricated. Time of death between 1am and 3am."

Temple found himself breathing a sigh of relief. "So are we on the same page?" he asked.

"That barring some phenomenal piece of evidence or overnight change of half-a-dozen legal statutes," Hodge said. "We have nothing to prosecute her on?"

"Something like that, yeah."

"GSOC are saying the same thing. Okay, well I'll give Sergeant Burrows a ring, let her know –"

"Actually, Michael," Temple cut in. "Do you mind if I tell her? She asked for my help and I'd like her to know I stayed involved."

"Stealing my limelight, Kieran?" Hodge said with a snigger. "Never had you down for a glory-hunter."

"Sure why earn brownie-points when you can nick em."

"Go on then. You're just lucky I'm so modest."

"You are that, Michael. To a fault."

After he got off the phone, Temple glanced through his notebook. It jarred with him again, as he glanced down through Mia's statement, that in her ten years with the Gardaí, she had never had to take a life and now that she had, it wasn't even in the line of duty. And that it was the man who supposedly loved her.

"Did nobody think to warn her?" Hodge's words came back to Temple and he realised that he had been naïve in his reply. Nobody knew? Come on, of course people knew. Kate Dobson knew. Kate Dobson's father knew. And Alice Miller knew.

Alice Miller knew.

He flicked to a blank page and was about to start writing when he glanced up and saw Yvonne standing on the doorstep. She was saying something but he couldn't hear her over the engine.

"I said 'Would you like me to bring your dinner out to you?'" she said after he shut it off. "And the TV, maybe?"

"Sorry," he said, getting out of the car. "I was just going back over the day's activities."

"I'm sure you were," Yvonne said. "So, how's Mia?"

Temple walked up the steps and kissed his wife. "Can you at least wait till I get in the house before you start the interrogation?"

"It's been on the news, Kieran. Did she really kill someone?"

"What's been on the news?" he said as they walked into the house.

"That a Garda sergeant is being investigated for killing an intruder. No names were mentioned but…it was her, right?"

The better detective.

"Afraid so, yes. It was her boyfriend…Ex-boyfriend."

"Fuck. But what's it got do with you? Was he involved in a gang or something?"

"Okay, you can stop now," Temple said, annoyed at Yvonne's tone.

"What?" Yvonne half-heartedly tried to sound defensive.

"We both know she didn't ring me because I'm with the OCU."

Yvonne turned to him and she wasn't happy. "Yeah, Kieran, we do know that. So? Why did she ring you?"

"I'm her friend, that's why. She was panicking because, oh I don't know, there was a dead guy on her kitchen floor –"

"You're her friend? You haven't spoken to her for months. How are you her friend?" Temple didn't answer. "Kieran? Have you spoken to her?"

"No, of course not. You know I haven't." *No sense rocking that particular boat.* "But I'm certainly the closest thing she has to a friend on the force right now. She was in trouble and she needed help. So yeah, I don't mind that she called me."

"Well bully for you. So what, you're now investigating this friend? Is she going to end up in prison over this?"

"Highly unlikely. The guy she killed, the ex, was attacking her when she stabbed him. There won't be a charge."

"Oh. Well that's good," Yvonne's relief actually seemed genuine and Temple was momentarily surprised by her sympathy "Okay, so you won't have to deal with her anymore."

So much for sympathy.

"That's it?" he snapped. "Mia's going through the worst ordeal of her life and you're just relieved that –"

"Why should I give a shit, Kieran? It's tragic, okay, I get it. But why should I really care? Did she care about me last December? Did she give a single thought to how her actions would affect me? Affect us? No. So it's good that she's okay and that she isn't going to jail. But that's it. You promised to have no more dealings with her and now you can go back to keeping that promise."

Temple knew that, at this moment, he couldn't commit to that. "Look, this all happened less than twenty-four hours ago. I can't say that it's definitely over. I want it to be but I don't get to make that decision. But, honestly, in Mia's state-of-mind, do you really think she's going to be trying it on with me?"

Yvonne flashed a glance at him and he saw the guilt in her eyes. Not just guilt. There was something else. Accusation.

"Oh I get it," he said. "It's not Mia you're worried about, is it? For fuck sake, Yvonne –"

"Well what do you expect me to think?"

"That I'm your husband and I would never....Did you even

believe me when I swore – I swore! – that nothing happened?"

"Yes! Well…I know you've been talking to her since then, Kieran, which I just accepted because it was just talking and it was part of me trusting you. But then, she rings you in the middle of the night and –"

"And nothing!" he shouted. "There is nothing. And I'm not going to start trying to convince you of that all over again!"

Chapter 26.

Barely out of the gate, Temple felt bad and almost turned back. He was supposed to be the sensible one, the one who applied logic over emotion and who definitely didn't storm out in the middle of an argument.

But Yvonne's accusation had stung. And was hard to believe – she knew that whole mess last year had been Mia's doing and, not only had it gone nowhere, Temple had immediately told Yvonne what had happened, for fear that even concealment of truth would be construed as guilt.

Mia was attractive – beautiful even – he'd have to be a robot not to notice, but as far as he was concerned, she was his colleague first – or subordinate if he wanted to be cruelly accurate – friend second and attractive woman after all that. Of course he had been flattered by her compliments. They were true – he had been helping her become a better detective and he had made her transition into the OCU easier. But that was his job.

Temple asked himself, as he had done countless times in the last ten months, if he could have better seen the signs, put a stop to it before it had got so out-of-hand. And again, he came to the conclusion that her behaviour had changed so rapidly from friendly to flirtatious to seductive, he really had done everything he could. Her resulting transfer out of OCU, as heart-breaking as it was for her, was necessary.

From what he heard, she was settling in okay at the Technical Bureau but the rumour mill had been busy.

How this whole business would change everything? Only time would tell.

Of course, Mia might not want a career in the Gardaí anymore, Temple had to remind himself. If her job and her prospects and Garda politics had been anywhere on her mind twenty-four hours ago, they certainly weren't now. If he knew her, she'd be re-examining every minute of the ill-fated romance with Daniel Summers, wondering where it all went wrong. Or maybe she would just be reliving, over and over, that horrible feeling as the spike of that meat thermometer pierced his flesh. She might be agonising over what that meant for her, would she be prosecuted, end up in prison –

Temple suddenly remembered the favour he had asked Hodge. It meant that he was supposed to be telling Mia that she wouldn't be charged. He should have called her with that news straight after his conversation with Hodge but Yvonne standing on the doorstep, and their subsequent argument, had distracted him.

He put his hand to his pocket – but no phone. He could picture it right where he had left it, on the kitchen counter.

That's what you get for leaving in a huff.

He felt his hands clammy on the steering-wheel as he thought back to Yvonne. Those horrible days around Christmas when she had definitely suspected that something was going on between him and Mia and, although he thought his reassurances had satisfied her, she'd been harbouring doubts ever since. And all it took was one phone-call from Mia, even during a crisis, for those doubts to raise their ugly heads.

And now, as he steered his car on to the North Circular, he wondered what it meant that he was now on his way to see Mia.

~ ~

"Really? What, just like that?" Mia wasn't as relieved as Temple expected. But he could guess why.

They were sitting in the Sideline Bar of the Croke Park Hotel, a Gin and Tonic sitting in front of Mia. She continued to stare at the glass, having barely looked at him, even when he told her the news.

"This is a good thing, Mia," he said. "It's the right thing. You did what you had to do, you know that."

"Did I?"

"He was out of control. You really think you could have talked him down?"

"Maybe not, Kieran," Mia said, blinking back a tear. "But there's a big gap between talking him down and this, don't you think?"

Temple sat forward. "Look at me."

She didn't.

"Mia."

She held the stand-off for another second and then looked up from her glass.

"Were you trying to kill him?" Temple asked.

"Of course not, but –" Mia stopped and glared at Temple. "Wait, is this you doing your thing you do? Trying to catch me out? You tell me I'm off the hook and then give me just enough rope to hang myself with?"

"No, Mia. I'm trying to tell you –"

Mia pushed back her chair and stood up. "Go home, Kieran," she said and knocked back her drink. "Either arrest me and we'll do this officially or just leave me alone. No more fucking parlour games. I learned them from you, remember?"

She was understandably upset but Temple could also see that this wasn't her first drink of the evening. "Mia, will you sit down, please? I'm not trying to –"

"What are you even doing here, Kieran? It was.... what's his name – Hodge's job to tell me this. You're just...I'm not sure what you are –"

"Hey!" Temple said, louder than he meant to. "You were the one who got me involved in this. Let's not forget that, okay? You wanted a friendly face? Well, that's what I am so, yeah, of course I was going to come. I was worried about you!"

Mia must have noticed his embarrassment. She glanced around at the other customers, who were doing a poor job of ignoring them.

Temple gestured towards her seat. "Will you sit down please?"

Mia pointed at her glass. "I'm finished. And I'm tired of being the entertainment." She started to walk away and then turned back. "See you, Kieran. Thanks for everything. But you don't have to worry about me anymore."

Temple watched her unsteadily work her way across the room, thinking that that had been the second argument he had had with a woman in less than an hour.

What a day.

He considered going after Mia but knew there was no good reason. She was in a hotel and so, although tipsy, probably didn't need help getting to her room. And however upset she was over Daniel Summers, the fact was that Yvonne was right,

Temple wasn't really Mia's friend anymore. She had voided that when she put his marriage – and some say his career – at risk. Besides, she had friends – real friends – to comfort her. Alice Miller, for example. And at the end of the day, Temple had done what he was supposed to, help clear her of any wrongdoing in Daniel Summers' death.

So, okay, if she wanted to be left alone, he was happy to oblige.

He picked up the glass, only to realise that it was Mia's G&T and it was empty. He really needed a pint at this stage but he really didn't want to have it in some bland hotel bar. He knew there and then what he was going to do – get out of here, drop the car home, walk to the pub and get very, very drunk. And to hell with the lot of them.

Chapter 27.

"Mia?"

The thought of pints, as soothing as it was, vanished when Temple saw her sitting there, perched on an uncomfortable-looking lobby sofa. Her head was bowed and she had one palm pressed to her forehead.

She didn't look up as he approached. "What the hell am I doing, Kieran?" she said, her voice shaking. "Why do I keep fucking everything up?"

"Come on." He sat down and squeezed her other hand. "You don't keep fucking everything up. Stop being so hard on yourself."

"Yeah, I do," she turned to look at him, her eyes red and cheeks blotchy. "Every decision I've made in the last year has ended in disaster. All that stuff with you, then transferring into the fucking Technical Bureau and now this."

"'This'? Mia, 'this' was a seemingly nice and ordinary guy

who turned out to be a nutcase. How can that possibly be your fault?"

"Maybe it's karma then. Punishment for previous sins."

"Stop. You don't believe in all that. And if anything, you've been punished enough. You don't owe anyone anything. Not even the universe."

Mia gave him a weak smile as fresh tears came to her eyes. "But I killed him though, Kieran. I did. However you spin it, it is what it is. Because of me, Daniel's dead."

"Well, answer me the question that made you just storm out of there," Temple said, gesturing towards the bar. "Were you trying to kill him?"

Mia sighed with resignation. "No."

"No. I'm not saying that you can just brush it off and get on with your life as if nothing happened but, as hard as it is to believe, you will eventually forgive yourself."

"Huh," Mia said. "I have a lot of practice doing that."

"Ah Mia." Self-pity always annoyed him. Plus, they both knew one of Mia's weaknesses was being hard on herself.

"Have you forgiven me?" she asked.

This was one of the reasons he missed working with Mia. Her spooky ability to read his mind.

"Are you kidding? Look at where I work. I was a hero around that place for months."

"Kieran," she said with that 'give-it-a-rest' tone.

"It's fine," he said. "It'll be fine."

"For what it's worth, I'm sorry –"

"Don't," Temple interjected. "Just leave it."

"But I am sorry. It was all my fault and I want you to know that. You shouldn't blame yourself."

"I don't," he said before he could stop long enough to sugar-coat it. "But we're not kids, Mia. Pointing fingers and worrying about who's to blame? It's just a waste of time."

"Why are you angry?"

"Because you're only apologising now to make yourself feel better, that's all."

"No, I'm not. I feel bad for what I did to you. And what you must think of me. I just wanted…"

A fresh tear meandered down her cheek as her voice failed her. Before he could tell himself not to, Temple had pulled her in for a hug.

"Sorry," he said. "You really don't need me having a go at you right now."

"I just wish we still worked together," Mia said. "At least, with you around, this wouldn't be so hard. How am I supposed to go back to work in that place after this?"

"What are you talking about? You'll get all the support you need. You're the victim here."

"It doesn't feel like it. Feels like I'm going to have to face the staring and whispering and gossip all over again."

"No you won't…" Temple realised what she was saying. "Hang on, when are you thinking about going back?"

"I'm on tomorrow. Of course, I can't get into the house to –"

"Mia, you can't go to work tomorrow!"

"Of course I can, I'm fine –"

"You're not fine. Nobody who went through that could be fine. You need to take time to get over this. At least a few weeks."

"No Kieran, what I need is…you know…distraction…" She faded off as her resolve faltered. "I don't know, maybe," she said. "But I just couldn't face being in that house. Not by myself."

It dawned on Temple where they should have been having this conversation. "Hey what happened to you staying with Alice?"

Mia was surprised. "What?" she said. "That was never the

plan. Yeah, that's all they'd need right now."

"What do you mean?"

"Nothing. I'm just not staying with them. I'm fine here."

"Okay, well stay here then."

"What am I going to do with myself? Sit around moping…no thanks."

"I don't know. House hunting?"

Mia laughed as she wiped her cheek. "I think I prefer moping. Careful, or I'll make you come with me." She sat back and closed her eyes. "Uh. I think my hangover has arrived."

Temple stood up and put out his hand. "That and you haven't slept in thirty-six hours. Come on, bed-time."

Mia allowed herself to be pulled up and they walked towards the lift.

"Do you mind if I ask," she said "Did you tell Yvonne all this was going on today? That you were seeing me."

"She was okay with it," he said brusquely. He really didn't want to talk about this and was surprised, annoyed, that Mia had brought it up.

Sensing this, she blushed. "Sorry. Bad form." They got to the lift and she pressed the button. "I shouldn't be mentioning –"

"No, you shouldn't."

She turned to him, stood close to him. "Tell me though, honestly," she said, softly. "Did you never even wonder? Even for a second?"

"Wonder what?" Temple felt a bead of sweat on his face as Mia's sweet scent hit his nostrils.

"If you weren't, you know, married." She was whispering now. "Last year, when we…I know what I did was wrong, but I also know it wasn't completely a figment of my imagination."

She took another step forward. Too close.

"Mia, stop," was all Temple could manage.

She took his hand and kissed him on the cheek, then again

just below his eye.

"It wasn't, was it?" she said. "I could feel it, Kieran. And if we'd both been single….I could feel it, Kieran. Just like I can feel it now."

And then they were kissing. Her lips softly caressed his before they pushed his mouth open. At the moment, Temple couldn't stop this, didn't want to. He pushed his tongue forward to caress hers. His free hand ran up along her side and stroked her cheek, the nape of her neck, her hair.

The ping of the lift barely registered. But when Mia backed towards it and pulled him with her, his mind suddenly cleared.

"Jesus, Mia, stop," he said, breaking the kiss. She pulled him to her again but he pushed her back. "Come on. I said stop!"

Mia backed away and Temple recognised the look on her face, that mix of embarrassment and regret. That look that he had seen on her face before. That look he had worn himself once.

For an eternity, neither of them said anything. Temple considered just walking away and, if necessary, never speaking to Mia again. But he didn't.

Maybe he could just make light of it, turn it into a joke and –

"This has got to be giving you a big head, right?" Mia said, forcing a smile. "Every time we're together, I throw myself at you."

There she was again, reading his mind.

"Let's just put it down to sleep-deprivation and borderline-drunkenness," Temple said, returning the awkward smile. "It didn't happen."

"Yeah, let's pretend it didn't happen, as always," The bitterness was back in Mia's voice. "Well it is all over now, Kieran. You can go back to pretending you and me never happened."

As Mia stepped into the lift, Temple felt a sudden unease and sighed as he knew what it meant. But he couldn't ignore his gut.

He put his arm out to stop the lift door closing. "Thing is…"

Mia smiled seductively. "Thing is…what?"

"Daniel Summers. I'm not entirely satisfied that it is all over."

"What do you mean?" Mia said. She actually looked scared. "You just spent the last hour telling me that it wasn't my fault and that I'm a victim and –"

"That is what I'm saying, Mia. But – I'll put it to you this way – is it not a bit odd that nobody told you about Daniel's violent past?"

"What violent past? Who would tell me?"

"Alice Miller, for one. She knew all about it, how he slapped Kate Dobson? And yet she was perfectly happy for you and Daniel to get together, she even facilitated it as far as I can see –"

"Daniel had completely changed by the time we got together. Maybe Alice thought he deserved a second chance. She's a good person, despite what you might hear."

"Despite what I might hear? From who?"

Temple didn't miss Mia's 'I've-said-too-much' expression.

"Let it go, Kieran, please," she said. "This has nothing to do with Alice. It was me. I did it. And I have to live with –"

"Despite what I might hear from who, Mia?"

She sighed. She knew Temple. She knew him well enough to know that, once the teeth were sunk in, they were going nowhere.

"Well, Jude's mother, say."

"Jude's mother? I assume we're talking about more than just 'no-one-is-good-enough-for-my-boy'?"

"Her thirty-year marriage to Jude's father ended last year when he started having an affair."

"So?"

"As far as Mrs. Miller Senior is concerned, it was all Alice's doing."

Chapter 28.

June.

"You know, you look the spitting image of my son."

Walking through Meeting House Square, it took a moment for Jude to realise that it was his mother smiling at him. But she was too thin, gaunt even. Not two words he would have associated with her.

He suddenly remembered the missed called on his phone from two days ago. "Fuck, I totally forgot to ring you back," he said as he hugged her. She felt frail too and it reminded him of his grandmother in the weeks before she died.

"Yes, you did," she said, poking him in the chest.

"Sorry, sorry. Hope it wasn't anything urgent."

"No, just ringing to say Hello. Haven't heard much from you since your big night. Are you still annoyed with me about that bloody dinner party?"

"What? God no!" Jude said, wishing that it was completely

true. "I was never annoyed with you. You were upset, things were said. You've already apologised."

"I suppose Alice is still milking it for all its worth, oh-woe-is-me and all that?"

"Well right now, she's too busy enjoying her birthday."

"Oh right, so it is."

"But she isn't milking anything, Mum. She understands that – "

"I don't need her to understand," Geraldine snapped. "I don't need her sympathy, Jude. Or yours."

"That's not what I'm saying –"

"Some support from your father would be nice, but I suppose I have to get used to being without that too."

"What do you mean?"

"Let's just say, you're not the only person who hasn't been returning my phone-calls."

Jude's teeth clenched and he hoped his mother didn't see it. No such luck.

"It's okay," she said, kissing his cheek. "It's not for you to worry about." She looked at her watch. "Ah, I'm late. I'm going to see that new French film in the IFI."

"On your own?"

"Yes, Jude, on my own. I used to go to cinema on my own all the time, even before your father left. He couldn't stand the subtitles. 'I go to the cinema so I don't have to read', he used to say. So I'll be fine." She smirked. "Unless…you want to come with me?"

The guilt caught in Jude's chest. "Sorry, Mum. I have a late fish delivery coming in. I need to be there to make sure they don't try to offload any crap."

His mother squeezed his hand. "My son, the entrepreneur. Okay, well I better go."

"I'll call you later, I promise. For a proper chat."

"Only if you've time."

Jude watched his mother walk up the steps into the cinema and felt the guilt being replaced by anger. He took out his phone as he walked towards Eustace Street.

"Are you trying to be an arsehole or is it just another symptom of your mid-life crisis?" Jude surprised himself with this outburst – a year ago, he would never have talked his father like that. But a lot had happened since then.

"Jude? What's the matter?" The man was obviously just as surprised.

"Did you hear what I said?" Jude was relieved as, thankfully, his voice didn't crack.

"Yeah, I did. What's wrong with you?"

"It's out-of-sight-out-of-mind, is it?"

"Slow down, slow down. What are you talking about?"

"I'm talking about your wife! Remember her?"

"What about her? Is she okay?" He did sound genuinely concerned.

Too late, old man. "Oh, you care now, do you?" Jude was on a roll. "She's fine. Well, no, she's not fine but she'll tell you she's fine. The point is, she's been ringing you and you haven't bothered to take her calls? Or even return them? What the fuck is wrong with you?"

"Jude, wait –"

"Walking out on your marriage is one thing, Dad. It's shitty, but it's done. But you don't get to shirk your responsibilities. You don't get to pretend she doesn't exist!"

"Jude! I will not be spoken to like I'm –"

"She calls you, you answer, okay? Whatever she needs, you get for her. She needs a kidney? Well, you've got two."

Jude took a breath and waited.

"You finished?" his father said eventually.

"For now."

"I agree with you."

"Well that's just wonderful."

"No, son, when you're right, you're right. I have been avoiding her. She wouldn't talk to me or take my calls after…you know."

"After you went off and slept with someone else. Is that what you're trying to say? It's her fault that she didn't want to be your friend after that?"

"No, of course not. But when she eventually did ring, I was annoyed that, suddenly, she wanted to talk to me. So I didn't answer. It's no excuse –"

"No, it's not. So what are you going to do about it?"

The man sighed. "Jude, as hard as it is to believe, I hate how much I've hurt your mother. I really do."

Jude couldn't believe it. He actually felt a twinge of sympathy. "Well you're just going to have to live with that," he said and the sympathy was gone. "Or maybe talk to your new woman about it. I'm sure she'll pat you on the head and tell you everything's going to be okay. Goodbye."

"But, you know what, Jude? I get it. I've hurt you. And I get that you and your mother are, like, kindred spirits now or something. But that doesn't give you the right to bark at me like a dog. I am still your father."

You complete shit.

"Kindred spirits? What are you saying, Dad?" Jude did hear his voice crack this time, but he didn't care. "You're not the first person in the world to be unfaithful so that makes it okay?"

"Fuck, I'm not the first person in this family to be unfaithful. And I think your taking your anger with –"

"So? Infidelity is contagious, is that it?"

"Of course not, but you need to cop yourself on and –"

"I think your days of being sanctimonious are over, don't you? Now go and call your wife."

Chapter 29.

"Can I just say," Alice called out over the chatter around the table. "Excuse me? Can I just say thanks everyone for coming out – it's a bit short notice, I know. And also for not singing 'Happy Birthday'. For reasons I won't bore you with, I hate it."

Someone at the other end of the table started singing it but an animated glare put a stop to it. "Bad enough," she continued. "That I had to organise my own birthday party, but –"

"Where are all the men?" Mia called out and everyone laughed.

"The men," Alice replied, raising her glass. "Are where they should be. At work earning the money or at home minding the babies." A cheer went up around the table and a middle-aged couple at a nearby table looked over and tutted loudly.

"Now, let us drink and be silly," Alice said, clinking her glass against Mia's.

The party, for Alice's thirty-fourth birthday, was in fact a meal-for-ten at *Paul's*, the exclusive restaurant adjoining an equally glamorous hotel on Merrion Square. After Mia's impressively stealthy organisation of some champagne in the hotel bar, they had adjourned to the restaurant where they were received enthusiastically by the staff. And now they were now squeezed around a couple of tables in a nearby wine bar on Ely Place.

"Thanks again for organising the bubbly," Alice said to Mia. "That was definitely a nice touch."

"Hey, no problem," Mia said. "I just wish I had remembered earlier that it was your birthday. Not exactly fair that you had to organise your own party."

"You did it last year, remember? I think you're off the hook. Jude, on the other hand, is not."

"What, no present?"

"Nah, we're going to Paris for a weekend when things settle down. And he got me flowers."

"So, what's the problem?"

"Well, he wouldn't even take a few hours away from work to come and have dinner with us. Friday's their biggest night, blah blah blah." Alice suddenly looked embarrassed. "That's kind of why I made it a girls' night."

"I'm surprised we're not having the party at Jude's. I'm sure you'd get the family discount."

"That's kind of why I didn't," Alice said. "I don't want him feeling he has to lose out on a table for ten. He's having a hard-enough time making money as it is. And..." she then stopped herself.

"What?" Mia asked.

"Well I'm not sure how welcome I'd be at the moment."

"What, you two not all-loved-up?"

Alice just shrugged. She didn't know what to say.

"As in, like, real problems?" Mia asked.

No, we're fighting about you, Mia. Apparently, you're not good enough for his precious Daniel.

"Ah, you know, money, family – the usual suspects."

"The Miller way is the only way, right?" Mia said.

Alice gave her the now established 'I-get-it-you-don't-like-him' expression.

"Anyway, look," Mia said. "A night away from Daniel is probably not a bad idea either. I still don't know how to let him down gently, and I'm running out of procrastination excuses."

"So you've decided for definite then?" Alice didn't try to hide her disappointment. "You're not moving in?"

"It doesn't feel right. I want to make sure I can live with him before I decide to live with him. Now all I need is the right way to tell him that."

"Well if you want my advice –"

"Damn right. You got me into this mess."

Not for the first time tonight, Alice almost brought up Jude's big plan, the date with Ben Jameson but, again, she couldn't do it.

"Just rip off the Band-Aid," she heard herself say instead. "Don't pussy-foot around, just tell him. According to Jude, that's how Daniel likes to get bad news." *You might as well take some of the blame here, darling.*

"Easier said than done. You know me, I get all stuttery."

Mia then pointed towards the other end of the table, where Suzanne was chatting and smiling nervously. "I'm surprised you invited the scarlet woman."

"That's kind of why I invited her. She needs all the friends she can get right now."

"She seems to be okay at making friends."

It was only then that Alice shifted slightly and could see that the person talking to Suzanne wasn't actually one of their group. It was a man in his mid-forties. Suzanne, despite her constant smile, was clearly uncomfortable.

After a few moments, the man gestured towards the bar as he stood up. As he left, Suzanne picked her glass and took a very large drink.

Alice smiled. "Someone's in need of rescue."

"She seems to be doing okay." Mia said.

"Look at her, she's searching for a big hole in the floor to jump into." Alice stood up, grabbing her glass. "Come on."

As she walked up along the table, Suzanne gave her a relieved smile.

Alice sat down in the man's chair. "Got yourself a fan there, have you?"

"Des," Suzanne said as if she wasn't fully convinced that it was his real name. "Why is it that all men need for encouragement is an accidental moment of eye-contact?" She took another drink as her shoulders relaxed.

"I don't know, he's kind of cute," Mia said, as she pulled a chair over. "A haircut and a new wardrobe and you'd have something quite presentable."

Alice looked in time to see the man glancing over and giving an involuntary frown at the new arrivals.

Suzanne smiled. "I already have my project, thanks." She then looked embarrassed. "No offence, Alice."

"Not at all. I've always thought Brian was in need of a bit of Gok-Wan-ology. Of course, you could never say that to Geraldine."

"Still though," Mia was looking over towards the bar again, as the man picked up two drinks and headed their way. "Nothing wrong with a bit of harmless flirtation."

"I've never been good at that," Suzanne said. "Knowing what to say, body language, all that sort of thing."

"Ah don't overthink it," Mia said. "Just do what comes naturally."

Hearing something in Mia's voice, Alice glanced at her. She was wearing that particular smile, the smile that Alice had last seen a few months ago. At a wedding.

Chapter 30.

Jude had tightened his grip on the knife.

"Dad? What are you doing here?"

Brian took an involuntary step back and forced a smile. "Starting to regret coming to see you where there are knives."

Jude released the knife and it dropped on to the counter.

"Can...I come in, son?"

"It's half-two in the morning, Dad. How did you even know I was here?"

"Educated guess. Suzanne's educated guess - she's at Alice's birthday party."

"So you're feeling lonely." Jude turned off the light over the prep area and started wiping down the counter. "What do you want?"

"To apologise, mostly."

"Do you? Or does your girlfriend just want you to patch things up to ease her guilty conscience?"

"Suzanne has nothing to feel guilty about, Jude. It's me who –"

"Yeah, well I don't want your apology. I want…" Jude realised what he was about to say just sounded childish.

"You want what?"

Jude thought for a moment. "I want things the way they were," he said. That sounded better than 'I want you to love my Mommy'.

His father sighed. "Sometimes I want that too, son." He ventured further into the kitchen, allowing the door to swing closed behind him. "Life certainly was more straightforward then. But you can't help who you fall in love with."

"Oh please." Jude turned and glared at his father. He wasn't going to listen to this shit. The man certainly knew how turn on the 'poor-me' act. It used to work too, especially when it came to his own mother, Jude's grandmother, and the house that Jude had inherited. It used to work but not anymore.

"Of course you can help it, Dad," Jude said. "We all have free will, the last time I checked –"

"It's not that simple –"

"Yeah, it is. There was that moment you had to decide. To act on your stupid, selfish, mid-life-crisis-fuelled feelings or to do the right thing. And you chose stupid. Now the rest of us have to live with the consequences."

"Look, I'm trying to do the right thing here, Jude. Not Suzanne, me. I know that the easiest way to do that would be to proclaim it was all a big mistake and go beg your mother to take me back."

"Yeah, maybe you should do that. See how far you get."

"But it wouldn't be true, me saying that. So, this is the next best thing. Trying to make things right with you. Your mother needs more time to forgive me, or maybe she never will. But I really couldn't bear to lose you over this. I really couldn't."

Hearing the quiver in his father's voice, Jude looked over and, for the first time in his thirty-five years, saw tears in the man's eyes. If this was the 'poor-me' act, he was taking it up a notch.

"You can't just expect me to just sit back and accept it all, to just be happy about it. Can you?"

"I don't know. But do you think there'll ever be a time when you might be happy for me? For me and Suzanne?"

"No, Dad. I don't." Jude said. "But it's not like I'm never going to talk to you again. For a start, you're my bloody accountant."

"There are other accountants. And you haven't exactly needed my help –"

"Look, we're not going to be one of those families. The kind where there's a row one day and they never speak to each other again. Like –"

"My family? Me and your grandmother?"

"That's not what I meant. You did speak to her."

"Only when I had to."

"She was a hard woman, Dad."

"You'd know better than anyone. She was lucky to have you taking care of her, I should have told you that more often."

"Okay, you're just getting maudlin now."

Brian smiled, a mixture of amusement and relief. "Maybe."

They both fell silent, not sure where the conversation was going, where their relationship was going.

Eventually, Brian glanced around the kitchen. "This is the first time I've been here since it was a building site. Looks well."

Jude extended his arms dramatically. "This is my kingdom."

"You have anything to drink in your kingdom?"

Jude laughed. "As a matter of fact…" He turned and opened a cabinet door. He pulled an oval bottle from the back of the cabinet and proudly showed it to his father.

"Glenrothes," Brian was clearly impressed. "Is that –"

"The eighty-five." Jude smiled proudly as he took out a couple of tumblers. "A parting gift from Renato. Of course, I just use it for the trifles."

~ ~

"Can I make an observation?" Brian said when they both had over-filled glasses in their hands.

"Go on," Jude said with some scepticism.

"This room. I know it was an empty shell when I saw it last but shouldn't this kitchen be bigger?"

Jude sighed. "Oh that. Yeah, it's a slight bone of contention. My so-called 'silent' partners are becoming vocal. This redesigned kitchen was their first creative contribution."

"Is that a freezer?" his father asked.

Jude tensed. "Yep."

"Why do you need a big freezer? Surely most of it has to be fresh."

"They wanted it."

"Did *they* say why?"

"They were kind of sketchy on the details. Something about being-prepared-for-all-eventualities, whatever that means. It started off as a small thing, then they wanted bigger and this is what I ended up with."

Brian walked over and opened the freezer door.

"And it's half empty. Do you not think you need to push them for a reason? Even speaking as your accountant, any wasted space, somewhere down the line, means lost revenue."

"True –"

"Plus this place is your responsibility. It's your name on the paperwork. You should be in the loop of everything that's going on."

Jude pushed closed and locked the fridge door. "I know, but –
"

"They're your partners, Jude. But they're supposed to be your silent partners. They can't be let take over the place. Do they even have any experience in the industry?"

"It's actually not them I'm worried about. I'm more concerned that they're under instruction."

"What does that mean? From who?"

"A man called Graham Fanning. My partners have had dinner with him, here, the last three nights. Oh, and lunch on Monday."

"Graham Fanning….why do I know that name?"

Jude took a long drink, emptying the glass. "Probably because he's been in the papers, having survived three recent attempts on his life. And because he's one of the biggest drug dealers in the country."

Chapter 31.

October.

Temple took a deep breath as he walked briskly along Camden Street with Brian Miller. As much as he hated to admit it, he was struggling to keep up with the sixty-something-year-old man and was starting to regret his bravado. Mr. Miller's suggestion that he accompany him on his walk from Donore Avenue to George's Street seemed manageable at the time, even if Temple didn't know why such a thing was necessary – there were two perfectly good cars sitting right there.

"He definitely said Graham Fanning?" Temple asked, trying not to sound too out-of-breath.

"I take it you know who that is then," Brian Miller said.

"Safe to say." Of course Temple knew who Graham Fanning was, but it bothered him that the name was in Brian Miller's vocabulary. Or his son's.

"For God's sake," Brian said. "Why do these people…" He shook his head. "Why can't these people just make a mess of their own lives? Why do they have to prey on…Jude just wants to make a living doing what he loves. What's wrong with that?"

"This is how they function, sir," Temple said.

They look for a sucker. Someone with more ambition than patience. He almost said this to Brian Miller but then stopped himself – he needed to keep the man on-side.

"Function?" Brian's exasperation was clear. "Can't they function like the rest of us? Use their intelligence, go out and get a bloody job. That too much to ask?"

"Not everyone has what you and I might consider conventional intelligence, Mr. Miller," Temple said, fighting the urge to go further, to give the man a lesson in class gaps, to tell him that Graham Fanning had, in fact, left school at twelve, that he had been running with gangs since he was eight, that that was his formative education.

"I know that," Brian said defensively. "I'm just saying –"

"What did you say when Jude told you?" Temple interjected. "You know, about this association between his partners and Fanning?"

"My initial reaction was to go to the Guards. But Jude wouldn't hear of it. He wouldn't even admit that there was actually something to worry about. Fanning was just a regular customer, he said. Even when I reminded him that this regular customer, a known criminal, was in cahoots with his business partners, he was still adamant it didn't mean anything."

His business partners. Temple had missed this opportunity with Jude. He wasn't about to make that mistake again. "Yeah, what were their names again? The partners?" he asked casually.

"Em...Mr. Lewis and Mr. Curtis. Don't know their first names."

Better than nothing.

"Your son does have a point, Mr. Miller. Eating lunch isn't a criminal offence. And, until you find a body hanging up in it, having a big freezer isn't either."

"I know, I know. Which is why I told him to just walk away, that it wasn't too late to get out of the partnership."

"Maybe that's the right move," Temple said.

"Except that Jude said he didn't have the money to pay back what they'd given him. It was always his plan to buy them out eventually but not for a couple of years, not until he was well-established and making proper money."

"So his back's against the wall, then," Temple said. "Is he scared?"

"I have no idea. You know, maybe not. I am though."

"Mr. Miller, if Jude feels he has the situation under control, maybe he does."

"Could you not talk to him? You know what this Fanning guy is like, maybe you could persuade him to –"

"Jude has already turned down my help," Temple interrupted. "Besides, he's right, nothing illegal has happened. As much as we all dislike Graham Fanning, I can't chastise him for eating. But maybe I can ask around, see what I can find out about these investors. What else do you know about them?"

"Nothing. Can you believe that? I'm supposed to be Jude's accountant, and he doesn't even tell me who he's doing business with."

Brian Miller veered towards a door and pulled a set of keys out of his pocket.

No way, Temple thought. He hadn't touched on why he had come to see the man in the first place and after walking two miles at a speed that no doubt shortened his life, Temple was at least going to get some answers he needed.

"Before you go in, Mr Miller," he said.

The man turned to look at him, probably for the first time since they'd met.

"I was hoping you could clarify something for me. In relation to Daniel Summers."

"Sorry, yes," Brian Miller looked embarrassed. "We got completely off the point there, didn't we?"

What do you mean 'we'?

"The truth is, I'm about to speak to your wife –"

"Geraldine?" The man's mood was suddenly different, any trace of joviality gone. "What's she got to do with all this? In fact, what have either of us got to do with all this?"

"Your daughter-in-law is the connection, sir," Temple said and watched the man's apprehension definitely increase. "In the course of my inquiries, I discovered that you and your wife separated last year as a result of –"

"I had an affair," Brian Miller said, obviously deciding to face the interrogation head on. "But it's more than an affair now. You know that, of course."

"Do I?"

"You came to see me at her house?"

"Oh right. Well, the current status of the relationship is not what I'm interested in. What I would like to know is how you met Ms. Keane and, more specifically, how the affair began."

"We met at Jude and Alice's, sure. But it was a party and there were forty or fifty other people there."

"But your wife wasn't."

"No, she was at home with a migraine. Well, that was the official line. Truth was, herself and Alice weren't getting on. So I went by myself, out of politeness mostly, and I met a lot of people. Suzanne was one of them. She was working for Alice at the time."

Temple raised an eyebrow to show there was little point playing the whole thing down at this stage.

"Okay, fine," Brian said. "She and I probably did monopolise each other's time that night. We got on well. She was easy to talk to."

"Not to mention easy on the eye," Temple said and

immediately wondered if he had overstepped the mark.

But Brian just smiled. "I'm only human."

"And how did you go from that to leaving your wife for her?"

"I don't know. The usual way."

Temple folded his arms and waited. Vague answers were not going to do Brian Miller any favours.

Brian sighed, realising he wasn't getting away with them. "Well, it was Alice. She mentioned a few times after the party that Suzanne had been asking about me. I was flattered, curious maybe, but that was it. Then Suzanne and I bumped into each other on the street. I was out for my usual lunchtime walk, doctor's orders and all that. And there she was. Again, the conversation was just so easy and I suggested a quick drink after work. That led to lunch the next day and the day after that. A quick goodbye hug became a long hug, which became a kiss on the cheek –"

"Which became jumping into bed, I get it."

"There might have been a step or two in between," Brian said sardonically.

A little late for piety, Temple thought.

"Funny thing was," Brian continued. "She had never mentioned me to Alice, not once. In fact, she confessed that she had barely even remembered me."

"Until?"

Brian smiled. "Exactly. Until Alice started dropping my name to her."

So Mia was right, Mrs. Miller wasn't being paranoid, Temple thought. Alice *Miller was playing her part.*

"I don't get it, Inspector," Brian said. "I really don't see what all this has to do with Daniel Summers' death."

"I'm just trying to get a picture of everyone involved. For thoroughness."

Now who's giving vague answers?

"Well, in the interests of thoroughness, I want you to know that I'm happy." Brian opened the door and stepped into the musty hall. "I can say that in complete honesty for the first time in twenty years." Brian was now standing in the doorway and his stance in no way suggested an invitation inside. "You're saying Alice manipulated us? I say okay. In fact, all things considered, I say 'thanks very much'. Cheque's in the post."

Luckily for Temple, he wasn't one to be offended by having a door slammed in his face.

Chapter 32.

"I need a holiday. And a drink." Mia said. "But not necessarily in that order."

Alice smiled, detecting some of the old happy Mia standing on her doorstep.

"Wine's chilling as we speak," Alice said.

~ ~

"So, that's it," Alice said, after Mia had explained that, given the evidence and statements by people who knew Daniel, the D.P.P. had ruled the incident as self-defence.

"Mia? That's it?" Alice said again when she didn't get an answer.

"Yeah, sure," Mia said and took a long, purposeful sip of her wine.

"Well come on, what's up?" Alice wondered if she was missing something. "I thought you'd be relieved."

"He's still dead, isn't he?"

"It's not your fault. If he wasn't dead, you'd be dead."

"Maybe not. Maybe if I'd pushed him away earlier, not encouraged him –"

"Yeah, and if I hadn't introduced you to him, and if his mother hadn't given birth to him…who isn't to blame? Hindsight is a wonderful thing."

"It's not that simple."

"It really is. As I've said to you, so many times before, you really have to stop being so hard on yourself!"

"Funnily enough, Kieran Temple said the same thing to me."

"Did he now?" Alice considered asking Mia about Temple but stopped herself. She knew she'd get more from Mia by letting her talk about him in her own time. Besides, Alice already had what she needed.

"So when are you going back home?"

"To that house? Probably never."

"Oh, right. Of course." Alice suddenly knew where this conversation was going and decided she better just deal with it. "You know I'd invite you to stay here, but now that everything is so…you know…with Jude…" She faded off, the words she was thinking sounding strange in her head.

"Oh God, no!" Mia said, seeming genuinely surprised. "I wasn't asking you that at all. Kieran made that assumption all by himself. That's the last thing you need at the moment. I'm going to stay at the hotel again tonight."

Alice hoped her relief wasn't obvious. "And then?"

"I don't know. I was going to go back to work but that probably isn't the best idea. I need to get my head together. Maybe I'll go to Skibbereen, stay with Nina for a few days. I –"

She was interrupted by a buzz from the hall.

"Someone at the gate," Alice said with a frown. The only person she was expecting was already here. "Back in a tic."

She went to the intercom but, before she could speak, an identity card was held up to the CCTV screen. She pressed the button to open the gate.

"It's your mate," she called to Mia.

Mia appeared at the door, bemused. "My mate?"

"Detective Inspector Temple."

Mia paled. "What does he want?"

"Relax. He's probably just wrapping things up," Alice said. "You know, being meticulous."

Mia's obvious concern, or fear maybe, left Alice uneasy, but the three officious rings of the bell left her no time to think about it.

~ ~

"Good evening, Mrs. Miller," Temple was surprised that his smile was coming so easily.

"You're working late, Inspector," she said, stepping back to let Temple in. "Getting lots of overtime, I hope."

"It's a wet one tonight," he said, shaking the water off his coat.

"What can I do for you?" she said curtly. This was as far into the house as Temple would be going.

"Em, I was hoping –" Temple stopped when he spotted Mia standing at the kitchen door. "Mia," he said, feeling his cheeks flushing. "Didn't know you'd be here. Good to see you. How are you?"

"I'm okay, Kieran. I'm…how are you?"

The awkwardness was obvious to everyone in the room and, judging from her bemused expression, nobody more than Alice Miller. "You're not looking for Mia then, Inspector?" she asked.

"No, of course not. Why would I be?" Temple said, a little too defensively.

"Oh, okay," Mia said. "I'll…maybe I'll go then. That okay?"

It was only then that Temple noticed she was already holding her handbag. Given their last conversation, it was no surprise that she didn't want to be around for this one.

"Okay, yeah," he said.

"I was asking Alice actually."

Alice Miller was clearly taken aback by her friend's wish for a hasty exit. And for the definite coldness towards Kieran Temple.

"You don't have to," Alice said. "I'm sure this won't take long. Right, Inspector?"

Temple didn't get a chance to respond before Mia took a few steps towards the door. "Still, I've been in Inspector Temple's shoes. Last thing he needs is someone earwigging on an interview."

Interview. Thanks a lot, Mia. So much for catching Alice Miller off-guard.

Alice opened the door and Temple moved further into the hall to let Mia past. While she and Alice said goodbye, he busied himself by looking at some photographs on the wall.

"I'll, em, talk to you later," Mia said.

Closing the door behind Mia, Alice turned and smiled curtly at Temple. They both allowed a moment of silence to pass.

"These are nice," Temple said, gesturing towards the photographs.

"Yeah, I suppose." She allowed her gaze to linger on a frame containing five photos of herself and Jude. A holiday, on a sofa, on a hill-top, around a crowded dinner table, another holiday. All happy, all real.

Alice walked to the kitchen and Temple assumed he was invited to follow her.

"That middle one. That's Lough Tay, right?" he asked, once

again taken aback by the almost-blinding brightness of the kitchen.

Alice turned, impressed. "Yeah. You climb?"

"You must be joking. Used to go walking up there. Glendalough, Luggala, Sally Gap. With my wife when we first got together."

"You enjoy it?"

"Eh no. All I remember is the wind. Windy all the bloody time."

"There's no bad weather, Inspector. Just bad clothes. But yeah, that wind does go through you alright. So why did you do it?"

"Trying to impress her."

A brief smile crossed Alice's face. "Did it work?"

"She married me, didn't she?"

"Fair enough. Yvonne, isn't it?"

"Sorry?"

"Your wife's name?"

Temple felt uneasy and wasn't sure why. Maybe the mention of her name had reminded him that at present, and for about the third time since they'd met, he and Yvonne weren't talking to each other.

"Yeah, that's it," he said. He didn't really feel like getting into how she knew his wife's name. Mia had probably mentioned it. It didn't matter anyway.

"Is Mr. Miller –"

"What's she like?"

"Who?"

"Yvonne."

"She's, em –"

"Is she like Mia?"

Temple was tempted to let it happen, to find out what Alice Miller was getting at. But he pushed the urge aside – again, it

---

was irrelevant and, besides, he didn't feel like letting her know she was getting to him. He didn't even want to admit that to himself.

"Is Mr. Miller here?"

"Sorry, no." Alice's disappointment was obvious, even if she did try to hide it behind that tight smile. "He had to go to London for a meeting."

"Oh?"

"With Greg Rownes. You've heard of him, I assume."

"Of course. My wife has every one of his books, I'd say."

"It's a kind of a brainstorming session. By which Greg's going to tell Jude all the things he's doing wrong."

"You're not a fan of Mr. Rownes?" Temple asked.

"Only because I know him," Alice said without a trace of pretention. She walked into the sitting room and Temple took that as a silent invitation to follow her. She perched uncomfortably on the edge of a sofa, like she was the one visiting.

"So shouldn't we be doing this down at your station?" she asked. "You know, if it's an official interview."

Temple smiled, embarrassed. "Mia might have overstepped there, slightly. I just have one or two things to clear up. You know, before I go back to my proper job."

"Yeah, Mia mentioned you work with Organised Crime? Is that, like, gangs, stuff like that?"

"Sure, stuff like that."

"And you had time to get involved in this?"

Temple laughed. "Not really. But it's Mia so –"

"You must be really good friends to help her like this."

Maybe it was her tone, but Temple felt that unease again, that feeling that she was stepping over a line.

"We were partners for a long time."

"Partners."

"And friends, as you said." Temple opened his notebook to show that he'd be asking the questions from now on. "Can we talk about Daniel Summers for a quick second? You know, so I can get out of your hair."

Alice was almost smirking at this stage. "Sure. Go ahead."

"It's just one or two things, really," Temple said. "The relationship. What did you think of it?"

"What does all that matter? He's dead, Inspector. And not as a result of crime, as we now know."

"Indulge me."

"But you know what I thought of it. It's well documented that I, what would you say, facilitated it."

"Yes, that's what surprised me."

"What do you mean?"

"I mean, you put a lot of work into it. Getting them together like that."

"Besides persuading Mia to crash a wedding, there wasn't much to do."

"I don't think so."

"Inspector, please." Alice closed her eyes. "Could you just say what you want to say? You're the one who needs to back to your real job."

"I think that, once you had decided they were a good match, you were going to make sure they got together. I mean, that's what you do, isn't it?"

"That's what I…" Alice's expression hardened. "What are you accusing me of, exactly?"

"It's not an accusation. I'm just saying that you go to great lengths when you decide to get two people together. Mia and Daniel. Kate and Stephen. Your father-in-law and Suzanne Keane."

"God-damn it!" Alice hissed. "Will that woman ever let it go!"

"You're referring to your mother-in-law, Mrs. Geraldine Miller."

She glared at him. "Who else? How long did it take her to mention it, ten seconds?"

"It doesn't matter, does it? The fact is, you encouraged them, a married man, also your father-in-law, and a friend of yours, to have an affair, something that was obviously going to cause disruption. Is that what you wanted? Disruption?"

"And now, what? I did the same with Daniel and Mia? Pardon me, Inspector, but if you think that, you're an idiot."

Temple was okay with being insulted – it just showed him that he was getting somewhere.

"Brian and Geraldine were in trouble long before Suzanne came along," she continued. "They were at loggerheads since Brian's mother, Jude's grandmother, died and left this house to Jude and Brian barely put up a fight. Geraldine accused him of being spineless. Since then, it's been bad-to-worse. They barely spoke to each other. Brian flirted with anything with breasts, including me on more than one occasion. And the last time Geraldine cracked a smile was probably when the late Mrs. Miller Senior popped off. Brian and Geraldine were heading for the cliff, Inspector. Suzanne just helped –"

"You mean you just helped," Temple said and saw that flash of rage cross Alice's face again, the narrowing of the eyes, the pursing lips. "And what about Jude?" he continued. "Would he agree that his parents' marriage was 'heading for a cliff', as you put it?"

Alice took a deep breath and, to Temple's surprise, she smiled. "There's no underestimating the power of denial. But I think you know that better than anyone, right?"

"Mrs. Miller –"

"Look, whether Jude accepted it or not, it was happening. All I did was speed up the inevitable," she said. "But, yeah, it was enjoyable. There, I confess. Who was it said 'Mankind is the plaything of blind fate'? Well, why should blind fate have all the fun?"

Temple was almost impressed by this admission.

"I get it, okay? I'm no angel," she continued. "But, at the end of the day, I'm also not breaking any laws, am I?"

"With your little love-triangle project? No, you're not."

"Or with Mia and Daniel either. She –"

"I know Mia, Mrs. Miller. I know her well. And she would never go for someone like Daniel Summers."

"Really?" Alice said. The confidence was back. "And what kind of guy would she go for, Inspector? If you know her so well?"

Maybe it was the smirk, maybe it was the insinuation, but now it was Temple's turn to be annoyed. Pushing himself forward in the chair, he forced a smile.

"Let me make myself clear," he said, forcing calm into his voice. "I am ninety-percent sure that, without your intervention, Daniel and Mia would never have got together, would never have even met. That you encouraged their relationship in the full knowledge that they were inherently bad for each other and that it would it end and end badly. I'm also pretty sure that your continued involvement from that day to this meant that Daniel ended up –"

"Oh come on," Alice said, forcing a snigger. "You can't possibly think that –

"Yeah, I do. And as soon as I can prove it – and I will prove it – you will be held accountable."

The fixed smile faded as Alice shook her head. When it was clear that he was finished, she sat forward, mimicking his posture.

"Well let me make myself clear, *Kieran*," she said. "You really don't want to do that. It's bullshit anyway. Even if I did do what you're suggesting, it doesn't mean anything. Most relationships that end, end badly. And it certainly doesn't mean that I'm really responsible for any of it."

"We'll see," was all Temple could manage.

"No, we won't."

"I'm sorry?"

"See, I know you went to see Mia last night, Inspector. And I know that it didn't end with a hearty handshake. You might tell me that she instigated it, just like she did last year. That you were an unwilling participant, just like you were last year. But we both know that's not true, right?"

Temple opened his mouth to speak but no words came.

"You think that I fuck around with people's lives?" Alice said, sitting back and looking relaxed for the first time since his arrival. "You think I do it for my amusement? Well how far do you think I'd go for my survival?"

Chapter 33.

July.

Ah don't overthink it. Just do what comes naturally.

Mia was conscious of the presence in the bed beside her. And even in semi-sleep, she knew it wasn't Daniel.

Slowly forcing herself into consciousness, she managed to crack open her eyes again and found herself looking up at a detailed ceiling rose and a cheap chrome bar of spotlights. She lay there, feeling dazed, as the questions, one at a time, popped into her head.

Glancing down along the bed, Mia realised that the thin duvet was only covering her naked body from her belly-button down. She grabbed it and pulled it up to her neck.

Something tells me we're past self-consciousness.

She turned her head and saw the white blotchy back of a naked man. His hair was shoulder-length at the back, like he was trying to compensate for the growing bald patch. The shoulders definitely weren't as broad as Daniel's and, when she lifted the covers, she was looking at significantly flabbier buttocks.

Pulling the duvet back up to her chin, she slowly sat up and allowed her gaze to wander around the room, willing herself to recognise something, anything. But nothing was familiar, not the dull grey-white featureless walls, not the cheap MDF table with oversized flat-screen TV. The picture on the night-stand, of a girl, early-twenties probably, with black hair and intense eyes, certainly did not ring any bells.

"Can you tell me where the hell I am?" she asked the girl.

Her croaky voice, the first sound she had heard, caused the man to stir. As he rolled on to his back, she could see his face. And last night's activities came back to her with cruel clarity.

His attempt to flirt with the shy Suzanne. A consolatory shared cigarette with Mia outside the restaurant and then another. A messy kiss in the back of a taxi that had continued against a front door, up the stairs and into this room.

She could remember his taste, that all-too-familiar nicotine-and-whiskey combination from her youth. His attention had moved to her ears, neck and breasts as they fumbled with clothes. She could remember her hands on him, all over him and how, for an older man, he became excited so quickly, at just her touch in the right place.

Mia closed her eyes again and hoped, prayed, that that had been it. One premature male orgasm followed by immediate coma. But she knew they had gone further. She knew he had been inside her. And that she had wanted it, welcomed it, enjoyed every second of it.

The low intermittent buzzing broke the silence and Mia turned towards it. Her bag lay open on the floor, its contents spilling out on to floor. She reached down and retrieved the phone, forcing away the accompanying nausea.

Please don't be Daniel, she pleaded to fate before looking at the screen. She didn't have the wherewithal to come up with a convincing lie right now. And she certainly wasn't about to tell him the truth.

Mia sighed with relief when she looked at the screen.

"Alice," she whispered.

"Jesus, Mia, where the hell are you? I've been trying to ring you since last night! What happened to you?"

"I'm fine."

"You're fine? That's it? Where did you go? Did you get home okay?"

"Eh, no, not quite. I'm in…" No, it still wasn't coming to her.

"Where are you? Why are you whispering?"

There was a moment's silence as Alice joined the dots. Mia then heard a short laugh and detected a note of derision. "You have got to be kidding me. Really? You went home with Hugh Hefner?"

One thing came back to her. "His name is Des. And he's okay." She didn't like that she sounded defensive. She could have just denied it, pretended she was at home, and she could have made it sound convincing. But she needed to confide in someone about this and it might as well be Alice.

"I'm at his place," she said and glanced around the room. "I think. Well I hope it's his place."

She picked up a classic car magazine, looked at the cover and threw it back on the floor. "If it's a hotel, it's a pretty awful one. I'm sorry, Alice. I just –"

"Hey, you don't have to apologise to me," Alice said and Mia was surprised at how accepting her friend was of the situation.

"You won't tell him, will you?" Mia regretted the words as she said them.

"Mia, come on," Alice said, some hurt in her voice.

"Sorry. Hang on, what time is it?"

"Half-nine."

"Fuck, I need to get out of here," Mia said, looking around the floor for her clothes.

"Hey relax," Alice said. "Stay a while, why don't you? You can cook lover-boy some breakfast."

"Jesus, how can you find this funny?" Mia said, trying not to raise her voice. "What the fuck am I doing? Just when things were going well –"

"What are you talking about, 'going well'? Weren't you freaking out last night about how well things weren't going?"

"Look, can we not talk about this now? I better go. And Alice?"

"What?"

"Not a word to Jude either, I don't need him getting a crisis of conscience."

"Yeah, of course."

Mia hung up and, finding her underwear under the bed and the rest of her clothes in a pile, hurriedly dressed. As she was putting on her shoes and envisaging the imminent walk of shame, there was more movement beside her.

"Hey, good morning," she heard and looked over to the satisfied face looking back at her.

"Hi," she said curtly with her best polite smile.

"You dressed already?" Des glanced at the clock "It's only early."

"Yeah, I have to go. I have…" She started to think of an excuse, and then didn't bother. "I have to go."

"Oh okay. Well can I call you, you know, meet for a drink or something?" he asked. But it sounded half-hearted.

Mia nodded towards the photograph on the night-stand.

"Don't think she'd approve, do you?"

He glanced at the photo and emitted a brief but proud smile. "That's my daughter, Anabelle," he said.

There's always a twist. "You're married."

"It's complicated."

"She's not here, is she? Your wife? Asleep in the next room, maybe?"

Des laughed, a funny laugh which reminded Mia how she ended up here. "No, of course not," he said. "She lives in Galway. They both do. It's complicated."

"Isn't it always."

Des sat up in the bed and ran the back over his hand down Mia's back. "You don't seem too bothered. About me being married. Unless...you are too?"

"I have a boyfriend," Mia said.

"You do?" he said dramatically. "You mean you...you...you used me?"

Oh shit, Mia though, this I don't need. But I suppose I deserve –

But Des was grinning. "I...I...I feel so cheap! I'm going to have to have counselling. I may be scarred for life."

Mia started to smile but then remembered that it was this cheeky sense of humour, and that contagious laugh, that had got her into this situation.

She stood up and grabbed her bag. "Okay, well...." She trailed off.

"It's okay" he said. "It was fun."

She tried to look embarrassed, but there was little sincerity behind it.

"Thanks. Can you tell me one thing though?"

"Yes, dear."

For a very nauseating second, it felt she was talking to her dad. Not her dad, of course. But someone's dad.

"Where are we, exactly?" she asked, terrified that he would say 'Portlaoise' or 'Ballymena' or 'Abu Dhabi'.

He smirked, seeing her fear. "Relax, we're in Clontarf." He pointed towards the window. "Seafront is five minutes that way.

You'll get a taxi there no problem."

Mia started towards the door.

"Hey, you leaving this as a souvenir?" he said.

She turned to see him holding up a black bra.

"Thanks," she said dryly as she snatched it from his hand.

Mia walked down the unfamiliar stairs and out on to the quiet road. As she walked, she checked her phone. Eight missed calls from Daniel. Actually scared, she dialled her voicemail.

"You have six new messages. Received yesterday, 10:32pm."

"Hey baby, just giving you a call to see if you're having a good time. Talk to you later."

Daniel's voice sent another pang of guilt rippling through her.

"Received 1:16am."

"Hi, just checking that you're okay. Give me a quick call back or a text, just so I can go to bed."

"Received 3:01am"

"Mia, can you ring me back please. Alice isn't answering her phone either. I need to know that you're okay. I can't sleep."

"Received 3:33am."

"Jesus Mia, this isn't fucking fair. I'm worried about you. Will you just –"

Mia hung up and dropped the phone into her bag.

~ ~

Alice stared out the kitchen window, smiling to herself.

Wow, Mia, you are good. This was much quicker than I expected.

Alice wondered if she'd need to pander to Jude's whim at all now. Maybe Mia's actions, her own choice of an alternative to Daniel, would be sufficient.

But, as she heard Jude coming down the stairs, Alice knew he wouldn't accept this. Maybe it was because a good review from Jameson was part of the deal. Or maybe it was something else.

"Did you get her?" Jude asked, walking into the room.

"Hmm?"

"Mia? Did you track her down?"

"Eventually," Alice replied. "On her mobile."

"Where was she?" he asked.

"Didn't say."

"You didn't think to ask?"

"I'm not her fucking keeper, Jude." She immediately regretted her aggression, worried he'd see past it. "She was probably at Daniel's."

"Daniel's?"

Alice took pleasure in Jude's surprise. "Well," she said. "Where else would she be, right?"

Chapter 34.

Brian heard that loose floorboard upstairs above him and glanced at the crystal clock on the window-sill. Eleven-twenty-three. She had slept late. And he had been sitting here for nearly five hours.

Suzanne rarely slept past eight, even on the weekend, but at Alice's birthday last night she had let her hair down. She had come in around two and had made a drunken effort to go to bed quietly, during which she had instantly woken Brian. If he'd been in a better mood, talking to drunk Suzanne would have been fun. But, since getting home from making peace with Jude, Brian's uneasy feeling had grown into unashamed worry. So he had just kept his eyes shut and pretended to be asleep as Suzanne put herself to bed. But this pretence was as close to actual sleep as he got for the rest of the night and, around six, he gave up and came downstairs. He spent the next five hours in this chair, wondering what the hell he was going to do.

Jude had been right about one thing – Brian's action had definitely left others to live with the consequences. One of those was Jude himself, rushing into a business partnership without exercising one iota of due diligence. Something that a highly-skilled and ambitious chef might do, not something an astute businessman would. And when Jude had hired Brian to be his accountant, Brian saw this, not just as an olive-branch, but also a sign that Jude was realising his own lack of business acumen. Unfortunately, the accountant-client relationship had gone no further than a handshake, with Jude not even giving his father a set of books or telling him that he had gone into business with two men about whom he knew nothing and who, apparently, had some less-than-wholesome connections.

My actions, everyone else's consequences.

Hearing the bedroom door opening, Brian ran his hand through his hair, as if it would magically dispel the bleary-eyed worry from his face.

"Brian?" he heard Suzanne's croaky hangover-infected voice as she padded down the stairs.

"I'm out here, sweetheart," he said. She came into the sunroom, looking as half-asleep and hung-over as she sounded.

"Hey you," she said. "I must have been really out of it. I didn't even hear you get out of bed."

"I've been up a while," Brian said.

Suzanne smiled, was about to say something funny maybe, but stopped when she took a proper look at him. "Hey, you okay? What's wrong?"

"Nothing. I don't know…I'm just thinking."

"Brian." There was that warning tone that she had introduced into the relationship recently.

"I'm fine, honestly. Here, let me get you some juice."

She knelt down beside him, took his hand and lovingly kissed it. "It's okay, you can tell me. You're worried about Geraldine?"

Brian sighed, feeling the facade slipping. "Jude, actually. He's got himself involved in something and I can't help him –"

"Involved in what?"

"You don't want to know and I don't want to talk about it. But it's something that, if I'd my wits about me the last few months, I could have stopped."

"Your wits about you?" Suzanne sat back. "What, I distracted you from your real life, is that it?"

"Of course not. I mean, of course you've been a distraction, but in a good way –"

"That's not what it sounds like."

"Look, I'm not saying it's your fault, okay?" Brian didn't want to argue but she really wasn't helping.

She relaxed. "Okay, sorry. But it's not your fault either, Brian. Jude is an adult. He's capable of making his own decisions."

"His own mistakes, you mean."

"Well that's the thing about free will, isn't it?" Suzanne lowered herself gingerly onto his lap. "It can just as easily lead to mistakes as anything else. But come on, you've been saying since I've known you how independent Jude is. Do you really think he'd have listened to your advice?"

"I'm his father, I could have made him! I'm supposed to be his accountant as well. You might have been right about that, it was just a peace-offering. There was no real weight behind it."

"Don't think that's quite how I put it."

"After everything that wife of his put him through. And now everything I put him through. The restaurant is supposed to be his reward and even that's turning against him."

"Well maybe it's not too late. You know? You might still be able to help him now."

"I wouldn't even know where to start."

"Come on. This is you. The big fixer. I bet, since you've been sitting here, you've come up with half-a-dozen solutions."

It wasn't true but hearing her saying that helped. He smiled. "Gotta admire your confidence."

"What can I say, I'm a believer."

She was. Since the day they had met, she had always been positive and encouraging. Some cynical people, Geraldine for example, might say that she was just catering to a fragile ego. But it was much more than that.

"I love you." The words were out before he could stop them.

Suzanne sat up straight, clearly as surprised as he was. "You what?"

"I do," Brian said. "I'm sorry, I know we agreed that this wasn't to get serious too quickly. But I feel it, I have felt it since the start. And even with everything that's going on now, I still feel it. So it must be true, right? I know, I'm breaking the rules and I understand if –"

Whatever he had left to say was lost as Suzanne was kissing him, her arms wrapped tightly around his neck.

Chapter 35.

"What? What do you mean?" Any other day, this look of sheer confusion on Daniel's face might have been endearing. His eyes were wide, his brow furrowed. "I thought you were all on for moving in! You said you were!"

Alice's words of wisdom, to blurt out the bad news, was proving less than successful. Mia should have followed her instincts – the idea didn't feel right from the moment it had been suggested. Any confidence she might have had now abandoned her and that she had told him with such poise just left her feeling like a hypocrite.

"But living together is such a big change, Daniel," she said now, finally hearing that shake in her voice and taking comfort from it.

"Well if you didn't want to, why didn't you tell me when I asked? I mean…Jesus!"

"I don't know, I was –"

"Like, I'm a big boy, I could have taken it!"

All evidence to the contrary.

"I don't know, okay!" she said. "It was all so out-of-the-blue, I didn't know what to say. I wasn't stringing you along, I promise."

"You sure about that? Maybe you were. Maybe you just wanted to get my hopes up so your…fucking…rejection could have as much impact as possible. You knew what you were doing all along!"

Daniel's ridiculous melodrama aside, he had a point. Living together was never going to happen and she had known it from the moment he had asked her.

Just get through this, she told herself. *At least you're being honest now.*

"For God sake, Daniel!" she said, attempting his level of drama but not quite getting there. "You make me out to be some heartless bitch! What, I'm just out to hurt you?"

"Well, aren't you?" he yelled. He came right up to her, right in her face. And for the first time, Mia was a little bit scared of him. "Because that's how it looks from here."

"Why would I?" she said, fighting the urge to take a step back. "I'm mad about you. You know I am!"

To her relief, he turned away. "Yeah, I thought you were. I…I thought it was really good. And now you're ruining it!"

Mia could do nothing but stare at him, this pacing, rambling man. A man on the fucking edge. So not the person she thought she was going out with.

"Why, Daniel?" she managed to say. "Why am I ruining it? Why is not wanting to live together after just three months 'ruining it'?"

"Because –"

"I want this to last," Mia wasn't done. "So, you know, maybe

I'm trying not to rush it, to keep things at a more consistent pace –"

"Consistent! Consistent with what? Your idea of the 'perfect relationship'? We kiss on this day, we sleep together on this day, we live together on this day, is that it? Maybe you better give me a copy of your schedule so I know when I can hold your fucking hand!"

"Grow up, will you!" As quickly as she'd been afraid, she was now just annoyed. "What do you mean, my idea of the perfect relationship? So what, we have to do everything by your standards instead, is that it? Or you'll lie down on the floor and have a tantrum like a little baby? Yeah, that's normal!"

This outburst seemed to catch him off-guard. He started to say something but Mia was on a roll.

"I'm part of it too, you know?" She continued, forcing calm into her voice. "Of this. I should get to have some say –"

"Are you?" With two steps, he was back in her face again. "Are you part of it, Mia? Were you part of it last night?"

"What does that mean?"

"Where the hell were you? I was ringing you and –"

"You know where I was," she said, managing to hold his gaze. "Alice's birthday." She prayed that the guilt wasn't written all over her face.

If it was, Daniel was too distracted to notice. "And what about after that, huh? Where were you then? You didn't come here. And you didn't go home. So where were you?"

"What do you mean, I didn't go home? What makes you think that?"

"Well, did you? Tell me you did and maybe I'll believe you."

"Okay, you're just being a prick now," Mia hoped that attack might actually be the best line of defence. "What, you think I was fucking someone else? Is that what this is about?"

Daniel took a step back, thrown by Mia's sudden crudity.

"What are you...stop –"

"Okay fine, Daniel, I was, okay?"

"Mia, I mean it –"

"I was fucking someone else! Yeah, we were at it all night. We –"

The pain exploded across Mia's jaw, through her eyes before enveloping her head, her shoulders, her whole body. The power and surprise of Daniel's slap threw Mia off-balance and she hit the floor.

There was silence. And stillness. From everywhere. The room. The house. The whole city seemed to be waiting.

Mia stared at the ceiling, blinking fast as the waves of nausea came at her faster and stronger. She felt she would have no choice but relent, turn her head and vomit on Daniel's cream carpet. But, as she felt that urge dissipate, Mia was able to stand up and walk to the door.

"Mia, wait," Daniel said quietly, taking a step towards her. But, as she spun around, her fury made him recoil.

"Don't!" she barked. "Don't say a word. Not one. Don't say a word to me ever again. Don't come near me. Ever. Again!" Her voice was breaking, she was crying and she had to get out of there.

Out of the room, almost to the front door before she felt a dull, then sharp, pain around her upper arm. She froze as the pain took her breath away.

"Don't go, Mia," she heard Daniel say quietly in her ear. It was his vice-like grip burning her arm. "Don't leave."

Mia prayed for a steady voice. "Let go. Let go, Daniel. Let go, right...fucking...now."

Then the snag on her arm was released and she was out. Out the front door into the driveway, she willed the tremors running up and down her entire body to stop. This throbbing, that had now centred itself to her upper jaw and upper arm, was more than just pain.

Everything was different now.

She got into her car, locked the doors and drove away.

Oh God oh God oh God. Mia blinked, a long blink to try to quell the tears. *Not this, never this.*

She tried to wipe the tears away but they were coming too fast and, by the time she reached Irishtown, she could barely see. She turned on to a side street and pulled to the kerb.

And then Mia screamed until she couldn't breathe.

Chapter 36.

In the five minutes that she was dealing with the annoying know-it-all customer, Alice had missed three calls on her mobile. It rang a fourth time as she was getting back to her office and, after she stared at it for a few seconds, curiosity finally got the better of her.

"Hello?" she said in her polite I-don't-know-who-this-is voice.

"Alice? It's Daniel."

Fuck it. Never answer an unknown number. "Oh, hi."

"Have you spoken to Mia today?"

Yeah, she was in a stranger's bed at the time. Why do you ask?

"Eh, no, I haven't, Daniel. I'm sure she's –"

"We had a fight." He sounded weird. Panicked. "It was bad, Alice."

Alice felt a coldness run through her. But she felt something else too. "What do you mean 'bad'. What happened?"

"It was my fault, I over-reacted. But there was no warning. She just said it out of the blue…"

Alice closed her eyes and sighed.

You had to come clean, didn't you Mia?

"Daniel, it was nothing, okay? She told me. It was just sex, it didn't mean anything," Alice said

"What? What was just sex?"

"She's hardly going to leave you for him. She loves you, I know she does –"

"Alice, what are you talking about?"

She froze. *Shit. Wait, does he not know?*

She didn't have to wait long for the shoe to drop.

"Mia was with someone last night?"

She listened to Daniel's laboured breathing as she tried to think of something to say. "Dan –"

"I don't care," he said.

This threw her. *What do you mean you don't care? How could you not care?*

"What I did," Daniel continued. "What I did was…I have to find her, make sure she's okay."

What I did.

"Daniel? What the hell happened? What did you do?"

"I didn't mean to. But she pushed me." He sounded like he was crying. "It all happened so fast…I…"

And then Alice knew exactly what had happened. It couldn't be anything else.

She also knew how she should be feeling at that moment. Angry, sick, maybe guilty. But she didn't.

"There is only one thing you can do right now, Daniel," she was saying before she could stop herself. "Find her. Make her forgive you."

There was silence from the other end of the line.

"Really?" Daniel said eventually. "Are you sure? Should I not

_"

"Be strong. Be assertive, Daniel. It's the only way she'll see that you're truly sorry."

"Em, okay. I suppose…" Daniel was confused and, all things considered, Alice couldn't blame him. "I mean, I am truly sorry," he said. "I only hit her once. It all happened so fast, it doesn't even feel real."

I only hit her once. Hearing him say those words finally brought the bile to Alice's throat and, for a moment, she wanted to do a U-turn, tell Daniel to fuck off and never speak to her or Mia again. But she didn't.

"So you better go and deal with it, Daniel," she said instead. Hearing the door to the gallery open, she felt some relief, she now had a reason to end this horrible conversation. "Look, I have to go, I have a customer."

"Eh right, ok, right," he said. "Okay, listen, thanks Alice. I mean it. You're a good friend, to both of us."

Yeah right, she thought, let's see how good a friend I am when I have a change of heart and call the Guards.

Unable to say something more comforting – or anything at all for that matter – Alice hung up. She tried to summon the emotions that should have been there – disgust with Daniel and pity for Mia. She willed these feelings to come to her, feelings that would come as second nature to anyone else.

But they wouldn't.

She closed her eyes as a wave of exhaustion washed over and she considered just closing up early and going home. She suddenly remembered she had a customer waiting.

"I'm sorry to keep you waiting," she said as she walked out of the office. "I was on a –" She stopped when she saw who was admiring the recently hung Therese MacAllister.

"Geraldine," Alice said, not able to hide her surprise. This was maybe the third time Jude's mother had ever visited the gallery. "How are you?"

"I'm wonderful," she said, turning to look Alice up and down as she always did. "I love your top. Very….bohemian."

Alice fought to overlook the thinly-cloaked insult. "So what brings you into town on a Sunday afternoon?"

"Oh, pleasure, pleasure. What else should bring anyone anywhere?"

Alice was surprised by this upbeat side to her mother-in-law, something she hadn't seen for some time.

"It's Oscar Wilde, dear." Geraldine said, glancing around the room as if she was standing in the middle of a landfill.

"Didn't think he'd be quite your thing," was all Alice could manage in retort.

"That's the thing about you," Geraldine said with a tight smile. "You've always had a very two-dimensional view of people."

Alice returned the smile. "Some people, maybe. I suppose I –"

"You need to fix things with Jude, Alice."

Alice was taken aback. "Fix things? I don't know what you mean."

"Yes, you do. The way you two are heading? I've seen it before, many times. And unless one of you sorts it out –" She paused and Alice knew that the woman's patronising tone was coming. "Well, I don't have spell it out, do I?"

"Maybe we're not exactly all over each other at the moment. But…"

She faded off, not sure that she should actually say what was on the tip of tongue.

Geraldine looked at her. "But…but what?"

"I'm just surprised. I'd have thought you'd be delighted to see this."

"You're right. Nothing would make me happier than to see the back of you. We both know that."

Thanks for sugar-coating it. I love you too.

"But it's not up to me, is it? I know my son and, despite everything that's happened, he still loves you. I can only imagine why. In fact, maybe it's because of everything that's happened."

Alice couldn't resist. "And what makes you think I still love him?"

"I really couldn't care less, Alice," Geraldine replied with unsettling certainty. "When all is said and done, and as much as I hate to admit it, you and Jude are better off together than apart."

"Better for who?" Alice asked, even though she knew the answer.

"For him, of course. He needs you and, right now, that's all that matters."

Alice's disdain for her mother-in-law, which she had been keeping in check, suddenly came to the surface and it took all her willpower not to lash out, to pick one of the topics she knew would sting and just go for it.

"And what about my needs?" she asked instead and then cursed herself for sounding whiny.

"As I said, irrelevant." If Geraldine was going for dismissive, she had nailed it. "There comes a time in every woman's marriage, especially nowadays when all the rules and roles are blurred, when she has to be the traditional wife. Sacrificing and subservient. Believe me, I know what I'm talking about."

Alice laughed, she couldn't help it. "Give me a break, Geraldine, it's just the two of us here. When have you ever been sacrificing or subservient?"

"My dear, what do you think I'm doing these days? My husband is having a fling and, in case you hadn't noticed, I'm letting it play out. Because when someone has an itch for twenty years, the easiest thing is to just let him scratch it."

Chapter 37.

October.

"…I just need to speak to him for a second."

Walking through the Mountjoy Station lobby, Temple turned when he heard the familiar voice. "Mr. Miller," he said. "You looking for me?"

"What do you think?" Jude Miller's cheeks were flushed.

"Okay." Temple was taken aback by the man's aggression. "How can I help?"

"You can help, Detective Inspector, by telling me what the hell you think you're doing."

~ ~

"You were in my house last night," Jude said. They were now sitting in one of the station's meeting rooms, a better place to have this conversation than the very public lobby.

The man was still irate, although the edge had come off it.

"Weren't you Inspector?"

"I was."

"Threatening my wife."

"Threatening?" *I wasn't the one doing the threatening.* "Eh, no. What Mrs. Miller might have picked up on as –"

"How can you think she had something to do with Daniel's death? It's ridiculous! You had her scared out of her mind –"

"If you would let me explain –"

"How would you feel if I went to your superiors and told them you were making unsubstantiated accusations? They wouldn't be too impressed, I'd imagine."

Right, enough of this.

"Mr. Miller." Temple's own voice was now raised, which clearly caught Jude off guard. "I didn't make any accusations, unsubstantiated or otherwise. What I did do, however, was suggest to your wife that this is more than a simple case of self-defence. If there someone else involved – whoever that person might be – that they will be held accountable."

Jude was less angry and now mostly just confused. "What the fuck are you talking about? Mia's already admitted to it! You're trying to take some of the attention away from one of your own people. This is just cronyism taken to a whole new level. You people protecting each other to the end, right? Even when it isn't fucking necessary!"

Temple had known that this would eventually come up but it annoyed him anyway. Of course there was a certain urge to protect Mia but not to the point of doing what Jude was suggesting. "Mr. Miller, I would advise you not to say anything you might regret –"

"Look, Inspector. I knew Daniel, okay? He was my friend, sure, but he was far from perfect. I've seen him in action before. Jealous, obsessive –"

"Violent?"

"Well…yeah, there were times –"

"So you agree with your wife? That he got what was coming to him?"

"What? Of course not! Did Alice say that?"

Temple shrugged.

The tension on Jude's face quickly dissipated to acceptance. "Look, you can just stop this," he said. "I'm never going to say – "

"Do you really believe her motives were honourable?"

"What? Whose motives?"

"Your wife."

"Yes! She –"

"Do you really believe that she got Mia and Daniel together, thinking they'd be suitable? That they would be good for each other?"

"She must have," he said, trying to sound resolute but not quite pulling it off. "Why else would she –"

"'Maybe she was getting bored creating perfect couples and decided to mix things up.' They were your words, remember?"

"Jesus, I was joking when I said that. You know I was."

Temple didn't miss the undercurrent of pleading in the man's voice.

"Maybe. Or maybe you were using a nice little half-joke to tell me something. Something you couldn't bring yourself to say outright."

Jude laughed. "I'm really not that clever, Inspector. And why the hell would I do that anyway? I know our marriage isn't perfect but I'd have to hate Alice to do what you're suggesting."

Temple made a point of sitting back in his chair. *We're just having a chat. Nice and friendly.* "Your marriage. How is it not perfect?"

Most people would have missed it, it was quick, but Jude's eyes flicked to the right. Here comes the lie.

"I don't know. The usual ways. Cap-left-off-the-toothpaste sort of things."

The vague answers again. Must have been a family trait. Temple stared at Jude, the same technique he used on the man's father.

"Okay, okay," Jude said with frustration. "For one thing, I didn't like the way she treated my mother. How's that for typically Irish?"

"Some clichés exist for a reason, Mr. Miller. What way did she treat your mother?"

"Ah, this whole thing over the house. Remember I told you it's been in the family for four generations?"

Temple nodded.

"Well, it skipped one."

"So I heard. Your wife was vocal on the subject."

"Was she?" Jude was unimpressed. "Nice to know she's so happy to talk about someone else's private business."

"She's your wife. Maybe she thinks it is her business."

Jude shrugged. "So, did she mention that I inherited the house from my grandmother? That it was a source of great stress and irritation for my parents? Funny thing is, it was my mother who took it worse. Contesting the will was a pointless exercise, Dad knew that. Whatever else can be said about my grandmother, she was meticulous. And smart. Smarter than Dad, even in death."

"So what's this all got to with your wife?"

"Nothing, except that Mum never got over the whole thing and Alice likes to rub it in her face any chance she gets."

"And you're okay with that?"

"At the beginning, sure, I let it happen. I was pretty pissed off with Mum. But I eventually called 'enough'.

"But your wife –"

"Alice was like a dog with a bone, wouldn't let up. And the

more I asked her to drop it, the worse she got."

"She resented your parents. For trying to evict her from her home. She was married to you so she was fully entitled to be there."

Jude stared at Temple for a moment. "Yeah, maybe."

"Why else would she sabotage your parents' marriage?"

Jude laughed. "What? Come on, who told you that, Dad? Alice didn't sabotage anything. He did that all by himself, trust me."

"You don't believe that. You know she was involved."

Temple paused, waited for Jude to object again. He didn't.

"And you've been punishing her ever since."

This time, he did speak up. "Punishing her? How am I doing that?"

"In the same way she did it to your parents. The relationships she engineers, you destroy."

"Okay, now you really are clutching at straws. I don't give a shit about her little matchmaking –"

"Oh I think you do. You tried to break up Kate and Stephen Dobson, that little lie you told him about her having a bit on the side. And, when that didn't work, you went after Daniel and Mia."

"Hang on –"

"You probably figured Daniel would be better off in the long run. Sure, he'd go off the deep end a bit, stalk Mia, maybe even hurt her. There's no love lost between you and her, so you figured if she got a bit of a beating, what harm. But the real one to suffer in it all would be your wife when –"

"Okay, STOP!"

His bellow reverberated around the small room. Temple sat motionless, awaiting one of two outcomes – an apology or a tirade.

It was actually somewhere in between. "I never tried to split up Kate and Stephen."

"Sure you did. They told me you did. You told Stephen that Kate was seeing someone else."

"I told Stephen I saw Kate with another guy, that's all. And that Alice had seen her snogging the same guy a few days earlier. We just wanted him to be aware of what he was getting into."

"We?"

"Me and Alice. And we figured it'd be better if it came from me as I was his friend."

"Did you see Kate snogging this guy?"

"No, they were drinking pints in Neary's."

It only struck Temple now and he was annoyed with himself.

"Was it the same guy that Alice says she saw him with?"

Jude was annoyed again. "Says she saw him with? What are you saying, that my wife is a liar –"

"Was it the same guy?" Temple wasn't going to let him change the subject.

"The way she described him, yeah."

"Did she describe him though?" he asked, just to confirm the hunch. "Or did you describe him and she picked up on it?"

This threw Jude and a look of sadness and betrayal swept across his face. He quickly covered it with irritation. "What exactly are you saying, Inspector?"

"So Alice tells you that she saw Kate snogging some guy. And you just believe her."

"Of course I believed her. There was no reason not to."

"And then she convinces you to be the bearer of bad news –"

"Me and Stephen were friends. It made sense."

"But it cost you that friendship. You were even banned from their wedding."

Jude, exasperated, started to speak but nothing came to him. He stared at the table for a few seconds before closing his eyes.

Temple suddenly felt guilty. Here was a man doing the valiant thing – confronting his wife's accuser. Jude was being a hero and Temple, in return, was being a bully and an opportunist. Time to pull back.

He sat back in the chair and crossed his legs "I hear you were in London."

Jude glared at Temple with considerable disdain. "Yeah. Is that against the law now too?"

"No, your wife mentioned that you were meeting an old friend. Is he going to help you with this investor situation?"

Jude suddenly stood up, almost knocking over his chair. This reaction was not what Temple was expecting.

"Inspector, my partners are none of your business, okay?" Temple wasn't sure, but he thought there was a definite thread of fear through the chef's voice. "And you've been trying to get a rise out of me since I got here. Do you think I'm going to talk to you about that?" He turned towards the door and then paused. "I assume I can go? You're finished unfairly assassinating my wife's character?"

"Unfairly?"

"Inspector, Alice and me, we might not be perfect. But don't think for a second you can turn me against her. Because that's never going to happen. So, when it comes down to it, you're outnumbered."

Temple smiled. He had to admire Jude Miller's guts. "Okay. One last question before you go though. If you don't mind."

Jude opened the door and stood with his back to it, to show that this would definitely be the last question.

"When did Mia and Daniel break up? Like, officially? I forgot to ask her before she left."

"That's an easy one. Dollymount Strand, Mia's summer party. They do that daft midnight-swim. The relationship definitely ended that night. Well, you know, for her it did."

"For her? And what about for Daniel?"

"For Daniel? Come on."

"What does that mean?"

"Isn't it obvious by now? For him, the relationship never ended."

Chapter 38.

August.

"Hello? Earth to Alice?" Mia said, looking at her friend.

Alice was leaning against the kitchen counter, running her finger around the rim of her wine glass. "Sorry, what?"

"I hope it's sunny wherever you are," Mia said. "This is supposed to be a party, you know. I know it's early but you could at least try and be festive."

"Sorry, you're right," Alice said, forcing herself to perk up. "Party party. Let's have some music."

She went into the sitting room to the stereo. "What time are you expecting people?"

"I don't know, what time do people go to parties in Dublin?"

"Same as anywhere else, depends on the party," Alice called from the other room. "And how popular the host is. In your case, I'd say 2am, if you're lucky."

"Thanks, I love you too," Mia said. "Well I'm doing the swim at midnight, even if no-one else is here by then."

"You know, of all the things to pack up and haul across the country," Alice said, flicking through a rack of LPs. "A collection of dusty old records would not have been high on my list," She picked out Forty Licks by The Rolling Stones and took a long look at the record player. "I'm not sure I even remember how to use one of these."

"That's because you are an uncultured slave to technology," Mia replied.

"It's the twenty-first century, darling," Alice said as she came back into the room. "Get with the program."

'Street Fighting Man' started playing in the other room.

"Nice," Mia said, clinking her glass with Alice's.

"So, is he coming?" Alice blurted.

Mia visibly tensed. "Yeah, probably," she said, shrugging her shoulders a little too emphatically. "Said he might be meeting some people beforehand and would call in after. I don't even know what that means."

"Maybe he's moving on with his life or something," Alice suggested. "Or he just wants you to think he is."

"Already? I don't even know if we're officially broken up. That would be moving on pretty quickly, don't you think?"

"Well where are things now? Have you seen him since…" Alice was unsure of the politically correct way of saying 'he punched you in the face'.

"No," Mia said. "I mean, we're talking again. He's been on the phone every day this week. Most of it is him saying sorry and begging me to forgive him and all that. And I tell him I have and he says sorry again and we eventually talk about something else just to show that we can. It's all getting a bit repetitive, to be honest."

"So if he comes here tonight, is that you back together?" Alice asked, her eyebrows raised.

"I don't know, maybe. Not sure if I can trust him anymore."

You can't trust him anymore? He wasn't the one who slept with someone else.

"Trust is kind of important alright," she said.

"Maybe I just need some time," Mia continued. "You know, to sort –"

She was interrupted by Alice's mobile phone ringing.

"It's about time," Alice said under her breath. Then, to Mia, "That's Jude, back in a minute."

She walked out into the garden as she answered. "Where the hell have you been?" she said. "I've been trying to get you –."

"To tell me Mia's all set for her hot date?"

"No, it's not about that –"

"Time's a factor here, honey. Most of the work has been done for you –"

"Jude, will you just listen to me! There was this guy at the gallery this afternoon, acting weird –"

"Guy? What guy?"

"I don't know. First he was just standing out front staring in at me. It was really starting to freak me out. And then, as I was closing up, he came in and started asking questions."

"What kind of questions?" Jude said. He was anxious and something told Alice he already knew something about it.

"It was fairly normal at first," she said. "He was admiring the paintings, asking how much they were, that sort of thing. But then he started talking about the gallery, whether I owned it, if it had plenty of insurance. I asked him who he was and he said he was a friend of yours."

"A friend of mine? Who was he?"

"He wouldn't tell me his name, even when I asked. He just started talking about you and the restaurant and how much money did I think it was making."

"Well was he a Guard? A detective maybe?"

"How am I supposed to know what a detective looks like?"

Alice said. "He was wearing, like, jeans and a scruffy tee-shirt. So, no probably not. But…" Hearing herself saying it all out loud, Alice started wondering if she was just being paranoid.

"But what?" Jude sounded stressed, even scared maybe.

"It's just, he had this weird look on his face the whole time. Like he knew he was scaring me. Like he was enjoying it."

There was no response from the other end of the phone.

"Jude? What's going on?"

More silence.

"Jude!"

"I don't know, Alice! It might be something to do with my partners. Something they're involved in, and now they're using me and the restaurant to –"

"To what?"

"There's some weird stuff going on. Money, cash, that isn't going through the books, is being used to buy stock. I –"

"Jesus," Alice exclaimed, trying not to raise her voice. "What's it got to with me? With the gallery?"

"I didn't think they knew anything about you, I promise. I mean, you've never met them and it's not like we talk about personal stuff. Look, don't worry, I'll take care of it."

"Jude, don't do anything stupid, please." Alice said. "This guy…this guy was fucking scary, okay? Maybe we should go to the Guards –"

"No! No, we can't. Look, Alice, we don't even know –"

"But if we just –"

"Just let me take care of it, okay?"

"Take care of what, Jude?" Alice was panicking but she didn't care. "Please talk to me! I'm scared!"

"Alice? Baby? We need to just stay calm, okay?" Jude said. "Can you stay with Mia tonight? You're at her party, right?"

"Why…what, do you think they know where we live? Jesus, Jude!"

"No, I don't. Honestly, I don't!" Jude said. "But you're scared and I'll be home late. So just stay with Mia, please?"

Jude's soothing tone was not having the desired effect, maybe because it didn't sound genuine.

"Okay. Yeah, maybe," Alice said.

"But don't say anything to her about this, okay?" Jude said. "Not to anyone."

Alice laughed, she couldn't help it. "What would I even say?"

"Everything will be fine, I promise."

Right now, she was finding it hard to believe him.

"Bye," she said and hung up.

She didn't even bother to tell him that she believed him. He didn't believe himself, by the sound of it. And as she stood there, staring into Mia's garden, she was angry with him for patronising her.

Why could you not just tell me the truth?

There was something going on at the restaurant, something illegal. And, thanks to her strange and disturbing visitor, Alice was now involved.

If Jude had come clean, told her everything he knew, then maybe she could help him. Or at the very least, she could help herself.

This wasn't exactly the first time she had thought about leaving him – there was a time when it was on her mind every day – but it was the first time that the motivation was fear.

Realising that her continuing absence from the party might be conspicuous, she turned back towards the house. She was startled to see someone at the door.

"Shit. Daniel!"

"Sorry, Alice, didn't mean to scare you."

She immediately wondered how long he had been there. From his stupid grin though, she guessed he hadn't heard the conversation.

"You didn't scare me. What are you doing here?"

"What do you mean? I was invited," he said, defensively.

"I thought you weren't coming till later. Didn't you have a thing?"

"Yeah, I blew that off. I figured this was more important. People have arrived. I'm here to bring you –" he held up a glass of champagne " – this and drag you in for a toast."

Alice took the glass and knocked back the contents.

Daniel sniggered. "Eh, okay. Good thing I brought so much of it."

"Good thing," she said and started to pass him into the house.

"Wait a sec, wait a sec," he said, lowering his voice. "I wanted to say thanks for your help with…you know, the other day?"

"I didn't do anything," Alice said, her gaze fixed on Mia in the kitchen. ""I just told you what you already knew."

"I know and –"

"But I tell you Daniel," she said, giving him a look that made him take a step back. "If you ever do anything else to hurt that girl –"

"I won't, I promise," he said, putting his hands up. "Lesson learned. I will never harm a hair on her head."

"You better not. I'm sure she'd be interested in learning about some of your past exploits."

"Exploits?" Daniel's eyebrows went up. "What, Kate? Mia knows about that, she's okay with it –"

"Something tells me you didn't tell her the whole story," Alice said. "And who says I have to stop at Kate. Who's to say that you didn't have a few other girlfriends that you took your frustrations out on. Never underestimate the power of exaggeration."

"What? Why the hell would you do that?" Daniel said, clearly shocked. "I know what I did was wrong, but Mia has forgiven and forgotten and –"

"Well I haven't forgotten," Alice said. "And I won't stand by and watch you fuck up her life. I was ready to accept that you were a new man, that you had sorted out your shit. Even though people don't really change, in my experience. And the bruise that Mia thinks is hidden behind make-up? Well that just seems to prove that I was right."

Alice reached for the door-handle but Daniel beat her to it. When he didn't open the door, she looked at him. "I can make your life miserable. I can be very resourceful when I want to be."

"Why would you go to all that trouble for little old me?" he asked, forcing a smile.

Her reply wiped it off his face. "Because I'd enjoy it."

Chapter 39.

The sea was cold, much colder that Mia had expected. Colder than previous years too, she was sure. Nonetheless, she followed her own advice and ran in, diving into the dark water as soon as it was deep enough.

The air was freezing too and it was this reason she gave for not being naked. They were still quick to remind her it was a cowardly break from tradition. She wore a tee-shirt and shorts and told herself that the bruise on her arm, left there by his grip, still visible, had nothing to do with her wanting to keep some clothes on. It didn't make her weak.

It did not.

The other souvenir Daniel has left her with, redness on her cheek, was also stubbornly hanging in there but could be concealed with make-up.

Mia was less-than-impressed that the same people accusing her of cowardice were not even prepared to get their feet wet, let alone swim. And now here she was in the water with the one person she didn't want near her.

She had known this the second Daniel had arrived at the party. The sight of him had made her cheek throb and her heart race. His touch, the light kiss on her other cheek, had left her cold, numb. And as she swam out, circled slowly and then back towards the shore, she could hear his breathing behind her, the water lapping around him as he tried to keep up.

Fuck you, Daniel. Fuck you, fuck you, fuck you. This is supposed to be my night.

This had always been her favourite night of her year. Starting off as a typically rebellious event of her teens in Strandhill, it was especially fulfilling later when her parents got wind and banned it. And then, when she came to Dublin, it became a night of cleansing, of rebirth, when she removed – and ritually destroyed – whatever she was wearing. A night when she swam as she was born and emerged from the sea refreshed, renewed.

But now, as she sat with him on the sand, listening to the waves lapping, she didn't feel refreshed or renewed. And she didn't feel annoyed or angry or sad either. Much worse than all that, she felt nothing. For that detachment, that numbness, on this of all nights, she could not forgive.

She would never forgive.

"….when she wants to be," Daniel was saying.

"What?"

"I said Alice can be kind of scary when she wants to be."

Mia smiled. "Yeah, she's very protective of me. What did she say to you?"

"I told her not to worry," he said and Mia wondered why he had ignored the question. "That what happened was…well that it would never happen again."

"Yeah," Mia said.

"And I meant it," he said running the back of his hand down

her arm.

Mia turned to face him. She wanted to be looking at him for this conversation.

"Really, I promise," he continued. "I've learned my lesson. I never want to hurt you again." He did mean it, she could see that. But it didn't change anything.

He leaned in and kissed her. It was a tentative kiss, he clearly knew he was lucky to be here. Mia paused and then found herself reciprocating, the excitement and passion of him momentarily flooding back to her.

But after a few moments though, she pulled away. She had to or she never would.

"Thing is," she started to look away but then forced herself to maintain eye-contact. "I'm not sure I want to just pick things up where they were. I've had time to think things over and I think we should take a break."

"What?" Daniel sat back in an effort to read Mia's expression. "What do you mean, 'a break'? Are you kidding me?"

"No. I'm not," she said, enjoying the strength in her voice.

"I don't understand. I thought…I thought everything was okay."

"It is okay, but –"

"I thought we were getting back together here. I said I was sorry, you know I did. And you forgave me!"

"I did. I do forgive –"

"And you invited me here…to what? I thought we were getting back together and now – what – you're breaking up with me? Over what, one mistake?"

"It's not just what happened last week, Daniel," she stammered, seeing a familiar look on Daniel face, a very familiar look. "I'd been thinking about it, even before then, and –"

"I don't fucking believe it! You invited me here to dump me?"

"No! I mean, when I invited you, I didn't think that I was –"

"Jesus, Mia, I love you. You know that, right?"

"I know, Daniel, but it's not as simple as –"

"I love you! And you love me. Don't you?"

This time she had look away. He wasn't making this easy.

"You told me you do. And now you're telling me…"

He sat there on the beach, doing the same heavy breathing as when he was trying to swim, his foot twitching feverishly.

Mia turned to him. "You know this is the right –"

"You fucking bitch!" Daniel yelled.

Mia suddenly felt her eyes stinging, a deep, piercing pain. "Ah, Daniel! Fuck!" she screamed. "What are you doing?"

The pain was excruciating, and she could feel the sand on her face, smell it in her nose.

"What am I doing? What am I doing!" She could hear him moving, standing up. "I'm leaving."

Mia tried to look at him but she still couldn't open her eyes. She rubbed them but that only made it worse.

She sensed him kneeling beside her and she held out her arm so that he could help her up. Instead, he just spoke softly in her ear.

"Let's see you make your way home blind, you cunt."

And then nothing, just the sound of the waves on the shoreline.

"Daniel?" she called out as tears of pain and panic ran down her cheeks.

"Daniel, don't leave me here. Daniel, please!"

Chapter 40.

Brian was taking it all in stride.

It was now four months since that day he'd arrived home to an empty house. Arrived home to find his belongings packed into three matching Goyard suitcases and stacked neatly at the top of the stairs. With a note that simply said 'Don't Call Me'.

Brian had had to laugh – or at least smile. Even in this moment of heartbreak, of betrayal, Ger had managed to have a sense of humour – she had wanted to throw out those suitcases for years, despite his protestations that they were worth a fortune. Now she was getting her way, although she probably never imagined she'd be throwing him out with them.

Before Brian could think, to react, to try and talk his way out of it and probably make things worse, he had turned on his heel and gone to Suzanne's.

And had been living there ever since.

With those months past, Brian was starting to think of himself as that person he was pretending to be – the bachelor enjoying the early stages of a blossoming romance. He was dressing younger, *Lyle & Scott, Alexander McQueen* and even *Tommy Hilfiger*, and wearing aftershave for the first time in twenty years.

Of the people in his 'real life', only Jude had tried to remind him that that life was still there, that it wasn't going anywhere. Even after that angry phone call from his son, Brian had managed to justify his continued inaction. He told himself that it was best to let everyone cool down, to gain some perspective, so that calm and logical conversations could be had. That justification, and telling himself that Geraldine was okay, that she was a survivor, had been working.

It was denial, of course. He knew that.

He knew it because, as he lay awake at 4am the last seven or eight nights, when his shields were down, that was when the reality crept in. The reality that nobody, no matter how 'strong' they might be, could just get on with life after what had happened. What life? Ger's life for the past thirty-two years had been as his wife.

As he arrived at Suzanne's and took out his newest and prized possession, the key to her front door, Brian forced himself to make a decision.

I'll talk to them. To all of them. It's time to face the music.

He turned the key in the lock.

After the weekend.

"Honey, I'm home," he said with a smile. This private joke of theirs probably was starting to get old.

No reply.

"Suzanne? You here?"

"I'm in here, Brian," he heard from the kitchen. "We have...a visitor."

"We? I didn't think 'we' would be getting visitors yet," he

said with a laugh as he walked into the room.

"Just this one," Geraldine said.

Brian stood, frozen, staring at his wife. He looked over at Suzanne whose awkward smile was painted on. She looked like someone being held hostage.

"Trying to decide which of us to kiss first?" Geraldine asked.

"How…" was all he could manage.

"Does it matter?" she said confidently.

As the shock faded and he took in the surreal sight – his wife and his mistress at the same table – his nice little plan, his nice little life, seemed ludicrous.

"What do you want, Ger?" he asked, the over-compensation making him sound cocky and stupid.

"What do I want?" she asked. "What I want is for you to come home and for this…this 'thing' to stop." She cast a look of contempt in Suzanne's direction.

No way Ger, Brian thought, *you don't get to bully her.*

"'This thing', Geraldine?" Brian asked, managing to match her scorn. "I don't know what you think –"

"I know exactly what this is, Brian," she interrupted him. "I know you, remember? You're a boy with toys! The quad-bike in 1997 that held your interest for, what, a month? The boat you nearly bought last summer?"

She leaned over and gave Suzanne's hand a squeeze. "It's not your fault, dear. You're a hobby…a…a train set. And this little boy has a short attention span."

She looked at Brian and her expression – detached, cold – rattled him.

"Now I've been patient," Geraldine continued. "I've given you time, all these months, even when you were pathetically at it behind my back. Like I wasn't going to find out, I know more of your secrets than you do. So it's time for you to come home and let life get back to normal. See if you can prevent your son hating you. And, who knows, maybe I'll even forgive you someday too. That's what we do in this family, right? Forgive?"

Her words were barely registering. Brian couldn't take his eyes off Suzanne, who was taking on-board – and possibly even believing – what Geraldine was saying. If he didn't do something, he was about to lose her.

"This isn't a fling," He was at Suzanne's side in two steps and he put his hand on her shoulder. As if they had rehearsed it, she put her hand over his.

Geraldine's demeanour slipped.

"It's real, Ger." He kept going before she had a chance to interrupt. "We're together. And we love each other."

In silent confirmation, Suzanne squeezed his hand.

Geraldine started to laugh – a forced laugh – but Brian didn't flinch.

"But –" Geraldine said but could say no more as the reality occurred to her. "No, you don't."

"I'm sorry, Ger," Brian said. "But we do. Do you not see it?"

"But.... you're a train-set," Geraldine said with a shake in her voice. Her trembling jaw betrayed the plummeting confidence.

She suddenly stood up and cleared her throat. "Well...I don't believe you. But, maybe you need more time to..." She wiped the beginning of a tear from under her right eye. Suzanne instinctively rose too.

"I better be off then," Geraldine said lightly, like she had called around for a cup of tea. Brian felt a jab of pity and then one of guilt. But it was for the best, he told himself, the best for everyone and necessary in the long run.

At the door, Geraldine paused. "You seem to have your feet firmly under the table here," she said without turning. "So I'm going to stay at the house. I'm the one who made it a home, after all."

"Geraldine, we need to talk about this, you know, there's stuff to –"

"Goodbye, Brian," Geraldine said. She walked out of the room and he jumped as the front door slammed. And then there was silence.

"Are you okay?" he eventually asked.

Suzanne turned to face him. "Are we really doing this?"

He held his hand out to her. "I am if you are."

She took his hand and he pulled her to him, wrapping his arms around her as the sense of release, of freedom enveloped him.

After a minute of silent embrace, she looked up at him. "I guess we're going steady."

~ ~

Geraldine sat in her car, the initial panic of 'We Love Each Other' dissipating. She was still right, even if they weren't ready to admit it. It was just an affair, a fling that would fizzle out. She found herself saying it to herself, first under her breath, then out loud. "It's just a fling. It's just a fling."

But the more she said it, the louder she heard the words, the less she believed them.

Suddenly, the pain was back. That stinging behind her left eye, like she had just been stabbed through it. It was a pain she had first felt ten years ago when Catherine died.

Her friend. Her sister. Well, okay, her sister-in-law.

If only you were here now, she thought, you'd sort out that brother of yours. It's the least you can do – you talked me into marrying him.

The headache was supposed to have been a one-off. At the time, her doctor had promised her that it was. But, since Christmas, it was back with frequency and vengeance and, when it hit, she felt she might pass out.

She closed her eyes for a moment, begging the pain to leave

as quickly as it had arrived. She opened her handbag and pulled out a silver card of tablets. Just holding them helped.

Co-codamol – take two tablets four times daily.

Geraldine flipped the card and inspected it. Four left, half-a-day's supply. She wondered if Doctor O'Leary would renew the prescription so soon.

One at a time, she popped the four pills out of the card, put them in her mouth and swallowed them. She then sat back, closed her eyes and she waited for herself to return.

Chapter 41

Mia hadn't been to rehearsals for far too long, long enough to forget how much she missed the choir. But not long enough that she had forgotten how to sing.

And she did sing and sing loud. It was a good thing that they weren't practising 'Pie Jesu' or 'Nearer My God to Thee', because she would have sung loud anyway. She needed to.

But thankfully they were working on Wagner and Mia's loudness was matched by everyone else's.

And now as she sat with the others in Thai Orchid on Phibsboro Road, the exhilaration and adrenalin that had built up over the last two-hours were making way for general happiness. Not exactly something she had felt recently.

"Well you young people can go partying if you want," Peter was saying. "But, my friends, I am going home." To be emphatic, he yawned.

"Young people," Mia said. "You're twenty-nine!"

"Okay, well you and me are the oldies, Mia," Peter said. "Those two are probably off into town."

"Jesus, you're living with Rachel what, three weeks?" Angela said. "And you already have your slippered feet up on the footstool. Does she bring you cups of tea and shortcake biscuits too?"

"Jesus, I would murder a shortcake biscuit right about now," Peter said.

"That's it," Barry said, grabbing Peter's wrist and pretending to take his pulse. "I'm calling it. Time of death, 11.35."

Angela raised her almost empty glass. "Great, let's drink to the dearly-departed. I never knew Peter as a man. But I did know him as an old man."

Laughing, Mia stood up and grabbed her coat. "Come on old man, you can walk me home if you're going."

"We caaaan't go home now," Angela said, right on cue. "Sure it's only early! McGowan's for one, come on."

"Angie? No," Mia said. "Maybe for you, it's early. Some of us need our sleep."

They said goodbye and Mia playfully linked Peter's arm as they walked towards home.

"So have you seen the asshole since…" he started and, immediately embarrassed, faded off. "Sorry, I shouldn't call him that, but it's hard to –"

"Hey, go nuts," Mia said. "I have. And no, I definitely haven't seen him, taken his calls, replied to his texts. Not making that mistake again."

"You know, I'm with the Revenue now, remember. Give me his PPS number, we can exact some revenge Peter-style."

Mia forced a laugh, mostly to dispel any urge to take him up on it. "No thanks. I just don't want to even think about him anymore. That's revenge enough."

They walked up Phibsboro Road and on to Connaught Street, chatting about tonight's rehearsal and Peter's new job. As they approached the house, Mia suddenly found herself feeling nervous. It annoyed her – she'd never been afraid of being on her own before and now the thoughts of that house, quiet and empty, were making her uneasy. *Fuck you Daniel, you are an asshole.* She tightened her grip on Peter's arm.

"Well, here we are," he said, opening the gate for her. "Your knight in shining armour."

"That you are, sir," Mia replied. "Sure, what would a damsel do without you?"

Reaching the door, she turned and gave him a hug, which thankfully he returned without any trace of discomfort. "Thanks for the text-badgering, making me come tonight," she said. "I needed it more than I realised."

"Hey, no problem, and next time I need cheering up, you better be there to force me to do something I don't feel like."

"You better believe it," she said. "I'm a woman and a guard. Interference is both my nature and my job."

Another quick hug and Mia went in. She was relieved that Peter stayed on the step until she had the door closed and triple-locked – she had had two extra locks fitted the day she got home from the hospital – and she hoped that a door being audibly locked didn't come off as rude. But Mia had the impression that Peter wasn't the type to worry about such things.

Standing in the dark hall, Mia fought the urge to turn on the light, turn on all the lights in the house. She knew that if she did that, she'd be doing it forever. And she wasn't going to become one of those people who slept with the lights on, one eye open with a knife under the pillow.

So instead, she stood there in the darkness, stared at it and forced it into benevolence. And then slowly walked up the stairs to bed.

~ ~

Standing on the doorstep, Peter listened to the locks being turned and regretted not jokingly inviting himself in. He then instantly felt guilty – he knew what such an impulse meant and he didn't like himself for it. Bad enough that Rachel was insecure about Mia, without him having the urge that would prove her right.

He turned and walked quickly out on to the street before the less logical part of his brain could start making suggestions again, like knocking on Mia's door.

Come on Pete, he thought, *you've finally got your shit together. You know you want to be with Rachel. She's perfect! She gets you, how many women in your life could you say that about? You've figured that out now so don't even think about fucking it up. You –*

The fist came out of the darkness and smashed into Peter's face, knocking him against a car and on to the ground. Dazed, he automatically tried to get up but a sudden and agonising pain exploded through his chest. It spun him over on to his back and his cheek banged against the wheel of the car. As Peter's brain tried to make sense of what was happening, another burst of pain rippled through him from his stomach. He could feel the wet sticky blood running over his cheek. He instinctively tried to pull his knees up to protect himself as he realised that someone, a person, was actually doing this to him. Someone was beating him up.

"Please, stop," he started but a kick to the groin ended his plea. He retched and tried again to pull his knees to his chest.

"She's fuckin' you now, is that it?" a male voice shouted, accompanied by another burst of pain in his stomach. "She's moved on, has she? That was pretty quick, don't you think?"

Peter was grabbed by the shirt and dragged into a sitting

position against the car. "Pity she had to lower her standards with a shitty little fucker like you!"

He could barely make out the words that were being spat at him, only hearing echoes bouncing around his head. A light somewhere above him danced from one side of his vision to the other. *Am I in a room? I thought I was outside –*

"How about you, you enjoy it?" the voice said and the echo boomed around his brain. "Was she good? Everything you ever dreamed of?"

"No," he said, not even sure if the words were coming out. "We didn't –"

"No! No?" Even if he couldn't hear every word, the anger in the voice was unmistakable and terrifying. His head jerked violently to the left and he could make out a form in front of him, a silhouette obscured by the street-light. The pain throbbed through his face and head.

I wonder where Rachel is. Maybe she's upstairs. Rachel baby?

He could smell something, mint maybe. It was warm, like someone's breath.

"Well, if she's such a disappointment," he heard very close, right in his ear. "It should be really easy to follow my advice."

Why are you saying this, baby? You sound weird. I need to sleep…

Peter winced as he felt his hair being pulled. He moaned as something grabbed his testicles and squeezed them hard.

"Stay the fuck away from her, okay?" the person said. "And I might just let you keep your balls."

And then there was stillness. No movement or sound or feeling of anything.

Peter lay against the car and tried to take a breath. But there was no air out there for him.

Anyway, I don't need to breath, I just need to sleep. Once I get some sleep, I'll be okay, I'll be right as rain then….

It overwhelmed him, the tiredness. His body was moving but he wasn't making it move. He wondered where he was going, maybe upstairs to bed. As he slowed to a stop, he felt the cold surface on his sore cheek, his sore ear, his sore everything. Peter wondered, as his eyes closed, why his pillow smelled like tarmac.

Chapter 42.

Jude looked at the clock. 1.50am.

Leaning against the prep table, he rubbed his eyes and looked at the clock.

Still 1.50am.

That ethereal sensation that only came from lack of sleep was setting in. He had been up since five and hadn't stopped all day. Constant motion and concentration on food and customers and deliveries would leave less time to think about all the other stuff.

All that other stuff that now, at 1.50am, he couldn't ignore.

For the last hour though, all he needed was bed. His own bed, in his own house. But he couldn't bring himself to go to it. Like so many nights lately, it was the one place he couldn't bear to be.

Jude knew that he should just accept that he had got what he wanted – Daniel and Mia were broken up. But if he did accept that, then he'd have to accept the cause of the break-up and that

Daniel almost blinding Mia was okay. That it was okay that she had spent three days in hospital, that she was now terrified of him. That all was okay because the net result was achieved. The ends justified the means.

But Jude didn't want to face that, he refused to. Mostly because he knew that all that shit could have been avoided.

Yes, he could fixate on Alice instead, on her reluctance to do what she had been asked, what she had agreed to do, if somewhat reluctantly. If he could blame her for all of this, it would just be easier.

Or maybe it was all bullshit and he was just after a good review.

Jude didn't like the idea that he might be beholden to that asshole Jameson for anything. He didn't like that he'd pimp out Mia in order to get it, as Alice had suggested. If he would do that, go that far, what does that make him? It makes him no better than Jameson. It makes him no better than –

Go on, say it. It makes you no better than Alice.

There were times that he had given her the benefit of the doubt. She didn't really know what she was doing, she couldn't have known what harm she might be inflicting. But Alice knew what she was doing. Alice always knew what she was doing.

Jude had come to the conclusion over the years that Daniel was unlucky in love and that was just his thing. There were people like that. People for whom, whatever choices they made or whatever circumstances were thrust upon them, there would always be a bad outcome.

With Daniel, some of this bad luck was self-inflicted. His intense on-again-off-again relationship with Kate had come crashing down after four years. And from the little gossip Jude had engaged in, he had learned that any romances before Kate were equally messy, ill-conceived and ill-fated.

But with Mia, it wasn't luck. Their paths should never have

crossed and they probably never would have, but for the intervention of someone who was just trying to relieve her boredom. Someone who should have known better. No, someone who did, most definitely, know better.

It wasn't a good sign that he was taking the most comfort by blaming his own wife. In truth, he had suspected for years that his marriage might not stand the test of time and, as this became more apparent, he wondered, maybe for his own warped amusement, what the final catalyst would be.

Perhaps his irreparably damaged pelvis, caused by numerous rugby injuries, which ruled out any chance of their having children.

Perhaps Alice's insistence that that she didn't mind, that not having a family was 'no big deal', even though he could see it in her, in her body language, how much it hurt just to say that. Perhaps it was her refusal thereafter to ever talk about it and the distance that grew between them until barely a word was spoken on any subject. That was until the day Alice's behaviour suddenly changed and she became loving and attentive. The day he became suspicious.

When a wife becomes loving and attentive and it makes you suspicious, something is definitely wrong.

He could remember that look in her eyes as they made love for the first time in months. That look that still haunted him to this day. It wasn't love or passion or lust.

It was guilt.

She had denied the affair, of course she had. She denied it for a week, horrified by the accusation. And Alice was usually a good liar, a fabulous liar. But she couldn't lie to him. She had her tells and Jude knew them all.

On the day he planned to confront her again, she came in, sat on the corner of the bed and confessed. It had been going on for two months apparently, with a customer at the gallery. It was nothing serious, the occasional bit of fun in a hotel room.

But with that 'occasional bit of fun', had come complacency.

She was pregnant.

So she was coming clean, not because she wanted to, but because she had to. Not for Jude's sake, but for her own.

That would be the end for most marriages, wouldn't it? Jude thought. *It should have been the end. Except that –*

Quiet laughter coming from the dining room cut through his thoughts. He realised that the two men were still there, polishing off another bottle of wine.

He looked at his watch again and, knowing there was little else for him to do, he decided that it was time to face his demons and just go home. He would have to ask the men to leave now. Or maybe he would just drop the keys on the table as he passed by. He turned off the lights in the kitchen and at the Passe. When he pushed through the kitchen door, they were already standing, putting on their coats. He wondered why, even in the middle of the summer, they wore the heavy woollen overcoats.

Maybe men like these are always cold.

Each giving him an identical short wave, they disappeared out the door onto the street. Jude stopped in the middle of the room and allowed himself one last scan of the place. It was to ensure that all lights and appliances were turned off, but also, it was the nightly reminder that this was his kingdom. His responsibility, his ward, but most of all, his opportunity.

The orange glow of the streetlights cast an eeriness over the room. As his scan of the room came full-circle, he jumped. There was someone outside the window, looking in. As his eyes adjusted and he realised who it was, Jude sighed.

Out on the street, he ensured that all the locks were secure and then turned to face this visitor.

"Daniel."

"Hey."

"What are you doing here? It's two o'clock in the morning, man."

Jude started walking up towards Dame Street, not really wanting to have this conversation right now, if ever. Daniel followed him.

"I just needed to talk to someone, Jude, and -"

"Well I would recommend a good psychiatrist, you'll find them in the phone book. Don't forget the silent 'P'."

"Why are you being like this? I thought you were my friend," Daniel said with a hint of inebriation.

Jude spun around.

"Friend? Friend!" He was shouting before he realised it. "My friends don't slap their girlfriends around and then try to blind them. People who do that sort of thing are not my friends. And what did I hear about you beating up someone? A guy from her choir?"

"Hey, I didn't do that, that wasn't me," Daniel said, trying to sound hurt.

"Oh, give me a…the guards might have to believe you, just because the poor bastard didn't see your face, but I don't. You're a sick man, Daniel, and you need help."

"I do need help, I do," Daniel said, relieved that someone understood him. "I need your help. Help me get her back."

Jude laughed. "Are you fucking kidding? You're kidding," he said. "You should not be let near her ever again. Or any woman for that matter."

Jude walked on.

"Oh, I get it," Daniel said, walking behind him. "I see what this is."

"Do you?" Jude said, uninterested.

"You're jealous," Daniel said with a nasty laugh. "You're in love with her? Just like I am. Just like every other man who knows her. And now that you've ruined things for me, you can –

"

"Ruined things for you? The only person who ruined things for you is you. Go home. You're embarrassing yourself."

"Hey, I'm talking to you!" Daniel shouted.

Jude was shoved in the back with enough force that he lost his balance and fell on his knees. Before he could get up, Daniel pushed him down and was sitting on him, pressing his knees into Jude's back. Jude could feel Daniel's breath as he spoke in his ear.

"It was you who ruined it, Jude," he said with terrifying, feral anger. "You and that stupid bitch wife of yours, with her threats that're supposed to scare me. I am going to get Mia back. She wants to be with me. She just doesn't –"

Daniel suddenly grunted. Jude felt the weight lifting off him and he rolled over to see Mr. Lewis and Mr. Curtis, each holding one of Daniel's arms and dragging him towards the wall. They slammed him against the building and lifted him so his feet were off the ground. Curtis used his spare hand to grab Daniel's neck in a stranglehold and Lewis delivered a hard punch to his ribs, and then another.

Jude was about to tell them to stop but hesitated, deciding that Daniel might benefit from some of his own treatment. More punches were delivered and the grip on Daniel's neck tightened. He coughed, struggling to breathe, as he thrashed with his legs. Jude pulled himself to his feet, still trying to get some air into his lungs.

As the two men continue to punch him, Daniel started slipping back down towards the ground. Curtis paused to get a better grip and Daniel managed to pull his arm free. He lashed out with his fist and connected with Lewis' ear. The man was taken aback and lost his grip. Daniel lunged forward and wrestled Curtis to the ground with his entire weight. As he did so, he punched with both fists into the man's torso. The man exhaled loudly as the air was forced from his lungs. Lewis recovered his composure and grabbed Daniel, pulling him up and slamming him back against the wall. Curtis was immediately on his feet and he approached Daniel with real anger on his face.

Jude started to turn away, leaving Daniel to face the music, but something caught his eye. Curtis had something in his hand, something glimmering under the dim streetlights.

"No, wait," Jude said, moving towards them. Curtis had his hand pulled back and there wasn't a hint of hesitation about stabbing Daniel.

Jude grabbed the man's wrist. This was definitely not part of any plan. "No!" he yelled. "No! Not happening." He pulled Curtis's arm back and managed to loosen his grip. The blade, a small flick-knife, fell from his hand and bounced on the footpath.

"Let him go," Jude said, hearing fear in his own voice. "Now!"

After a moment's hesitation, they released Daniel and he dropped down on to his feet. He stood there, looking dazed.

"Daniel," Jude said with forced calmness. "Go. Walk away. Right now."

Daniel was possibly about to say something, but obviously saw the fear in Jude's eyes. He turned and started walking, before breaking into a run.

Jude stood, in silence, looking from one man to the other, Curtis wearing a defiant smirk, Lewis slightly embarrassed. Not showing any emotion, Jude kicked the knife with the side of his foot and it dropped off the footpath on to the street.

Then, without a further word, he turned and walked away.

Chapter 43.

Luggala was quiet. As it should be at two in the morning.

Alice knew it was dangerous, stupid even, to drive up there on her own in the middle of the night. She might as well have painted the words 'Attention Murderers' on the side of the car. But having gone to bed at ten and stared out the window for two hours, she knew that fresh air was the only thing that would help.

She had considered ringing Mia to see if she'd go with her – her friend had needed her company often enough in the last few months so asking for a little payback wouldn't have been uncalled for. But in the end, she didn't call her, conceding that she just wanted to be by herself.

Alice hadn't even intended on going far. She assumed she'd walk to the end of the road, maybe as far as the Dodder again, and that would be it. But, before she knew what she was doing, she was in her car, driving out through Rathfarnham and up into the mountains.

The place was quiet but Alice was unprepared for the extent of that quiet. Not a single call of an animal or bird, not the distant hum of a motorway, nothing. Alice stood by the car for three, four, five minutes, waiting to hear anything, then willing to hear anything.

She hoped that she would stand there for those few minutes and breathe, and with each breath, the sadness and fear and panic would disappear off into the trees, like they were home.

But they didn't. If anything, surrounded by all this nothingness, she felt that the sadness and fear and panic were her only companions.

It was fight-or-flight time, that was clear. With all the other stuff going on, all the other bullshit, there was only one part of her life that really mattered. Jude. And after the drama and trauma and the affair and the baby and the choices they had both made, their relationship came down to this very simple question.

Should I stay or should I go?

It had been with her since the unwelcome visit at the gallery and every time she thought about it, she came to a different conclusion. So as she stood there looking at nothing and listening to nothing, she knew it was time to decide, to just leave all logic and reason aside and pay attention to that voice she normally ignored.

But she couldn't hear it now. Her instincts were letting her down at the one time she needed them most. Maybe they were sulking, refusing to cooperate, having been disregarded for so long. Or maybe they were whispering to her the answer she didn't want to hear and she was subconsciously ignoring them again.

And then the answer was there. Maybe it was a Eureka

moment or maybe she was forcing it, but it was there. Of course she was going to stay, it was her only option. After everything they'd been through, everything she'd sacrificed, to walk away now would be the ultimate concession. The admission that she had wasted the last five years. That guy coming to the gallery meant nothing – even if he was threatening her, as ludicrous as it sounded, she knew that Jude loved her and would never let anything happen to her.

Alice instantly felt protected and safe and confident. She wanted, more than anything else, to see Jude, to tell him she loved him and that everything would be okay.

As she drove back down, she prayed that this renewed feeling wouldn't fade, that it was the new beginning for her, for them both, that they could just focus on starting their marriage afresh. Maybe a restart of Jude's career as well – maybe he could just walk away from Sixteen Eustace, go back to working for Renato. She might be able to convince him of what everyone else had already realised – as good a chef as he was, Jude Miller was not a businessman.

But he was stubborn, she knew that. It wasn't going to be just a case of her saying to him 'I love you, let's start over' and he would just go along with it. A sign of faith would be needed.

Ben Jameson.

She knew that, with everything that had happened with Mia and Daniel, she would have to give them time before getting them back together. There was more to be got from that relationship, but she would have to be clever about it. So in the meantime, she could show Jude her commitment to him, her willingness to make him happy, by setting Mia up with that god-awful man. Anything between them would have a short lifespan anyway, two, three dates tops. She might even be able to use it to have some fun with Daniel.

As she approached the gate of the house, she groaned. "Ah,

not this again."

She pulled up on to the footpath and looked across at their gate. Their neighbour, Mr. Dexter, had fallen into the habit of parking his car outside their house and, once or twice, had parked too close, thereby blocking the entrance. Alice had eventually visited him and delicately raised the subject. But it had clearly fallen on deaf ears and Alice didn't relish having to repeat the request, perhaps more forcefully. Maybe she'd send Jude this time.

It was ridiculous, the car was completely blocking their gate. But then Alice noticed something – it wasn't Mr. Dexter's old Opel. It was a silver Mercedes CLK. It was Jude's car.

"Jude, what the hell are you doing?" she muttered.

Alice walked over and found that the car was positioned so close to the gate that she could not even squeeze past it. She took out her phone and was about to dial when she heard a strange sound coming from the car, murmuring and scratching. She moved around to the side of the car but the windows were fogged up. A wave of panic washed over her when she noticed a red-brown streak across the inside of the window.

"What the hell?" Alice yanked open the door. The heat and the smell of rancid meat hit her first and she instinctively put her hand up to cover her nose and mouth. Something dropped out of the car on to her foot. She looked down and screamed as two more large rats scurried out. As they did, she felt a sharp sting to her ankle.

Screaming, Alice backed away from the car. She lost her footing and fell backwards on to the path. She watched, horrified, as the wave of rats spilled out of the car and scattered in all directions.

Chapter 44.

The ambulance was already there by the time Jude arrived. Alice was sitting on the back ledge while the paramedic examined her foot. Jude saw something in her face he wasn't used to – fear. He watched her for a while, feeling the pain and panic that she was feeling. She sensed his stare and by the time she met his gaze, the emotion was gone. She just stared back at him blankly, not even flinching when she was given an injection.

Like all those other times, Alice insisted on hiding herself from him.

Jude still felt the urge to console her, to reassure her that it was going to be okay.

Even if he knew it wouldn't be.

~ ~

Alice sat at the kitchen table, with so much to say and no idea how to say it. Two Garda detectives had just left. She had given them a statement, which hadn't really told them anything that wasn't already pretty obvious.

Jude had told the detectives that no, of course he had no idea why someone would steal his car, fill it with rats and lamb-carcasses and leave it outside his house.

"It's them, isn't it?" Alice said, now that they were finally alone. She rubbed her ankle where the rat-bite still stung, despite the painkillers she had been given. "Well, isn't it?" she repeated when Jude did not reply.

"Alice, don't. Please."

"Don't? Don't what? Say what we both know? These people are –"

"These people are my partners. And they've just shown me, shown us, what they're capable of!"

"Why did they do this? Everything was going okay, wasn't it?"

"Who knows? Who knows why these fuckers do anything?"

"Don't give me that. Something must have happened."

Jude's expression, one of fear, contrition, guilt, confirmed Alice's suspicion.

"They're taking everything," he said quietly.

"What? What does that mean?"

"Everything the restaurant makes, I have to give to them. Minimum twenty grand a month."

"But…but you can't. How are we supposed to –"

"Live? Yeah, that was my question."

"And what did they say?"

"That it was my problem. And when I pushed them on it? Well, they suggested I shouldn't do that. And this –" he pointed outside towards the car "– is just to show why I shouldn't do that."

"Ah Jude no," Alice couldn't accept this. "They wouldn't –"

"Yeah, Alice, they would. So now do you think I'm in a position to argue with them? Or tell those guards what happened?"

"Well...well maybe you don't have to tell the guards. I could do it. Or –"

"It doesn't matter which of us does it! They're watching you as well. And probably Mum and Dad too. That's why they sent someone to the gallery. To show that it wasn't just me they had under their thumb."

"I'm not part of this, Jude. You have to tell them –"

"You're my wife, Alice, and if they decide to use you to control me, or to punish me, or to test me, then that what's they'll do."

Alice couldn't believe what she was hearing. This wasn't their lives, being extorted, being threatened, being attacked. That sort of thing happened to...to...other people, people who deserved it, people who chose to get involved in crime.

Or people who allowed themselves to get involved in crime, she realised. People who weren't smart enough or diligent enough to know what they were doing, what they were getting into before they got into it.

People like Jude.

The doorbell startled them both. It took a moment for Alice to recognise it, in fact. The front gate, with its own buzzer, was normally the first line-of-defence but with the gate now open, the front door was now fully accessible. The feeling of complete vulnerability swept over Alice again.

"Stay here, I'll go." Jude said, his calm sounding forced, unnatural.

He went into the hall. "Who....who's there," Alice heard him stutter as he approached the front door.

There was silence.

"Jude?" she heard herself say, a definite shake in her voice.

The front door slammed and she heard a familiar voice. Brian walked into the kitchen.

"You rang him?" Jude asked her as he followed his father into the room. Alice only then remembered that, while she was waiting for Jude to arrive, she had called Brian and asked him to come over.

"I'm sorry Jude, but you need to talk to someone about this. Please, tell your father what happened."

"Yeah but how could you possibly think that –"

"Just tell him!"

Jude looked from his wife to his father and realised he had little choice. He relayed to Brian what had happened and what he had just told Alice about his partners.

The man stood, his back straight, his expression stony-faced. "Jesus Christ," he said after Jude had finished.

"I know, I know. It's crazy. But if you have any pearls of wisdom, now would be the time to –"

"How could you do this?"

"Brian," Alice said. "That doesn't help –"

"Help? I think we're beyond Daddy's help by now, don't you?"

"We're not asking you to click your fingers and magically fix everything but –"

"You know what, Alice" Brian interrupted her. "I appreciate that you rang me, but can I just talk to my son now please?"

Alice was taken aback but the surprise was short-lived. This was Brian all over.

"Fine," she said. "But just help him, will you?"

"In private?" Brian gestured towards the door.

"No, Dad," Jude said. "She should be here."

"Maybe he doesn't think I'm entitled to have my say in this," Alice said. "Is that it, Brian?"

"Why would you want to, Alice?" Brian said scathingly. "You

haven't exactly shown much interest in the restaurant up to now. Or any part of Jude's happiness, for that matter."

"Oh, I see," Alice said. "You're bringing that up now –"

Jude put up his hand. "Okay, cease fire, both of you."

"No, Jude," Alice said. She wasn't going to be the one to back down. "It always comes back to this. But it amazes me that he still thinks he can get up on his high horse about the sanctity of marriage? You're such a fucking hypocrite, Brian."

"Excuse me?" Brian said.

"Alice, stop." Jude put himself between them. "I mean it."

"He sat at this very table preaching and moralising about what an awful person I was. The sermon went on for hours, remember Brian? Remember what you said? How you had built a marriage that, despite its ups and downs, had lasted all those years and surely, if you could make it work, then we could too. Remember that? And I believed you! I took it to heart, we both did, and we made it work! And now what? Turns out, you don't believe your own fucking words!"

Jude was obviously shocked by her outburst. But there was also something else showing on his face - relief. Relief that she was saying what he never could.

"You have some nerve, missy," Brian said angrily. "You have some bloody nerve! You think this is the same thing? You think that me and Suzanne being in love is the same as you flinging yourself at some random guy off the street? Don't you dare sully us with your carry-on!"

"Jesus!" Jude cut in. "Do you not think we have more pressing matters to be talking about?"

But Brian wasn't to be stopped. "You would have gone on with that forever, wouldn't you Alice? The only reason you stopped was because neither you nor your fancy-man had enough cop-on to take proper precautions. And remember the mess that left us in!"

"Us? I don't remember you suffering too much at the time."

"I discovered my daughter-in-law was pregnant with some stranger's child! You think I wasn't suffering?"

"That's enough! I mean it," Jude said. "Go home, Dad. You've managed to make a bad situation worse, as usual. I cannot believe you are dredging all this up again."

"Me! She started it!"

"Dad! I mean it! Leave, now!"

Jude's aggression was enough to give Brian pause.

But it was too late. Alice couldn't stop herself. "Well you're suffering now, aren't you," she said. "You're the one causing misery now, not me. You're the one destroying the family. And I, for one, am delighted. And all I had to do was put one pretty face in front of you. Just once. You're pathetic, so you are."

She watched as her words, words that had to be said because they were true, sunk in.

Jude's shock was slightly more that she expected. "All you had to do?" he said.

Shit.

Had she just said that? Yeah. It was out alright. Alice watched Jude as he took it in, the words that confirmed his fear.

"Alice? All you had to do?"

Brian was smirking. He was actually enjoying this. "You know what she did, son. The same as she always does. Same as all those other couples. She decided that two people should be together and then worked tirelessly to make it happen. The fact that one of them was married was irrelevant."

"It's bullshit, Jude," Alice tried but she heard no confidence in her own voice. "He's just trying to pass the buck, as usual. He –"

"But it wasn't irrelevant, was it Alice?" Jude said. "The fact that one of them was married was the whole point. You set out to hurt Mum, didn't you?"

Alice could feel his glare but couldn't bring herself to look at him.

"Of course she did, Jude!" Brian said. "You know she blames your mother for –"

"You need to go, Dad," Jude said quietly.

"But –"

"Right now."

Alice glanced at Jude. Right now, he was not to be argued with.

Brian saw it too. "Okay, son. You're right, I'll go."

Throwing another scowl at Alice, Brian walked out of the room. She watched Jude, hoping for some glimmer of reassurance from him. But without a word, he left behind his father.

Alice sat in the silent kitchen, waiting for Jude to come back. She wondered if this would be it, the fight that brought everything out, that would include words that couldn't be taken back, that would end up defining their relationship.

Or maybe he'd just say nothing and it would be the newest thing to be ignored. Another Miller family scandal never talked about.

Alice waited. And waited.

You're my wife, Alice. If they decide to use you, then that what's they'll do.

Jude's words came crashing back into her mind.

They'll use you to control me, or to punish me, or to test me. You're my wife.

And then Alice knew what she had to do.

Chapter 45.

Mia was nervous. It was because she was waiting. She hated waiting.

That's what you get for always being early.

She really wasn't sure why she was here at all. It had all started a few days ago with a phone call from Alice, asking if she'd be open to going on a date with a friend of Jude's. The idea of it had left Mia completely cold but, using her usual powers, Alice had convinced her to meet the guy for 'an innocent lunch'. Twice that morning, Mia had almost cancelled but knew that, by doing that, she was just prolonging the issue. If she had nothing else, Alice had tenacity and the date was going to happen at some stage. So Mia might as well get it over with. She could then tell Alice that he was boring or annoying or, the vaguest and most satisfying of all excuses, 'there was just no spark', and that would be it.

She knew very little about Ben Jameson, mostly what she had gleaned from their phone conversation the day before. She did also know that he was married with one child, a son. This, she had learned from the ludicrously self-serving profile in Gourmet magazine – he had sidestepped the issue when she had asked. But, as Alice had been quick to point out, this was just a lunch and it didn't have to mean anything if she didn't want it to.

Not that it mattered that he was married. Having relationships with married men had never bothered Mia. She didn't have to feel guilty as she wasn't the one cheating. There was also the benefit that there was less chance of any real emotional attachment with a married man, which was exactly what Mia needed right now.

No emotional attachment.

So with all these comforts at her disposal, she didn't know why she was still nervous. Maybe it was just first-date jitters.

Or maybe it was because, after this lunch, she was finally going to visit Peter in hospital. She hadn't seen him since the attack, couldn't bear to see him, couldn't bring herself to acknowledge the reason he was in hospital with concussion, a broken nose and three cracked ribs. That it was her fault.

If it wasn't for her, he would be fine. He would have gone surfing the next day, had a nice weekend with Lucy. He'd now be in work, in the new job he had fought so hard to get.

If she hadn't asked him to walk her home, if she hadn't hugged him on the doorstep, if she hadn't got involved with that monster Daniel in the first place.

Daniel. The Gardaí, two uniforms from nearby Mountjoy station, had questioned him about it after she had told them, without going into any great detail, that he was her 'recently-estranged' ex-boyfriend and wasn't taking the break-up well. But, because there was no witness and Peter could not remember a face, or a voice, or much else about that night, they were unable to charge Daniel with anything. But Mia knew. She knew it was him.

She had thought about ringing her friend and ex-colleague Kieran from the Organised Crime Unit but, in the end, dismissed the idea. There was probably nothing he could have done and their relationship was somewhat strained at the moment too.

Out of the corner of her eye, Mia saw a man bounding up the stairs and turning to survey the restaurant. Mia recognised his face from the magazine and also, she realised, from Jude's restaurant opening.

"You're late." Mia stood as he approached the table. He wasn't but this borderline aggressive style of flirting seemed to be his way and Mia was happy to participate

"Well, we're not all public servants who can just faff off to lunch at half-twelve," he said with a slight smirk after they had exchanged the customary first-meeting cheek-kiss. "I have a real job."

"Oh yeah," Mia said sarcastically. "Eating, and then talking about it. I hear they're bringing out a Nobel Prize just for that."

"They should," he replied. "It's not easy."

Mia was about to laugh but realised he wasn't joking.

"So, can we expect VIP treatment today?" Mia asked.

"Maybe," he said. "I was supposed to ring them, tell them I'd be here in an official capacity." He winked. "I kind of forgot. Oops."

Mia laughed before she could stop herself and was pleasantly surprised.

"Wow," he said as they sat down. Mia hoped that this smirk wasn't a permanent facial expression. She liked confidence. Arrogance, not so much.

"Wow?" she echoed.

"Did you look this good at Miller's launch?"

Mia decided to play along to see if, in fact, the man's arrogance was just an act – in her experience, it nearly always was.

"Are you kidding?" she said. "I looked much better that night. This is me in work-mode. I would have been dressed up for a big fancy affair like a restaurant opening."

He poured a glass of water for himself and took a sip. "If this is you in low-key, I can't wait to see the shiny version again."

Easy there, tiger, she thought, *it's the middle of the day here.*

"And who says you're going to?" she said.

"Let's just say I have a feeling," he said.

She smiled. The cockiness was starting to grow on her.

"So," he said, after they had placed their orders. "It's ages since that night, how come you finally decided to take my call? I was about to give up."

"Well, for one thing," Mia said. "I was seeing someone. And – "

"The grumpy guy?"

Mia was impressed that he remembered, and also somewhat bothered that he did.

"He wasn't that grumpy."

"I used to play rugby with him back in the day, he was always grumpy. What's his name again?"

This took Mia by surprise. "Daniel. Daniel Summers. You used to play rugby with him??"

"Well, not with him. He was Clongowes, I was Terenure."

"Huh," Mia said, wondering if this was something she needed to worry about. "Anyway, we broke up recently."

"I'm sorry to hear that," Ben said, making no effort to sound sincere. "Was it bad?"

"It was fine. We wanted different things," she said. "Yeah, I wanted a little bit of space, and he wanted to beat the shit out of me and become an obsessive asshole."

Mia was surprised that she was being so upfront and blunt with someone she had just met. It clearly caught Ben Jameson off guard too and, for a few seconds, he just looked at her. Mia wondered if he would just make an excuse and bolt.

"So," he said. "Not really the same interests then."

Mia laughed again. This was getting interesting.

"So, I'm what, the rebound man?" he continued. He was trying to be flippant but there was no disguising the hope in his voice.

"Well right now," she said, raising her glass of wine. "You're the wannabe rebound man. Reckon you're up to the job? I have very high standards."

"For…rebound guys."

"For everything."

He clinked his glass against hers. "I don't doubt it for a second."

~ ~

More than two hours later, they stood outside, under *Fallon & Byrne's* canopy, waiting for the rain to stop. Ben was looking sheepish, or trying to, for letting their 'quick lunch' stretch so long.

But Mia didn't feel guilty. She was having fun for the first time in a while. And if it was happening at lunchtime on a Tuesday, so be it. She hoped he felt the same but, unusually, couldn't quite read his body language.

"Well, I better make a move," she said. "All that public-service business won't do itself."

She leaned in for another polite first-date cheek kiss. But instead, he kissed her on the lips. A soft but hungry kiss, his tongue flicking along her upper lip. She initially wanted to pull back - it was too soon, it was too suffocated - but after a moment, she couldn't help but give in, to reciprocate.

Then, as dramatically as it had started, the kiss was over.

"Okay, well, nice to meet you at last," he said casually. "Maybe we can do this again sometime. Or dinner maybe."

Mia regained her composure almost as quickly. "Yeah, great, would love to," she said.

"Bye," Ben said and started to walk away.

"Actually," Mia said and he turned back. "Maybe you could come over to my place on Saturday? You know, I could cook."

"You cook?"

"No, not really."

"Yeah, okay," he said. The smugness was back and Mia now found it compelling, maybe even arousing.

"Great."

"I'll call you," he said and walked away.

She stood, watching him cross the street, picturing him smirking confidently to himself. She considered her unplanned and rash invitation and wondered if she was doing the right thing. She knew why she'd done it. There were a few reasons but it was mostly because he was the complete opposite to Daniel.

"To hell with it," she said out aloud.

~ ~

Across the street, in the doorway of a closed-down shoe-shop, a homeless man sat huddled on the ground, in vain attempt to protect himself from the elements. Standing beside him, another man, wearing a similar but infinitely cleaner raincoat, kept his head tilted to keep the rain off his face. He would occasionally glance up and across to the restaurant, at the two people chatting awkwardly.

He winced when he looked up and saw them kissing. He

closed his eyes and managed to suppress the nausea before it arrived. He kept them closed and wondered if the panic attack would be bad.

But it didn't arrive at all. Not the dizziness, not the dryness in his mouth, not the sense that the buildings were closing in around him. Maybe it was because, when he looked over again, Mia was on her own. The man, who Daniel had vaguely recognised when they emerged on to the street, was now walking away towards George's Street. Daniel's focus went back to Mia and he wondered if that was a smile on her face.

Mia turned and walked in his direction and, even though she was on the other side of the road, he dropped his head in case her gaze wandered over.

He almost started to follow her. The urge to confront her, to make her give him another chance, was overwhelming. But that wasn't the best thing to do. He turned on his heel and headed back towards his car.

Mia wasn't the one he needed to confront.

Chapter 46.

What would you like to chat about? Sport? Weather? Infidelity?

It seemed to Geraldine that Brian had given her just enough time to regain some strength before he called her. He needed to collect some of his things and 'maybe they could have a chat'.

The confrontation at his fancy-woman's house had not gone well. It had backfired quite badly, in fact. Since then, she had been functioning on automatic pilot. She had even managed, for the most part, to not tell people that her marriage was in trouble. She even refrained from telling the G.P., going as far as talking about Brian's health when it came up.

The reward for this outward strength was the renewed prescription and the packet of Co-codamol now standing on the kitchen table, like a soldier ready for battle. Ready for when the pain returned, as it did regularly now. She had taken some this morning, just after Brian's call, when the stinging behind her eyes had come on so suddenly that she thought she might pass out. The two pills had dulled it to a mild ache.

She knew better than to think that this visit was going to lead to reconciliation. It was what she wanted of course but seeing him with her, how united they were, had made her realise that it was more than just an affair. It wasn't just a phase. It was a relationship.

The memories, having been relegated to the back of her mind over the years, had returned in the last eight months. Being single was not something Geraldine ever wanted for herself and she had made it her business to always be in a relationship. This had occasionally meant that she had been with men who weren't good for her, but she preferred that to being on her own and she comforted herself with the knowledge that she never fully gave herself, heart or soul, to any of them. This was until, on her twenty-sixth birthday, she completely fell in love with her best friend's brother. A breath-taking romance followed and Geraldine was surprised when Brian made it clear that his feelings for her were as strong. The eight months between them meeting and marrying and the years that followed had been the happiest time of her life.

She wondered if Brian ever took time out of his happy new life to remember those days and if –

The doorbell surprised her.

He's taking this formal approach a bit too far, isn't he? she thought, stuffing the painkillers into her pocket as she stood up. *First a phone call asking permission to visit and now this? Is he going to have his solicitor with him too?*

"Jude!" she said in surprise when she opened the door. "What are you doing here?"

"That's a lovely greeting," Jude stepped in and gave her a hug.

"I don't mean it like that, you know I don't. It's just that, well, I'm expecting your father."

"Yeah, I know. That's why I'm here."

She saw his pale complexion, his sunken eyes. "Jesus, you look terrible, Jude. Are you not sleeping again?"

"An hour last night," he replied, as he flopped down in the old armchair in the kitchen. "But it's a whole hour more than the night before." It was only that he seemed to notice her. "You don't look so good yourself. Are you okay?"

"I'm fine, love," she lied. As she said it, she felt the dull pain strengthening. "Your dad'll probably be here in a minute."

She put the kettle on and looked out the window, pretending to wait for the water to boil. As she did, she took out the card of pills, popped out two and swallowed them.

She turned around and smiled at Jude. "How's Alice? Does she know you're –" She stopped when she heard the familiar sound, one she used to take for granted. A key in the front door.

"Geraldine?" Brian called. His voice sounded different. Nervous, lacking its usual confidence.

He walked into the kitchen and stopped short when he saw Jude.

"That look of surprise is becoming a habit, my dear," Geraldine said with a tight smile. "Tea?"

"Em, yeah sure," Brian said, as he tried to sound relaxed. "I wasn't expecting to see you here, son."

"Well, I wasn't sure I'd ever see you two together again," Jude said. "And I need to tell you both something."

"That's a bit dramatic, isn't it?" Brian said, sitting down. "But your mother and I need to discuss the situation ourselves before we –"

"Let him speak, Brian," Geraldine interrupted him.

"You need to hear this first," Jude said, "Before you make any decisions. Before you do something that can't be undone."

Geraldine was about to tell him that they were already past that point. Instead, she took her own advice and let Jude finish.

"The fact is...well, all of this that's going on? It's my fault."

"How is it your fault?" Geraldine said.

"Don't be silly, Jude." Brian said, folding his arms. "Of course it isn't."

"The other night with Alice's...performance? She was obviously involved in getting you and Suzanne together."

Geraldine was confused. "What are you talking about? What do you mean, involved?"

"She more or less admitted it, Geraldine," Brian said. "I was there."

"She set it up, Mum. She made it happen. In fact, from the day she met Suzanne, I'd say she's been planning it. Planning to break up your marriage."

"What? Why? Why would she do that?"

"Lots of reasons. But mostly....well, I think she wanted to punish you. To punish all of us. And I should have seen it coming."

"How could you have?"

"I should have had my eyes open. I had convinced myself that things were back to normal. Everything seemed okay."

"Jude, no." That comforting authority was back in Brian's voice. "It wasn't your fault. But it doesn't matter anyway. It doesn't matter whose fault it is –"

"Of course it does!"

"No love," Geraldine knew where Brian was going. "The damage is done, do you not see that?" she said. "Pointing fingers won't achieve anything now." She looked at Brian, trying not to glare. "We all had our individual parts to play."

"You didn't," Jude said. "That's the worst part, you did nothing and you're the one suffering the most."

"Come on now, don't be naïve. You know what I did. What I made Alice do."

"You didn't make her do anything!" Jude stood up and

turned towards the window. "Did you make her sleep with that guy? Did you make her get pregnant?"

"But I did make her get rid of it. I forced her to give up the one thing she's always wanted!"

"No, you just made it clear that she could not bring that baby into this family. You didn't force her. She could have had it. It was her choice."

"It was no choice. She would always choose you, Jude. And doesn't that count for something?"

Geraldine knew that Jude had asked himself that question many times since Alice's affair, since the pregnancy, since the abortion. He had tortured himself with it over and over. And he had convinced himself that, after the choice his wife had made, the sacrifice she had made, he owed it to her to be there, to make it work.

But as Geraldine looked at him now, his fortitude, that certainty that he should do the right thing, was no longer there. And it broke her heart.

Chapter 47.

Jude walked into the house and wondered why he could hear music. It was faint but it was definitely there. He took a step back outside, wondering if it was coming from next door. But no, it was inside. In the sitting room, in fact.

"Alice?" he said, closing the front door behind him. No response.

The room was in darkness and he thought that she must have left the music on when she went to bed. He crossed to the stereo and jumped when he saw the silhouette sitting by the window.

"Alice?" he said. "What are you doing? Did you not hear me calling you?"

"I heard you," she replied quietly. Ice tinkled as she took a sip from her glass.

"Well? What's going on? Why are you sitting here in the dark?"

"Just thinking."

He sat down beside her on the chaise longue. "Are you drinking whiskey? You never drink whiskey."

She didn't reply, just took another sip.

"This has to stop, Jude," she said evenly, not looking at him.

"There's nothing I can do, Alice."

"Of course there is. Go to the Guards, tell them everything. I mean everything, since the day you met those guys."

"Tell them what? These guys, they haven't done anything illegal. All they are is two businessmen who have generously invested in a restaurant and –"

"What about their money? Where did that come from?"

"Come on Alice, they're not stupid. Their money will be clean. And by the time anyone traces it back to –"

"Let me make this simple for you, Jude," She turned to face him. "Either you go to the Guards, or I will."

"Alice –"

"You said it yourself, I'm involved now. I'll tell the Guards that they threatened me, came to my gallery, made me feel unsafe –"

"You can't –"

"I might even exaggerate it a bit, say there were two of them, they had me cornered in my office, wouldn't let me leave –"

"Alice, stop!"

"Jude, I'm just –"

"Don't you see what would happen if they even got a sniff that we were talking to the Guards?" He stood up, stood over her. "If you even filed a report? My partners would, at most, be questioned. Not arrested, just questioned. No proof would be found and that would be the end of it. And then these two men, who have no problem with violence, would know that I tried to shaft them."

"What are you saying, they'd kill you?"

He sat back down. "They need me. You know, to be the face of the business. To be the legitimate name over the door and the chef in the kitchen."

Jude took Alice's hands in his, looked into her eyes and waited for the penny to drop. He didn't have to wait long.

"Wait...you're saying....they'll hurt me?"

"I don't know, okay? I wouldn't have thought so before they came to see you, to show me that they could get to you -"

"So you are saying that!" Alice was panicking and Jude squeezed her hand.

It didn't help. "Well...well...we just have to get out of here then," she said. "Leave Dublin, Ireland even. Just go."

"Alice -"

"No, Jude! We have to."

"We can't leave, Alice. Seriously. It's too late -"

"How can it be too late? We just go to the airport right now and -"

"We do that? We're running for the rest of our lives. Me leaving means them losing a ton of money and that's all they care about. These people don't forget. They'll either find us or they'll wait for us to come back. They'll wait forever. And then they will kill us."

Jude had never seen this much fear on Alice's face. He had the urge to just tell her it was okay and that he'd fix it. But he knew there was no point - she wouldn't believe him anyway.

"We have to just keep going," he said softly, rubbing her shoulder. "That's our only option now. We have to see it through."

He noticed that Alice suddenly didn't look scared anymore. She looked suspicious. And now angry.

"You fucker," she said. "This is nothing to do with them hurting us or coming after us or anything like that. This is about your fucking ambition!"

"No, it's –"

"You have your precious restaurant now." She was up off the sofa now. "It's all part of the great Jude Miller career plan and you're not going to let a little matter like personal safety get in the way of that."

"You're wrong. This is me thinking about personal safety. About us being smart and not just letting instinct take over. You think I haven't considered leaving –"

"Oh, just stop! You're just making me feel like more of an idiot than I already do."

Jude's eyes were drawn to something near the door. He gave his eyes a second to adjust. "What is that suitcase doing there?"

Alice turned to face him, her arms folded. "It's mine. And it's packed."

"Packed?"

"I took yours down from the attic too. Are you going to use it?"

"No, I told you, we can't –"

"Maybe you can't," she said, the anger starting to slip as fresh tears came to her eyes. "But I can."

She pulled out the handle of the trolley bag.

"Was it a specific moment, Jude?" she said. "A day, maybe? When your career became more important than me?"

"Alice, don't –"

"Maybe it was the day I wanted to have a baby and you and your mother made me give that up. Or maybe it was the day I so effortlessly ruined your parents' marriage."

Jude was crying now too, he couldn't stop it. She wasn't going to make this easy.

The truth was, he knew the answer to her question. What's more, she did too.

Leaning on the handle of her case, she stood in front of him. "You say it or I wi –"

"My career was always more important." .

Chapter 48.

From the Millers' house in Castleknock to Connolly Hospital in Blanchardstown was a fifteen-minute drive. It took the ambulance six. To Brian, who was now running beside the gurney into the A&E, it had felt like hours.

An hour earlier, he had run his hand over the stubble on his face and wished he had taken some things from the house the day before. The conversation with Jude had distracted him.

Jude.

Brian hated that his son was blaming himself for what had happened and wondered if just putting his own hand up and accepting responsibility would be the best thing for everyone, even if he knew that it wasn't really that simple.

He thought about this as he looked at the reflection of his unshaven face in the office window. He had been using his electric razor for weeks now and he really needed to have a proper wet shave. His wooden-handled razor, a Christmas present from Jude, was still at home – what used to be home. Plus there was that book, Mandela's biography, by the bed, that he really wanted to finish. So, with the auditors having left a few minutes earlier, Brian decided to treat himself to an early finish and drive out to Castleknock.

When he walked into the house, he called Geraldine and got no answer. Upstairs, he was surprised that the bed was unmade and the room untidy, unusual for her. As he started back down the stairs, he realised that he had, in fact, seen Geraldine's car when he arrived.

So where is she?

He found out when he walked into the kitchen.

Geraldine was slumped at the table. She might have been asleep except for the vomit pooled at her mouth.

"Oh Jesus!" Brian ran to her and started gently shaking her. "Ger? Ger! Wake up sweetheart." Getting no response or even movement, he pulled her up into a sitting position and immediately noticed that she was cold, her lips a horrid shade of blue.

Brian wasted no more time. He called for an ambulance.

~ ~

As the gurney was being manoeuvred into the hospital's Resuss area, a nurse pulled Brian aside, having to almost prise his hand away from Geraldine's.

"Sir, are you her husband?" she asked.

"Em, yes, yes I am," he said slowly. "Well…we're separated," he added.

"Okay, well when was the last time you saw her? The last time anyone saw her."

"I don't know, I saw her yesterday. She was fine! I mean, I think she was."

"Well we need to ascertain when this happened."

"When what happened? What's wrong with her?" Brian said, his voice cracking.

The nurse tried to lead him from the room.

"The doctor is trying to find that out now," she said softly. "Is there anyone you need to contact?"

Brian nodded and, turning away, pulled out his phone and looked at it in his shaking hand. He knew he had to call Jude, tell him what was happening. He just wished he knew what the hell that was.

~ ~

Twenty-five minutes later, Jude was sprinting into the A&E, almost running into an old man who was talking to a nurse. He was past him before he realised that the old man was his father. The despair and confusion on Brian's face left him cold.

"Dad? What's going on?"

"Jude! Oh, thank God," his father said. "I'm just filling out these forms here, but I'm not even sure what I'm supposed to –"

"Well what have they told you? Is she okay?"

"Just that she may have taken an overdose of something. Painkillers, maybe. They made me leave while they…" His voice stopped working.

Jude turned to the nurse for some reassurance – anything – but she was gone.

"I don't understand!" his father suddenly erupted. "She was okay yesterday, right? How could this happen?"

Seeing his father like this, Jude had to fight to stay calm. "Dad, you need to relax, okay? We don't know what happened yet –"

"Will everyone please stop telling me to relax! You were with her yesterday, after I left. Did she seem alright?"

"I don't know, Dad. I was only there for a while but she seemed fine. She said she had a headache, she was going to have a lie-down. I –"

Jude turned when he heard someone clearing their throat behind him, a woman in her early thirties.

"Mr. Miller, I'm Doctor Rashid, I'm looking after your wife."

Jude stepped forward. "I'm her son, Jude. What the hell is happening?"

"Well, it looks like your mother took a large dose of a prescription painkiller, Co-codamol. The paramedic brought this in from the house."

She showed them the box of pills.

"It says it was prescribed two days ago but there are already half of them gone."

"Oh, Jesus," Brian said, putting his hand to his forehead.

"When she came in, she was unconscious but she was breathing. We gave her oxygen and fluids and we're waiting to see if she responds. We've taken some tests for liver and kidney functions, to determine what damage has been done."

"Oh Jesus," Brian said again.

"As far as we can tell, from the rate of ingestion, it could have been an accidental overdose. The test results will be back soon and, in the meantime, we are giving her some drugs to counteract what she took."

"So, what?" Jude said. "Is she going to be alright?"

"Does she have any medical conditions? Something that requires this strength of painkiller?"

"No," Brian said. "Nothing. Well, she gets headaches sometimes. When she's run down or stressed. But she…" It dawned on him what might have caused it. "Oh, God!"

"It's okay, Dad," Jude said, sounding much calmer than he felt. He turned back to the doctor. "Is she going to be alright?" he pleaded again.

"We don't know right now, but she's lucky." The doctor offered a reassuring smile and it worked. "If you hadn't got there when you did, Mr. Miller, she probably would have died."

Jude gave his father's hand a reassuring squeeze.

"We've sedated her and moved her to a Recovery bed," the doctor said. "You can see her now if you want but, as I said, she is heavily sedated."

They followed the doctor to the ward, where Geraldine lay in a bed, her face still grey and thin but some colour in her lips. A tube crossed her face, supplying oxygen to her nose.

Brian immediately went to her and grasped her hands in his.

"Ger?" The shake in his father's voice was not something Jude was used to. "Ger, love, I'm here, okay? I'm not going anywhere."

Jude was about to follow him in the room when the doctor stopped him.

"In cases such as this," she said. "We always recommend a psychological consultation. Particularly as your father mentioned that she was stressed –"

"What? Why?" Jude said. "You said it was an accident. She doesn't need a –"

"I said it could have been an accident, yes. But we can't rule anything out." She paused. "You father mentioned that he and your mother are separated, is that right?"

Jude nodded.

"And is that a recent development?"

"Late last year, they –" Jude didn't like what the doctor was suggesting. "No, she would never…" The words caught in his throat.

"I'll send someone to talk to you," the doctor said. "In the meantime, you can stay with her for a little while. But she really needs to rest. And I really would prefer it was one person at a time."

Jude entered the ward and stood a few feet away from the bed. He watched his father sitting there, holding his mother's hand to his face.

After a few seconds, Brian sensed his presence. "Jesus, Jude," he said. "What the hell am I doing? How have I let our lives get so messed up?"

Our lives? Jude thought. *Your life was pretty good, all in all.*

"I don't know, Dad," was all he could manage without saying something he might regret. "I'll be back in a minute. I need some air."

"I think maybe I…" his father asked, looking away from Geraldine for the first time. "I mean, will she ever forgive me?"

Looking at Brian's face, a face that was finally accepting responsibility, Jude had to urge to just tell his father that of course she would, that everything would be okay.

But, even now, he couldn't bring himself to say it. He could barely bring himself to look at the man.

~ ~

Jude walked for twenty minutes with no idea where he was going. It was only when he was approaching a shop that he realised what he needed more than anything. For the first time in six years, he bought a packet of cigarettes.

He sat on the low wall outside and smoked one and then a second, straight after. They didn't help.

He couldn't believe that this was happening. At a time when he should have been happy and proud and excited, it was all turning to shit. With everything he had done, all the risks, all the sacrifices, he sat there and asked himself what was the fucking point of it all.

Chapter 49.

"I was wondering when you and I might have this little chat," Ben Jameson said as he walked into the reception area of Irish Gourmet.

"Hey there, Freckles," Daniel said and Jameson fought a wince as his hand was squeezed.

"Nobody has called me that in seventeen years, Dannyboy," Jameson said, returning the compliment of the rugby-school nickname. He wished it had been something more derogatory. "No prizes for guessing why you're here."

"You want to go somewhere more private to talk about it?" Daniel asked.

"Talk?" Jameson said, feigning surprise. "And I thought we were going to go out back and duke it out like the old days."

They exchanged tight smiles and it was clear that neither would like nothing more than to swap a few punches. Instead, Jameson pointed towards a nearby meeting room.

"If you're here to give me your blessing, Dannyboy," Jameson said as he dropped into a chair. "Let me save you the trouble –"

"I just want to offer you some friendly advice, that's all," Daniel interjected, the polite smile falling away.

"Advice? Okay, well this should be interesting."

"You should be careful, Ben. I'm serious. She's dangerous and she will fuck up your life if you give her half a chance."

"Well that's the difference between you and me, Dannyboy," Jameson said with a smirk. "I don't give women the chance to fuck up my life. I keep things nice and simple. That way, nobody gets hurt."

"Except maybe your wife?" Daniel said, raising his eyebrows.

Ah why did you have to mention that? Jameson though. *Now I am going to have to hurt you.*

"It doesn't really surprise me that a guy like you can't handle Mia," he said. "She's complex. Bit of a riddle, as they say. And, yeah, she possibly is a little messed up. Beautiful women always are. You're naïve not to have seen that in the first place. How long were you together, five months? Jesus, my two-year-old would have had her figured out in half that time."

"This is all very interesting but –"

"It's the same reason you were always a shit rugby player, Dannyboy." Jameson was enjoying himself and he saw no reason to stop. Dannyboy Summers should have known better than to come here in the first place. "You always expected the best of people. Whenever someone grabbed you by the balls, you were surprised!"

Daniel didn't look as put out by the accusation as Jameson as hoped. In fact, the fucker looked a bit smug sitting there. He decided he better just finish him off quick so he could get back to work.

"So let me offer you some friendly advice, Dannyboy, since we're being all *friendly*," he said. "Why don't you go and get yourself some nice plump little woman who'll appreciate you and treat you well, cook your dinners and even satisfy your morning glory on the weekends. And you can leave the beautiful, unpredictable, 'dangerous'" – He laughed as he mockingly repeated Daniel's word – "women to guys like me. Because, frankly, they're wasted on you."

That should do it, Jameson thought. But, to his surprise, the smirk was still there, on Daniel's face. Maybe he hadn't been listening. He was about to continue when Daniel took out his mobile and started scrolling through his phone book.

Jameson didn't know whether to be amused or annoyed. "I'm sorry, am I missing some…" He faded off when Daniel turned the phone to show what was on the screen.

"That look familiar, Freckles?" he asked.

"What?" Jameson said as he fixed his gaze on the phone. And to his shock, recognised the number. "What the fuck?"

He tried to grab the phone out of Daniel's hand but it was pulled away. "What are you doing? Where did you get that?"

Daniel pressed the button on the phone and put the phone to his ear.

"What am I doing?" he said, moving the phone away from his mouth. "I'm showing you what 'guys-like-me' are capable of." He then glanced at Jameson. "She'd be at home now, right? Probably just back from collecting your son. Cocoon Childcare in Terenure, isn't it?"

"Jesus, Summers!" Jameson said, nearly climbing over the desk towards him. "Stop being a dickhead! Hang up the phone, for fuck sake!"

Daniel put up his hand to silence Jameson as he spoke into the phone. "Hello, Mrs. Jameson? Hi, my name is Daniel Summers, I'm a friend of Ben's."

He paused and looked at Jameson, who could feel the colour draining from his face as a bead of sweat dropped from his underarm and ran down his side.

"Okay! Okay!" he hissed. "Just hang up, please!"

Daniel stared at him for another few seconds and then turned his attention back to the phone. "Actually, can I call you right back? Thank you so much. Bye."

He dropped the phone on the table and gave Jameson a friendly smile.

"Look!" Jameson said, trying to sound aggressive but knowing he was beaten. "You want me to stop seeing Mia?"

"With immediate effect."

"Why?"

Daniel leaned in so their noses were almost touching. "None of your fucking business."

Jameson had seen that look on a few peoples' faces before. And it always meant that he was in trouble, that he was beaten.

"Fine," he said. "It's over."

"What, just like that?"

"Yeah, sure. To be honest, it is getting tiresome. You're right, you know," he said, trying to sound friendly and familiar but just coming off pleading and pathetic. "Turns out, she is too messed up, even for me!"

Daniel sat there and stared at him, not a hint of emotion showing. "It's over?"

"Over! Done," Jameson said quickly.

"So if I ever see her again, I won't see you with her?"

"Definitely not! I'm a married man, you know? Got to grow up sometime. And I love my wife." Jameson looked into Daniel's eyes, made sure he had his attention. "I do, Dan. I love her. I wouldn't want to hurt her, you know?"

Daniel continued to stare at him for another few seconds, before pushing himself up off the chair.

Hoping his relief wasn't too obvious, Jameson came around the table and opened the door. He offered his hand and, after a

moment, Daniel shook it.

Before Jameson could release the grip, Daniel pulled him close. "Now, wouldn't you agree that Mia's dangerous? Because of her, your wife almost found out that you're a lying adulterous asshole. See? She almost ruined your life already. Now you know how I feel."

~ ~

Jameson sat in the meeting room, staring at the wall. He couldn't go back to his desk looking like this. The others would think he was dying or something. They'd have never seen him like this before, sweating and upset. He would stay here for a few minutes. He didn't want to worry them.

His own behaviour had surprised him. How often had he told himself that he didn't care if Miranda found out about his 'extra-curricular activities'? Surely it would simplify his life. From the day he was flirting with the hotel wedding co-ordinator, he had suspected that marriage wasn't really for him. But now, here he was, faced with the possibility of her finding out. And it terrified him.

Maybe, he thought to himself, *I'm finally growing up and am ready to be one of those boring responsible people. Maybe I need to put a stop to all this bullshit.*

Ending this thing with Mia would be a good start.

He wasn't doing it for Summers, he told himself. That asshole was just bluffing, he wouldn't have had the balls to tell Miranda. But still, just having a dodgy ex-boyfriend sniffing around was giving himself more trouble than he needed.

Time to end it. It's run its course anyway. I'll call her after work and -

His mobile vibrated in his pocket and he fished it out. Reading the text, he laughed. "You dirty girl, Mia," he muttered as he tried to think of something equally smutty to send back.

Time to end it. Yeah, right.

Chapter 50.

October.

Temple turned to look at the clock.

But there was no clock.

No Kieran, that's in the other room, remember? Beside your own bed.

He looked at his watch instead and was reminded of Jude Miller's Patek Philippe. And he realised how ludicrous that pang of jealousy had been. It was bullshit.

No, Kieran, what's bullshit is this. You sleeping in the spare room. Punishing Yvonne for doing nothing wrong. Not a thing.

She had a right to be suspicious, to be worried. And he had chosen to be immature, to ignore her instead of reassure her, to go to bed in here instead of in their bed where he could pull her to him, plead with her to forgive him, to trust him, to believe his promise that he would never see Mia Burrows again.

But instead, here he was. In an uncomfortable, stupidly narrow bed. All by his own doing.

He looked at his watch again. Great. *I've to be up in three hours.*

Having gone to bed at midnight and then lain awake until two, it pissed him off that, just after four, he was awake again. Wide awake.

He heard the extractor fan in the en-suite come on – Yvonne was up too.

Temple knew what he had to do. But he also knew what he couldn't do, which was tell Yvonne what had happened at the hotel. That particular truth would not set him free.

The extractor shut off – it was now or never. He swung himself out of the bed but froze as he heard the master bedroom door opening. Footsteps padded across the hall and he heard a light tapping on the door.

"Hiya," he said.

The door swung open and Yvonne stood there in that very cute green-and-grey striped woollen night-shirt. An overly-affected sulk adorned her face. "So, are you going to punish me forever?"

She knew him so well.

"You should be punishing me."

"You didn't do anything," she said, coming in and sitting on the edge of the bed. "Not really."

He shook his head. "I don't know." He started rubbing her shoulder. Picturing Mia's face at the hotel lift, he tried to push it away, and with it any guilt. "Whatever it was, I'm finished now. It's finished."

"Really?"

"She was cleared. And now she's gone. Out of Dublin."

"For how long?"

"It doesn't matter, I won't be talking to her anymore. I'm no longer her friend, okay?"

"Okay."

"So even if she does come back –"

"Let's," Yvonne interrupted, "just stop talking about her." She ran her hand up along his arm. "I don't even want to think about it anymore. I mean, I can't keep blaming you for what happened, can I? Because it was nothing. Compared to what might have happened. Compared to what most men would have let happen."

Temple pulled Yvonne to him, into his lap, and hugged her tight. "Well most men aren't married to you, are they? Most men don't have it so good."

She hugged him back and the relief and joy hit him hard.

"That bed in there is freezing," she said and kissed his ear, then his neck.

"I can imagine," Temple said.

Her kisses moved to his chin and then his lips. They were wet, warm, hungry. "So, Inspector Temple," she whispered. "Did we ever christen this room?"

"Are you kidding? Loads of times."

"Funny that," Yvonne said, pulling his tee-shirt up over his head. "I really don't remember."

Chapter 51.

Greenland Industrial Estate in Baldonnell, near the Aerodrome, was a late bloomer amidst Ireland's economic recovery. Many of the businesses, haulage firms mostly, had long since closed their doors during the recession and few had returned. The result was a half-full estate with entire roads lined with vacant units.

It was on one of these deserted roads that Temple now drove, splashing through the potholes in the un-maintained tarmac. As he reached the dead-end, the front doors of a black Range-Rover opened and two men emerged.

The driver, known as Percy, was a tree-trunk of a man in his early thirties who wore a dark grey suit and navy tie. He left his door open and stared at Temple's car as it approached.

The other man was shorter and slightly overweight. Wearing a pair of khakis and polo shirt, he looked like he just come off a golf course. He was leaning against the Range-Rover, lighting a cigarette, and wore a well-practised air of self-importance.

"D.I. Temple," the man said, as Temple got out his car. "How is the life of law enforcement treating you, my friend?"

"You know how it is. The crimes are the same, it's just the scumbags who vary slightly." Temple replied. "Got rid of the Humvee?"

"Yes, was attracting some unwanted attention," Graham Fanning said with a smile. "From people in your line of work, mostly. This is much more, eh, subtle, wouldn't you agree?"

"I suppose," Temple said. "How's Calista?"

"She's great," Fanning said enthusiastically. "It was her birthday last week. Twelve, can you believe that?"

Temple nodded. "And how is she?" he repeated.

Fanning's smile faded. "The same, I guess. Scarring on her neck has faded and the doctors are talking about trying these new hair implants from the U.S., say they'll be able to match the colour of her real hair." He paused, to indicate that that was the end of the good news. "But, you know, her face is still…" He winced and then glanced at Percy, who was busy pretending not to hear the conversation. "How about you?" he then asked Temple.

"No change. Don't even see it anymore really. Sometimes I even forget which arm it is." They both emitted a short and unconvincing laugh.

The pause that followed left Temple remembering that day. Six years gone, it was a day he still thought about all too often and would for the rest of his life.

He had been trailing 'pub-owner' Fanning, who was suspected of being in a position to make a large Ecstasy purchase. The Gardaí were struggling to curb the Dublin narcotics trade and under pressure to secure some high-profile arrests.

It was dusk and Fanning was sitting in his car outside a house in Drimnagh, talking to a young woman. Temple was at the entrance to the estate, sitting in a dirty unmarked Peugeot with Mia Burrows, watching the conversation. This wasn't the buy, more likely it was Fanning doing the ground work, maybe recruiting some street-traders for later on.

A dark green Fiat Punto drove past them into the estate. Temple noticed how slowly it was moving and, more notably, that the registration plate was unreadable. The car proceeded up the road and, as it drew parallel with Fanning's BMW, an object was thrown through the open passenger window.

With the front wheels smoking, the Fiat sped away. At the same time, a flash of light from inside Fanning's car was followed by a loud bang. The BMW burst into flames, the interior instantly engulfed.

Without even thinking about it, Temple had started his car and sped to the blazing BMW. As he skidded to a stop and jumped out, the driver's door opened and Graham Fanning rolled out on the ground. He rolled in the grass a few times but actually didn't seem to be on fire. Temple was about to make a hasty retreat when he heard a terrifying shrieking coming from inside the burning car. Fanning was trying to stand up and was screaming 'Calista! Calista!'

Temple turned and yanked open the back door of the car. The intense heat and the black billowing smoke made him recoil, coughing. But the screaming was now even shriller, and Temple lunged forward, reaching his right arm into the inferno. The pain was agonising but his arm felt something on the seat. Not even knowing what it was, Temple yanked it out on to the road.

It was a small girl, five or six years old, and her long blonde hair and clothes were on fire. Ignoring his own burning jacket, Temple dropped the girl down on to the grass verge and started rolling her over and over and patting the flames with his arm. The dampness of the grass eventually put the fire out and he turned her over.

The sight of her face had made him retch.

As Temple stood in this windy industrial estate, he could taste the bitterness in the back of his throat again. He glanced at Fanning, suddenly anxious to get this meeting finished.

"I need a favour, Graham."

"I'm listening," Fanning said.

"Lose interest in Jude Miller and his restaurant."

"What's that?"

"Come on, Graham, I'm too cold to play games here. *Sixteen Eustace?* In Temple Bar? You know it?"

"Sure, had a couple of meals there. Good sea bass."

"Yes, well you, or rather, two of your guys, have an interest in the place. A financial interest, I assume. I need them to, you know, walk away, that's all."

"That's all? If a couple of my associates have decided to invest some of their hard-earned money –"

"Give me a break," Temple said, getting annoyed. "We both know that if your 'associates' are involved in this place, it's not because their accountant told them that restaurants were the way to go."

"Still though, that's a pretty big ask there, Kieran."

"I don't come to you for the little stuff, Graham."

"Fair enough. Do you mind if I ask why you're so interested in the place?"

"Need-to-know, I'm afraid. You know how it is."

Fanning continued to stare. Need-to-know-basis wasn't going to be enough.

"The proprietor is suffering from a conflict of loyalties. I'm trying to provide some clarity."

"You're getting to sound more and more like me every day, d'you know that?" Fanning said, flicking his cigarette and pushed himself away from the car. "So I guess we're going to be having these little meetings forever, you and me?"

Temple paused and stared at Fanning for a second. "Not forever," he said. "The day you look at your daughter and don't think of me, you can stop taking my calls."

Chapter 52.

September.

Daniel hoped a run on Sandymount Strand would help his hangover.

It was a bad one. From about three o'clock the previous afternoon, he'd been craving a drink. He had wondered who he might recruit to keep him company but, as the day came to an end, he couldn't think of anyone he wanted to call. That was his own fault, of course. A life-long habit of Daniel's was to fall off the planet whenever he was ensconced in a new relationship. The difference now was that the one person he could always rely on was also gone. The days of sitting in the pub with Jude, drowning sorrows or laughing them off, would be no more.

So, with nobody to call and no desire to sit in some pub by himself, Daniel had spent the evening on the sofa with a bottle of wine, a bottle of Captain Morgan's and the TV. By the time he had fallen into a fully-dressed drunken slumber, his mood was such he intended to stay in bed for the whole weekend. But after a slow waking at lunchtime on Saturday, that idea seemed like it had been someone else's. With much difficulty, he had coaxed himself out of the bed and on to the beach.

He was greeted by a strong wind, which initially made his head pound. He ran the length of the beach and back twice without stopping and only then started to feel human. But as he stood trying to catch his breath, the symptoms, headache and nausea, suddenly returned. Jude was walking towards him.

"Thought I might find you here," he said, stopping just within earshot.

"Yeah, needed some air. Rough night," Daniel said. "I've been meaning to text you."

"Yeah?"

"Heard about your mother. How is she?"

"She's okay," Jude said. "Bored and tired of the all the fussing. Just wants to go home."

Daniel looked away and waited, knowing he couldn't delay the inevitable any longer.

"Listen, Dan, we need to sort this out."

Daniel didn't want to sort it out. He just wanted to forget the whole bloody thing. But Jude wasn't the type to let that happen.

"I don't know what happened, Jude. I just –"

"Me neither," Jude said. "Those guys? They were just protecting me, you know? Maybe they took it too far, but they wouldn't really have hurt you or anything."

Daniel blinked in surprise. He couldn't believe it, Jude was apologising to him.

"I just wanted to make sure that you didn't go the Guards," Jude continued. "You know, if you're okay and all."

It was definitely an apology. More so, Jude was even asking for a favour. Thinking fast, Daniel put his hand to his neck and rubbed the spot where the finger-marks had, by now, faded. "It's still a bit sore," he said, with a pained expression. "And they had a fucking knife? They –"

"Come on, they were just trying to scare you!" Jude said, sounding desperate.

"That's not how it looked from where I was standing."

"You were attacking me, remember? So let's just leave it, okay?"

Daniel was silent for a moment. "You and I are friends, right?" he said.

"Of course," Jude said, looking relieved.

"Well then, okay, let's just forget it if we're friends. I need a friend."

"I know you do, and I want to –"

"You know, with everything that's going on with Mia." Daniel interrupted him, continuing to study Jude's expression.

"Don't be thinking about her. You're better off without that one. You know she's seeing someone else already? She's –"

"Nah, that's over," Daniel replied proudly. "The guy told me himself."

"Who? Ben Jameson?"

"Yeah, we go back. I dropped into his office the other day, told him what was what. I thought he'd put up more of a fight but he just –"

"Daniel, for fuck sake!" Jude was suddenly angry. "What are you doing? You and Mia are finished! She doesn't want to have anything to do with you anymore, you know that!"

"No, that's not true, Jude. Alice told me that Mia misses me, that she wants to see me. So I'm going to see her at the weekend, Alice told me where they'd be –"

"For fuck sake, Daniel, Alice's playing you! She has been since the start –"

"If I say the right thing, I'll talk Mia round. I know I will –"

"No," Jude said. "It's time to stop. Let this go. It's over."

Daniel looked at Jude and could not hide his disappointment.

He was not going to get the support he had hoped for. He turned and started walking away.

"I'm serious, Daniel. Drop it!" Jude said, following him.

"I don't need your blessing, Jude," Daniel called back over his shoulder.

"No, but you're asking for it." Jude said and then stopped walking. "I'll warn her."

Daniel spun on his heel and could not suppress the anger.

"No, you fucking won't!" he said aggressively. "She can't know I'm coming. Why do you even care?"

"Because I'm not going stand by and let you hurt her again. Which you obviously will!"

"Let me?" Daniel shouted. "You won't let me? Who the fuck are you! You can't stop me. You won't stop me."

"Oh? How can you be so –"

"Because if you try, if I even get a hint that you intervened, I'll tell the cops about your buddies. Don't think I won't. I still have the bruises."

He could see the despair and resignation on Jude's face but he didn't care. "I can't really remember their names though," he continued. "So I'll just point the Guards in your direction, okay?"

Whatever chance there was of reconciliation was gone now, but Daniel realised that it was a sacrifice he was happy to make.

Jude stood and stared at him for a few seconds. Then, without a word, he just shook his head and walked away. Daniel watched him climb the steps to the promenade.

"Fuck him," Daniel said and turned back to continue his run. He didn't need Jude. He didn't need anyone else.

He just needed Mia.

Chapter 53.

"I can't believe that you still have this photo," Brian said. "It must be, what, twenty-five years old."

A photograph, of two people hugging a small boy, had slipped out of Geraldine's wallet and landed on the bed.

"Twenty-seven," she corrected. "Taken in the garden in your mother's house. Jude was six."

"Yeah, that whole summer, he refused to take off those wellies. Didn't he even wear them to bed a few times?"

"Oh God, yes! How do you remember that?" Geraldine asked, laughing.

"I remember that he used to kick me if I tried to take them off, that's what I remember!"

"Stubborn as a mule, just like his father," Geraldine allowed her hand to brush against his. Brian had noticed that this morning, for the first time in months, his wife did not have a cloud hanging over her and that she actually seemed happy.

And he hoped he knew why.

The events of the previous eleven days had made him take a step back and look at his life and, although he still didn't know what would happen in the long term, at least things were headed in the right direction.

"What time is the doctor coming?" he asked. But he didn't hear her answer, distracted by his phone ringing. He looked at the screen and blushed.

"Go on, answer it," Geraldine said.

"I can call her back."

"It's fine."

"Okay," he said. "Won't be long."

He walked out of the ward as he answered the phone. "Hiya."

"Brian, where the hell are you?" Suzanne wasn't happy. "We're supposed to be having lunch."

"Lunch?" Brian looked at his wrist. No watch, he'd left it at home again. A present from Suzanne a few weeks ago, he had to admit he found it a bit heavy. "What time is it?" he said.

"Nearly half-one! Oh my God, you're still at the bloody hospital, aren't you?" Really not happy.

"Yeah, I am. Sorry. It's just that they told her she could go home and I'm helping her get packed and sort out the insurance, you know. But I can be there in twenty minutes. Where –"

"Look, don't bother. It's easy to see where your priorities lie."

"What do you mean, 'my priorities'? She's my wife, Suzanne, and right now, she needs my help."

"There are other people in her life too, not just you. I mean, you've been practically living there all week."

"I know, but –"

"You can't feel guilty for what happened. It wasn't your fault."

This annoyed Brian. He had hoped Suzanne would have been

a bit more supportive and patient, given the circumstances. But he was also annoyed because she was right. He was blaming himself.

But his constant attendance by Geraldine's bed wasn't just an act of contrition and Suzanne knew that as well as he did. They would need to talk about it, but this wasn't the time.

"Look, I'll come over later and we can talk then, okay?"

"Come over?" Suzanne said and Brian realised that he had let slip a little more than he'd intended. "You live here. What do you mean 'come over'?"

"I've offered to stay with Geraldine for a few days," he said quietly. "To, you know, help her, until she's better. It's only fair –"

"No, it's not," Suzanne said angrily. "Stay with? You mean 'Move back in with', don't you?"

"I don't know. I'm just –"

"I'll make this easy on you, okay?" Suzanne said and her stern tone surprised him. "What we had was good, and I mean that, it was really good, better than we deserved maybe. But I don't need all this...all this complication. Let's just call this what it is."

"Look, can we –"

"It's okay, Brian. Your wife needs you and, more to the point, it looks like you need her. I'm not angry – okay, I am – but I'm trying to be realistic."

There were a few moments of silence as Brian struggled for something to say. She saved him the trouble.

"Goodbye, Brian." She didn't wait for a reply.

Brian stood, staring at the phone, wondering if he should call her back. But he could not think what he might say if he did.

Geraldine was mostly dressed when he came back into the ward.

"Everything alright?" she asked.

"Yeah, sure," he said, but knew she wouldn't believe him. "I don't know, I think maybe me and Suzanne are…" he faded off. "Finished. I think Suzanne and I are finished."

"Oh. That was a bit sudden, wasn't it?" Geraldine said and seemed almost sympathetic. "Well, you know, maybe some alone-time might be good for you."

"Yeah," he said and then realised what Geraldine had said. "Alone? Well, I thought, maybe if the next few days go well, I could –"

"What?" Geraldine said. "Eh, I don't think so. What, you think that's it? You can just put a plaster on this and it will just heal itself?"

"No. Look, I know what I did to you was unforgivable and you –"

"No," Geraldine interrupted him. "That's not the point. It is actually forgivable. I decided – I'm not sure when exactly – that I do forgive you. But you've made me think about what I want in my life. And it's not you anymore."

She looked at his greying face and injured expression.

"Don't give me that look. You don't have the right," she said, folding her arms. "Now I would appreciate a lift home if that's okay but it probably isn't a good idea for you to stay. It wouldn't be, you know, fair."

As his wife gave him a polite and distant smile, the truth dawned. Her pleas for him to stay for just a few more minutes, the nostalgic conversations, her suggestion that, maybe, he stay at the house with her for a few days.

None of it had been real.

And now that the carpet had been pulled from under him, Brian knew that he deserved no better.

Geraldine breezed past him. "Grab my bag, there's a good man."

Chapter 54.

October.

As Temple was walking out of the Temple Bar multi-storey, his phone rang again. He tutted, knowing who it would be. Third time in the last hour. He thought about letting it ring out again but the D-Super's persistence was legendary.

"Superintendent."

"Fuck sake, Temple, where are you?" Hickey said.

"I'm –"

"Because four times this morning I was in your office at your desk to talk about the Moroney phone taps. And guess what? You weren't there."

"I'm just –"

"And I'm hearing rumours that you're still on that Mia Burrows thing."

Fuck, Temple thought. *So much for staying under the radar.*

"Seriously, why are you pissing about on something that was closed twenty-four hours ago?"

"I'm just…tying up some loose ends," was all Temple could think to say. He knew it wouldn't help.

"Well D.I. Hodge – remember him? Yeah, he's the one in charge of that investigation. According to him, there are no loose ends. It was self-defence, wasn't it?"

"Yes, of course. But there's just one…"

Temple heard the D-Super sigh – that really annoying thing he did when he was fighting to control his anger. "Temple? Listen to me. No, there isn't. You ended up on this thing by accident because you and Burrows used to be…whatever you used to be. But back to work now, Temple, back to your real work. My desk, Moroney phone taps, three o'clock."

Even if Temple had a good excuse not to be back at the Square at three, he didn't get a chance to offer it. Hickey was gone.

As he approached the restaurant, wondering how many lines of defence there would be between him and Jude Miller, Temple spotted the man himself emerge from a side-door, lighting a cigarette.

"Inspector," Jude said. "Didn't expect to see you again. I thought you were finished."

"Let's just say the file is still on my desk," Temple said. "Didn't see you as a smoker."

"Yeah, I'm bringing it back into fashion," he said. He nodded towards the door. "We're crazy in there these days, it was the only way I can justify a minute of me-time."

"Spare one more?"

~ ~

"So what d'you think of my kingdom?" Jude asked as they sat down at the small and cluttered desk, gesturing towards the kitchen they had walked through.

"As you said," Temple said. "Busy."

"Well we got a glowing review from someone fairly influential a few days ago. It's amazing how grown people will just so easily do what they're told. Listen to this music, drink this beer, eat in this restaurant."

"That would be Mr. Jameson?"

"Sorry?"

"The 'someone influential'."

Jude started to look surprised, but his expression quickly changed to resignation.

"But didn't he already write a rather scathing review last month? "Temple continued. "I don't know him that well, but he doesn't strike me as a U-turn kind-of-guy."

"I can be persuasive."

"You can? Or your partners can, maybe."

Jude immediately looked nervous, or at least more nervous than before. "No, this time it was me," he said, clearly trying to sound relaxed. "I do still have some influence, you know."

"It's just that…"

"What?"

"Well, I heard about that thing with your car. Very *Godfather*."

"For fuck sake," Jude stood up and turned away, a sign that the big lie was coming. "That was nothing to do with them. It was probably just kids –"

"Give it a rest," Temple said. He pulled an envelope out of his jacket pocket and fanned out a number of grainy black-and-white photographs on the desk.

Jude stood with his back to Temple, until the curiosity got the better of him. "What's this?" he said.

"I noticed them that day I met you outside your house. Cameras. Your next-door neighbour, Sean Dexter? Nice guy, breeds owls."

When Jude didn't respond, Temple went on. "Sean's

somewhat wealthy children have become understandably worried about him in his advancing years. Have spent a ton of money on a security system, including CCTV. One of the cameras, luck would have it, points in the general direction of your front gate."

Temple pointed at one of the photos, showing the back of a man's head as he was getting out of Jude's Mercedes, and then another clearly showing his face as he took a large cloth sack out of the boot, opened it and threw it on to the driver's seat. He was in his early forties with greying hair and he wore a large woollen coat. "You know him, don't you?" Temple asked, looking at Jude, waiting for his reaction. "One of your partners, right?"

For a minute, Jude said nothing, just stared at the photos.

"So what?" he eventually said. "This doesn't change anything. It's not like I'm going to press charges. You probably know who these people are, what they're like. They did this as a warning? Fine, I'm warned!"

"Well, the landscape has changed somewhat," Temple said slowly, gathering up the photographs. "You won't be answerable to them anymore. They're going to leave you alone."

Not for the first time, Temple saw the colour drain from Jude's face. Not the response he was expecting.

"What do you mean, leave me alone?" Jude said, "They've sunk a lot of money into it. It's not like I can just write them a cheque –"

"Don't worry about it," Temple interrupted him. "Don't get me wrong, I would suggest you pay them back at some stage. You know, when you can afford it. In the meantime though, you'll be left alone."

Temple wondered why it was such hard work for Jude to look relieved. "How did you –"

"Let's just say Mr. Fanning and I have an understanding.

Money is one thing. Honour is something else."

"You and Mr. Fanning…" Jude said and then sighed and closed his eyes. "You talked to Graham Fanning."

"I did."

"I don't understand. Why would you do that for me?"

"You know why," Temple said. "I need to close this thing properly, Jude. Your friend Daniel deserves that. And you're the only person who can help me do it. Because you're the only person who knows who's really to blame."

Jude threw up his arms in exasperation. "How…how can I do what you're asking? We're not perfect but…she is still my wife."

"How can you not?" Temple said. "What happens the next time she gets bored? We'll have another body on our hands?"

Jude closed his eyes, the pain sweeping across his face. Temple almost felt bad but knew that he couldn't afford to pull his punches right now. "Or another painkiller overdose and a week spent in hospital? She started that chain of events too, didn't she?"

As he watched Jude, the pain slowly vanished from the man's face. He opened his eyes and looked coldly at Temple.

"What do you want to know?"

~ ~

It had been a bit of a cliché, Jude didn't mind admitting it.

He'd been in London, working at the Dorchester, for nearly a year and had finally allowed himself to wallow in homesickness. It had surprised him how it had taken hold, slowly enveloping him over time, to the point where an Irish accent or the occasional smell of Guinness on the Kentish Town Road would nearly bring a tear to his eye. Living in Camden definitely didn't help.

He never expected to feel homesick – it was London, he'd been there dozens of times before the move and had lived much further away before that. He figured there'd be a few pangs but that they'd fade quickly. But the dissatisfaction in the job and increasing sense of anonymity and loneliness left him missing the intimacy of the smaller city, even if he didn't specifically miss his family.

On one of his rare days off, he had found himself in a crowded Japanese restaurant off the Tottenham Court Road, wondering how he would talk his way into a job in Dublin if he just bit the bullet and went home. He glanced up from his Bento box to see a blonde woman come in. He knew he was staring as she waited for service and then asked for a table – with an Irish accent.

Jude glanced at her again as she sat down nearby and polite smiles were exchanged. When she asked to borrow the soy sauce from his table, he had picked up the accent again.

"Nice to hear a voice from the old country," he said, passing the bottle.

Probably surprised by his accent, the girl smiled. "I'm actually from Essex, but I find men respond better to something more exotic."

"Exotic?"

"And Arabic is too hard. Promise you won't tell anyone?"

Jude laughed. "I will take it to my grave."

They sat in that restaurant and talked for hours. She was based in Dublin but on a six-month placement in London. Unlike Jude, she loved her job but, because of the antisocial hours, she didn't get home much and had made few friends.

After the long lunch, they had walked through the tiny streets of Covent Garden and along The Strand to the river, talking about food, travel, art, everything and nothing. It might not have been Paris or Rome, but London proved to be just as effective. Jude had fallen in love that day. And for the next six months, they had barely spent a spare minute apart.

Jude wondered now, as he walked along by the Liffey, why he was thinking about all that again, it had happened a long time ago. He should have been thinking about now, about Alice now. The woman who had had changed so much since they had met. The woman who had found comfort with another man when the one she married proved less than effective. The woman who had set her mind to destroying his parents' thirty-year marriage. The woman he had just betrayed.

There was a time – many times – when she could have chosen a different direction but didn't. So, as the image of his mother in a hospital bed flashed through his mind, he was comforted to think that, thanks to the conversation he had just had with the diligent Inspector Temple, Alice would finally be held accountable.

Jude sensed the car behind him before it crawled past. Slowing his pace and then stopping altogether as he got to the junction, Jude closed his eyes, shook his head and smiled.

The car, a Range Rover, had already turned into Saint Augustine's Street and stopped in front of him. The passenger window glided down.

"Hello, Mr. Fanning," Jude said quietly.

"Hey, Jude," Graham Fanning said and smiled, nodding approval at his own pun. "You must get that all the time."

"Not as much as you might think."

The back door of the Range Rover swung open.

"You and I have something to talk about, wouldn't you agree?"

Chapter 55.

"I stabbed him, Kieran."

"I told him to leave me alone. That it was over. Why wouldn't he just listen to –"

"Mia! Who did you stab?"

"Daniel! I stabbed Daniel!"

Temple sat his desk and listened to Mia Burrows' panicked words bounce around his head. He had just replayed the 999 call to make sure that nothing had been missed, that she hadn't said anything that he might have missed or seemed unimportant but now might mean something. But despite having replayed it half-a-dozen times, nothing jumped out at him.

He was now staring at the blank white-board, the one he had hi-jacked two days ago and had just been wiped ahead of his conversation with the D-Super at three.

Speaking of which, he knew he had to focus – he had been thinking about little else but Daniel Summers long after this case should have been squared away.

Jude Miller had told him about that last conversation he'd had with Summers, the one on the beach, and only then did the extent of the man's obsession with Mia become clear. His unwavering conviction that, despite everything – physical evidence, his friends counselling him, then warning him, then turning on him – he had remained certain that one more conversation with Mia would do the trick. The refusal to give up at any cost.

At any cost.

A call to the Mater A&E had confirmed that Daniel Summers hadn't exactly been a saint, especially towards the end. A record of treatment, mentioning a few thousand grains of sand that had to be washed out of Mia Burrows' eyes. The week-old bruise on Mia's cheek that had been noticed by the doctor treating her eyes, but that Mia had insisted 'was nothing'. And Peter Clarke – a friend of Mia's – who was still recovering from a ruptured spleen, a broken nose and three cracked ribs after a brutal attack. There was a good chance that, under different circumstances, Daniel Summers might be awaiting trial himself right now. But whatever he had done or what he was going to do, he didn't deserve to be dead. Temple still believed that.

He didn't blame Mia, she had done what she had to do. No, he had his sights squared on someone else and was in no doubt of her guilt. Unfortunately, at this moment, he didn't have nearly enough to charge her with anything. And his last option was leaving him less than happy with himself.

The phone on his desk buzzed.

"Inspector Temple? Is Inspector Temple there?"

"Yes, I'm here."

"There's an Alice Miller in reception."

Not so unhappy as to stop him though.

~ ~

"I hope this isn't going to take long, Detective Inspector. I really do have a busy day." Alice was going on the attack from the off. That might make it easier.

"No, of course not," Temple said, leading her into the interview room. "Just a few minutes. I'm just tying things up. You know, for the file."

"For the file." She didn't sound convinced.

Temple sat down at the table and when she didn't follow suit, he gestured to the empty chair. "Please."

Reluctantly, she sat. She'd made her point.

"Actually, can I just say before we start," she said and Temple felt the mood change.

Surprisingly, she looked embarrassed. "I'm sorry for what I said last time."

"Last time."

"That stupid threat I made. I was just upset, you know. I –"

Temple put up his hand. "No explanation needed. I understand that this is a difficult time. It's actually the reason I asked you to pop in. I wanted to let you know that you're no longer under investigation. You know, for any involvement in his death."

Alice allowed herself a quick smirk. "Really? What changed your mind?"

"Well, I –"

"Or did you ever really suspect me in the first place?"

"Sorry?"

"You were trying to deflect attention away from Mia. It's understandable, given your relationship with her."

"My relationship –"

"I mean your professional relationship. But you've obviously realised there was no need to find someone to blame. Self-defence is especially tragic that way. There are no culprits, just victims."

"Well I wouldn't say that."

The sadness, whether real or affected, disappeared from Alice Miller's face. "You wouldn't say what?"

Temple sat forward and rested his elbows on the table. "That there are no culprits. I still think someone else was involved."

"Who?"

Temple sat back and enjoyed the moment. "I can tell you this now because the wheels are already in motion," he said. "We're about to arrest your husband on charges of money laundering, handling and sale of stolen goods and, most importantly, conspiracy to kill Daniel Summers."

~ ~

Alice Miller stormed out the door and walked quickly through the garden in front of Harcourt Square Station.

"Alice, wait," Temple called, a few steps behind her. "We need to talk about this!"

"No!" she yelled back over her shoulder. "You're sick, you know that? This is obviously some personal vendetta against us. In fact –"

She suddenly turned on her heel and started back towards the door. "What's the name of your superior? I'm putting a stop to this right now."

Her hand went to her handbag where the corner of a white envelope was visible. Temple grabbed her wrist as she tried to pass.

He pulled her in front of him. "This is not personal," he said through gritted teeth. "You want to talk to my superintendent?

First floor, third door on the left. But he and I have already consulted and we agree we can bring these charges."

"I don't understand! Why do you think Jude has anything to with what happened to Daniel? They were best friends."

"We think Daniel found out what was going on at the restaurant, what Jude was involved in. He might even have been blackmailing Jude. But Jude knew Daniel's biggest weakness – Mia – and he used that to break him. A white lie here, a rumour there. Within a few short months at Jude's hands, Daniel went from being a confident man in a happy relationship to an obsessive paranoid wreck. Your husband pushed Daniel to the edge, Alice, and then over it."

"Oh, come on," Alice was trying to sound confident but it was barely holding. "Do you realise what you're saying? That he would do such a horrible thing to his best friend? Even if he had the ability –"

"He had the ability. We both know that."

Alice looked confused.

"Kate and Stephen?" Temple said. "They nearly called off their wedding because of him. It's safe to say he has form."

Temple watched as Alice realised what was happening.

"What…what about the other charges?" she said. "The…the money laundering? The stolen goods?"

"What about them?"

"Can you make them stick on their own?"

"I'm sure we can, yeah. But it'll be easier with the conspiracy –"

"I did it," Alice said.

Temple was surprised. He figured he'd have a bit more work to do than this. "You did what?"

"Daniel and Mia. It was me. I sabotaged their relationship. Jude had nothing to do –"

"It's okay, Alice," Temple said, trying to force as much

sympathy into his voice as he could. "You don't have to protect him. It's not like he'd do the same for you. He's practically been telling me it was all your fault since I met him."

"It is my fault. Please, you have to believe that."

"Why should I? What possible motivation could you have?"

"They deserved it."

This caught him Temple off guard, that she was willing to make such an admission.

"They deserved it? Daniel deserved it? He's fucking dead, Alice! How could he possibly deserve that, Alice? Or Mia? Her life is ruined."

"After what they've done, both of them? They don't get to be happy."

"What have they done? Alice, what the fuck have they done? Daniel just –"

"Daniel spent the last twenty years screwing up women, that's what he did. Every girl he was ever with ended up hurt. Kate told you what he did to her. If he did that to her, God knows what else he's –"

"So he deserves to be dead?"

"Yes! No, I mean…I never thought it would go this far. I didn't think he'd –"

"And Mia, what did she do?"

"Come on, Inspector. You of all people know what she did. She nearly cost you your marriage last year. Maybe your career too –"

"She didn't nearly cost me anything, Alice! Don't pretend you're doing this for me."

Alice pulled her arm away and Temple realised that he had been gripping her wrist.

"I'm not doing this for you," she said. "You see, Inspector? Daniel and Mia were so alike, they were destined to be together. They fucking deserved each other."

"And what about Kate?"

"What about her?"

"You did some of this for her. You wanted to hurt Daniel because of what he did to Kate."

"So?"

"So why did you make up lies about her, to break up her and Stephen?"

Alice looked at him confused.

"Kate was supposedly seeing someone behind his back?" Temple continued. "You fed all that to Jude and then pushed him to tell Stephen?"

A brief relenting smile appeared on Alice's face. "That relationship was a mistake from the start. My mistake. I rushed into it, I was trying to take Kate's mind off the Daniel nightmare. I never figured she'd end up engaged to the idiot. I was doing her a favour."

"Alice," Temple could actually feel a weight lifting. "Do you realise what you're admitting to?"

"Sure," she said quietly, but with way too much confidence. "But it doesn't matter. You're not going to –"

"Inspector?" he heard behind him. He turned to see Garda Paddy Malone, standing at the door.

"What?" Temple barked.

"You're looking at a restaurant down on Eustace Street, aren't you? In connection to our buddy Graham Fanning?"

Jesus Paddy, you and your subtlety.

"Hold on," Temple shouted. "I'll be right back," he said to Alice, who now looked worried.

"Is that Jude's –" she started but Temple had already turned away and was walking back towards Malone, giving him the finger-across-the-throat signal to shut up.

"It's all over the news, boss," Malone continued, not getting the hint. "The place is on fire."

Chapter 56.

"Declan McCormack here yet?" Temple asked a fireman, flashing his ID.

"He's around somewhere," the man said. "Check at the door. Don't go in though, there's still a lot of smoke."

Temple walked towards Sixteen Eustace, or what was left of it. The building itself stood as it had done for a few hundred years, but the charred brickwork above the glass-less windows and the black smoke wisping around the door suggested that very little remained inside.

The dozen calls to Jude's mobile, as they drove down from Harcourt Square, had gone straight to voicemail and Alice's panic had risen with each one.

Temple was able to find out that the fire had been reported at approximately five o'clock that morning and by the time the two units of Dublin Fire Brigade had arrived, the place was engulfed. In the hours that followed, during which it was eventually put out, nobody had seen or been able to contact Jude Miller.

This was the first time Temple had seen Alice so distressed and had almost felt relieved at the sight of it.

Despite her panic, Temple had managed to persuade her to stay at the Dame Street cordon while he went to investigate. And as he now walked towards the door of the restaurant, a man wearing a white helmet emerged. Declan McCormack, Dublin's Chief Fire Officer.

"Declan?" he called and the man turned to face him. "D.I. Kieran Temple, Organised Crime Unit."

"Sure, sure. Wait, what? Organised Crime? This is –"

"The owner is…well, he's helping us with an on-going investigation."

"You think this has something to do with that?"

"You tell me."

"Well we've got a dead body, if that's what you're asking. Extremely badly burned, at the back of what used to be the kitchen. We thought maybe it was a break-in. You know, a homeless guy looking for food. But no sign or contact from the owner. And now you're saying he's involved in something?"

Temple didn't know what he was saying. But a fresh bead of sweat trickled down his forehead.

He would have to tell Alice Miller something, a task that would not wait until the victim's identity was confirmed. In fact, she'd probably be the one to have to do that unpleasant job.

Temple started back to where he had left her but she wasn't waiting for him. Her panic had finally beaten her resolve and she was now running down the street towards him.

"Whoa, whoa, whoa!" He caught her by the shoulders and managed to stop her. "Alice, stop. Stop! There's nothing to see!"

"Where is he?" she screamed, trying to break free. "Jude? Jude!"

"Nobody knows anything yet. He may have been nowhere

near the place," he said, pulling her to him and turning her away from the restaurant. But even as he was saying the words, another bead of sweat betrayed him.

We've got a dead body, if that's what you're asking.

"Let me go, please!" she said through her tears. "I need to know that he's okay!"

"Shh shh shh," was all Temple could manage to say.

He heard two blips of a siren and looked to see an ambulance arriving. Before Temple could do anything about it, two firemen appeared from the building, a stretcher carrying a long black bag between them.

"Oh God!" Alice exclaimed and managed to break from Temple's grasp. She started towards the stretcher. "That's a body!"

"Alice, wait."

"Whose body is that? What's in that bag?!"

The two firemen stopped and glanced, confused, at this woman striding towards them. They looked at McCormack, who quickly measured the distance to the ambulance and gestured for them to back-track.

But they were too late. Alice reached them and started to unzip the bag.

One of the two firemen tried to get between her and the stretcher but she managed to pull down the zip. The bag opened to reveal the heavily charred remains of what was probably a man.

"Oh Jesus!" Alice recoiled in horror and Temple wasn't sure what was worse for her, the sight of a burnt corpse or the chance that it was Jude.

She was now crouching with her hand across her stomach as she gagged and retched between sobs. Temple put a comforting hand on her back.

He gestured to the firemen to move on. They started to zip up the bag.

"No, wait," Alice said, with surprising strength.

"There's no point," Temple said. "He's so badly burnt. You won't know –"

"I'll know."

She stood up, took a breath and turned to the stretcher.

The chief hadn't been exaggerating. The face was unrecognisable, the shape of the head and length of the remaining hair merely suggesting that it was a man. The height and build were the same as Jude's but also the same as a few thousand others in the city.

Standing beside Alice, Temple looked down along the corpse and was surprised by the consistency and extend of the damage. It was only when he got to the ankles that he saw the first possible confirmation of Alice's fear. She caught Temple's eye. "It doesn't mean anything," she said. "It was a restaurant, everyone wears those. He –"

As she stopped abruptly, Temple looked at her. Her lips quivered and big fresh tears rolled down her cheeks. He almost missed what she was looking at.

The earring.

Jude's black stainless-steel three-pointed star, the last remnant of his youth, might have been camouflaged against the blackened ear lobe but was still visible.

Definitely coming apart now, Alice sobbed loudly as she reached out to touch the charred face. Temple got to her just in time.

"No, Alice, don't," he said, pulling her away. "You can't touch him."

"Please," she said, trying to free herself. "Let me just…"

He turned her away, hugged her tight and let her cry into his chest. This was the woman, an hour earlier, he was about to arrest. For something that seemed ludicrous now, trivial.

As Alice sobbing slowed, Temple loosened his grip. She must have realised then who she was hugging, as she aggressively pushed him away.

"You did this," she said. "Jude was innocent, he was a victim! And because of your meddling..." Unable to say anymore, she turned and walked away.

Temple decided to let her have a moment. There was nothing he could say that would help. Because the fact was, she was right.

You did this. Jude was innocent, he was a victim!

Alice's words bounced around inside his head as he watched the firemen zip up the bag and wheel the stretcher to the ambulance. She was right, he had caused this. He'd lied. He had danced with the devil. And now the whole thing had gone to shit.

Glancing up towards the top of the street, he tried to pick Alice out of the growing crowd of rubberneckers. Not seeing her, he gestured to a uniform guard, who handed him her radio.

"Who's at Dame Street? Hello?"

"Garda Murray here."

"Detective Inspector Temple. The woman coming up to you from the scene, hold her there."

"Sir?"

He sighed. "There is a woman, very distraught, on her way to you. Don't let her out."

"I'm sorry, sir. My partner....my partner just let her out on to the street. Hang on, he's gone to look for her. Sorry, we're not normally expected to keep someone inside the –"

"For fuck sake," Temple said and started walking towards the street. "She couldn't have got to you by now. Unless she fucking ran –"

Damn it.

"Sir?"

"Did you get her?"

"I'm sorry, sir. She must have got into a taxi or something. She's gone."

Chapter 57.

As he marched into the Crumlin pub, Temple told himself he was calm enough to get the job done. He wondered if he should have taken a bit of time, maybe go and find Alice Miller first. But once he had explained the situation to Michael Hodge, Temple knew that this was his next port of call. He knew that walking into this place angry could mean his death, cop or not, so he had forced himself to take deep controlled breaths as he drove. By the time he was pulling into the car park, he felt sufficiently composed.

Unfortunately, it didn't last very long. At the sight of Graham Fanning's confident smirk, the composure evaporated.

"Kieran, I hear you've been trying to reach –"

Temple grabbed Fanning by his lapels, pulled him out of the booth and slammed him down on the table.

"You fucking son of a bitch!" Temple shouted as the two bouncer-bodyguards pulled him away.

Fanning lay on the table for a moment, completely shocked. This was, no doubt, the first time in a while he had been man-handled like this. Eventually he pushed himself off the table and stood nose to nose with Temple, a bemused 'You're-either-completely-brave-or-completely-stupid' look on his face.

"Careful what you say about my mother, Kieran," he said, stepping back and straightening his suit. "I doubt she'd like to know what you think of her." He waved a hand towards the two men. "Let him go, let him go."

Fanning sat down in the booth as a fresh cup of coffee was put in front of him. He gestured towards the seat opposite him. Temple didn't budge.

"Now, what is this about?" Fanning said.

"You know what this is about. Jude Miller, that's what this is about."

"What about it? I asked around, none of my people are involved." He took a long noisy sip of his coffee. "Anyway, didn't that place burn down last night or something?"

"Yeah it did, Graham. You had two of your boys in there pulling Jude Miller's strings or whatever. And when you found out that he was talking to me, you got fucking scared –"

"Hey –"

"And torched the place!"

"HEY!" Fanning bellowed. "I don't get scared! Certainly not of a little piggy like you! You think you have me over a barrel, don't you, Kieran? Snap your fingers and your own personal gangster will do your bidding? Well, I have limits, okay?" He took a long deep breath and exhaled slowly, as if he was practising some anger management exercise. "Yes, I know what you did for me and I'm eternally grateful. But don't push your luck. Now, if I say that none of my people were involved in that restaurant, then none of my people were involved in that restaurant. And a fire, Temple? That's not the way I do things.

You of all people should know that I have a certain aversion to fire."

As much as that was true, it didn't prove anything.

"So what?" Temple said. "It's not like you'd be getting your own hands dirty anyway. You send some of your lap-dogs to do it."

"I'm serious, Kieran." He gestured towards the floor with one finger. "There's that line again and you're about to cross it. I'm going to say it one more time, I. Did. Not. Do. It. Would have been counterproductive, anyway."

Temple decided he'd made his point. He sat down in the booth. "What does that mean, exactly?"

Fanning was smirking. "You really don't get the role you've played in all this, do you? Before you and I had that little rendezvous in Baldonnell yesterday, I knew almost nothing of Jude Miller or his restaurant."

"Before yesterday?"

"Restaurants aren't my thing. Pubs, maybe, but not restaurants. Too unpredictable."

"If that's true, then why –"

"Because your boy was obviously saying I was. That I was using his place for what, money laundering or something? Saying that to you. And there's nothing worse, in my opinion, than defamation of character. Won't stand for it."

"So you –"

"I went and had a chat with Jude, to find out what he was up to."

"Was this one of your usual kind of chats?" Temple gestured towards Percy, who was standing at the bar, eating crisps.

"Just a chat, Kieran. conversation. But the boy wouldn't say a word, apart from telling me what I already knew. Even when my Percival got up nice and close, nothing. He's got balls of steel, I'll give him that."

"So, what, he told you nothing, I'm to believe you just accepted that?"

"Course not. I gave him a choice." He smirked again. "Well, three choices."

"Which were?"

"He could tell me what he was up to. Or I could make him tell me – Percy has some…interesting techniques. Don't you, Perce?"

The big man just shrugged.

"Or," Fanning continued. "He could turn his big lie into a big truth."

"He could pay you."

"What would you call it, poetic justice? Irony? He's blabbing to the world and his wife that I'm his partner? Then, make it so."

"And he went for that option?"

"I was as shocked as you are, believe me. I assumed such a threat would just loosen his tongue. But no, he was all up for paying me. Even offered me a lump sum up front. I was to call in today, have another lunch, and collect it. Of course, I should have known better. I'm obviously getting a bit punchy in my old age."

"You think Jude burned the place down himself?" Temple had to admit, the thought had occurred to him to him too.

"How else would you explain it?"

"I'm still not convinced it wasn't you. And if he did it himself, how would you explain the fact that his smouldering remains were pulled out of the building less than an hour ago?"

Fanning's look of surprise was brief. "Huh. That does add a wrinkle. But we both know what fire is like, don't we Kieran? One second, it's a few sparks and before you know it, you're standing in the middle of an inferno. He was a chef, a good law-abiding citizen. Not an experienced arsonist."

Fanning pushed himself out of the booth.

"Where do you think you're going?" Temple said. "We're not finished."

"Yeah, we are Kieran," Fanning said as Percy handed him his coat. "You know I didn't burn down that place. And now that I've let you work out your frustrations, I have a meeting." He started towards the door. "Stay, have a drink, on me."

Chapter 58.

"What did you mean, 'almost nothing'?"

Fanning had almost reached the Range Rover before Temple caught up with him. He turned around, his patience clearly being tested.

"Kieran, seriously. I'm getting annoyed now –"

"'I knew almost nothing of Jude Miller or his restaurant'. That's what you said. Almost nothing."

"I had a few lunches there. So what?"

"In his restaurant? Just walked in off the street, did you?"

"Isn't that how restaurants work?" He looked at Percy. "Well that's how it works for me." The big man smiled.

"But no, Kieran," Fanning continued. "I was invited, if you must know. Now can I please –"

"What, he just rang you out of the blue?"

"Not him. Girl rang me on his behalf."

"What girl?"

"I don't know. Some girl. Told me she was from this fancy new place in town and would I like to be their guest for lunch."

"You didn't think that that was a bit strange?" Temple said.

"It was a bit strange she didn't invite me for dinner," Fanning said. "But I suppose a free meal is a free meal."

"So you went?"

"Of course. And, I tell you, it was good. Best I've ever had, maybe. Good service too, attentive but not in your face, you know the way. And Jude even came out afterwards, introduced himself, we had a drink. Proper VIP stuff. And that was it, nothing else till our chat yesterday."

Temple squinted. "Bollox."

They stood there in the cold car park, staring at each other.

"Yeah, okay. Okay!" Fanning said, clearly frustrated at how much he was giving up in one go. "He said I was welcome to come and have dinner anytime, on the house!"

"On the house. That didn't surprise you?"

"Nothing surprises me, Kieran. But, yeah, I should have smelled a rat."

Interesting choice of words. Maybe I'll get back to that later.

"Meaning?"

"Well he offered, so I went. And he came out again, joined me for dessert. We get talking again, restaurants, pubs, how to make money in a recession, all that. He's bringing out different wines for me to taste –"

Temple cleared his throat. Fanning took the hint. "Anyway, so conversation turns to travel and holidays and out of the blue, he starts asking about passports, whether if I knew anyone who…" Fanning faded off and looked guilty, like what he was about to say would incriminate himself.

"Anyone who what?"

"Anyone who can provide false passports," he said, as if that was obvious.

"False passports?" Temple was starting to wonder if they were talking about the same person. "Jude Miller. Jude Miller was asking about false passports?"

"Passports, birth certs, death certs, drivers' licences, curly-wurlies, the whole selection box."

This was obviously crap but there must have been a point to it. A punch-line, maybe – Fanning always did have a weird sense of humour.

"For who? Him?"

"Nah, two other guys."

"He give you the photos? You know, for the passports?"

"What are you talking about? What would he give them to me for?"

"But you saw them though."

"They were on the table before I could stop him."

Temple remembered what was still in his pocket from his last conversation with Jude Miller. He took out the envelope and emptied the photos on to the bonnet of the Range Rover.

Fanning picked up one of the photos and peered at it. "Yeah, he might be one of them alright."

"Who were they? These guys."

"He didn't say. Although the other one, not this guy, looked like someone I know."

"Who?"

"No-one, really. A junkie who used to buy…I mean, a gentleman I used to do business with. Lewis May."

"Lewis May. But he's not one of your crew?"

Fanning snorted. "You're joking."

"So what about these passports? You agreed to get them?"

"Of course not, I denied all knowledge," Fanning said. "You know, 'What-would-I-know-about-that-sort-of-thing' and all that. But your friend, Mr. Miller? He'd done his homework. I was impressed. And so, with the right blend of persuasion and a very nice *Bordeaux* Superieur, I gave him the guy I know in London."

Jude's in London today, Detective Inspector.

"You just gave him some guy? No questions asked? What guy?"

Fanning couldn't have looked more smug. *"The Guy I know In London* isn't a guy. It's more of a…service. A phone number."

"Come on, I haven't time for –"

"It's a beautiful system really," Fanning said. "Some paranoid forger came up with it in the nineties. His father was a telecoms engineer. One number on an exchange, shared by a wide circle of people. Every time it's dialled, it picks a different phone to ring. None of them know each other. So the wealth is shared evenly around the community and everyone remains anonymous, protected from people like you. It's genius. I wish I'd thought of it."

"Why you telling me this? Is this not one of your trade secrets?"

"Nah, rumour is Scotland Yard have got wind of it. Nothing they can do, no-one they can arrest. The guy who set it up? Died in 08. Still though, that'll be the end. Shame really."

"What's the number?"

"It won't do you any good."

"You'd be surprised."

"Even the number changes every few weeks. Any one I give you will be dead by now, Jude was supposed to give me the new one. And you wouldn't get the same person anyway and whoever you do get won't have a clue what –"

"Okay, okay, I get it," Temple said. "So he was getting the passports and whatever just for these two?"

"Yeah, sure. Well, maybe for himself and the woman too."

"Woman? What woman?"

"I don't know, he didn't show me photos of her."

Great.

"But I saw him with a woman, outside the back door round on Essex Street. And from the way they were together, the familiarity or whatever you want to call it, I guessed she was his wife."

"His wife? Alice. You sure –"

"But from the way she kissed him, she definitely wasn't."

Another woman? Jude?

Temple had only known him a few days, but he didn't seem the type to have an affair, even amidst a failing marriage.

"What did she look like?"

"Blonde. Hot. And..." he faded off.

"What?"

"For some reason, unpleasantly familiar."

"You knew her?"

"Fucked if I know from where though. She just left me feeling...uneasy."

"Uneasy? You?"

"Yeah I know. Go figure, right?"

Temple stood in silence, running his finger over the grainy photographs, wondering if they were talking about the same guy.

Fake passports? Another woman?

He took a step forward, offering Fanning his hand. "Sorry about, you know, earlier. I was upset."

"If I took offence at every little thing," Fanning said with a smile. "I wouldn't be the astute businessman I am today. But," he squeezed Temple hand until it burned. "You only get one."

Fanning held his hand and his stare for a few seconds before letting go. Temple turned towards his car.

"So, are we done?" Fanning called to him. "You and me. Is that it?"

Temple didn't stop walking. "Tell Calista I said hello."

"Hey, hold on."

"Come on Graham," Temple called over his shoulder. "I have to get back to work."

"You're not going to believe this," Fanning said. "I just remembered where I know her from. Jude's woman."

Temple turned back. And, yeah, Fanning did suddenly look unsettled.

"Not a happy memory?"

"Just when you said Calista. The day you pulled Calista out of..."

Five years later and he still couldn't finish that sentence.

"What about it?"

Fanning looked a bit puzzled. "Jude's blonde was there. I'm sure of it."

"What?" Temple didn't get it. "How could she have been there? She worked for you?"

"She wasn't there with me, Kieran. She was there with you."

~ ~

As Temple sat into the car, he was pissed off with Fanning again.

She was there with you.

It was bullshit, it had to be.

Mia.

Definitely not. How could Fanning remember back to that day, the most horrific and stressful of his life and even register that someone else had been there? Know what that person looked like? And then make a connection with someone he saw, from a distance, five years later? No, not possible. The brain does strange things to you when you're stressed.

And, technically, it was possible. Jude and Mia did know each other. She was his wife's best friend. It wouldn't be beyond –

No! No, no fucking way!

He'd have picked up on it. He had mentioned Mia to Jude, and vice versa, plenty of times over the last few days. Not once had he seen a flickering eyelid, a blushing cheek or even a dilating pupil from either of them.

Besides, Mia was in a relationship, albeit a dysfunctional one, with Daniel Summers. What, she then starts an affair with her best friend's husband while also sleeping with the restaurant critic?

It's daft! And –

And then he realised that it wasn't daft at all. Had it been anyone else, it would have been. But it was Mia, the same Mia he'd known for six years. And this fit her like a glove.

His phone, lying on the passenger seat, buzzed with a text message. It was from a number, not a name, and one he didn't recognise. And it was a picture message.

The picture brought an instant cold sweat to his forehead.

Taken from across a hotel lobby. Him. And Mia. At the lift.

Temple jumped as the phone rang loudly. The same number as the picture message. He stared at the phone for a few seconds, willing himself to answer. For the first time, he had no idea what to do.

"Mia?"

"Guess again."

"Alice? What the fuck –"

"I'm sorry, Inspector," Alice Miller said.

He could barely hear her, the noise of the wind breaking through her voice.

"Alice, what are you doing? What is this photo?"

"You and I need to talk, don't you think?"

"Okay, sure. So talk."

"Not on the phone."

"Well, where are you?"

"You can hear the wind, can't you? You know where I am."

Chapter 59.

He was driving too fast, Temple knew that. More than once, he had had to steer into the ditch to avoid hitting an on-coming car. But he didn't slow down.

As he came around a bend, he spotted the gravel lay-by that was used as a car park. There was only one car parked there, Alice Miller's Mini.

Just as the phone-call suggested, the wind was strong, sharp on his face. He tried to ignore it as he started up along the rough path. He had nothing with him for this and if this weather got any worse, he'd be in trouble. Even on this shallow slope, the leather soles of his black brogues were slipping under him.

After about twenty minutes, now sweating and breathless, he reached a place that looked vaguely familiar. He realised it was the spot from which that photograph in the Millers' hall, the one of Lough Tay, had been taken.

It was for this reason that he expected to find Alice here, but she wasn't. And Temple now had no idea what to do next. Earlier calls to her phone had gone straight to voicemail and now he wasn't getting a signal either. He spun around a full a circle and in a moment of annoyance and desperation, called her name. After a few seconds of listening to the wind, he heard her.

"Over here."

He spun in the direction of the voice and saw her.

"Jesus, Alice, I thought….Are you okay?"

"Of course I am, Kieran," Alice said. She was completely calm, serenely calm. "It's okay if I call you Kieran, right?"

"If you want to, sure," As he approached her, he could see that she was standing at the edge of the sharp cliff-face. "Can you come away from –"

"That's what Mia calls you, isn't it?"

"What?"

"She calls you Kieran."

"Yeah, I suppose so. We're friends."

"That's how these things always start, isn't it? Friends."

"Alice, please. Just take a step away from the edge, will you?"

"You're colleagues, right? Partners, even. Then you're friends. Good friends, that's what you tell yourself. You get close, maybe have a few stressful days on the job. She cries, you hug her, make her laugh. Your hug turns into a kiss, not a 'friends' kiss on the cheek –"

"Alice, what are you talking about? Nothing –"

"Nothing happened? You turned her down again? Just like last year when you disgraced her, forced her out?"

"I didn't –"

"Made her take that horrible job you knew she'd hate. Ruined her life. Just like you've ruined mine!"

"Look, stop. I'm not trying to –"

"You went after Jude even though you knew he hadn't done anything wrong. Why, Kieran? Just to get to me?"

"I went after Jude because –"

"For what? What did I do, really? Had a bit of fun, messed around with people's relationships? Daniel and Mia? Brian and Geraldine? If these people were so fucking happy and secure, do you really think my interference would have made any difference?"

"Alice! For once this isn't about you, okay? Jude isn't innocent. Maybe I did do it to get to you but…the fact is, Jude was up to something in that restaurant. And I think Mia was somehow involved –"

Alice laughed. "What, Jude and Mia now? They've known each six years and suddenly now they're having an affair? You really are clutching at straws!"

"I don't know, but –"

"Just stop okay! You lose. It's over. These people were using him and now, thanks to you, they've killed him. And you're going to pay for that."

"Please, let's just talk about this. Just come away from the edge."

"Why?"

"Why? Because I don't want you to fall, that's why."

"But I didn't fall, Kieran." That eerie calm was back. "You pushed me."

Without another word, Alice Miller fell backwards and was gone.

Chapter 60.

"Alice! Jesus!"

Temple ran to the edge of the cliff, dropping to his knees as he got there. He looked down, bracing himself for the worst but, to his shock, Alice wasn't a dead and crumpled mess at the bottom of a ravine. Instead, she lay on a grassy ledge a few feet below, rubbing her ankle.

"Jesus Christ!" Temple said, lighted-headed with relief. "Are you okay?"

"Of course I'm okay," Alice said confidently.

"Why...why did you do that?"

"To make a point," she said. "To make you realise that I'm serious."

To make me realise you're fucking crazy.

"What are you talking about?"

Alice tried to stand up but, unable to put weight on her ankle, dropped back down on the ledge.

"How does this sound, Kieran?" she said, wincing in pain. "I have photographs of you and Mia in that hotel the other night. You've seen them, you know what they suggest. I've demanded that you leave me alone, that you accept that what happened to Daniel was self-defence and nothing more. That if you don't, I would send the photos of you and Mia to your boss –"

"Wait –"

"– and to Yvonne. They'd be pretty damning for both your career and your marriage, I'd say. So you follow me up here to get the photographs. You threaten me and, in my anger, I say I'm going to send the photos anyway. I'm unpredictable like that. You lose your temper and push me over. Not realising that this ledge was here to break my fall. You tried to kill me but it didn't quite work. That one is called 'Attempted Murder'."

"Alice, we both know that –"

"So you want to send me to prison for turning Daniel into an obsessive psychopath? Go right ahead. We can be cell-mates."

"That's all very interesting, Alice," Temple said. "Except that you forgot one detail. Just a small thing really."

"What detail?"

"Me." D.I. Michael Hodge stepped forward to the edge and looked down at Alice. Temple enjoyed watching the smugness disappearing from her face.

"Who –"

"I'm with him."

"Sorry," Temple said. "Figured I needed some back-up on this one. Unless…is there any reason he'd want to kill you? Do you have photos of him in a compromising position?"

Alice stared up defiantly at Temple for a few seconds. She then closed her eyes and shook her head in resignation.

"You know, I was going to just drop it, Alice," Temple said. "I really was. I decided that we had all been through enough, even you. But right now, I'm thinking you can just go to hell. And I'll be adding blackmail to the charges."

He stood up and turned to walk away.

"No, wait," Alice called out, desperation in her voice. "Wait, please! The photographs, you can have them. They're in my bag and …"

Alice tried to stand again but her twisted ankle couldn't support her and she dropped back down. The ledge under her suddenly moved. The rain-weakened earth under the ledge shook and, under her shifting weight, it succumbed.

"Kieran! Oh God!"

Temple looked down as the ground beneath Alice dropped away and, screaming, she fell with it.

"Help!" She managed to grab some brush sticking out from the soil.

"Shit!" Temple dropped down on to his knees, all thoughts of his little victory forgotten. "Alice! Hold on, I'm coming!" Without thinking, he stared scrabbling down along the near-vertical cliff.

"I've a tow-rope in my car," Hodge called down to him. "I don't know if –"

"Just get it!" Temple shouted back.

The brush in Alice's right hand suddenly came away from the loose rock-face and she screamed again.

"Alice! I'm coming to get you. Can you hear me?"

"Please! I can't hold on!"

"Yes you can, Alice! You hold on!"

Temple felt the fragile cliff loosen as he crawled over but he didn't stop. Hearing Alice's blood-chilling scream below, he lifted his hands away and let himself slide down the hillside, praying that he would be able to stop when he got to her.

Digging his feet into the soil, he slowed his descent and stopped just above Alice. Her left hand was gripping a clump of grass but her right arm and legs was flailing frantically.

"Okay, Alice, I'm here. Grab my wrist."

"I can't!"

"Come on. Look at me. Look at me!"

Alice looked up at him, at his hand just above her. She reached up and managed to find his fingers, to intertwine them with hers.

"No, Alice, my wrist. You have to –"

Suddenly the clump of grass tore away and Alice's other hand lost its purchase. She jerked downwards and Temple was pulled sideways, causing one of his shoes to slip out of its shallow groove. His sweat-soaked hand was pulling away from hers.

"Kieran, it's slipping! I can't hold on, please help me! Pleeeeease!" Alice begged.

He grasped at her with his other hand but could not reach. There was a small rock jutting out on the far side of his right arm and he stretched across himself to try and get it. But it was too far. His shoe slipped again – it was about to come away and, when it did, there was nowhere to go for both of them but down. His only hope to save himself was to grab the rock with his right hand.

The hand that had Alice.

Only the tips of their bent fingers connected them. He tried to reach down again with his left hand to grab her wrist but didn't even come close.

He found himself looking into Alice's terrified eyes with nothing more to offer her, pleading with her. But only her own horrified realisation looked back at him.

His foot lost its tentative hold and, like he was no longer controlling them, Temple felt his fingers straighten out. Alice seemed to hang there for a moment before she fell away from him. Paralyzed, Temple watched Alice Miller fall faster and faster before vanishing over the edge and into the ravine.

As he started to fall himself, his now free right hand instinctively grabbed the nearby rock. His body rotated and, before he realised it, he was now the right way up and holding on to cliff-face.

"Kieran!" Hodge was calling from above. "Are you okay? I can't see you!"

The words barely registered. Picturing only Alice Miller's terrified dying stare, Temple let out a long desperate roar.

Chapter 61.

Temple sat at his desk and resisted the urge to even blink. He knew that, if he did, he'd see nothing but Alice Miller's face. It was only three hours since her death and it would be a lot longer before he'd see anything else behind his eyelids. It didn't matter how many people told him that it wasn't his fault.

And despite another piece of friendly advice, he had gone back to work instead of home. He had told himself that he needed to distract himself but, in fact, it wasn't doing the trick. Every time he looked at the computer screen or reached for one of the dozen-or-so files on his desk, her face, her terrified eyes, popped into this head.

The phone rang and he sighed with relief, hoping this would give him a moment of respite.

"O.C.U. Temple."

"D.I. Temple. Declan McCormack."

"Declan. What have you found?" He was in no mood for even

basic pleasantries. "Was it arson?"

"I'd have to say no. We've only done a cursory inspection but if you ask me, it was an accident, most definitely. *Crepes Suzette.*"

"Excuse me?"

"That's what caused it. Well, something that involves a pan and a high-temperature naked flame. Your guy lights the brandy, flames go into the extraction system where all the grease and crumbs and all that are. Boom."

"Aren't those things supposed to be cleaned out regularly?"

"Yeah, and I'm supposed to have a full head of hair and weigh fifteen stone."

"So you found nothing to suggest that it was started on purpose? Accelerants or –"

"No, nothing. Except…"

"Except what?"

"Well, that restaurant has only been open for what, a few months, right?

"Five or six, yeah."

"Not very long for the extractors to be full of shite. Even if they were never cleaned, it would take years for the enough grease to build up to cause a fire. Maybe he cooks a lot of duck."

"What are you suggesting?"

"I'm not suggesting anything, Inspector. Just making an observation."

"Cheers. I appreciate your observation."

"Anything on our victim?"

Just that his wife is dead too.

Alice Miller's terrified face flashed through Temple's mind.

The door to the office opened and Michael Hodge stuck his head in, spotted him and headed his way.

"Em, not yet," Temple said to McCormack. "The pathologist should have it by now though. Thanks for the heads-up, Declan."

He hung up as Hodge arrived at his desk.

"How did you get past security?" Temple made a brief attempt at a smile.

"I told them I was the postman," Hodge said, leaning against Temple's desk and dropping a white envelope onto it. "I think this might be yours," he continued, the voice lowered. "It was in her back-pack. For someone pushed off a cliff, she was very careful to stash it securely under a bush. So would you have?"

"Would I have what?"

"Let her off? Walked away?"

Temple threw a 'Oh-come-on' look at Hodge, who just shrugged his shoulders. "Depends what's in those photographs, I suppose. Speaking of which, I had a look on her phone. You know, looking for next of kin. Now that her husband is no longer with us."

"And?"

"No photos. None of you, anyway. She must have deleted them before she died."

"She must have? She thought to do that before she framed me for trying to kill her?"

"Suppose so, right?" Hodge pushed himself off the desk, avoiding eye-contact. "Take care of yourself, Kieran. Don't let the bastards get you down."

"Cheers," Temple said, fidgeting with the edge of the envelope. "A few pints one of these days?"

"You're buying," Hodge said, starting towards the door. He then turned back, "Oh by the way, some woman was looking for you this morning. Left three messages at Mountjoy."

"What woman?"

Hodge fished in his pocket and pulled out a Post-it. "Someone called…Barbara."

"Well if she's calling your station, it's probably about Daniel Summers."

"Fuck sake, is this thing ever going to be finished?"

"Don't let my D-Super hear you say that. I'm already on his shit-list for staying on it this long."

"Yeah, me too."

"Just blame me."

"I did." Hodge snorted. "Do you know who I reckon was the best person to investigate Daniel Summers' death?"

Temple sat back, put his hands behind his head and raised his eyebrows.

"Daniel Summers."

"What does that mean, Michael?"

"He was Mister Organised. To the point of obsessive, according to his employer. Would have made a good detective, I think."

"I'm sure," Temple said dryly, hoping Hodge would pick up the hint that he was losing interest in this small talk.

"Seriously," Hodge said. "You know, Arthur Conan Doyle used to say the reason Sherlock Holmes was such a good detective was that he was obsessive. He was also a sociopath, but that's beside the point. You know our man Daniel had a will that he reviewed or changed every six months?"

This threw Temple. *Every six months?*

"Did you see it?" he asked Hodge. "The will."

"No, should I have?" Hodge then picked up on Temple's train of thought. "You think he made Mia Burrows a beneficiary?" He snorted again, his preferred expression of derision. "What, she killed him for this nice car and a wardrobe full of Hugo Boss suits? The boy was comfortable, he wasn't exactly rolling in it."

"No, I suppose not," Temple said and squeezed his eyes closed. "I don't know what I'm thinking."

"I told you, Temple, go home," Hodge said. "This has been, as they say, a fucked-up day." He handed Temple the post-it. "After you make a phone-call, of course."

"It wouldn't kill you to ring her, you know."

"She asked for you."

"Lazy pup." Temple looked at the name and phone number, but neither rang a bell.

"Better be careful," Hodge said, starting towards the door. "You're losing track of all your women."

Temple watched Hodge leave and glanced down at the Post-it again. 'Barbara 014921314'.

Every six months.

He wasn't sure why he couldn't shake what Hodge had said about the will. He told himself not to rush to judgement, that his instinct had been wrong in the past.

He flicked through his notebook and found what he was looking for. The name of Daniel Summers's solicitor.

He took a deep breath before reaching for the phone.

Chapter 62.

Temple felt a horrible lump in his throat as he hung up the phone.

He sat back, sucked his lower lip through his teeth and wondered if it actually meant anything.

Yes Detective Inspector. Mr. Summers did change his will. He added someone.

"No. It doesn't," he said out loud. "Mia probably didn't even know."

And it didn't change the evidence. Everything he saw in Mia's house and everything he heard from Mia, from the Millers and from the Dobsons. It all pointed to the fact that Daniel Summers attacked Mia and she defended herself.

Then why the lump?

It was ten-to three and he was going in a circle. It was time to move on. He needed his brain free of Daniel Summers and Mia Burrows before the D-Super arrived. If he was lucky, the face of

Alice Miller might even leave him alone for a few minutes. One last thing to do, then it was on to Moroney and those wire taps. He reached for the post-it.

"Hi, is that Barbara?" he said when the phone was answered.

"Eh, yes," a middle-aged voice said with some trepidation. "Oh, is that Inspector Temple?"

"It is, Madam. I'm sorry, have we met?"

"Forgotten me already, Inspector. Barbara Caldwell? Mia's neighbour? We met the other morning when –"

"Yes, of course. Mrs. Caldwell."

"Barbara, please," she said flirtatiously.

"Okay, Barbara," Temple said, allowing himself a brief smile. "Thanks very much for helping Ms. Burrows that day. I know she appreciated it."

"Ah it was nothing. She's always been so good to me, that girl. Helping with my bins and –"

"So how can I help?"

"Well," Mrs Caldwell said sharply. She obviously didn't like being interrupted. "I just wanted to let you know that Mia's...friend was at her house last night."

"Her friend?" Once again, Alice's face appeared in front of him.

"Yeah, you know. Her.... boyfriend, partner, whatever the word for it is these days. You know him. The restaurant guy."

Jameson. "What, he called to the door? Mia's still away, isn't she?"

"No, he went in. At four o'clock in the morning, no less."

That was odd. Jameson had never even been invited to stay over. Now he had his own key?

"I got up to let the cat in," the woman continued. "She never knows what she wants, that animal. She's out, she wants in. She's in, she –"

"Do you know how long he was there for, Barbara?"

"Let me see. Yes, he was just going in when I opened the door. I would have gone over but I wasn't dressed or anything. And I heard the door close again ten, fifteen minutes later. You really have to give that front door of hers a good hard slam. Fair dues to him, he got it first time. Of course, he's been in and out of that house a lot the last year or so –"

"The last year?"

"Ah yeah, at least."

"And you're sure it was Mr. Jameson you saw?"

"Jameson? No no, that's not his name, is it? The guy with the restaurant? The chef."

The phone nearly dropped out of Temple's hand. "Jude Miller?"

"That's it."

~ ~

"It's time. Make the call."

~ ~

"Paddy! Paddy?"

Garda Paddy Malone stood up from his desk.

"What?"

"Tell me you got something on Lewis May?"

"Who?"

"You know, your man…the name I got from Fanning."

Malone sat down and fiddled with the mouse and peered at the computer screen. "Hang on."

Temple was frantically flicking through his notebook, hoping that he'd taken out the pages for the file.

He stopped and went back a page.

"Jude Miller, Alice Miller," he whispered to himself. "Married two-and-a-half years. Together…"

He heard Alice Miller's voice in his head. *They've known each other six years and suddenly now they're having an affair?*

Together – four years.

So they knew each other before Alice?

"No Alice," Temple said out loud. "They're not suddenly having an affair."

"Lewis May, D.O.B. 1st June 1962," Paddy called over from his desk.

Temple stood up. "Go on?"

"Currently no-fixed-abode. 1997 shoplifting and disturbing the peace, '99 armed robbery, 2002 more shoplifting, possession-with-intent. Few small things since then, that's it. Thing is though…"

"Thing is though," Temple said. "He's dead?"

Where one goes, so must the other.

Paddy looked surprised. "That's why they pay you the big bucks, I suppose," he said. "How did you know that?"

Temple's mobile started vibrating again and he fished it out. He'd have to tell Yvonne he's call her back.

But it wasn't Yvonne. The call was coming from a blocked number. And this was his own personal phone – besides his wife, only a handful of people knew it even existed. He let it ring out.

"When was May's body found?" he asked Paddy.

"Pulled out of the Liffey at the Four Courts just this morning. Couple of his fellow down-and-outs IDed him."

"How'd it happen?"

"Accident, looks like. Or maybe it was a drug thing. He might have been spotted on Wellington Quay with some guy in a hoodie –"

"Might have been?"

"You trust these junkies?"

"Who IDed him?"

Hickey looked at the screen. "Name on the statement is Bertie Ahern. Someone has a sense of humour."

"Jesus. Anything we do know? What about known associates?"

"Yeah," Malone clicked his mouse a few times. "Here we go. Two. Nora Mackey, AKA Chastity, local brasser, he was caught engaging in a 'lewd act' with her on Prices Lane last summer. And Curtis McDonagh, him and May came out of Cloverhill around the same time, late 2000. Current whereabouts, unknown."

Temple laughed, he could not stop himself.

Curtis and Lewis.

Jude, you arrogant bastard. You didn't even change their names.

~ ~

After hanging up, he sat his desk and stared at the mobile, hoping that he hadn't just missed his chance. Just as the pessimism was setting in for real, it rang again.

"Hi Mia."

On the other end of the phone, Mia Burrows laughed.

"I was hoping you'd figured it out," she said.

Chapter 63.

Daniel sat at the kitchen table and felt the blood sticking his fingers together. It was less the pain of his cuts and more the sounds coming from the bedroom above him that were causing him to wince.

These unbearable grunts and moans went on for so long, each one penetrating him as he sank lower and lower in the chair. He wasn't even comforted by the prospect of calling Ben Jameson's wife and telling her what he was up to. He wasn't sure that she'd believe him but – no, she would, he'd make sure she did.

A deal's a deal, Freckles. He would enjoy making that call.

Eventually, the sounds stopped and, after a few minutes, he heard them coming downstairs. His head suddenly cleared and he managed to sit up as the front door opened. That was the fucker leaving.

Now we can talk, Mia. Sort everything out.

The anticipation caused his stomach to clench. He wanted her to come in, relishing the look on her face. But she didn't. For another eternity, there was no sound at all and he wondered if she'd already gone back upstairs.

He jumped as the loud buzz of the doorbell broke the silence and the front door opened.

What the hell, he thought, *is the horny bastard back for more?*

"Jesus, I thought he'd never leave," a voice said. A familiar voice. It wasn't Ben Jameson. It was someone who shouldn't have been here, ringing Mia's doorbell in the middle of the night.

What the hell are you doing here, Jude?

A few seconds of silence passed and Daniel wondered what was going on. Was this dizziness extending to full-blown hallucination now?

But he wasn't light-headed now, everything was clear. And, at that moment, he knew. He could barely believe it, but he knew. Everything was clear.

He heard the door to the sitting room open.

"Can you stay?" Mia asked, in that room now. He could hear her voice more clearly.

"Yeah," Jude said. "Unless – you haven't invited Alice over for breakfast or anything, have you?"

Mia laughed "No. Hey, guess what, the stuff from London arrived today."

"Excellent, let's have a look," Jude said. "Jesus, you think Lou would have shaved for the passport. He's supposed to look like a businessman, for fuck sake."

"Don't worry about him, he'll be fine. He's even learning his lines now."

"Oh my God, look at your hair. It's faaaabulous daaahling!" Jude said

"Ah come on, it's not that bad!"

"It's pretty awful," Jude said, laughing. "No, no, I want to look. Typical."

"What's typical?"

"Even with truly awful hair, you still manage to be beautiful."

The sudden pause in conversation brought tears to Daniel's eyes. They were kissing – he could hear Mia making that little sound she always did.

"God, I missed you," Jude said and the sour sting of bile came to Daniel's throat. He swallowed but that just made it worse.

"Have you heard from Alice?" Mia asked.

"Nah," Jude said with maybe a trace of sadness. "I doubt I will. Not for a while."

"You are still her husband."

"It doesn't matter. You know what she's like, Mia. She's leaving me for the same reason she does everything. Pure unadulterated selfishness. We're relying on it, remember? All this 'danger' I was bringing into her life? That's all she could see the last few weeks, especially when I involved the gallery."

"Suppose," Mia said.

"What?" Jude said. "You're not worried she knows about us."

"It's just…that whole business with your parents. It felt like she was retaliating or something. Punishing you. And not just for the abortion."

Listening to this surreal conversation, Daniel realised he needed to do something. He pulled out his phone and started the voice recorder. He didn't even know if it would work, if it would pick up their voices through the wall but he had to at least try, if only to prove to himself that he wasn't going crazy.

"Please, trust me," Jude said. "Look around you. It's working. Everything is happening exactly the way we thought it would. You're hardly going to be her friend now after what she did to you. And in a few weeks, after my partners have mysteriously fallen off the face of the earth and the restaurant is mine again, you and I can gradually become friends –"

"Okay, okay. I get it."

"We just need to stay focussed, that's all I'm saying."

"And what about Daniel?"

His heart jumped at the sound of Mia saying his name. He almost dropped the phone.

"Well, he didn't turn up at your girl's night out tonight, did he? It's finally getting through to him. You just keep seeing the horny critic for a few more weeks, just to be sure."

"What do you think he'll make of you and me getting together?"

"Who, Daniel? I really don't give a shit."

"Jude, come on, don't go all macho –"

"I don't. After what he did to you, him and me are finished. And if he comes near you again, I'll fucking kill him."

Suddenly, a loud clatter made Daniel jump. This time, he had dropped his phone and it bounced noisily on the tiled floor.

"What the hell was that?" Mia said.

His eyes closed, Daniel listened as the kitchen door opened.

"Oh my God, Daniel!" He opened his eyes to see Mia's shocked face looking back at him. "What are you doing here?"

"Daniel! What the hell?" He wasn't hearing things. It was definitely Jude.

Daniel watched him as he followed the trail of blood across the floor to the broken glass door.

"Did you....did you break in?" Jude asked.

"Mia, I'm sorry," Daniel said. "I had to see you."

"Are you serious!" She was really angry now. "Jesus Christ!"

Not that he cared. He watched as realisation gradually hit home and Jude and Mia exchanged worried glances. Their nice clean plan had just gone sideways.

"Dan, how long have you been sitting here?" Jude asked.

"Long enough," Daniel replied.

Another worried glance.

"Just get the fuck out of here, okay?" Mia said. "Just forget what you think you heard and leave, okay?"

This was the first time Daniel had seen panic on Jude Miller's face. The poor man was obviously surprised that Mia was telling Daniel to go. It didn't matter anyway, Daniel wasn't going anywhere. This was just too good.

"Forget what I think I heard?" he said. "Is that the best you can do? You two are having a thing? This takes the biscuit, Jude, it really does. I know I accused you of fancying her, but this? It's no wonder you kept trying to warn me off."

"Daniel, shut up!" Mia was trying to maintain her anger but it was slipping. She was using it to cover something else – fear. "You just broke into my house! Do you even realise how…how…"

"So what are you going to do, Sergeant Burrows, arrest me?" Jude took a step towards him. "Daniel –"

"Sure, go for it. Arrest me. Actually, can I get my phone-call now? I think I'll call…Alice."

He leaned down to get his phone but Jude beat him to it.

"Fuck, he was recording us," he said, seeing what was on the screen.

"Won't hold up in court, I'd say," Daniel said, wincing as the movement made his hand burn like hell. "But it doesn't really need to, does it?"

"Sorry, Dan," Jude said coldly, dropping the phone back on to the floor. "I'll buy you a new one, okay?" He raised his foot and Daniel winced as Jude stomped down hard on the phone. He then kicked it against the wall and, weakened by the stomping, it broke into bits.

Mia had turned away and was standing against the kitchen counter. "You don't really want to ring Alice anyway, do you Daniel?" she said. "Come on, just say it. Tell me why you're really here."

Daniel stood up, the resignation in her voice giving him strength. She was right – he didn't care about his phone or about Alice or even about whatever this thing was with Jude.

"Mia, I just want what I've always wanted," he said, taking a step towards her. "I want you." Just looking at her, her back and her beautiful slender neck, he knew he loved her as much as ever.

"This thing with him," he said, glancing at Jude. "What is it, really? It couldn't possibly be anything like what we have."

"What we have," Mia echoed. "So what are you saying? If I come back to you, you'll forget about everything you just heard?"

He was standing right behind her now and could barely believe that he was this close to her again. That everything could be this good again.

"You're right, Mia," he said. "I don't even know what I heard. You know, I'm injured, I'm light-headed. I was probably just imagining things, right?"

Mia was silent. She was finally seeing sense.

"Okay," she said quietly.

"Okay?"

"Okay, I'll come back to you. Of course I will."

His heart swelled as he heard those words. Hearing the door close behind him, they were finally alone. Even Jude had realised how it had to be.

"Really?" he said excitedly, putting his hands on her shoulder, urging her to turn around.

"Really," she said. "I love you. You believe that, right? That I love you?"

"Of course I do," he said.

She turned to face him and Daniel felt the exhilaration and anticipation that he had missed so much. "And I love you t –"

The pain was back and it stole his breath. But it was a

different pain, a strange burning. Not in his arm, but lower, in his side, below his ribs. And it wasn't a mild sting but a ferocious agony that spread through his chest and enveloped his whole body. He inhaled but nothing happened. He couldn't breathe, couldn't think.

Looking away from Mia's sad eyes and down, he didn't get it. A circular stainless-steel display, like on a meat thermometer. But where was the rest of it? Where was the spike?

He jerked and gasped as the thermometer was pushed further, deep inside him.

But this can't be true. If it was, I'd be dead and...

The room was spinning too fast now and he just needed to sit down. Just for a second, to catch his breath. As he looked back at Mia's face with that strange mix of regret and acceptance, the pain faded. It was only tiredness that consumed him now. He just needed to sit for a second. Or to lie down, he didn't care.

His knees found the floor, then his hand, his shoulder, his face.

I love you, Mia.

Chapter 64.

"Come on, Kieran," Mia said after a long silence. "The suspense is killing me."

"I don't understand," Temple said. "Why are you telling me this?" His voice was steady, with no emotion, and that was annoying – at least that could have been a hint to himself of how he was feeling.

"Because I need you to understand –"

"To understand."

"Yeah, to understand why. Daniel was about to ruin everything. Two years of planning down the drain because he couldn't get it into his head that –"

"So it was all Daniel's fault then?" At last, some anger.

"That he was there, yeah!" Mia said. "I sure as hell didn't invite him."

"You sure about that?"

"What, you're saying I invited him over and then made him

break in?"

"You did stand to benefit from his death though, Mia," Temple said. "Financially, I mean."

"What are you talking about, the will? I have no intention of ever –"

"Not the will, Mia," Temple cut in. "You don't want Daniel's apartment or his car. I'm talking about the life assurance."

"Hey, I never asked him to do that," Mia said, a crack in her voice. "I never wanted his money."

"But you decided you'd take it though, didn't you? You didn't invite him around, that's fair enough. Your real boyfriend, your lover, your life-partner – let's just say 'Jude' – was coming over to finalise everything. So when you saw Daniel sitting there, that was when you decided. You were going to get what you deserved. From him."

"Kieran, please. Don't –"

"He made you miserable for all those months and it was payback time."

"He left me no choice! He had heard everything that me and Jude were doing –"

"No, Mia! No. That man was putty in your hands. You could have convinced him of anything. If you'd told him you and Jude were…rehearsing a play, he'd have accepted it."

"Don't say that," Mia said. "Daniel wasn't stupid."

"No, but he was suggestible. With you, he was. You knew that. And you killed him anyway. It wasn't self-defence, we know that. But it wasn't self-preservation either. It was greed. And it was punishment."

For a few seconds, there was no sound from the other end of the line. But Temple knew she was still there.

"Doesn't matter, Kieran," Mia said eventually. "You have nothing you can use. You can't prove I even knew about the life assurance. Even if I did, we were split up – it would be a safe assumption that he had taken me off the policy."

Mia then took a deep breath. *"After eight months of physical and psychological abuse, the woman's ex-partner then attacked her in her own home. Assuming he would kill her, the woman was forced to defend herself and, in doing so, fatally wounded her attacker. That sounds plausible to me, Kieran."*

"Sure. How about this though? After eight months of bullshit, the woman decided to punish her boyfriend –"

"He wasn't my boyfriend!"

Mia's outburst echoed and distorted the line. He was finally getting to her.

"He wasn't my boyfriend," she said again, with forced calm.

"That's the whole point, isn't it?" Temple said. "Daniel was never part of your plan, was he? He was part of Alice's plan. And it pissed you off that you had to go along with it."

"We didn't have to –"

"Yeah, you did. You said it yourself, she tried to set you up with people before. If you kept resisting, she might have got suspicious. So you go out with him, throwing her off the scent that you were, in fact, fucking her husband."

"I am not fucking him! You say it like it's…I love Jude."

"Does he love you?"

"Of course he –"

"Because he gave you some pretty bad bruises the other night. That was him, right? Because we both know it wasn't Daniel. So if that's what you think love is, you're in for –"

"Jude didn't want to do that, I made him. It was the only way you'd believe the self-defence. The idea of it made him sick. He's never hurt me, not once. Not in –"

"Six years? That's how long it's been going on, isn't it? Since your stint in Scotland Yard? I should have made the connection really. Some detective I am."

"You did."

"I did what?"

"You did make the connection. That night we got drunk and…"

As she faded off, Temple felt himself tense. He really didn't want to go back to that night again. He wondered it was relevant or if she was just trying to distract him.

"What about it?" he heard himself say.

"You worked it out. That my guy in London, as I called him, was back in Dublin and that I was seeing him again. And I let it slip that he was married. You were so disappointed in me."

Temple tried to recall the conversation. He could remember the night alright – it was the end of a particularly bad week, when a supposed slam-dunk operation went south. In true Irish style, Temple and Mia had chosen to drown their sorrows in beer and whiskey. As inhibitions dropped and they both tried to think of something other than work to talk about, Mia might have said more about her personal life than she should.

But right now, none of it was coming back to him. He could remember the kiss – that was never going away. Had started innocently on her doorstep, just a consoling hug that they both needed. Before he could stop it, it was something else and they were inside Mia's house, heading for the bedroom. They both knew what would have happened if Temple's moment of clarity hadn't put a stop to it.

"So, that kiss and everything that came after it? Me racked with guilt, confessing to Yvonne? You losing your job! That was all you just covering your ass?"

"I don't give a shit about my job! You knew about me and Jude! I had to distract you from that. I did what I had to –"

Temple laughed. "I didn't know anything, Mia. I really didn't. I was pissed!"

There was silence.

"So…" Mia said eventually.

"So you fucked everything up for no good reason. Congratulations."

More silence. Temple hoped that Mia was feeling just a little bit stupid.

"You played your part too, Kieran," she said. "You weren't entirely innocent."

"I suppose."

"Speaking of which, when did you and Graham Fanning become such good friends?"

"I wouldn't exactly say we're friends," Temple said. "But yeah, he does me the occasional favour."

"That's what you thought you were doing, right? Asking him a favour? To leave Jude alone. But, instead, you were tipping Fanning off."

"That's the funny thing about a criminal, Mia. He could be a convicted mass-murdering bastard. But you accuse him of doing something he didn't do? He might –"

"He might kill you. Yeah, I know," Mia said. "That's exactly what we thought was about to happen. Jude nearly had a heart attack when you told him you'd spoken to Fanning. Came this close to confessing to the whole thing."

"But Fanning didn't want to kill him."

"It might have been kinder than what he did want."

"For you to pay him for the rest of your lives? So you torched the place instead."

"We'd no choice. Surely you can see that."

"You had a choice. You had a choice not to kill Curtis McDonagh. That was him pretending to be dead Jude, I assume."

"I don't know which was harder, punching a hole in a dead man's ear or convincing Jude to give up the earring."

"Cold, Mia."

"What, you think Fanning would have just left us alone

because the restaurant was gone? Jude had to be dead."

"And Louis May? His sodden corpse was recovered this morning. What do you call that, collateral damage? I mean, that's it, Mia. You and Jude are no longer a Garda sergeant and a struggling chef."

"What does that mean?"

"Now, you're just a couple of murderers. You could have just left the country. No-one had to die."

"Fanning –"

"Fanning's priorities are different now. He doesn't give a shit about money. His claim on the restaurant was on principle, to teach Jude a lesson. But, without hesitation, you just –"

"Without hesitation? Of course there was hesitation. We're not –"

"Monsters?" Temple smiled and then laughed, he couldn't help himself. "Yeah, Mia. That's exactly what you are. And I'm coming after you. Or maybe I'll have another little chat with Fanning. He and I work well together."

Another moment of silent reflection from Mia.

"You're not going to do that." She was back to being annoyingly self-assured.

"Why, because I hold a torch for you or something?"

"No, of course you don't."

"So what then?"

"For the same reason you were never susceptible to my charms, Kieran. No matter how hard I tried. Because you love your wife."

"My wife? Are you threatening me –"

"Do you think Alice's the only person to have those photographs? Where do you think she got them from?"

Fuck.

Temple glanced at the envelope recovered from Alice's backpack as he realised what had been bothering him. Her name and address were written on it, but only then did he recognise the writing.

"Jude is so much more than just mountains and lakes," she said. "He's also a damn good paparazzo. So if I get even a sniff of you behind me…well you know the rest."

Temple sat back and rubbed the palm of his hand against his forehead.

You got me, Mia. Well played.

"So what's the plan now?"

"Well, I can't really give you too much detail, you understand," Mia said. "But we're taking your advice, Kieran. We're leaving. The restaurant is gone and Jude with it. That's the way it's going to stay. I'm in Cork or Cornwall or Cuba, you're not exactly sure where, recovering from my ordeal. One homeless guy is dead, another one is missing. I doubt any division is going to blow its budget on that one."

"Jesus, Mia, how did you do this?" Temple decided that he might as well admit it. He was impressed. "I mean, how did you even bankroll it?" Temple said. "Since we both know there were no silent partners, no drug money from Graham Fanning."

"The old-fashioned way, Kieran," Mia said. "The banks are lending again, didn't you know? Especially to someone with ten years' cheffing experience, a detailed business plan…oh and full ownership of a house valued at two-point-six million."

"The house. You put it up for collateral. But Jude loves that house, he'd never risk –"

"No he doesn't. He did love it, right up until the old woman left it to him in her will."

"That was a bad thing?"

"The conditions were a bad thing. He could never sell it. One final 'fuck you' from her to the whole family. But the fact is, our plan actually started the day he was handed the deeds to the house. And now the insurance pays off the bank-loan –"

"And the house?"

"Granny forgot to include one thing. What happens to the house if Jude dies. I guess she loved him too much to think about that. The house goes back to its morally rightful owner."

"Brian Miller."

"Some justice should come out of all this mess."

"Mess? Is that what this is?"

"This wasn't how it was supposed to be! Me and Jude were supposed to end up together, in that house. With Alice gone by her own volition – we just put a little something to spook her and let her show us her true colours. Then we'd leave it a few months and then slowly 'start' to see each other."

"You'd have done that to her? She was your friend."

"Friend? She set me up with Daniel, someone she knew would hurt me. Some friend."

"So you had it all sorted."

"Until three nights ago. Then it all got…"

"Messy. So you rang me," Temple said, now realising the extent to which he had been used. "You figured I'd easily believe the self-defence story and I'd steer the likes of Michael Hodge in that direction."

"No, Kieran. I got you involved because I knew you'd end up involved anyway. But, left to your own devices, you'd probably have figured out what was going on. So we gave you Alice, got you fixated on her."

"She's dead, by the way." He wasn't sure if he had planned to tell her, but it was out now. "Alice."

It was Mia's turn to be speechless. "Wha…" she said eventually. "How?"

"She died trying to punish me. For killing Jude. You should have seen her, she was so angry. About the death of the man who, according to you, she didn't love."

"I…I didn't really mean –"

"How do you think Jude's going to feel about it?"

She was thinking about that for a few seconds. "You know what, Kieran?" she said. "I think he'll be okay. He didn't love her. He'll shed a tear, maybe, but he'll get over it."

"So she fulfilled her purpose as a lightning rod."

"Hey, we wouldn't have needed her if you weren't so good at your job."

"Cut the flattery, Mia. Clearly I'm not that good or we wouldn't be having this conversation."

"Yeah, maybe. Speaking of which, it's time to say our goodbyes. They've just called my gate. One-five-two. Bit of a walk."

"Come on, Mia. You don't expect me to believe you're still in Dublin."

"Maybe. Doesn't really matter, does it?"

As maddening as it was, she was right. "This is not over," was all he could think to say.

"Okay, if you say so," she said. "Look, don't beat yourself up. And if you behave yourself, no-one needs to know how close you came."

She was waiting for a response, taunting him with silence. Temple decided not to bother, not to give her the satisfaction. She could have the last word, he didn't care.

"See you, Kieran. It's been fun."

Epilogue.

Temple put the good wine glasses on the table and stood back. That was everything.

His hand went into his pocket, touching the corner of the envelope, and reminded himself of what he was about to do. But he still glanced at the fireplace, with its fire now hot enough to quickly incinerate the photographs if he threw them in.

But that wasn't the job at hand. Instead, he would show them to Yvonne, admit what had happened in that hotel and free himself from Mia's grip. He might also have to show them to the D-Super, but he'd cross that bridge later.

Considering what he was about to do, Temple wondered why he was now standing at the hearth, holding the envelope. He wondered would Yvonne believe him, that the kiss had just been a set-up, part of Mia and Jude's game. He glanced back at the table and remembered all the dinners they had had there, watching TV or just talking. It was sitting there, a few months after they'd bought the place, that he had proposed. And he couldn't shake the feeling that her seeing the photos – actual proof of something physical between him and Mia – would just be the end.

Hearing the front door slam, Temple pushed the envelope into his pocket as Yvonne walked into the room.

"Hey you," she said.

"Hi," he said.

She frowned. "You okay? You look…weird."

"Thanks. You look gorgeous."

"Yeah right. You sure you're okay?"

"What? Can't a man compliment his gorgeous wife?"

"Of course he can." She gestured towards the table. "What's all this?"

"Scallops with chilies. Fillet steak and chips. And a 97 Faustino One."

"And The Good Wife box-set?"

He loved that mischievous smile. "Already in."

She came over and kissed him softly. "You do know how to make a gal feel wanted. I'll go change. Five minutes."

Hearing her going up the stairs, Temple pulled the out envelope and stared at it, willing it to tell him what to do. But he knew what he had to do.

~ ~

The Montreal Airport Police responded immediately.

A woman, added just that day to The Interpol Worldwide Wanted list, was currently strolling through the Departures Concourse. Details on her were brief, so the commander on duty decided to take no chances. He dispatched the armed unit to apprehend the woman.

For someone who knew she was being pursued, the woman seemed calm.

"Ma'am, armed police!" The commander said himself as he approached the woman wearing a beige linen suit and carrying a back-pack on one shoulder. "Please place the bag on the floor and put both hands to the back of your head."

She stopped abruptly and, for a moment, looked deep in thought. The commander stood directly behind her with two of his men, one on either side. They edged forward so she could see that they were armed.

For an eternity, nobody moved. The entire airport, all of Canada, seemed to be waiting. Then the woman let the bag fall from her shoulder. She put both hands behind her head and interlocked her fingers. The commander stepped forward and pushed her on to her knees and then down on to her chest.

A crowd of people had gathered and were watching the commotion. Among them was a man with greying hair and a goatee, wearing shorts, sandals and a grey tee-shirt under a loud Aloha shirt. As the suspect was being cuffed and led away and the crowd dissipated, the man gave a 'what-is-that-all-about' look to the person beside him before strolling towards the boarding gates.

As he approached the first cluster of gates, the man suddenly had a feeling that he was being followed. After what he had just seen, he put it down to paranoia but, as he walked on, the feeling grew. He started moving faster and, just ahead of him, he spotted a corridor to his left. He ducked in and pushed his back against the wall.

A few seconds later, the suspected pursuer strolled past. He reached out his hand and, grabbing the person by the wrist, pulled her to him.

"You were supposed to meet me in Reykjavik," Jude said before kissing Mia. A comfortable and passionate kiss.

He looked deep into her eyes and, for a moment, was back in that crowded Japanese restaurant off the Tottenham Court Road.

Nice to hear a voice from the old country.

"Sorry about that," Mia said. "I got nervous, I decided to wait for you here instead. Besides, I've been in Reykjavik nearly a week, that place is boring!"

"Wow, that hair isn't nearly as bad as it looked in the passport. How are you, Colette Thomas?"

"That, Alistair Thomas, is because it's not a wig this time," Mia said.

They both laughed and then hugged, a long hug as they allowed the relief to envelop them.

Jude and Mia started walking towards the departure gate, allowing themselves the luxury of holding hands, something they hadn't done in public for a long time.

"So where's the money now?" he asked.

"Still waiting for the final clearance, but should be in the account by the end of the week."

They found their gate and checked the screen, which told them that there was a twenty-minute delay.

But they were in no hurry.

~ ~

Hearing Yvonne going up the stairs, Temple pulled out the envelope and stared at it, willing it to tell him what to do. But he knew what he had to do.

Looking at Mia's hand-writing one last time, he dropped the envelope on to the fire.

THE END.

What did you think of BURNING MATCHES?

Leave a review on Amazon by visiting
www.paulfitzsimons.com/amazonreview

Leave a review on Goodreads by visiting
www.paulfitzsimons.com/goodreads

Lightning Source UK Ltd.
Milton Keynes UK
UKHW020532241118
332859UK00001B/70/P